In the light of darkness

Elizabeth Rex

Chapter 1

The persistent ringing of the phone jolted Ann out of her erotic dream. Irritated at the abrupt awakening, she reached over for the phone in the darkness of the room. She pressed the phone to her ear and muttered a sleepy 'hello.' The urgency in the voice on the other side of the phone caused Ann to sit bolt upright in bed. 'I am so sorry to wake you, guv, but can you get over here as soon as possible? We are at the home of a Tom Casey who has been murdered. The address is 27 Chapel Street, Belgravia. SOCO are on their way. The coroner is here already,' said Sergeant Hughes. Ann memorized the address, then replied, 'Oh alright, I will be there as soon as I can.' She gazed lustfully at the athletic shape of her still sleeping partner's body beneath the sheets. She pulled on some clothes and hurried off out of the door to her car parked in front of the house. The rain pelted down as Ann Dixon sped to the address in Belgravia. Ann slowed down as she approached a house, where two squad cars were parked. She parked her car next to a car she recognised as the coroner's in front of the house. She walked towards the front door, never failing to turn heads as her long shapely legs and the flick of her head caught the attention of the police officers milling around outside the house. SOCO had arrived and were assessing the crime scene inside the house. Ann bent under the police cordon of blue and white tape, walked to the front door of the house, where Sergeant David Hughes came forward to greet her. He handed her some overshoes which she slipped on and walked into the house. The scene inside the house defied description. The naked, blood stained body of the victim that hung upside down from the bannister resembled a carcass at an abattoir. Rivulets of blood pooled beneath the victim's head. The bloodied figure could only be defined as human as his arms and legs were splayed outwards.

The victim had been placed in an upside- down position which had been secured by ropes. His face was almost completely obscured by the blood which had cascaded over it from the numerous wounds on his abdomen and legs. 'Hi Ann, glad you could come. Your super asked us to call you as you have had experience with this type of murder. The victim is Tom Casey, the owner of the house. His housekeeper, Mrs Smith found him at 6.15 this morning and alerted the police,' said Tim Jones, the coroner. The copious collections of clotted blood around the trauma sites on the body, suggests he has been tortured for a long time.

I would imagine death was between 4am and 5am,' continued Tim. 'Do you know the cause of death?' asked Ann. 'I would say virtual exsanguination, and cause of death probably strangulation. I can tell you more after the post mortem. There is a distinct pattern of an inverted cross on his neck which might have been made by the ring the murderer was wearing at the time of the strangulation,' he continued. Ann moved to have a closer look at the body. Sergeant Hughes commented that the knots in the rope suggested that the killer might have served in the navy. There were multiple cuts visible on the torso and legs. The extensive bleeding and formation of clots around the wounds suggested that the cuts were made while the victim was alive. It was clear that the murderer intended to inflict severe suffering prior to death. Ann knew from her many years of experience of such brutality that it had all the hallmarks of a revenge killing. The room was in total disarray. Chairs were overturned and draws pulled out onto the floor. The tastefully furnished room with notable paintings on the wall paid testament to the exquisite taste of the owner. Ann surveyed the rest of the room. Large blood stains and patterns of spatter on the sheer white carpet looked like a macabre painting. SOCO bagged and labelled all the items they found strewn around the floor. They photographed the scene, the victim and any items of relevance. 'You might want to look at this guy. It is a code book. SOCO found it stuck to the underside of the desk top,' said David. 'Yes, tell them to bag it. I am sure we will find someone to decipher the code. Let's go talk to Linda Smith,' replied Ann. 'Mrs Smith, I am Chief Detective Inspector Dixon, my colleague, Sergeant Hughes and I promise not to detain you longer than necessary and the paramedics are waiting to attend to you when we are done,' said Ann. 'What time did you get to the house?' Ann urged. A tearful Linda Smith informed Ann that she had worked as a housekeeper for the deceased. She explained that she had arrived at 6.15am and discovered the murdered victim. She also said that her employer was a lawyer who lived alone and was single. When asked when she had last seen Tom alive, Mrs Smith said that she had cooked dinner for her employer at 6pm that evening. She knew that he dined alone on the night of the murder, because he asked her to prepare the table only for him. He usually had a friend join him to play bridge. She told Ann that Tom Casey had three other brothers. He also had a sister who was deceased. When asked, Mrs Smith obliged by giving contact details of George Casey who was Tom's elder brother. Ann thanked Mrs Smith and told her the police would be in touch if they needed any more information. Ann and David returned to the scene of the crime. An enormous bookshelf housed an impressive array of books. There were also a vast number of books on the occult. The murdered man was still wearing his Cartier watch. His wallet and mobile phone lay on the coffee table near to the body. Ann instructed the forensic team to speed up their gathering of evidence around the body as the coroner was keen to get the body to the mortuary. A man's boot print, size 10 was found at the edge of the carpet. All items collected, were photographed, labelled and bagged. 'I want all kitchen knives collected, tagged and bagged,' she added. It took four policemen to lift Tom Casey's body off the banister, as he was heavily built. The body was placed into a bag and transferred to the mortuary. 'I will call you when I am ready to do the post mortem. Come on I'll walk you to your car,' said Tim as he headed for the door. 'I see you still have your Renault. She is still in pristine condition,' remarked Tim as he got into his car. 'Yes, it gets so little use as I drive around in cars from the Met for much of the time,' added Ann as she jumped into the passenger seat. She was besieged by a group of reporters as soon as she was inside her car. She was bombarded with a flood of questions from the media. "You will have to wait for an official press release from the superintendant. 'There has been a murder, but it is too soon to draw any conclusions about this case. Now please get away from my car, I have work to do,' shouted Ann. The reporters surrounded the car like a mob of protesters, ignoring her request. She urged David to drive away swiftly. 'Bloody vultures, they can smell carrion far better than the feathered species,' said Ann with disdain. 'Let's find Stephen Edwards, and ask him to deal with the press,' said Ann. 'Good idea, guv, I will see if he is in his office while you park the car,' replied David. 'Good, that will buy me time to grab a quick cup of coffee,' said Ann, smiling as she envisaged the satisfaction she would derive from the black liquid which she often substituted for food.

She returned to her office and hastily poured herself a large cup of coffee from the machine. It gave her an instant lift and pacified the pangs of hunger to some degree. She raced through her emails and replied to the urgent ones. Then she rang the number of one of the brothers of the victim. There was a short ring, and then a man answered. 'George Casey, how can I help?' replied the man on the other end of the phone. 'Hello, this is Chief Detective Inspector Ann Dixon of the Metropolitan Police. I wonder when it would be convenient to see you, Mr Casey. It concerns your brother, Tom,' Ann said. 'Good Lord, what crime has Tom committed?' came the concerned reply. 'Well I cannot tell you over the phone as it is a delicate matter, but it is very important that I see you urgently,' Ann continued. I will give you the address, and you can liaise with my secretary about my availability,' said George. Ann scribbled down the address and promised to contact his secretary. Ann managed to secure an appointment with George for 3pm that day. Just then, David popped his head around the door. 'The super is in his office, if you are ready to see him now guv,' said David. Ann grimaced at the thought of meeting with her boss. Stephen Edwards disliked having women in the police force and hated having them in authority He always managed to erode Ann's confidence and reduce her to a mumbling wreck during their meetings. Her hands were clammy with the adrenalin suffused anticipation of the meeting. David sensed her anxiety and added, 'It's okay, guv, he seemed to be in a good mood when I saw him,' added David. 'That will change as soon as I step into his office. Oh well better get it over with, no point in delaying the agony,' said Ann nervously, as she headed for Edwards office. She knocked and waited to be invited in. 'Come inside,' boomed Edwards. Ann walked in, greeted him and at down. 'There's been a murder. Sir. Our victim, Tom Casey is a 45year old white male. He was tortured and then murdered in his home. The housekeeper found the body at 6.15am this morning. The victim has 3 brothers and a sister who is deceased. Victim must have let his killer into the house because there was no sign of a forced entry. The extent of the injuries suggests the victim was tortured for a considerable length of time. The position of the body was hung upside down from a bannister and the large collection of books on the occult suggest a link to the occult. The extent of the torture suggests a revenge killing. The coroner thinks cause of death was strangulation, but he will tell us more after the post-mortem. I have contacted one of the siblings, George Casey. I have not told him about his brother's death. I have an appointment to see him this afternoon at 3pm. We had the press at the victim's house this morning demanding answers. I wonder if you could call a press conference at your earliest convenience, please Sir,' said Ann. Edwards did not look at Ann during the entire time she spoke. He continued to doodle on the paper before him. She had to ask him loudly if he needed to know more about the case, to attract his attention. He looked up at her and said, 'Dixon, the Met does not pay you to speculate. I need hard evidence and don't take a bloody lifetime gathering it. I want a result in the shortest possible time and don't fuck up. I will sort out the press. Now get out of my office, I am very busy,' he shouted. Ann was furious at his disinterest and lack of respect but remained civil and left the room calmly. David joined her in her office and knew instantly that she was upset. 'Arrogant pig, he gets worse every day. He thinks we have to tolerate his rudeness because he is the stressed father of a child with special needs. He is oblivious to anyone else's needs,' continued an infuriated Ann. David pacified her by promising to buy her lunch after their interview with George Casey. 'That sounds great, let's get the team together in the incident room. I need to brief them on the murder. David set about informing his colleagues that Ann had called a meeting at midday. They began setting up photographs and details of the murder on the board and on computer screens in the incident room. The officers gathered promptly at midday for the meeting. Two teams headed by Detective inspectors Ian Roberts and Alfred Tobin were present. Ann called order as the officers continued to talk among themselves as Ann tried desperately to get their attention. She banged a book on the table forcing them to attention. 'Alright, everyone, our murder victim, Tom Casey, a 45year old white male was tortured then murdered at his home at 27 Chapel Street, Belgravia. There was no forced entry, so we assume the victim let his killer into the house. The motive was not burglary even though the chaos at the scene of the crime, suggests it was. The victim's Cartier watch, laptop and phone, was still in the house. It appears that the killer might have been looking for something. It might have been the coded book which we found stuck under a desk. Forensics have I formed me that the book is written in Witch's code. Presumably one or more of the brothers might be able to decode the book. The killer must have missed it in his panic to find it as he hurriedly pulled out the drawers of the desk. Our officers discovered the book by chance when they replaced the drawers of the desk, and saw it carefully stuck under the desk top. Someone obviously knows about the existence of the book and is keen to have it. Perhaps the victim was tortured to reveal the whereabouts of the book, or the murder possibly was a revenge killing, judging by the degree of torture. The mark on the victim's neck, an inverted cross, and his being strung up upside down, suggests a link to the occult. There were many books on the occult on his bookshelf. The degree and savagery of the murder suggests a revenge of some kind,' she stressed. She delivered her talk, pointing to pictures taken at the crime scene. 'Are there any thoughts on the murder or any questions?' asked Ann scouring the room for feedback. Various questions were asked about items found at the scene. 'Ok, here's what I want you to do,' she added.

She organized her team into units and assigned them various tasks. 'I want D.I. Roberts and his team to question work colleagues and friends of Tom Casey. D.I. Tobin needs to interview the neighbours and friends who accompanied Tom Casey to his various social engagements. Check if anyone saw anything out of the ordinary. I want you to interview Mrs Smith, the housekeeper again. She was too distraught on the morning on the murder to give to us a comprehensive statement. She will be able to tell you what is missing. She may be able to give you more information. Sergeant Hughes and I will interview all the brothers. We are meeting with George Casey today. If there are no more questions, I will arrange another meeting when I have the post mortem and forensic reports. Now get on with it quickly, because the super wants a rapid result,' urged Ann. DI Roberts and Tobin paused outside the incident room for a brief discussion. 'I can't stand that cow. Who the hell does she think she is ordering us about,' protested Detective Inspector, Roberts. 'She might be a woman, but she has more balls than most men in that position. I would like to remind you that she has an impressive record. If you bothered to read her profile, you would know that she was one of the first UK detectives who got a murderer prosecuted by the analysis of plant DNA. Her persistence resulted in solving a murder case which baffled the senior members of the force. She got a conviction using plant DNA to solve a very baffling murder case which stumped the best of her male colleagues. Her impressive service for MI6 prior to her joining the force and her training with the Special Forces has contributed to her achieving superb results in her career. She also speaks five languages fluently. Name any man in the force who can match her. May I remind you, before you judge her for her gender, look beyond that and you will be astonished at her professional acumen,' said Tobin. 'What about that arrogant prick, her sergeant. He thinks he has been elevated to the rank of DI,' remarked Roberts. 'Hughes is not just a pretty boy. He served in the Royal Engineers for 5 years before joining the force. He has served in Iraq and has proved himself admirably in the force. Ann requested that he join her team because of his impressive record. Their relationship is totally professional because as you know she has a female partner,' continued Tobin. 'Never mind their great achievements, I can't stand them,' said Roberts. The briefing had taken longer than Anne had anticipated, so she was grateful that the traffic was not heavy, so she and Sergeant Hughes got to Surrey in time.

They arrived at an attractive mock Georgian house, in Surrey. 'You'll never be able to afford this on your salary, guv,' teased David. 'I am very happy in my humble home, thank you,' replied Ann. They walked through the landscaped garden to the front door and rang the doorbell. A large, bearded man opened the door. Ann stuck out her hand to greet the man and said, 'You must be Mr George Casey, I am Detective Chief Inspector Ann Dixon, and this is Sergeant David Hughes,' George Casey shook Ann's hand and ushered them into the house. George motioned for them to sit down and offered them a drink. Ann declined the drink politely. Now what has my brother done that makes your visit so urgent?" George enquired. 'I am afraid, I have bad news, Mr

Casey, Your, brother, Tom was murdered last night,' said Ann. George sat down, shocked at the news, but maintained his composure. Ann continued, immediately informing him that his brother was tortured before the killing. George absorbed the news, shocked and troubled. 'Did your brother have any enemies or someone you know might have wanted to harm him?' asked Ann. 'No actually, Tom was well liked by all his colleagues and friends,' 'Did your brother owe anyone money or was involved in financial schemes which might have put him at risk? Did a disgruntled client from his legal business bear a grudge,' enquired Ann. George said that Tom lived a clean life and would not have put himself at risk in any way. He confirmed that Tom never married, explaining that he just never found the right girl. Ann studied his expression, before asking, 'When did you last see your brother alive?' George thought for a moment, before saying, 'I think about a week ago." 'Tom asked me about a hedge fund investment he was interested in pursuing. He had become rather bored with his job and wanted to pursue something more exciting', he added. 'Did you get along well with your brother, and did he get along with his other siblings?" enquired Ann. 'Yes, of course, there was no animosity amongst the brothers, and we adored our sister, Yvonne, who died 3 years ago, God rest her Soul,' he continued. 'The only person who caused friction in our family was our brother-in-law, Luke Cowan. He is a rather an arrogant fellow,' George added with disdain. "He was obsessed with our sister, and resented the fact, that we, her brothers were close to her,' he lamented. 'Did your confrontations with Luke lead to violence at any time?' Ann enquired. 'Well it got pretty close to physical violence, but did not actually end in anyone getting hurt,' said George. 'Where would I be able to contact Mr Cowan,' enquired Ann. 'He is based at Chelsea Westminster hospital. My secretary has his number. I will ask her to let you have it,' he added. 'I would like to interview your brothers. Could you give me all the contact numbers please?' continued Ann. "I'd be delighted to,' and began writing down the names addresses and contact numbers Ann required. "Mr Casey, where I would like to know where you were between 3am and 6am am this morning. 'I had dinner with friends and then went to my private club until 4am,' he explained. Can your friends corroborate your whereabouts?' asked Ann. 'Yes indeed, here is my friend, John's telephone number, he drove me home around 5.30, stayed for drink, then left,' said George. 'We will need you to come to the mortuary to identify your brother's body at your earliest convenience,' said Ann. George agreed and an arrangement was made for him to call at the police station the next day. George's other two siblings, Jake and Nathan shared a house in West London. Ann thanked George for his cooperation and said she would be in touch if the police needed any more information. She shook hands and left accompanied by David Hughes.

They climbed into the car. 'Hedge fund, they should rename it unlimited funds, did you see the Lamborghini parked outside?' David remarked. 'Be happy with your lot and stop envying other people's wealth,' she scolded. 'Speaking of happiness, how about some food?' asked Ann. She spotted a café, parked the car and asked David to get the food. He returned with two large burgers and they sat in silence while finishing their food. Only when they were both sated, did they resume their conversation about their interview with George Casey. Ann asked David what he thought about George. David replied that he wondered if George was exaggerating the animosity towards Luke Cowan. Ann agreed and stressed the urgency to get Luke Cowan's side of the story. Ann dropped David off before returning to her office where she did some more work on her laptop, then headed home. A fragrant fusion of spices wafted through the living room as Ann entered the house. 'Hmm that smells divine, what are you cooking?' said Ann as she kissed Josie in the kitchen. 'Your favourite my darling,' replied Josie with a cheeky grin. 'When you have stuffed yourself with my love infused cuisine, you can show your appreciation by conjuring up a suitable dessert,' she suggested with a cheeky grin. Ann laughed, slapped Josie on her bottom and headed for the shower. They sat down to dinner catching up on the events of the day. Ann told Josie about the murder victim omitting all the gory details. The doorbell rang. 'Are you expecting anyone?' Josie enquired. 'No, I don't think anyone would arrive unannounced,' replied Ann. Josie answered the door and emitted a joyful whoop. 'Oh Adam, how wonderful to see you,' shrieked Josie flinging her arms around the tall handsome, blonde caller at the door. Ann rushed to the door as she recognised her brother's voice. She embraced him warmly. He stood grinning at the women's overwhelming outpouring of delight. 'Oh, my favourite people. I missed you so much,' said Adam. 'When did you get back?' I only expected you next month,' gushed Ann.

I left because things were getting rather hairy in Afghanistan,' replied Adam. 'Have you finished your book?' urged Josie. 'Yes, my third and last I hope,' replied Adam. 'You have lost weight. Come along, let's get some proper food into you,' said Josie leading him by the hand to the dinner table. Adam was a journalist. He had seen many atrocities in the war zones of Bosnia, the Gulf war and Afghanistan. He was Ann's only sibling. They were very close. He adored Ann's partner, Josie. They chatted during the meal, catching up on one another's news. 'Where are you staying?' Josie asked. 'I wonder if I could bed down here for a few nights as my flat has been rented out,' Adam continued. 'Absolutely fine,' both women chorused.

Ann reviewed details of the murder on her desk the following morning. Her concentration was broken by a member of staff who informed her that George Casey had arrived to identify his brother's remains. Ann stopped what he was doing and took George to the mortuary. George went through the motions of identifying his brother's remains. He maintained his composure even though the battered corpse hardly resembled the brother he once knew. 'Do you have any leads on the killer?' George enquired. 'No, we have no leads at present, except to say that your brother let his killer into the house as there were no signs of forced entry. It suggests he might have known his attacker. We doubt whether it was a burglary because expensive items belonging to your brother were not taken, although the disarray at the scene of the crime suggests the killer was searching for something. We suspect it might have been a book written in some sort of code as it was stuck under the desk top which had drawers pulled out, but the killer missed seeing the book. Do you know anything about this book?' asked Ann. George frowned, remained silent for a few moments, and enquired, 'I wonder if you would let me have the book. My brother was very meticulous about his books,' he stressed.

"I am afraid I cannot let you have it as it is part of the evidence and must remain with the forensic department until we have completed our investigation. It would be helpful if we can find someone who can decode the book. I am sure the book has some connection to your brother's death,' said Ann with an enquiring stare. 'I cannot decode the book and I don't know who can help you, but I would like it returned to me as soon as your investigations are complete, Inspector,' replied George. 'By the way, here is Luke Cowan's number,' he added. Ann thanked him for coming to identify the remains of his brother and escorted him out of the building. Ann was keen to interview the other brothers and especially Luke Cowan. She surmised that the answer to the killing might be lurking within the family. Ann went to find David to remind him that they should arrange to see the brothers as a matter of urgency. He told Ann that he had managed to contact the younger brother, Nathan who explained that as he and Jake shared a house, he said he would arrange for Jake to be present at the meeting too. 'I managed to arrange a meeting with both brothers on Thursday at 7pm,' declared David proudly. 'Are you able to make it for 7pm on Thursday, guv?' 'Hmm let me check,' said Ann as she flipped though her diary. 'Yes, I am free from

5pm. Let's meet at my office around 6.00 on Thursday. We should be able to get to West London by 7", she replied. David parked the car at an attractive terraced house in Fulham. Ann rang the bell.

A tall athletic looking, man answered the door. Ann identified herself and flashed her badge to confirm her identity. The man introduced himself as Jake Casey. He invited Ann and David into the living room and called to his brother Nathan to join them. Ann informed the brothers of Tom's demise and offered her sympathies. Nathan broke down in tears at the news, but Jake remained unemotional. Ann asked where the brothers were on the night of Tom's murder. Jake replied that he worked as a paramedic and was on duty. Nathan said he was at the pub until, midnight, after which time, he went to his girlfriend's home where he stayed till the next morning. 'I will need names and contact numbers to check your alibis,' said Ann. 'Yes, of course, we will give you the information you need,' said Jake. 'How did you get along with your brother, Tom?' enquired Ann. 'I got on well with Tom. We did not live in each other's pockets, but we got together quite frequently at family gatherings and for the odd drink. We had our differences, but not to the extent of needing to commit murder,' he replied. 'What about you, Mr Casey, did you get along with Tom", Ann asked Nathan. 'Oh yes, I was very close to my brother. He was like a father to me after our parents died,' replied Nathan tearfully. Ann paused for a moment, then asked, 'I understand from your brother George that none of you got along with your brother-in-law, Luke Cowan.' asked Ann. 'Oh, that Bastard, scowled Jake. He should have died instead of our sister,' said Jake with vehemence. 'There wasn't a moment of peace when he was around. Our sister was very disheartened by the way in which he disagreed with us. We got into many verbal battles with him. My brother, Tom despised him with a vengeance. In as much as it devastated us, it was a kind of relief when Yvonne died because it cut the connection we had with Luke. He thinks too much of himself. He thinks everyone is beneath him,' complained Jake. 'Do you share your brother's opinion,' Ann asked Nathan. 'No, I had no fights with Luke. I know he loved our sister very much,' replied a red eyed Nathan. 'Of for goodness sake, my brother is too tolerant,' replied Jake. Ann listened intently, making notes as they spoke. Jake did most of the talking, interrupting Nathan in mid conversation sometimes, and answering for Nathan before he had a chance to reply. Ann thanked the brothers, warned them that she would need to take a cheek swab, for their DNA to exclude them as suspects. David waited until they had reached the car, before he spoke. 'Do you think Jake interrupted his brother because he wanted to stop him from divulging anything,' he asked. I think it was just his arrogance, assuming that Nathan was not intelligent enough to answer the question, but I suppose you may be right in thinking it might be part of a cover up,' said Ann. 'Did you notice the number of books on the Occult on the bookshelf?' enquired David. 'Yes, George Casey had enough books on the occult to fill a modest library, so I am not surprised that his brothers share the same interest,' added Ann. 'Let's get in touch with the formidable sounding Dr Cowan,' said Ann. 'Shall I ring him guv?' asked David. 'No, let me do it as I think this guy will insist on speaking to a senior member of the team,' she said. Ann dialled Luke's mobile number which rang for a while before he answered. Luke Cowan sounded very charming on the phone and not like the monster the brothers made him out to be. Luke agreed to meet with Ann and nominated the hospital lecture room as he was on call, and unable to go home. Mr Luke Cowan was an eminent orthopaedic surgeon. He was tall. His muscular body strained against his tight fitted shirt. His blond hair swept back, made him appear rather dashing. Ann moved forward to shake Luke's hand and introduced David to him. Luke motioned them to sit down and he pulled up a chair opposite Ann. He fixed his gaze on Ann as she spoke; his piercing blue eyes unsettled her. He had a disarming smile which he used as part of his seduction strategy.

David noticed how Luke frequently diverted his gaze to Ann's shapely legs. This incensed David who began to nurture a dislike for this lecherous man. Ann informed him sympathetically about the demise of his brother-in-law. He stared at Ann unflinchingly and completely devoid of emotion as she briefly outlined the circumstances of Tom's death. Luke reclined in the chair and measured his words as he spoke. 'Why are you telling me this?' I have nothing more to do with the Casey family after the death of my wife. I cut all ties with the brothers when my wife died,' he explained. 'Well Mr Cowan, it is routine police procedure to question everyone who is involved with the family, even ex-in-laws,' Ann explained. 'Can you verify where you were between 3am and 6am on Thursday, Mr Cowan?' enquired Ann. 'I was in the operating theatre until 11pm; went to the office to catch up on some paperwork, then went to sleep in the doctor's room,' explained Luke. 'Can anyone vouch for your whereabouts?' enquired Ann. 'Yes, a colleague, Dr Worthing met me in the corridor as I emerged from my office around 2am,' he continued. 'I will need the contact number of your colleague please,' replied Ann. Luke gave her the number and location for Dr Worthing. 'You don't believe I had a hand in Tom's death, do you?' he asked. 'No, but since you had many disagreements with the victim and his brothers, we have to exclude you as a suspect,' explained Ann. 'Oh, I get it, they have told you about our disagreements, haven't they Inspector?' he retorted. 'Why have they not told you how possessive they were over their sister and how they ruled her life and how insanely jealous they were of my love of her,' he continued, the veins; stood out prominently on his forehead as he tried to stifle his **anger**. Ann spotted an opportunity to catch him off guard and immediately asked the question, 'Did your animosity towards your brothers-in-law drive you to the point of committing murder, Mr Cowan?' Ann probed. The effrontery of her question brought Luke to his feet and he lunged towards her shouting, 'Good God! how dare you make such an outrageous accusation?' he demanded to know. His once calm composure replaced by unadulterated rage. This violent outburst mobilised David to his feet and he placed himself between Ann and her would be assailant. Ann remained in control and calmly qualified her statement by saying, 'It is a perfectly reasonable question. It is documented that powerful, repressed emotions can drive some people to commit murder,' she continued. Ann watched his response carefully. 'Well it seems they neglected to tell you about their sister's ex- boyfriend, Sam Cain,' he said. 'The brothers gave him the beating of his life when they discovered that Sam was sleeping with their sister,' he continued. 'You should ask Sam how much he hates the brothers. There's where you should be looking for the murderer, Inspector,' he added. 'Where will we find this Mr Cain,' Ann enquired. 'His number will be in the phone book,' replied Luke. 'We will require your fingerprints and a swab for DNA testing to exclude you from the list of suspects, Mr Cowan," Ann explained. 'Bloody hell, the police always chase the wrong people and leave the real criminals to freely roam,' he said angrily. 'When do you want to do your samples,' he fumed. Ann remained unfazed by his outburst 'Tomorrow if you are available please,' said Ann. Luke checked the time on his watch and apologised that he had to take his leave to attend a meeting. He told Ann that he would be available should he be needed for any more questions. Ann remained polite, thanked him and left. 'This guy has a very short fuse, guv. It would not be difficult to provoke him, and he has enough anger towards the brothers to do serious damage,' said David. He certainly is a very volatile character. Let's see what forensics have found,' replied Ann. 'We have to meet with Sam Cain. He might just provide an important missing piece of the jigsaw,' she said hopefully.

She returned to her office to document her interview with Luke Cowan. She was in the throes of getting most of her paperwork done, when the phone rang. It was Tim Jones requesting her presence in the mortuary for the post-mortem examination on the body of Tom Casey. She called out to Tim, apologising for being late, hurriedly donned protective clothing and moved over to the table where the body of Tom Casey lay. Tim was dictating into a recorder suspended overhead. He had confirmed that the cause of death was asphyxiation due to strangulation. He confirmed his findings by stating that the victim's hyoid bone had been fractured during the strangulation. He drew attention to a circular pattern on the right side of the victim's neck. He suggested that it resembled a pattern of an inverted cross which might be the impression of a ring. Tim deducted that the killer had used his hands to strangle the victim, and that he wore a ring, which seemed to have been turned around on his finger, facing the inside of his hand. The imprint of the pattern was transferred to the victim's neck as the killer clasped his hands around the victim's neck and squeezed with tremendous force. The hyoid bone is fractured. An impression of four fingers on the side of the neck confirms that the victim was strangled. The presence of petechial haemorrhages in the eyes suggests cause of death as being strangulation. A trace of glove powder suggests that the killer wore gloves. 'There are bruises at the side of the mouth where this linen strip kept the mouth gag in place,' he pointed out. There is a pattern of bruising around the shoulders and around the groin, also across the body. This is consistent with the rope that held the victim onto the bannister. There are bruises on the wrists and ankles where he probably was restrained. Your murderer knows how to tie his ropes. He could have had naval training,' added Tim. He pointed to the missing strips of flesh which were cut out, from the victim's thighs. 'These missing pieces of flesh presumably were kept as trophies by the killer. There are holes in the bones of the legs and arms which appeared to have been made by an electrical drill,' he continued.

The drill bit found at the scene fits the holes in the legs. Linear cuts matched to a chisel found at the scene, was used to join up the holes drilled in the bones by dragging the chisel along the drill holes. The victim's hands and feet were a bloody mess as the bruising and bleeding suggested that the industrial staples inserted, were done pre- mortem caused great damage to bone and flesh. The victim's penis is slit in four sections, from the tip to the root, splayed open, it resembles a starfish. Hmm! must have been bloody excruciating especially as the poor sod was still alive when this was done,' added Tim grimacing as he imagined the pain endured. 'All the hallmarks of a personal grudge, a punishment, I would think,' said Ann. 'There were numerous linear cuts all over the body which suggested that the killer began the torture with the small cuts, possibly done with a razor or scalpel which caused profuse bleeding. The intermittent clotting around the sites suggests the cuts were made ante mortem. The killer then made deeper incisions to the dermis which he knew which would cause severe pain. The condition of the organs suggests the victim was a relatively healthy individual,' said Tim. Tim's final comment was that he assumed, judging by the precision of the strips of flesh cut out of the body, must have been done by someone who was a skilled butcher or someone with medical knowledge, as the incisions missed the major blood vessels in the abdomen, causing maximum pain and delayed death. He told Ann that he had sent off samples of blood and bone marrow taken from the drill bit and chisel found at the scene. Toxicology report did not reveal any drugs in the victim's system. Alcohol levels were minimal. Ann stayed to discuss the details of the case with Tim for some time after the completion of the post-mortem.

Tim promised that he would send Ann a detailed typed report as soon as he could. She thanked him and left. She returned to her office to complete all her paperwork regarding the post-mortem. She recalled details of her interview with Luke Cowan and tried to piece together parts of the puzzle, by recalling what he said and his reaction. She made a note of the contact details for Sam Cain, which Luke had given her, and dialled the number. A male voice answered. 'Hello, this is Sam Cain,' 'Mr Cain, I am

Detective Chief Inspector Ann Dixon. I wonder if you can spare the time to have me visit you as I am investigating a murder?' said Ann. There was a brief pause on the other end of the line. 'Are you sure you have the right number?' came the reply. 'You are Mr Sam Cain of 12 Bentley Road, Battersea?' enquired Ann. 'Yes, this is he,' replied the voice. 'I will get right to the point, Mr Cain, a man named, Tom Casey, whose sister you once knew, has been murdered, and we have to interview you and everyone who were close to the Casey brothers,' she continued. There was another brief silence, after which time, Sam Cain spoke. 'How about 10am on Wednesday?' Sam replied. 'That would be good for me too, see you then,' said Ann. The ringing of her phone interrupted her thoughts. 'Hi busy lady. Fancy a game of squash?' said the voice at the other end. 'Hello Owen, good to hear from you. Oh. Yes, I would love a game. Maybe I can get rid of some of the stress which is taking over my life. What time?' She enquired. 'Will 6pm be good for you? 'asked Owen. 'If you are free afterwards, we can grab a bite to eat,' said Owen. 'Great, see you then,' she replied. She phoned Josie to inform her that she would not be home for dinner.

Ann enjoyed the rigors of playing squash. She felt that it was her only means of lashing out at all the frustrations she suffered. Sweating profusely and breathing heavily as she battled to keep up with Owen's command of the game, Ann finally collapsed on the squash court, admitting defeat. They showered and changed for dinner. 'Your case is dominating the news these days,' said Owen. 'I wish it wouldn't. It is the bane of my life. I get any support from my superintendant. He is the rudest bastard on the planet,' she continued. ''Perhaps you should consider returning to MI6 with us,' said Owen encouragingly. 'Absolutely not, I am done with that lot. I love my work. I just wish I did not need to deal with such a mindless idiot as my boss,' she complained. 'You were a fantastic operative and I am sure a great cop. Don't allow them to get to you. Just follow your instincts,' he continued. The phone rang as soon as Ann reached her office. It was the forensic pathologist who informed her that they were able to lift off a good set of fingerprints off the drill bit and the chisel found at the scene of the crime. She was also told that the blood and bone marrow found in the groove of the drill bit, was a match to Tom Casey. The next morning, Ann mobilised her team to get fingerprints and cheek swabs from the Casey brothers and Luke Cowan. She told them she would take swabs and fingerprints from Sam Cain. David accompanied Ann to 12 Bentley Road the next day. Ann stood at the door for a few minutes while David Hughes parked the car. Then she rang the doorbell. A stocky, man answered the door. Ann introduced herself and her Sergeant to Sam Cain who invited them in.

Ann glanced around the living room quickly, before taking a seat next to David on the settee. Ann wasted no time in getting to the point of the matter. She repeated the reason for her visit and asked Sam if he could substantiate his movements on the day Tom Casey was murdered. He said he was at home, but there were no witnesses to support his claim. When questioned about his relationship with the Casey brothers, Sam explained how he was beaten by the Casey brothers when the brothers realised that he was dating their sister. He expressed deep loathing for the brothers as he showed Ann the scars he still bore as a result of the vicious beating. 'You see the Casey brothers thought nobody was good enough for their sister. They hated me because they thought I was not wealthy enough to marry their sister,' he said. 'Surely, Mr Cain, you must have built up a certain amount of resentment towards the Casey brothers if they beat you and humiliated you over time?' 'I would say that is a motive for murder in my book,' said Ann fixing her gaze on him. He shuffled uncomfortably, replying with a stammer, 'I disliked the brothers, but not enough to murder one of them. They are a wicked bunch of brothers. You should speak to their old neighbour in Nottingham.

He can tell you how cruel they were to animals, torturing and murdering those poor creatures during their satanic rituals. They also tortured the girls who were naïve enough to venture into their clutches. Who knows one of them might have murdered their own brother,' replied Sam. 'Do you know about the existence of a coded book which belonged to Tom?' asked Ann. 'I don't know about a coded book. I do know that Tom had many books on the occult, but I did not know about a book in particular", replied Sam. You should talk to Jack Slade, their neighbour. He knew them well enough. He may even be able to tell you about the book in question. He has enough dirt on them to put them in jail. 'Jack Slade will give you an eye witness account of what the brothers did to their own sister. I am not saying another word,' he replied nervously, sitting down to compose himself. Ann waited for him to recover from his outburst. 'What do you do for a living Mr Cain?' 'I work for an insurance company. It is rather boring work. Thankfully I can lose myself in my love of woodwork. I have made most of the furniture in this room,' he said. Ann fixed her gaze on a handsome coffee table and cabinet in the room. 'You are very talented Mr Cain, the work is exquisite,' remarked Ann. 'Thank you, I do all the work in my shed at the back of the house,' replied Sam proudly. Ann listened intently then said, 'I am afraid, Mr Cain, we will need you to come to the police station so that our forensic officer to take your fingerprints and swabs for your DNA so that we can exclude you from the investigation,' said Ann. 'We will need to speak to you again, so don't leave town,' she added. She asked for Jack Slade's address, which he gave willingly.

Her phone rang as she got into the car. It was Edwards. 'Dixon, I have organised a press conference for this afternoon at 2pm in the briefing room. You had better be there,' he shouted. She barely had time to finish her sentence when he put down the phone. 'Rude bastard, I hate it when he does that to me,' said Ann in frustration. She glanced at her watch and realised they had just about an hour before the press meeting. 'Let's try to contact Jack Slade while we are waiting,' she said to David as they headed for her office. She listened while David dialled the number Sam had given her. A frail voice answered the phone when David finally got through. 'May I speak to Mr Jack Slade please,' said David. 'Yes, this is he. Who am I speaking to please?' asked the voice. 'It is Detective Sergeant, David Hughes from the Metropolitan Police, Sir. I wonder if I could pay you a visit, at your earliest convenience please,' asked David. There was a brief silence, then, Mr Slade asked, 'Why do you need to see me?' sergeant?' said Jack Slade. 'We are investigating a murder of one of your ex-neighbours and we thought you might be able to tell us a bit about the background of the Casey brothers,' continued David. There was consternation in his voice when he replied. 'I don't know if I could do that, Sergeant Hughes. Those boys are bad bunch and it is not my life's worth to get involved,' he replied. Ann was becoming irritated at David's procrastination. She took the phone from him and introduced herself to Mr Slade. She spoke in a charming tone of voice. 'Hello, Mr Slade, I am DCI Dixon, so sorry to bother you. We understand your concerns about helping the police, but I assure you your help will be invaluable to us and of course everything you say will be kept in the strictest confidence,' she assured Mr Slade. Her seduction worked and he agreed to meet with them early the next morning. David wrote down the address as Ann repeated it while Mr Slade spoke. 'Thank you, look forward to meeting with you tomorrow,' said Ann. David smiled as he said, 'Ever thought of working for the United Nations guv?' Ann swung around at the remark, laughed and hit him on the head with a folded newspaper. 'Ever imagined yourself back in uniform, Hughes, watch your mouth,' she admonished him. 'Get a decent car to drive us to Nottingham tomorrow,' she ordered. 'We had better grab some lunch in the canteen because there's no knowing how long the press meeting will last,' she added. They discussed their meeting with Sam Cain, during lunch, and worked out a strategy for their next move.

'Better not be too direct with the questions when we meet with Mr Slade. He may clam up if he feels threatened,' she warned. They mulled over the evidence, and spent some time going over the details of their interview with Sam. The briefing room was filled with the buzz of eager newsmen and women who waited patiently for the superintendant to appear. A momentary hush prevailed when Edwards entered the room. He outlined brief details of the murder omitting details which would harm the progress of the case. His statement was followed by a barrage of questions from the media. 'Superintendant, do you have a suspect?' Why was the victim tortured?' Do you have any leads yet?' Why has it taken you so long to release a statement to the press?' he continued. Edwards waited for a suitable pause in the questioning then answered. 'We do not have a crystal ball to lead us to a suspect or tell us why the victim has been tortured. My officers must be given time to pursue information and rely on scientific evidence to help them find the killer. The police do not have an obligation to keep the media informed day and night whenever a crime is committed. They need time to process the evidence, so that they can able to inform the press which hopefully will result in the killer being caught. I have no further information at present, except to assure you that my officers are doing everything possible to find the murderer who committed this heinous crime. Ladies and gentlemen if there are no further questions, I am now concluding this meeting, 'said Edwards as he got up from his seat and began walking out of the room. Some persistent members of the media continued to fire questions at him, but he kept tight lipped and walked out of the door. Ann and David followed hastily as the media began to question them. 'Who was that short journalist who refused to back down?' David asked. 'That's the poison dwarf for the News of the World paper, Amy Baker. We have crossed swords many times and she hasn't forgiven me. No doubt she will follow this case doggedly purely to score points with her boss and hopefully try to get me discredited,' replied Ann. 'She sounds a nasty bit of work. You should steer clear of her, guv,' said David. Ann completed her backlog of paperwork and headed home. Josie was away for a few days, so she indulged in a takeaway dinner and a glass of wine and settled for an early night. David collected her at 7am and they set off to their meeting with Mr Slade. They reached Edwinstowe, Nottingham at 10.30am. The house was hidden from view amongst a clump of trees near the edge of the forest. The house appeared in a state of neglect. Paint peeled off the guttering and there were large cracks along the outside walls. The garden was overgrown with weeds and there were rusted car parts strewn at the back of the house. Ann and David took a brief look around, before ringing the doorbell. There was a momentary pause before an elderly bedraggled man opened the door. 'Who are you?' he enquired. 'Good morning, we are from the Metropolitan police. We would like to speak to Jack Slade please,' said Ann cheerfully as she flashed her identity badge. 'I am Jack Slade, come in,' he said. Ann introduced herself and David as she flashed her identity badge and followed him into the house. Jack took a cursory glance at the document and invited them to sit down. The inside of the house was unkempt and in urgent need of a clean. Jack apologised for the untidy state of the house, explaining that he neglected to keep it tidy after the death of his wife three years ago. He offered them tea, which Ann politely declined, explaining that they had coffee on the way over. 'So, which one of the Casey brothers has died?' Jack enquired. 'Tom Casey was brutally murdered last week,' explained Ann. 'I am hardly surprised, he got what he deserved,' said Jack. 'Oh! that's a rather harsh statement Mr Slade,' exclaimed Ann. 'Not at all if you knew how wicked they all were,' continued Jack. 'Mr Slade, we have information about the brother's having tortured animals and women. They also practised satanic rituals. Can you give us your version of events?' said Ann. 'Oh ay, I will tell you about the Casey's alright,' he said. He got up out of his seat and went over to the window. He pointed to a large white house a few hundred yards from his own. "That is where the Casey brothers lived with their parents. Their mother was an actress and spent lots of time away from home. Their father was a lawyer for Lloyds of London, so he commuted each day. The boys were cared for by a nanny. They were very wicked. They tortured killed small animals in the forest, including some of the neighbour's pets. 'How do you know so much about their behaviour, Mr Slade?' asked Ann. The boys used to take my tools and hide them in their garden shed to annoy me. I would go looking for my stuff in their backyard. That is how I happened to see what they got up to when their parents were away. They brought girls off from the streets, tortured them and then had sexual orgies with them. They moved their activities into the basement of the house, because the women screamed so much. They finally moved their rituals to the forest where they had the freedom to continue their perverse practices undisturbed. The most unforgiveable crime was the sexual abuse of their sister. I only know about what they did because their sister ran away from them one night and sought refuge at my house. She was terrified and told me not to say anything to anyone.

The boys had a cousin, James. He was as evil as the rest of them. I suppose his father being a Nazi does explain his cruel streak. He mixed with drug dealers and some very shifty fellas," continued Mr Slade. Their mother and father were killed in a car crash just when the boys started their careers. We heard that they were practising satanic rituals in the forest. Nobody dared go to watch the goings on out in the forest because it was believed the boys posted guards near the ritual site, who stopped anyone getting near the rituals. It was said the guards were a force to be reckoned with, so nobody ventured near the scene of the rituals. The terrible things that were done to the women by those lads, is beyond belief,' he continued. His eyes were filled with tears as he remembered the distress of their sister. 'Mr Slade, the police would label you a voyeur for watching these activities, and an accomplice in some ways, for not reporting the abuse,' said Ann.

'Believe me Inspector, I would rather spend time in jail then suffer the wrath of Casey's,' he added. 'Do you remember anything else Mr Slade?' asked Ann. 'Yes, would you believe for all their violent behaviour, George Casey and his brothers created a beautiful rose garden at the back of the house and tended it every day. I could not believe that men who embodied such perversity could produce such a beautiful garden,' added Jack. 'Did you know any of the girls who were brought to the house?' asked Ann. 'No, they were foreign girls who lived rough on the streets. Choosing such girls gave the boys carte blanche to use and abuse the girls as they pleased,' he continued. Jack thought for a moment. 'I do remember a Russian girl named Saskia who befriended my son. She got friendly with the Casey boys, and was seen at their home frequently. She then suddenly vanished, and we never heard about her again. Perhaps you should speak to my son, Andrew. He would be able to tell you more. However, Andrew lives on the Costa del Sol in Spain, but comes to see me at Christmas,' he continued. 'We would like to speak to your son. Do you have an address?' asked Ann. Jack shuffled over to a chest of drawers, riffled through some papers and produced his son's address and telephone number. 'Perhaps you could warn your son that we will be in touch. Thank you for your help. Here is a contact number if you remember anything more that will help in our investigations,' said Ann. Ann did not want to stress him any further.

She thanked him for his help and left with David. 'Wow these Casey's are a bad bunch,' exclaimed David. 'A bit like the Mafia,' said Ann." We need to have another meeting with the rest of the brothers," she said. They got back to London by early evening. Ann could not escape her meeting with Steven Edwards. She headed for his office as soon as she arrived. 'Where the hell have you been?' I have sent numerous messages and tried calling you several times,' he complained. 'Sorry sir, we have been busy interviewing. Sergeant Hughes and I have just come back from a meeting with the next -door neighbour of the Casey brothers when they lived in Nottingham,' she explained. 'I trust it wasn't a wasted journey,' he said. 'No on the contrary, it was most useful as we discovered facts about the Casey brothers that were valuable to our investigation,' she continued. This piqued Edward's curiosity and he pressed her for more information. She told him what Jack Slade had said. She was amazed that it held Edwards attention to such a degree that he did not interrupt her as she spoke. When she had finished, he asked if the information had brought her any nearer to finding the killer. She told him that she was still awaiting the outstanding forensic results. She promised to keep him informed of all matters pertaining to the case. 'Well keep me posted and give me a shout when you have heard from forensics,' said Edwards.

Josie was late for a meeting with an important client, so she raced to her appointment, speeding across the red traffic light. The driver of an ambulance which came out of the hospital gates was unable to apply breaks in time to avoid a collision. Josie's car was rammed from passenger's the side but thankfully nobody was hurt. The tall handsome driver stepped out of the ambulance grinning as he mocked Josie's driving skills. She was too embarrassed to reprimand him for criticising her driving skills. He stuck out his hand, introducing himself as Jake Casey. 'I am so sorry, I was speeding to a meeting,' said Josie apologetically. 'No real damage to the ambulance, but your lovely red Porsche has taken a bit of a knock,' added the ambulance driver. 'Let's swap details and I will get my insurance to sort it out,' replied Josie. 'No need to stuff up your no claims bonus, I have a better solution. My name is Jake. 'If you would agree to have dinner with me, I will tell my boss I was hit by a guy who drove off,' said Jake. 'I don't think I could do that,' replied Josie. 'Why, ever not? A pretty woman like you must be beating away the men from your door,' said Jake. 'I am in a relationship actually, so I can't accept your invitation,' replied Josie. For heaven's sake it will only be dinner, not a marriage proposal. A small price to pay for my silence, don't you agree,' he continued. Josie thought for a while, and reluctantly agreed to meet him for dinner in a few days. They exchanged phone numbers, but Josie warned him not to call her. He teased her about being afraid of her partner. She drove off feeling terribly guilty for planning to do something behind Ann's back. She pacified herself by thinking", no harm done, it will only be dinner. Josie was racked with guilt. She knew Ann would be incensed at her for entering into an illegal arrangement but there appeared to be something genuine about the man she had met by accident. She hurried home, her thoughts in turmoil. Glad that she had survived her meeting with Edwards, Ann headed for her office, completed additions on her laptop and headed home. 'I hope you have prepared a humungous meal, I am starving,' said Ann as she entered the house. 'Of course, my darling, I have prepared your favourite,' replied Josie. 'Good, I'll just jump into the shower and then you can have all my attention" Ann shouted as she ran upstairs to the bathroom. Josie followed Ann into the shower and engaged in a frenzy of passionate love making that left them breathless. 'Oh, someone was starving, remarked Ann grinning cheekily. 'Serves you right for deserting me in the early hours of the morning, replied Josie. The two women got dressed and headed for the kitchen. The two women caught up on their news and Ann talked briefly about her trip to Nottingham. The familiar sound of David's car hooter sounded outside. Ann dashed about collecting the files she needed to take with her for the day's work. "Sorry to keep you waiting. I never remember to put things where I can find them in the morning," she said. Josie waved them off at the door, and they headed for the office.

'I managed to get George Casey to meet with us this morning,' David informed Ann. 'He was not pleased, but agreed anyway," said David. 'Good, we will have a coffee, and go to his house afterwards,' said Ann. George Casey was still in his dressing gown when they arrived. He seemed irritated but remained civil and invited them into the living room. 'Thought I had told you everything I know at our last meeting, inspector,' said George. 'You were very helpful, but we need to clarify a few things we have learned from someone helping us with our enquiries,' continued Ann. George swung around and demanded to know who Ann had been talking to. 'Never you mind who it was, we need your version of the story,' said Ann. 'I don't like your tone, Inspector. What have they been saying to you?' He demanded to know. 'Let's say we know about the satanic rituals in the forest and the encounters with foreign girls by you and your brothers, Mr Casey," she said. 'We are normal healthy men with an interest in women, since when has this been a crime,' enquired George. 'Yes, I agree, but we have been told that your relationship with the girls defied the terms of normality. We believe that you and your brothers used the girls in your rituals, and that you tortured the women to satisfy your perverse needs,' retorted Ann. 'That's a preposterous accusation. I trust that you have firm evidence to support your accusations. I will consult with my lawyer about bringing charges against the police for slander,' shouted George, his face crimson with anger. 'We have a credible witness who will testify against you,' replied Ann triumphantly. Her statement forced George to back down. He composed himself, and said, 'I am quite within my rights to practice as a Satanist in this country. You will find it hard to prosecute me on the grounds of my unorthodox religion,' he continued. 'Of course, there is the question of you and your brothers having had an incestuous relationship with sister. She had related her harrowing ordeal to our witness. Do you have a feasible explanation for this accusation, Mr Casey?' said Ann with some conviction. George shifted in his seat uncomfortably. He was silent for a few moments before replying, 'You don't have a case, Inspector. My sister is dead. Where is the evidence?' he continued boldly. 'Don't be so sure Mr Casey. You will be surprised how the law can make a case stick, given the right circumstances,' she said.

He smiled at her confidence. 'Let me tell you, nobody will ever testify against me,' he said. 'You will have them silenced if they do, will you?' she continued. 'Those are your words inspector, not mine,' he continued. My answer to your question is, No Comment," he said emphatically. Ann realised they would not get the information they hoped for, so she thanked George for agreeing to meet with them and took her leave. 'I wanted to thump him at one stage, Guv," said David. "No point in doing that David. George Casey has wealth and power. He probably uses force to ensure people toe the line. We did promise Jack we would be discreet,' added Ann. The phone rang just as Ann got to her office. It was Peter Drew on the line. "Got some fascinating news, Ann,' said Peter. 'The fingerprints on the drill bit belongs to Sam Cain,' he said. 'The blood and bone marrow is a match to Tom Casey,' he continued. Ann asked if Luke Cowan had been in to tender his fingerprints and DNA. She was told he had done very early that morning and his DNA was no match to any of the forensic evidence at the scene of the crime. Ann immediately went to the incident room to find the senior officers who were assigned to the case. She found D.I. Tobin at his desk.

Chapter 2

"Alf, I just had a call from forensics. They have matched the fingerprints on the drill bit and the chisel to Sam Cain. I am going to see Edwards now to get an urgent warrant to search his house. Contact the rest of the team, fill them in and tell them to be on standby to accompany me to the house when I have the warrant. David joined them in the incident room and was briefed about the latest details. 'Stick around, David I want you to accompany me to Sam Cain's house. But first, give me a few minutes to brief Edwards. The news had already reached the superintendant by the time Ann walked into Edwards' office. 'I believe you have a suspect, Dixon", said Edwards sarcastically. 'Yes sir, I am on my way to arrest Sam Cain, and I need you to get a warrant issued to search his property please,' said Ann politely. 'Alright, you can pick it up in the morning. Make sure that there are no hitches. Now get on with it,' he growled. Ann left the room fuming. "Bastard, he gets worse with each passing day. A smile would probably crack his face,' she grumbled. 'Come on guv, you know he will never change,' replied David. 'Let's go and tell Sam Cain the bad news,' added David. 'We had better check on his whereabouts first,' said Ann. David called Sam and informed him that the police wanted to pay him a visit on an urgent matter. Sam told David that he was at home and would be happy to help with their enquiries. He was pottering in the garden when they arrived. He looked at them quizzically as they got out of the car and walked towards him. 'Good afternoon Mr Cain. There has been a dramatic development,' said Ann. 'We have matched your fingerprints to a drill bit and chisel used to torture Tom Casey and his blood was found on the drill bits,' added Ann. 'I would like you to accompany us to the police station for further questioning in connection with the murder of Tom Casey. 'Cuff him Sergeant Hughes,' ordered Ann as she led the way to the car. 'A warrant will be issued to allow the police to search your home,' continued Ann. Sam looked stunned. He attempted to protest but thought better of it. He followed the officers slavishly in silence, into the car. They drove Sam to the holding cells where, Ann and David accompanied him to the interview room. Ann went in alone with Sam. She informed him that their conversation would be recorded. He nodded in acknowledgement of her statement. The bright light in the room accentuated his pallor. 'It is 10.30 am on the 11th of March 2005. I am in the interview room with Mr Samuel Cain who has been brought in as a suspect in the murder of Tom Casey. Ann read Sam his rights, ensuring it was logged onto the recorder. 'Mr Cain, are you aware of the serious nature of the charges you are facing?' urged Ann. 'Yes, I think so, but I am innocent. I would never resort to murder even if the Casey's and I had our differences,' he stammered. 'You have no alibi on the night of the murder and your fingerprints are on the weapons found at the scene of the murder. Can you explain how they got there if you claim you are innocent,' continued Ann. 'You had motive and opportunity. We know that you could not have lifted Tom onto the bannister by yourself, so did you have an accomplice, Mr Cain?' Ann probed, leaning forward across the table in an intimidating manner, to unnerve him. His shoulders drooped with despair and he began to shake with emotion. 'I didn't do it. I did not murder anyone. You must believe me,' he implored Ann. 'The evidence seems to link you to the murder of Tom Casey. We will keep you here in the holding cells until we have searched you house. If we find more incriminating evidence on your property, it will enable the prosecution to build a very strong case against you. You will then appear in court and be formerly charged,' said Ann. Sam's distress and the fact that he could offer no additional information to either confirm or refute the charges against him. Ann terminated the interview and instructed the officer in charge to take Sam to the holding cell.

The buzz of the CID team could be heard along the corridor as Ann approached the briefing room. She banged the door loudly to get their attention as she didn't feel like shouting to make herself heard. They obeyed and sat down to listen to what she had to say. She began by informing them that she had Sam Cain in custody on the strength of the fact that his fingerprints were found on some of the murder weapons and that she was waiting for a warrant to search his home. 'Okay I need to hear what you have found out,' she said. Detective Inspector Alfred Tobin told her that his team interviewed Tom's neighbours. He said that the neighbour heard loud voices on the night of the murder. They also reported hearing classical music played around midnight. They did not take too much notice as they were used to Tom playing his music loudly, however, the music lasted for 3 hours until 5am. They were rather puzzled at the late hour of the music. They did not see anyone leave the house. They also did not see any strange cars parked at the house. Tobin informed her that Tom Casey's laptop and mobile phone did not have any significant information relevant to the murder.

Detective Inspector Ian Roberts reported that he had interviewed Tom's work colleagues, a close friend and associates of his company. There were very positive comments about him, and nobody could think of a reason for his death. He added that he discovered that Tom's bridge partner was also his lover, but the lover was away in Scotland on the night of the murder. Linda Smith confirmed that nothing had been stolen from the Casey home. Ann informed her team that she was waiting for a warrant to be issued to search Sam Cain's house. She told them that she would convene another briefing after the house search. The team gathered in groups and began to discuss their assignments. The warrant was granted later that day. Ann, David, D.I. Roberts and D.I. Tobin and the forensic team descended on 12 Bentley Road. Ann sent her officers to various parts of the house and instructed them to be meticulous in their search. Many books, relating to rituals of the occult, were found on the bookshelf. Sam's clothes were, and many other items in the house, were bagged for evidence. Ann and David Hughes concentrated on the tools in Sam's garage. He found a work bench and an array of chisels, screwdrivers, nails, and a staple gun and a drill. David Hughes called Ann to witness the collection of tools. 'I want you to bag all the tools,' said Ann. The forensic officer groaned at the command because there was quite a considerable number of tools in the garage. 'No excuses just do as you are told. How the hell do you expect to do a proper investigation if your work is shoddy?' Ann shouted. 'I don't bloody care if you are here all day. You will do a thorough job,' she added. A size ten shoeprint was visible in a patch of grease near the door. The search lasted 7 hours before the exhausted Ann and her team locked the house and took all the evidence they had collected. Ann had a good working relationship with the head of the forensic laboratory, Peter Drew. She went to meet with him and implored him to get the samples processed urgently. They discussed details of the case over a cup of coffee in his office. 'Old Edwards been on your back again, Ann?' Peter enquired with a smile. 'When is he ever reasonable about time limits?' Ann replied, scowling. He is pushing for a result because I am heading this investigation.

If it was a man in charge, I am sure it would have been different,' replied Ann. 'You shouldn't allow that old fart to get to you. Stand up to him. This is your investigation, and when you have caught the killer, Edwards will reap the benefit and you will be lucky if he says thank you,' said Peter, putting his arm around her for support. 'Listen, I won't let you down. My team will work overtime to get you the results by tomorrow afternoon,' he said reassuringly. True to his word, the results from forensics arrived promptly at 2pm the next day. She opened the envelope anxiously and read the contents. She walked to the incident room where David and Ian Roberts were examining some details on the board. 'Listen up, guys, I have the forensic reports from Sam

Cain's house. Get my team here now please. She briefed David and Ian on the reports while waiting for the rest of the team. It was short notice, so only eight members of the CID could attend the meeting. 'Thanks for coming,' said Ann. I have the reports on samples and items collected at Sam Cain's house,' said Ann. 'The drill and staple gun had been washed, but contained small traces of blood and bone marrow, which was a match to Tom Casey. The fingerprints on the staple gun and drill matched those of Sam Cain. The shoe print had traces of blood belonging to Tom Casey and carpet fibres from the carpet at the scene of the crime, but the shoe size did not match that of Sam as he wears a size 8. I do think he might have had an accomplice. The fact that it would have needed two people to lift the victim onto the staircase. I can confirm that according to these results, we do have a murder suspect and Sergeant Hughes will accompany me to the holding cells where I am going to formerly charge the suspect,' said Ann gathering her bag and papers as she prepared to leave the room. David and Ann made their way to holding cells.

She seated herself opposite Sam in the cell and informed him that the forensic results confirmed that his drill contained blood, bone marrow and tissue samples of Tom Casey, and that she was charging him with the murder. 'Mr Cain, you have the right to remain silent. Anything you say will be taken down and will be used in evidence against you. You have the right to appoint a lawyer, if you do not have one, the court will appoint one for you,' said Ann. Sam Cain stared at her in total disbelief that he had become a suspect in a murder case. He sank to the ground crushed by the news. Ann waited until he had composed himself sufficiently to speak. 'I did not murder Tom Casey,' he protested. Ann waited for him to calm down, before she spoke. She informed him that he would be held in prison until he appears before a judge to be formerly charged, and that he would be moved to a secure prison. She advised him to contact his lawyer in the meantime. Sam Cain looked a pathetic figure as he sat bent double in the brightly lit cell. It seemed that he was unable to comprehend anything she said at the time as he was overcome with shock. Ann was puzzled that she felt a measure of pity for him, for he did not appear as a heartless killer. But then, perhaps, he was driven by exceptional circumstances to commit murder. Ann and David returned to her office. She was surprised that she did not feel triumphant at finding the murderer. It all seemed so surreal. She slumped in her chair. 'Catching killers is exhausting stuff, hey guv? 'I think you need a double whiskey, 'said David. 'I agree, but a strong coffee will do nicely please,' replied Ann. They chinked coffee cups as David offered his congratulations. The boss will be pleased", said David enthusiastically. 'Don't remind me, I had better inform misery guts personally before he gives me an earful,' she replied woefully. She traipsed off to Edward's office triumphantly. She envisaged his discomfort at her success. She smiled at him as she entered his office. 'What do you want?' he sneered. 'I came to inform you sir that we have arrested Sam Cain for the murder of Tom Casey. His prints were found on the murder weapons in his garage and his drill had Tom Casey's blood and bone marrow. Her statement distracted him from his paperwork. He looked up and said. 'Splendid work Dixon pull up a chair and update me,' he said in an unbelievable civil manner. 'Well actually, sir there's not much more to tell. I will have a full report on the case on your desk tomorrow morning,' she added. He was annoyed at her brevity, just when he wanted more time to talk. 'The team are joining me for a celebratory drink at the Horse and Hounds in Pimlico at 7pm sir. You are most welcome to join us,' she added, and left the room with a great feeling of satisfaction that perhaps she had conveyed to Edwards the humiliation of being dismissed. The news of the arrest and charge spread through the station like wild fire. The police station was virtually deserted as most of the force migrated to the pub. The officers crowded around the bar. They cheered Ann as she walked into the pub. She acknowledged their enthusiasm with a wry smile and joined them at the bar. She was joined by Peter Drew who offered his own compliments for her diligent work. She thanked them for their hard work and support. Someone shouted, 'Three cheers for the guv'nor.' Everyone joined in the singing of 'She's a jolly good fellow.' David announced that he proposed that Ann should buy everyone a least two rounds of drinks. She replied, 'Don't push your luck,' David, you'll be back on the beat tomorrow,' she scolded. He officers roared with laughter and pointed a warning finger at David. She was surprised to see Edwards walk into the pub. He joined her at the table. 'Seems like you have done a good job, Ann, Congratulations,' said Edwards. It made her flesh crawl sitting in such proximity to a man who treated her appallingly and now wanted to be nice to her because her hard work made him look good. 'I have arranged a briefing with the press and television crew in the morning at 8am. Meet me in the briefing room at 7.30,' he said. 'Okay, I will be there,' she replied. She thanked him politely but made her excuses that she needed to go home. He tried to persuade her to stay, but she declined called to David to drive her home. Ann was very pensive in the car. 'What's on your mind, guv?' David enquired. 'Something's missing about this case,' she replied. 'I don't understand the bit about there being superimposed glove prints on the murder weapons. Why would Sam handle the weapons with bare hands, then use gloves?' It just does not make any sense,' she said. 'Perhaps he used gloves to hold the weapons while he was washing off the blood and forgot to remove all his fingerprints,' replied David.

'Look, guv, you nailed the villain. The forensic evidence is irrefutable. Get a good night's sleep and things will be different in the morning,' he said. 'Okay, thanks for the lift. See you in the morning,' said Ann as she got out of the car. Josie was asleep when Ann got home. She snuggled next to Josie in bed, not bothering to undress as sleep overwhelmed her. Josie had already left when Ann scrambled around the bedroom trying to put together a suitable outfit for the press meeting. 'Oh God, Josie why are you never around when I need your help,' she muttered to herself. David's persistent hooting added to her stress and she shouted out of the window for him to stop being bloody impatient. She jumped into the car, still applying her make up. 'Do I look alright to face the cameras David?' She asked as she adjusted her jacket. He threw her a swift glance and reassured her that she looked very smart. She scrambled out of the car, realising she was already ten minutes late. David feasted his eyes on the way her dress hugged the curvaceous contours of her body before he alighted from the car. Edwards glared at her. 'Why the hell can't you get out of bed in the morning,' he spat. 'Sorry sir,' she muttered apologetically. 'Do you have the report I left on your desk yesterday?' she asked, in an attempt to cover up his preoccupation with her late arrival. 'Let's go and face the press,' he replied as he led the way into the briefing room.

They were met by a sea of flashing lights. Edwards began to release his statement. 'The CID murder squad, led by DCI, Ann Dixon yesterday arrested and charged a man with the murder of Tom Casey. He will be formerly charged by a judge over the next few days and moved to a secure prison. Are there any questions?' Edwards asked. The media lunged at Edwards and Ann with their microphones held aloft and began to fire questions. 'How did you catch the killer, superintendant?' 'The murder weapons contained evidence linking the killer to the murder,' replied Edwards. 'DCI Dixon previous reports stated that the police suspected there might have been two killers. Do you think the murderer in custody acted on his own or did he have an accomplice?' asked Amy. 'We are still continuing our investigations and we will continue to question the suspect, in an attempt to establish if he had an accomplice,' replied Ann. 'The nature of the killing suggests a link to the occult. Do you think you should be pursuing Satanists connected to the victim to find a possible second killer?' Amy Baker urged. 'We cannot draw any conclusions about a second killer at present and it would not be worth wasting police time and money pursuing weak leads which do not guarantee an arrest,' replied Ann. Realising that Amy Baker was angling to trap him with her questioning, Edwards brought the meeting to a close. He thanked everyone for their time. This sparked even more questions, and with howls of protest, but he was determined not to answer any more questions. He and Ann exited swiftly through the side door. Edwards told Ann that he was pleased with their performance at the press meeting. He told her he would let her know when Sam Cain would need to appear in court to be formerly charged. They parted in the corridor and she walked to her office. Her phone rang as she sat down at her desk. 'Who is the greatest detective in the world?' said the cheery voice on the other side. 'Josie, it is so good to hear from you. I missed seeing you this morning. I wanted to tell you before you heard it from the media,' replied Ann. 'It's okay, I am so proud of you. By the way, I am going to have dinner with a client, so if you are early, don't wait up for me,' said Josie. 'Enjoy, see you in the morning,' added Ann. Sigh! I guess I will just have to join the queue of all your admirers,' said Josie. 'Don't sound so glum. I will make it up to you,' replied Ann. 'Promise, promises. I will hold you to that,' said Josie. David knocked and entered carrying two steaming cups of coffee. 'You read my thoughts, wonderful man,' she gushed, nurturing the cup in both hands and savouring the first precious mouthful. Ann's mobile rang as she downed the last drop of invigorating coffee. It was the chief super, Michael Heath.

He offered his congratulations and invited her for a drink at the pub in half an hour. She agreed but confessed to David that she had promised Josie that she would be home early. 'Come with me David, then I can sneak off while you keep him company,' she begged. He agreed and they drove off to the pub. Michael Heath was beaming all over his face as he shook Ann's hand and kissed her on the cheek. 'We are proud of you Ann, great job, well done,' he said enthusiastically. 'This is Sergeant David Hughes. He worked hard and should share the credit,' said

Ann proudly. Michael ordered the drinks and they wandered off to sit at the tables outside the pub. Ann updated Michael on details of the case. She thought for a moment, then said, 'Please promise not to share with Steven Edwards what I am about to tell you,' said Ann. 'You have my solemn word, fire away,' replied Michael. 'There are a few discrepancies which casts doubt on Sam Cain's guilt. I cannot put my hand on my heart and swear that he committed the murders. If he did, I think that he was just the lackey and not the main culprit. I believe we should gather further evidence in fairness to him and to justice,' added Ann. Michael listened intently and nodded in agreement. He smiled and said, you had better keep mum about your thoughts because you know Edwards will have your guts for garters if he knows there is division in his camp,' he added. 'Yes indeed, and that is the reason I advised Sam to hire a good defence lawyer. I will also continue to gather information about the case, in the interest of justice,' she assured Michael.

Josie parked her car and headed up the steps of the restaurant. Jake got up from his seat and greeted her with relish. 'I was afraid you would change your mind and not turn up,' said Jake. 'I am the guilty one, so the least I could do was to comply with your request,' added Josie. 'Did you get to patch up your lovely Porsche?' enquired Jake. 'Yes, they did a really good job. Can't tell it was damaged,' continued Josie 'What are you having to drink?' asked Jake. 'A glass of white wine would be nice, please,' replied Josie. Jake suggested Prosecco. 'Lovely, that would be very nice,' said Josie. 'What do you do for a living?' Jake enquired. 'I am a fashion designer,' replied Josie. 'Bright lights and glamour and lots of money, very impressive,' said Jake. '[You forgot to add that it takes plenty of hard work and mountains of stress too,' replied Josie. 'What does your partner do?' Jake asked. Josie hesitated before replying. 'She is in the police, a detective chief inspector, actually,' Josie announced proudly. 'I had better watch my step,' said Jake. 'Wow what a coincidence. I recently met a DCI who happened to be investigating the death of my brother,' said Jake. 'Your partner wouldn't happen to be the gorgeous Ann Dixon?' asked Jake. Josie blushed as she confirmed Ann's identity. 'Yes, it is,' she added. 'Wow fancy me crashing into the detective's other half. I wonder what she would say if she knew we were having dinner,' joked Jake. 'I am not going to tell her, as I know she will be very upset if she knows I accepted your invitation. Let's keep it quiet please,' pleaded Josie. 'Okay, I promise,' said Jake. 'Where did you meet the sexy detective,' enquired Jake. 'We met at a charity function. Ann has a friend, Owen Hammond who also happens to be my friend. I did not know that they met when they both served in MI6. Owen's brother is in fashion design, so he invited them both. Owen was the match maker for Ann and me. He arranged it so that I gave Ann a lift home that night and we fell hopelessly in love, and the rest is history,' Josie declared with girlish enthusiasm. 'Are you the same age?' Jake probed enthusiastically. 'Ann is 5 years older but that is insignificant as our love is so strong,' added Josie. 'Hey nosey, I hope you are not going to tell Ann that I have told you our life story,' pleaded Josie. 'Absolutely not, my lips are sealed,' Jake reassured her. 'It's not fair. There are you two stunning women, blissfully happy in a relationship. Here I am a lonely guy who would give his eye teeth to have either one of you,' he said dolefully. 'Too bad, I don't see how you, with your good looks cannot hold onto an attractive woman,' Josie remarked. Sigh! Problem is that they don't stay,' he continued. 'You will just have to tie them down before they escape,' replied Josie. Dinner progressed pleasantly. Jake's sense of humour and charm allayed her anxiety about the meeting. They laughed and chatted late into the night. As they were leaving the restaurant, Josie said, 'Well I hope I have paid off my debt by having dinner with you,' she said. Jake replied, 'Oh perhaps you will need to pay it off in instalments,' he said laughingly as Josie suddenly became serious at his remark. 'Of course, I am joking, but let's keep in touch,' he replied kissing her on the cheek. Perhaps we can speak from time to time,' he added. Josie nodded in agreement and headed for her car. She felt so guilty about her dinner with Jake, that she phoned Adam and asked him to join her for a drink. He was so concerned about the urgency in her voice, so sped over to meet her. 'Everything ok Josie?' You sounded stressed,' Adam said, as he joined her at the bar. 'Sit down, I had to talk to you,' she continued. 'Go on then, don't keep me in suspense,' he urged. 'Adam, I have done a terrible thing. I smashed into the ambulance driven by Jake Casey, the brother of Ann's murder victim. It was my fault. He suggested he blame it on a hit and run driver and in return I had to have dinner with him. Oh God, I was so afraid to tell Ann. In fact, I only found out who he was at the dinner. He confessed to have met Ann through the investigation into his brother's murder and I like a fool told him Ann was my partner. Please believe me it was just dinner. Nothing else happened. I did it to buy his silence,' continued Josie. 'Phew, Ann won't see it like that,' Adam advised. 'Oh Adam, I am so sorry I agreed to dinner. Shall I confess to Ann?' she asked. 'Lord, no, that is the last thing you should do. She will never trust you again. Did Jake ask to see you again?' 'No, he only wants to call me to speak sometimes,' she continued. 'Well that sounds okay. Just don't let Ann catch you out,' he warned.

'Don't worry you have not done anything wrong. Just keep his calls short and if he does not comply, I will persuade him,' he advised. Josie hugged him and thanked him and drove home. She slept on the sofa as she could not face Ann that night. She pretended to be in a deep sleep as Ann tried to wake her the next morning. 'Hmmm, must have been some dinner to leave you comatose,' Ann muttered under her breath. The reporters and members of the public worked themselves into frenzy, outside the prison gates, as the van carrying Sam Cain drove past. Their cameras flashed and there were shouts of 'murderer' as the van sped through the prison gates. The reporters chased after the van in their cars and rushed towards Sam as he was spirited away into court for the short hearing. A jacket was flung over Sam's head as he emerged from the van and entered the court through the side door. Despite the precaution, some reporters managed to take photos of the prisoner. He appeared deeply distressed from some of the photos which appeared in the papers the next day. Sam Cain had an excellent lawyer. He challenged the evidence against Sam, with impunity and proved Sam's innocence beyond reasonable doubt. The size 10 shoeprint in his garage was not his as he wore a size 8 shoe. The superimposed glove powder on the murder weapons suggested someone had worn gloves when handling the drill and staple gun. The evidence from Sam's next-door neighbour as having seen a tall man leave Sam's garage on the night of the murder, confirmed that a second person had access to Sam's tools.

The evidence was only admitted after Sam was already in custody. One of the neighbours went on a business trip the after the murder and was not available for questioning immediately after the murder. The police were only able to interview him on his return. The strongest evidence for his defence was that Sam could not have lifted the large framed Tom Casey onto the bannister by himself. The presence of the superimposed glove powder cast doubt on the evidence that a suspect would use his tools without gloves and leave his prints and then use gloves to handle the tools he used to inflict the torture. Sam's neighbour who had seen a tall man leaving the shed around 5,30am provided the final proof needed to overturn the evidence against him. Sam's lawyer presented a strong case for his defence. The judge was not able to dismiss the evidence put before him. The case did not go to trial. The judge dismissed the charges based on the new evidence for the defence. It was a relieved and elated Sam who was let out of prison that day. His sister accused Ann of gross negligence and incompetence and vowed to sue the police. Ann Dixon was pleased at the outcome but had to hide her true feelings from her Stephen Edwards, who was clearly vexed at the prospect of resurrecting an investigation that he felt should have been put to bed. Ann and David shifted uncomfortably in their seats at his office as he gave them the third degree voicing his disappointment at their bungled arrest. 'You can have the pleasure of facing the media with the chief superintendant,' he warned Ann. He carried on ad nauseam about the shortage of resources and the strain on the Met's finances. They were grateful when he evicted them from his office with a stern warning only to return when they could secure a viable conviction. David and Ann headed for the nearest coffee shop to recover from their lambasting.' Miserable bastard,' said David as he savoured the invigorating sips of coffee. 'Well we will just need to re-examine all the evidence and return to the scene of the crime,' replied Ann. 'There has to be something we missed,' she continued contemplatively. They returned to her office where she laid out all the evidence again and peered over every detail, looking for a connection to Tom Casey. 'Let's exclude Luke because he can only use powder free gloves because of his allergy to glove powder. Jake is the only one who wears size 10 shoes. We have examined his shoes, and none has s sole matching the print in Sam's garage. We need to consider if the perpetrator had an accomplice or that he was a very strong man,' said Ann. When they had finished, Ann called a meeting with her team. She pointed out all the details that had relevance to the case and impressed upon them the urgency to find more evidence. Ann told David that they ought to interview Jake and Nathan again and enquire about their cousin, James.

She managed to organise a meeting with the brothers for later that week. Jake seemed peeved at another interview, especially when she informed them that Sam was acquitted of the charge of murder. 'I don't know what more you think you can learn from us, Inspector, we have told you everything we know,' said Jake. 'I need to know more about your cousin, James. Do you know where he is at now?' 'He left for Brazil. He has business interests in Brazil. He has a sister, Susan with whom he stays in contact. She will be able to tell you more about his whereabouts,' said Jake. 'Do you know why he went to Brazil?' Ann urged. 'James is half German. His father was a Nazi during the war, and fled to Brazil, where he bought a house and lived there until 1965, when he changed his name to Muller and came to England where he met and married our aunt,' he continued. 'Do you know whether James participated in the satanic rituals with your brother's,' she enquired. 'I am aware that James and my brothers belonged to a sect who met regularly to practise their rituals in the forest, but I never joined in with any of it. Sam Cain hung out with them in the beginning, but after he had a run in with my brothers, he was excluded from the rituals. He might be able to tell you more than I can,' continued Jake. 'We have found a book with coded symbols at Tom's house. It seems that the killer was searching for this book on the day Tom died. Do you know about this book and do you know what it might contain?' Ann continued.

Jake stayed silent for a few minutes before replying, 'No I did not know about the book and I don't know what the symbols mean,' replied Jake, avoiding Ann's gaze. Ann sensed that Jake knew more than he was prepared to say, so she persevered with the questioning. 'Nathan, can you tell me anything about this book with symbols?' asked Ann. 'No, my brother was completely excluded from everything connected to the rituals because he was the youngest and very vulnerable,' replied Jake. 'Excuse me Mr Casey, I asked Nathan. 'I'm sure he can answer for himself,' said Ann curtly. 'Well my brother gets very upset at being asked questions he doesn't even understand. My brothers and I have always protected Nathan and shielded him from the evils of the world,' added Jake. 'That's very noble of you, but I still need a reply from Nathan as he is an adult and can answer for himself,' continued Ann annoyed at his constant interruption. Fearing that he might be the cause of an argument, Nathan interrupted by saying, 'I never knew what my brothers did in the forest although I knew they went there with some girls. Jake glared at him for giving Ann more fuel for questions. 'So! there were girls involved in the rituals. Tell me more,' Ann continued. 'I never met the girls, but I used to hide and watch from a vantage point when my brothers took them to the forest,' said Nathan. 'See that wasn't so difficult, was it?' Ann said reassuringly. Their conversation was interrupted by the ringing of Ann's mobile. 'Do you remember me inspector?' said the voice at the other end of the phone. Ann walked into the garden to continue her conversation in private. 'Oh God, Josie,' replied Ann, when she realized who it was. 'Hasn't madam forgotten something,' continued Josie cheekily. 'Oh no," exclaimed Ann as she remembered she had missed the launch of Josie's new designs. 'When pray, will her ladyship be putting in an appearance,' continued Josie, rubbing salt into Ann wounds as she squirmed with shame for disappointing Josie. 'See you in about an hour,' replied Ann. 'Just remember you will have to pay a forfeit of my choosing,' teased Josie. Ann smiled and promised Josie she would try to hurry to make it in time for the launch. David overheard some of Ann's conversation even though he continued to talk to Jake. He was silently envious as he wished he had been at the other end of the phone. He admired and adored her but had to keep his feelings under wraps for fear of alienating himself if she ever discovered the truth. He found her irresistibly attractive and her shapely body haunted him constantly. He hoped that by some miracle she would become aware of his feelings and reciprocate them. Alas! She was oblivious to his intentions and maintained a strictly working relationship. Ann returned to the room, looking rather flushed. She apologised for her brief absence and continued questioning Jake. They left reminding Jake to contact them if he remembered any significant details. David went very quiet during their journey, so much so, that Ann enquired if he was alright. 'I am fine guv, just a bit tired,' he lied. Ann dropped David off at the station and sped off to meet Josie at the launch. Ann's chic black trouser suit complemented her neatly cropped blonde hair. All eyes were transfixed on her. Her short blonde hair cut into a neat bob, her front forelock fell onto her forehead and the way she tossed her head backwards to flick her hair back. Josie moved forward to greet her, announcing her arrival proudly. She kissed Ann on the cheek, hugged her and pushed a glass of champagne into her hand. Ann enquired how the launch had progressed. 'Great! There was lots of positive feedback. Should have quite a few orders,' gushed Josie. Ann warded off the attentions of admirers, both male and female while Josie mingled. Ann found it most amusing at the speed at which her male admirers fled when they learned of her profession. Some of the female guests seemed more intrigued about what she did for a living and tried even harder to seduce her. The evening progressed pleasantly as she followed Josie who proudly showed her off to the fashion glitterati.

  Ann awoke early and sipped a cup of coffee as she turned her thoughts to what Nathan Casey had revealed about the meeting of the occultists in the woods. She knew that she had to witness the rituals for herself and she had to speak to George Casey. A pair of arms embraced her from behind, and a kiss in her neck announced Josie's presence. 'Early bird, how do you exist on four hours sleep a night?' enquired Josie. 'A lot on my mind, I suppose, damned murder case is very complicated,' complained Ann. She became very concerned when Ann talked about the satanic rituals. Josie knew that in her determination to solve a case, Ann had put her life on the line in the past. The doorbell rang. Josie opened the door to David who stood at the threshold drenched in the pouring rain. 'Come on inside," said Josie. 'I need the guv to accompany me urgently to a crime scene. 'Who is it Josie?' enquired Ann. 'It's your lovely sergeant needing your urgent attention,' replied Josie. Ann shot out of her chair, grabbed her phone and bag and joined David at the door.

They raced off towards the car. "Tell me on the way," said Ann as she jumped in the passenger seat. 'You are never going to believe this guv, George Casey has been murdered at his home,' said David. 'What the hell is going on?' exclaimed Ann looking flabbergasted at the news. Superintendant Edwards and D.I. Tobin were already at the scene of the crime. He walked towards the car as Ann and David arrived. 'Keep that lot at bay,' he ordered as he pointed to a group of reporters who were standing nearby. 'Tim Jones says the victim looks pretty smashed up. 'Take a look and get the report to me first thing tomorrow morning,' he snapped. Ann and David donned their overshoes and went into the house. Tim was bending over the body in the bedroom. He looked up as they entered. 'Seems like same modus operandi as the one who did Tom Casey,' he said. The cause of death is suffocation by strangulation. The familiar pattern of the inverted cross,' he continued. 'Percy, the gardener found the victim at around 7 am this morning He had worked for George Casey for the past 15 years. He says Jake Casey visited George around 6pm last night. Better leave the questioning for later. He seems very distressed about the murder at present,' he continued. Ann was ushered into George Casey's bedroom. His battered, bloodied body was sprawled in a heap on the floor His hands and feet had been crushed and broken and there was extensive bruising on the body. The bed sheets revealed evidence of sexual activity as the sheets were soiled with bodily fluids, and a streak of blood. 'Make sure you get all the evidence,' she urged. Ann examined the scene with David to make doubly sure that nothing was missed. The rest of the house seemed undisturbed. There were wine three glasses on the coffee table in the dining room. The forensic officer collected the fingerprints off the glasses. A DCI from the Surrey CID office was standing in the hallway as Ann came down the stairs towards the living room. 'Who the hell are you?' he demanded to know. 'I am DCI Dixon, who the hell are you? Ann answered with irritation. 'What are you doing on my patch?' he shouted. 'If you can bring yourself to ask my chief standing at the door, you might learn more and acquire some manners on your way over there, you bloody insolent arsehole,' Ann retorted indignantly. The man strode off angrily and went to speak to Edwards. 'That's put him in his place. Good for you, guv,' said David encouragingly. The reporters waited patiently for Ann to emerge from the inside of the house. They rushed towards her and fired a wave of questions at her. 'D.C.I Dixon, was George Casey murdered by the same man who killed his brother?' asked one reporter. 'Do you think you have a serial killer at large?' asked another rather impertinent reporter. 'It is too early to draw any conclusions at this stage.' replied Ann. 'Superintendant Edwards will release a formal report after the post-mortem,' Ann reassured them. Her statement seemed to placate them, and they dispersed reluctantly. Tim apologised to Ann for the behaviour of the DCI from the Surrey police. He explained that Edwards did not tell him Ann was drafted in to head the case. He told her that he would let her know about the date of the post-mortem. Ann and David stopped off at a café for lunch where they could discuss aspects of the murder uninterrupted. 'We had better build a water tight case David because we are going to have that bastard, Edwards breathing down our neck at every step,' warned Ann. They returned to Ann's office where she began to build a profile of the case, relying on input from David. 'Get the team for a briefing this afternoon and tell the forensic team I need their feedback by tomorrow. Meet me here at my office in an hour. First call will be the Casey brothers to inform them about their brother's death,' she said. David joined her an hour later. They tracked Jake down at work. He was shocked at the news but maintained his composure. He explained that he had stopped at George's house and was invited to join George and his daughter, Elaine for a drink at 6.30pm that evening. He explained that Elaine was spending a few days with her father. Jake told Ann that he left around 9pm and went home. He said that Nathan was at home too so he would confirm Jake's story. Nathan confirmed that Jake had come home around 9pm on the evening of the murder.

A buzz of excited voices signalled the preparedness of the men to take on the new case. 'We have another murder. I gather you have heard about the recent murder George Casey has been murdered in virtually the same way as he brother, Tom a few weeks ago. It is the same modus operandi. Tortured and then strangled leaving the imprint of an inverted cross. His ears are missing. The killer has presumably taken them as trophies. The victim was not alone during the attack. His daughter, Elaine had been visiting him, but she was nowhere to be found. We don't know if it was a double murder or if the killer has kidnapped the daughter. The brothers, Jake and Nathan both have alibis. I was unable to contact Luke Cowan as he is away at a medical convention. I will inform George's ex-wife, Eve who has remarried. We definitely have a serial killer at large,' she added. 'Ok, DI Roberts, you need to organise your team to interview the neighbours for their feedback. Check for strange cars or persons entering or leaving the house. DI Tobin, you get your men to interview the gardener, friends and colleagues of George Casey. He had golf buddies and some associates at the races. He also had a few female lovers whom he saw casually. Check if they have any grudges,' she added. 'If there are no questions, we will meet when I have news from the post mortem and forensics. Now get on with it,' she barked. Her mobile rang, and she checked that it was not Edwards, before answering. It was the detective constable at the police station. 'Guv, we just had a call from a woman called Eve Marshall. She says she is Elaine Casey's mother and is concerned that she is unable to contact her daughter since yesterday. I told her we only investigate if the person has been gone 24 hours, but she was very insistent that we find her daughter. I thought you might want to handle it in view of her daughter having the same surname as your murdered man,' he informed her. She took down the contact details thanked the constable. She immediately phoned the number she had been given. A tearful voice identified herself as Eve Marshall. She informed Ann that her daughter was visiting her father, George Casey yesterday and was not contactable since early evening. She told Ann it was very out of character for her daughter not to answer her phone. The realisation that Elaine's disappearance could be linked to her father's murder turned Ann's stomach. She paused for a moment before asking Eve if she could meet her urgently. 'Yes, of course Inspector, please come around in the next hour. We are at home,' said Eve. She rattled off details of her address which Ann scribbled down, thanked her and said she would call at the home shortly. David popped his head around the door. 'Everything ok, guv, you look as though you've seen a ghost,' he said smiling. 'Get inside and shut the door, I have just spoken to Eve Marshall, ex-wife of George Casey who reported her daughter Elaine missing since she visited her father yesterday,' said Ann unable to conceal her fears for Elaine's safety. 'Bloody hell, are you thinking what I am thinking, guv?' 'Yes David, we might have two murders,' said Ann, her voice quavering slightly. 'Come on there's no time to lose, get the car, we are going over to see Eve Marshall pronto", she added. David did not spare the horses, and for once Ann did not reprimand him for speeding. Eve lived in Finchley, North London. An attractive petite woman answered the door. Ann introduced David and herself. 'Have you found my daughter, inspector,' asked a tear strained Eve. 'I am afraid not. I am terribly sorry to inform you that your ex-husband has been murdered at his home last night.' Eve became visible distressed, shaking uncontrollably as she assimilated the news. 'Did they harm Elaine?' she was with her father for a few days", she enquired hysterically. 'Mrs Marshall, we do not know where your daughter is right now,' Ann explained. 'All we know according to Jake is that the three of them had drunks at 6.30 pm last night and then Jake left alone for home,' Ann continued. She waited until Eve was composed before continuing her questioning. "Would your daughter have gone off somewhere else without telling you?' Ann asked. Eve said that Elaine was a creature of habit and would not have done anything out of character. She added that Elaine was close to her dad, so she would have wanted to spend all the time with him. 'Even though my husband and I were divorced, George and I did not deny our daughter the love and care she deserved,' explained Eve. 'Did your ex-husband have any enemies?' Ann pressed. 'No, nobody that I know,' she replied. Ann thought for moment before asking the next question. 'Mrs Marshall, we have reason to believe that your husbanded dealt in the occult. Did you know about these rituals he and his brothers and friends performed in the forest?' "Good God no,' she exclaimed. 'George had books on the occult, but I never knew he indulged in such dark practises,' she said. 'Do you have a photograph of your daughter we can borrow please?' asked Ann. Eve disappeared for a few minutes and reappeared with a photo of her daughter. Eve handed the photo to Ann. Eve's husband arrived while they were talking. Eve introduced him to Ann and David. 'My husband, Harold is very close to Elaine,' said Eve. Ann directed her gaze towards Harold and asked him where he was the previous evening between 11pm and 4am. He said that he was at home with his wife. Eve confirmed that they watched TV till midnight, after which time we went to bed. 'When did you last see Elaine?' she asked Harold. 'Eve and I dropped her off at George's house two days ago,' he replied. 'Did you ever have any arguments with Elaine?' Ann continued. 'Whatever are you implying detective inspector?' asked Harold. 'Mr Marshall sometimes young girls do things out of the ordinary. No matter how well you think you know your daughter, she may do unpredictable things like disappearing for no apparent reason,' continued Ann. 'Did you ever argue with Elaine or have disagreements?' asked Ann. 'That's preposterous, we both loved Elaine and I never argued with her or caused her to be unhappy. My wife will vouch for that,' he exclaimed. Eve supported his argument. Ann nodded an acceptance. 'Does your daughter have a boyfriend or special friend,' asked Ann. 'She is studying to be a lawyer and did not want to be distracted, so she only has a few good girlfriends,' explained Eve. 'We would need to interview some of her close friends, so I would be grateful if you can give us contact numbers,' said Ann. Eve had a contact number for Elaine's close friends. 'May we have a look around your daughter's bedroom? We may find a clue to her disappearance,' said Ann. Eve hesitated for a moment then agreed. Eve led the way to Elaine's room. It was a spacious, tastefully decorated room. There were school photographs of Elaine, displayed on the dressing table. A collection of teddy bears adorned the bed. Elaine's laptop sat on a desk at one end of the room. Ann asked if they could take the laptop as it might hold some important information. Eve consented reluctantly. He also asked if she could have a hair brush belonging to Elaine for the forensic scientists to examine. 'What do you want with my daughter's hairbrush?' asked Eve angrily. 'We need to establish if the hairs on your daughter's brush matches the hair found at your husband's home,' replied Ann. Elaine reluctantly handed over the hairbrush. Ann informed the Marshalls that the metropolitan Kidnap Unit would liaise with them to set up a trace/intercept on their incoming calls that would be monitored by the technical support team Ann informed her that officers of the kidnap unit would park their operations van, near their home. Eve Marshall objected to this protesting that it was an intrusion of their privacy. It took great deal of persuasion on Ann's part to convince Eve that it was in the best interest of finding her daughter and that she would be advised to assist the police which ever way she could by agreeing to their methods of surveillance. Harold agreed with Ann and finally convinced Eve to agree to the plan.

'Do you have children of your own?' Eve asked Ann. No, I don't' replied Ann. 'I didn't think you did, judging by the way you assume that a missing daughter is not important,' replied Eve. 'It is a very unfair remark. I am not blind or insensitive to dealing with families who have gone through trauma or loss. I think my years with the force has given me enough skills to deal with these situations. Women with children are no more empathetic than those who have learned the art of compassion by involvement with traumatised victims like yourself,' said Ann vehemently.

'I think the Inspector is right. I am sure she will not handle any situation callously, knowing how much pain separation brings,' said Harold. 'I agree with your husband, Mrs Marshall. DCI Dixon will do her very best to find your daughter and will support you all the way. I have worked with her long enough to vouch for her absolute commitment and attention to duty,' added David. Ann shot him a surprised glance for his support.

'I give you my word that I will leave no stone unturned to find your daughter. My team are working around the clock to find her. I am sure we will be successful very soon. Meanwhile I need you to contact me if you can think of anything that will help us to find your daughter,' said Ann. Eve still thought Ann needed convincing about her love for Elaine. She showed Ann a family album pointing out the many years of happiness Elaine shared with Eve and George. 'My marriage to George ended because I walked away. I could not stand his controlling behaviour. He was insanely jealous, and it caused tension between us,' she continued.

'I am very sorry it came to that, but you are happy now and I am sure your life will be complete when we find Elaine,' added Ann. 'I am afraid, we must leave now. We will be in touch,' said Ann.

Chapter 3

Ann thanked Eve for her help and promised that they would do their very best to find her daughter. She waited until they were in the car before she spoke to David. 'David this case is more complex than we thought,' said Ann. 'Do you think the murderer has abducted the daughter?' asked David. 'That is very possible. Let's see what the boys at forensics have found",' she said. They sped off to forensics but were disappointed when the chief pathologist said he would only have all the information for Ann the next morning. David and Ann headed for her office. They stole past the office of Steven Edwards. His darkened office indicated that he had left for home. Ann sighed with relief that she did not have to confront her angry boss who had been trying unsuccessfully to contact her all day. Ann asked David to join her for dinner as Josie was away at a fashion show in Paris and she hated cooking. David jumped at the chance to spend quality time with Ann. She warned him that it would probably be a working dinner. He nodded in agreement and asked what type of food she liked. She said that perhaps they should head for a little Italian restaurant in Victoria. David phoned to reserve a booking, while Ann completed some work on her laptop. He dashed to his locker where he splashed on some aftershave, combed his hair and checked his appearance in the mirror before joining Ann outside her office.

They sped off to the restaurant together. They were ushered to their seats by a waiter. David perused the wine list and asked Ann what she liked to drink. 'Rioja would be nice,' David thought her choice was excellent and told the waiter to bring the wine. They surveyed the menu. Ann chose the butternut filled ravioli with seared salmon, and wild rocket. David opted for lasagne and a Mediterranean salad. Having placed their order, they sat back and savoured the wine. Ann looked across the table at David and asked him if his girlfriend complained about his long hours at work. He replied that he did not have a girlfriend as his unsociable hours chased away all the women he had. She sympathised with him and advised him not to give up so easily. He smiled then said, 'I suppose I am still waiting for the right girl.' 'Don't worry she's out there somewhere,' she reassured him. 'So near and yet so far, he thought,' as he looked at Ann, concealing his feelings for her. 'Your partner is a fashion designer, hey guv?' said David. 'Yes, she is held in high esteem in the fashion world,' replied Ann. 'She attained her degree in London and then spent some time in Milan and Paris gaining experience. Last year she was awarded an MBE for her contribution to fashion,' said Ann proudly. 'It must be difficult to maintain a relationship if you both are so busy,' replied David. 'Josie travels a great deal, but it works well for us as I work such long hours, said Ann. Embarrassed that he had perhaps probed into Ann's private life, he changed the subject. 'Do you think that doctor bloke, the Casey's cousin might not have gone to South America and is committing these murders, guv?' he asked. 'Well anything is possible right now. We need to establish if James has re-entered the United Kingdom before the murders,' she added. She used the serviette to make a rough sketch of the details of the case. Their dinner arrived and they tucked in hungrily.

They paused until after their meal before resuming their discussion. David stifled a yawn, at which point Ann announced that they went home. Ann reminded David not to be late in collecting her in the morning as they had an early start. David promised he would not disappoint her, said goodnight and drove off into the night. True to his word, David arrived early to collect Ann. Their first port of call was the forensic lab. Peter Drew, the chief forensic pathologist invited them into his office. He got them a coffee from the machine in the corridor and they all sat down to discuss the forensic results on the murder of George Casey. Peter revealed that the fingerprints on the wine glasses were a match to George, his brother Jake and an unidentified person. The bed sheets contained semen which belonged to George. The streak of blood belongs to a female who shares DNA with George Casey. Now brace your selves for this revelation. The DNA taken from the vaginal fluid on the sheets and on George's penis, and a few strands of hair in the bed, belongs to George's sibling, possibly his missing daughter,' said Peter. 'What the hell does that mean,' demanded Ann. 'It seems to point to the fact that daddy had sex with his daughter before he was killed,' explained Peter. 'Bloody hell,' exclaimed David. 'Carry on, what else?' said Ann. 'Blood at the scene all belonged to George. A sliver of material at the scene on the sheets is from a SOCO suit, so we are assuming that our murderer wore a protective suit. The size 10 bloody boot print at the scene, is army issue, so we might be looking for someone in the army or ex-army,' he added. 'We also found part of a broken finger of a rubber glove which had a partial print. The print belongs to Jake Casey,' he continued. Ann was flabbergasted at the new evidence. She took copies of the reports and made notes of her own as Peter continued. She glanced at her watch as she remembered that she had to be at the post-mortem midmorning. She thanked Peter for the report sped off to the mortuary.

  Ann apologised as she rushed into the examination room. 'Sorry, delayed at forensics,' she explained. Tim dictated into the recorder as he commenced the post-mortem. He began, 'This is the body of George Casey, a white male He is in good physical health. There are numerous bruises on the whole body suggesting the victim was repeatedly beaten with a blunt instrument after being subdued with a stun gun. The fingers of both hands are crushed. Degree of damage suggests use of a hammer or a similar heavy weapon. The toes of both feet are crushed. Both legs are broken above the ankles, probably with a sledge hammer and a block of wood wedged between the legs. Metal spikes driven through both knees. There is profuse blood loss and clotting at the sites suggests the wounds were inflicted while the victim was alive. Severe bruising on the face and body, several broken ribs and broken facial bones, suggests a beating of unparalleled brutality, while the victim was alive. His ears are missing, possibly taken as a trophy by the killer,' said Peter. 'I would say cause of death, asphyxia due to strangulation. Victim has petechial haemorrhages of the eyes. There are two identical black marks on the side of his neck. They look like burns from a stun gun. I would guess this was the killer's method of subduing the victim before the torture. The bruises on the neck, gloved fingers, and of course the unmistakable murderer's signature, the imprint of the inverted cross pattern. I would guess the killer put the ring on over his gloved finger to get a clear pattern of the ring,' he continued. 'Help me turn him on his front please,' he instructed. 'The victim's back was as bloodied and bruised as his front. Note the trauma to his anus. He was sodomized with an implement that had rough, raised spikes on the tip. I would hazard a guess that his rectum has been severely damaged by the implement. I won't know until I have opened him up,' he added. Peter proceeded with the Y surgical incision extending from the victim's throat to the pubic bone. This exposed all the organs in the thorax abdomen and pelvis. Peter began his commentary as he removed and examined each individual organ. 'The lungs are punctured by the broken third fourth and fifth ribs. The liver and the spleen are ruptured which indicates blunt force trauma, probably a large weapon, like a baseball bat,' he continued. 'Your killer's is a sadistic bastard, Ann. Seems he is sending us a message each time he kills,' he said. 'Do you have any ideas who the murderer might be?' he asked.   Ann shook her head and told him she thought the killings were liked to a satanic cult the brothers belonged to. 'Toxicology was unremarkable. There was a moderate amount of blood alcohol levels. He was on antihypertensive medication. There were no class A drugs in his body,' he confirmed. 'Well that's all I have for you now. I will send you a written report when I have completed the post-mortem,' he promised. She thanked him and headed for her office with David following behind. 'We had better have another coffee, don't think we are going to get lunch today,' she said. David fetched two coffees from the machine and placed them on Ann's desk. She sat down and checked her notes as she sipped her coffee. "Have you reminded the boys about the briefing at 3pm today?' she asked. 'Yes guv, I sent them all messages and left a reminder on the notice board,' said David. 'Well done, drink your coffee, we got to shoot off before Edwards gets back from lunch. He will go ballistic if he asks for the reports and I don't have them ready,' she said.

They entered the incident room where a team of officers waited to be briefed by Ann. The C.I.D squad who dealt with kidnapping was also present. Ann had photographs and details of both murders displayed on two boards. 'Good afternoon team. Listen up we have two murders and a possible kidnapping,' she shouted. Ann took her officers through the crime scene evidence and elaborated where appropriate. Comments such as, 'Sick fuck," was one of the comments which emanated from some of the officers when Ann informed them that evidence suggested that George Casey had had sex with his own daughter. 'I don't want inane comments guys, only intelligent positive feedback please,' said Ann. 'We don't know if George was forced to have sex with his daughter by the killer, so reserve your judgement gentlemen until we know the facts,' shouted Ann. 'I want you to interview Jake Casey as his fingerprints were on a wine glass at George Casey's house and on a broken finger of a rubber glove. Bring him to the station for questioning,' she ordered. 'I want you to interview Sam Cain and Luke Cowan too. Also check on whether Dr James Muller returned to England in the last month,' said Ann. 'Check the hospitals, just in case Elaine Casey was admitted at any time,' continued Ann. 'Get a team with sniffer dogs to search the woodland near the house. I don't want a stone left unturned,' she added. 'If there are no questions, hurry up and get a move on,' demanded Ann. The detective inspectors divided their men into groups and allocated various tasks to them. She reminded the men to them to get in touch with Interpol and circulate the photo of James Muller, and to check with the border squad to ensure James Muller has not left the UK. She gave them copies of Elaine Casey's photo and requested that a search be launched for her whereabouts. 'D.S. Hughes and I will interview Luke Cowan,' she said. 'It is vital you do not speak to the press on any account. Stephen Edwards will do the official press release tomorrow,' she added. A hum echoed through the room as the police discussed their tasks with their colleagues. Ann dealt with the individual queries from the officers before they embarked on their investigations. While Ann and David were busy planning their next move, her phone rang.

It was the traffic police who informed her that George Casey's Lamborghini was found abandoned a few streets from his house. Ann frowned, then turned to David and said, 'Why the bloody hell would George's car be abandoned few streets from his house from his house?' she enquired. She immediately informed the forensic officers and asked them to supervise the delivery of George Casey's car to the pathology garage. They complained that it was short notice but agreed as they did not want to increase Ann's stress levels. 'Let's try to get an interview with Luke Cowan today,' she told David. He immediately phoned Luke. The phone was on voicemail, so he left a message for Luke to contact him or Ann at his earliest convenience. He was surprised when Luke returned his call ten minutes later. 'To what do I owe the pleasure?' was Luke's sarcastic reply when David answered the phone. D.C.I. Dixon would like to interview you as another of your brother-in-law has been killed,' said David. 'We would like to know when it would be convenient to meet with you, Mr Cowan?' asked David. 'Why don't I meet you at the hospital canteen around 7pm, where can have a civilised discussion over a cup of coffee?' he enquired. David checked if the time suited

Ann, then informed Luke they would meet him at the hospital, at the agreed time. Ann spotted the disconcerting look on David's face as he finished the phone call with Luke. 'Mr Cowan is not your favourite person, is he David?' commented Ann. 'No guv, he gets up my nose with his arrogance and his condescending manner,' complained David. 'Hmmm must be a guy thing, I don't allow him to rattle my cage,' replied Ann. 'I will do the talking, to ensure you don't end up beating each other up,' Ann reassured him. 'Let's grab a bite to eat before we swan off to meet your favourite person,' said Ann with a mischievous grin. They sated their hunger with some Mexican food, drove off to the hospital. The crowded, noisy hospital restaurant was not the ideal place in which to conduct an interview, but Ann had to contend with the time and place afforded them.

Luke sauntered up to them and ushered them to a table. 'Ah it is the lovely Detective Inspector, nice to see you again,' said Luke as he shook Ann's hand. David mumbled a greeting but was instantly riled at Luke's manner. He enquired what they wanted to drink and fetched three coffees from the counter. 'Well what can I do for you this time, Inspector?' he enquired. 'George Casey was murdered two days ago, and we need to interview all the people immediately connected to him to exclude them from our list of potential suspects,' she explained. 'Oh, dear the Casey brothers seem to be dying like flies,' he replied. 'No need to be facetious, Mr Cowan, murder is a serious matter. I need to know where you were two nights ago between 11pm and 4am. 'I was at a medical convention during the day and spent the night with a woman. 'Can we have the contact details of this woman to verify you statement?' asked Ann. He replied, 'Yes of course, but you do realise that by interviewing this young lady you will ruin my chances of a relationship?' 'Yes, and I do apologise, but the police have to do their work in order to arrest the killer,' she said. 'So, each time a Casey brother dies, you are going to chase away my girlfriends with your questions,' he said with notable irritation.

He stood up in front of Ann in a confrontational manner. David jumped in between them and warned Luke to sit down. Luke backed down and laughed. 'Well Inspector, you seem to have quite a feisty Rottweiler to protect you,' he mocked. David moved towards him to strike him, but Ann stopped him. 'You should watch what you say Mr Cowan, we are doing our job and I will remind you that your job is to help us in our investigation,' continued Ann. Her tone of voice indicated that she would not tolerate his impudence. He apologised and asked if they had any more questions. 'We will contact you if we need to ask you any more questions,' she said. Ann thanked Luke for his time and accompanied David to the car. 'You shouldn't have stopped me guv, a good beating would take him down a notch or two,' said David gritting his teeth. 'If you had beaten him, you, would be giving out parking tickets instead of doing this job. Restraint is the name of the game,' she reminded him. 'It's late and I am completely bushed, can you drop me off at home please David?' pleaded an exhausted Ann. 'Sure guv, nothing more we can do tonight,' he said and drove off in the direction of her house. 'I will call you in the morning after my meeting with Edwards,' said Ann as she got out of the car. 'Good luck for tomorrow guv,' said David before he sped off.

Ann knew that Josie was back from Paris by the trail of designer carrier bags which littered the living room floor. Josie appeared wrapped in a towel, as Ann entered the kitchen. They ran towards each other and embraced and kissed. 'Hmm you smell divine,' said Ann as she kissed Josie's neck. 'New French shower gel, divine,' boasted Josie. 'I smell of the morgue, yuk, better head for the shower too,' said Ann as she began undressing and ran upstairs. Josie wrapped a towel over her wet hair and scoured the fridge for some food. She smiled as she only found a few dried bits of food. She knew that Ann never cooked. 'What would you like for dinner?' she shouted to Ann. 'Can't hear you, will be out of the shower in a jiffy,' replied Ann. 'How was

Paris?' asked Ann as she entered the kitchen. 'Fabulous and inspiring,' said Josie. 'I met a new designer who I am going to hire for my company. His name is Pierre and he is so charming and divinely handsome,' said Josie. 'Oh, trying to make me jealous, are you?' replied Ann. 'Got to keep you on you on your toes my darling makes the relationship more interesting,' teased Josie. 'Any leads on the murders?' enquired Josie. 'No, it is becoming a minefield with so many possibilities and no definite leads,' said Ann. She gave Josie a resume on what had been happening. They had similar theories on the murders. She always maintained that Josie should have worked on the force as her logic always made sense. Their discussion seemed to last for hours until Josie got up and said, 'I am officially declaring you off duty. We are going to watch a soppy romantic film and then, you must promise to be a very bad girl afterwards,' said Josie grinning cheekily. They settled in to watch the film and fell asleep on the sofa till dawn.

    Ann awoke first. She stood up and groaned with discomfort as the soft sofa made her back ache. She looked at the clock and panicked as she had barely half an hour to get to her meeting with Steven Edwards. Ann dashed about like a woman possessed as she struggled to find the clothes she wanted to wear. 'The world is conspiring against me, I can't find my shoes,' she complained to Josie, who had been woken by Ann's noisy efforts to get dressed. 'Bunk off work and come back to bed,' urged Josie, creeping back under the duvet. 'Can't, I have a meeting with the ogre, Edwards this morning. He will kill me if I don't turn up,' replied Ann. She kissed Josie hurriedly and dashed out of the door. Ann cursed at the heavy traffic as she sat idling and watching the minutes tick by. The hope of getting to the meeting on time was fading fast. When she finally got to her office to collect her reports, Edward's voice boomed down the corridor as he heard her voice and ordered her into his office. Whenever she delivered a report, he would ignore her verbal rendition and read the written report for himself. He never praised any of her efforts but was quick to condemn her omissions and mistakes. 'Where the hell have you been for the past few days?' Did you not get my messages?' demanded Edwards. 'Sorry sir, I have been up to my elbows in work. We have two murders, two Casey brothers and the possible kidnapping of the latest victim's daughter,' said Ann hastily. Edwards peered over the reports and thought for a while. 'Have the team come up with any sound leads for the murders,' he asked. 'No sir, I have ordered my men to bring in Jake Casey as he was the last to have seen his brother and niece alive.

A finger of a rubber glove with Jake's partial fingerprint was found at the scene of the murder. He has an alibi, his brother Nathan who claims they were both at home at the time of the murder," continued Ann. "The forensics report confirm that George Casey had sex with his daughter before he was murdered. We don't know if it was consensual sex or if he was forced to do it by the murderer. A partial size ten army boot print seems to belong to the killer,' said Ann. 'I have put out a nationwide search for Elaine Casey. We have no evidence she has been killed. We think she has been kidnapped by the murderer because she probably witnessed the killing. George Casey's car was found abandoned a few streets away from his house. I am waiting for the forensics lab to send me report of their findings in the car. Waiting to hear from Interpol if they managed to track down George Casey's cousin, James Muller, a doctor who used to work at Chelsea Westminster hospital,' added Ann. 'Why do you need to interview this man?' asked Edwards. 'He is the doctor who participated in the satanic rituals with the Casey brothers and we believe that he may be complicit in the murders because the brothers know about his involvement in the rituals,' explained Ann. 'And you know this how?' asked Edwards sarcastically. The young Casey brother, Nathan revealed James' participation in the rituals, but he won't testify. If we subpoena him, he might change his story,' she continued. 'Jesus what a family,' exclaimed Edwards. 'I have the bloody press release at 2pm today. Be there and I mean on time,' he ordered. Ann nodded in agreement and promised to meet him at 2pm in the press room. 'I think it is time to me to bring in a forensic psychologist, sir. I know of a very good profiler, Savannah Carey. She helped to bring a serial killer to justice very successfully, quite recently. She is rather unorthodox in her methods but if it brings us a result, it would help us to prosecute the bastard who has eluded us thus far,' she continued. Edwards looked at her with some annoyance that he did not think of the profiler first. Instead of complimenting her on her recommendation, he reprimanded her for proposing that he spend more metropolitan police money. 'Oh! for heaven sake bring in whoever you bloody like, but know if it blows up in your face, your will shoulder the blame for failure,' he scolded. David was waiting outside her door. Ann's flushed face said it all. She bore the scars of an unpleasant meeting with her boss. 'How did it go?' he whispered to her. 'Bloody awful,' replied Ann as she nudged him in the direction of the coffee machine. They helped themselves to coffee and headed for her office. She brought David up to date with her meeting with Edwards and outlined what he asked her to do.

He said that he would contact the profiler later that day. He told her that forensics wanted them to call in at the lab because they had an update on their examination of George's car. 'We had better go there after the press release as I was reminded not to be late,' Ann replied dolefully. Ann peered over the reports to familiarise herself with all the details as she anticipated that she would be asked questions by the reporters even though her boss headed the interview. The pressroom buzzed with the chatter of excited impatient newsmen. Steven Edwards called them to order and began his report. He told that the two murders bore the hallmarks of the same killer. He also told them that the disappearance of Elaine Casey was linked to her father's murder. His statement released a barrage of questions, all directed at Ann

"D.C.I Dixon, is this the work of serial killer?' asked a reporter in the front seat. 'We are treating these murders as linked, but we can only arrive at a definite conclusion when we have processed all the evidence,' replied Ann. 'How soon do you think you are going to catch this killer, or do you think he has outwitted you, Inspector? Has the Met's procrastination resulted in a second murder?' the reporters asked impatiently. 'The Metropolitan Police and all our affiliated teams are doing their very best to find the killer and bring him to justice,' continued Ann. 'Do you think it is a personal vendetta against the Casey brothers Inspector Dixon?' asked a female reporter. 'Well the fact that two brothers were murdered in quick succession, suggests a grudge or a score to settle,' replied Ann. 'D.C.I Dixon do you think Elaine Casey has also been murdered, or has she been kidnapped and held somewhere?' asked, Amy Baker. 'We have no evidence to suggest that Elaine have been murdered. There is a distinct possibility that she may have been kidnapped, but we are not sure,' stated Ann. She remained steadfast in her replies, much to the chagrin of her boss who appeared overwhelmed by their probing questions. Sensing that the reporters were not satisfied with their explanations, Stephen Edwards informed the press that there he was calling an end to the press interview due to lack of time.

     A roar of disapproval echoed around the room and some reporters persisted with their questions. Finally, Edward's voice boomed across the room. 'There will be no more questions, this meeting is adjourned,' he stated. The reporters flocked towards Ann in the hope of a last few fragments of news. She remained firm and refused to answer any more questions. She grabbed her coat and headed for the door with David close behind. They dashed for car with the reporters in hot pursuit. David grinned as they got to the safety of the car. 'The boss didn't like being shown up, hey guv?' said David. 'I did not tell the reporters to only ask me the questions,' replied Ann. 'He is green with envy because you are more popular with the press,' said David. 'Tough luck, that's his problem,' said Ann. 'We need to be wary of that Amy Baker. She is like a bloodhound; always sniffing out juicy bits of news and then using it to her own advantage. She has never forgiven me for the bruising encounter we had with the last investigation, and for being disciplined by her boss for using unlawful tactics to obtain information. I will also let you know that she is pretty pissed off because I rejected her advances,' declared Ann. 'Ouch that must have been a blow to her ego, as she rates herself as irresistible,' David added with a smile. 'Just remember, no private interviews to anyone,' warned Ann. 'I promise to keep my head down and my lips sealed,' said David. 'Let's shoot over to forensics, I want to hear what they found in Casey's car,' said Ann. Peter was peering into a microscope when Ann and David tracked him down. 'We fine tooth combed George Casey's car,' said Peter. Strands of female hair, belonging to a sibling of George Casey, probably his daughter, Elaine's hair found on the back seat of the car. Front seat had fibres from a SOCO suit. Also found mud and blood on the accelerator and at driver's side of car. The blood is a match to George Casey. Fingerprints on the steering wheel are no match to anyone we have on file. Possible indication that killer drove Elaine in George's car to wherever he took her then drove the car and abandoned it where we found it,' explained Peter. 'You had better ask the neighbours if they saw anyone leaving the house or heard a car driving off at around 4am that morning,' said Peter. 'I have my men working on that side of things,' replied Ann. She thanked Peter for his report and headed for the direction of her office. Detective Inspector Tobin was waiting for her as she opened the door. 'I have Jake Casey in the interview room guv. I thought you may want to sit in on the interview,' said Tobin. Ann nodded in agreement and followed D.I. Tobin. Jake looked dishevelled as they entered the room. He had been on night duty and seemed in great need of sleep. Ann greeted Jake and proceeded to turn on the tape recorder. She stated the date and time and the names of the persons present at the interview. 'Jake Casey, we have brought you in for questioning as part of a glove with your fingerprints was found in the bedroom where your brother, George Casey was murdered two days ago. Can you explain how a glove with your fingerprints happened to be at the scene of the crime,' Ann asked. Jake looked up in surprise. 'What do you mean my glove?' I only went to my brother's house on that night to have a drink at 6pm with him and my niece, Elaine. 'I came straight from work. I do remember finding a pair of gloves in the pocket of my uniform, which I had used on duty, in my pocket and discarding them in the kitchen bin.

George reprimanded me for bringing bacteria into his house,' explained Jake. 'So how do explain why only one finger of the glove was found in the bedroom where the murder occurred, if you say you put both gloves in the kitchen bin,' Ann pressed him for an answer. 'I went to have a drink with my brother and his daughter and left at 9.00. You are the detective. You work it out,' Jake replied sarcastically. 'My brother, Nathan can verify that I got home around 10pm and went to bed,' added Jake. 'Nathan has confirmed that you were home by 10pm, but her went out around 10.30 so you don't have a complete alibi. What was part of your glove doing in Georges' bedroom where he was tortured and murdered?' asked Ann. 'I don't know,' protested Jake. 'I think you sneaked out of the house before 11pm and returned to Georges' home where you tortured and murdered him,' replied Ann. 'Why would I do that?' asked Jake. 'Because you resented George for having sex with your sister, a resentment you harboured for years,' shouted Ann. 'D.I. Tobin leaned forward to grab Jake by the shoulder. Ann cautioned him and reminded him that his methods would be regarded as police brutality. David and Detective Constable Terence Holmes were watching the interview in the room next door. Terence Holmes leaned over David's shoulder and whispered,' Still got the hots for D.C.I Dixon I see., 'Fuck off, you bastard, you wish you can bang her,' retorted David. 'Isn't that what you are doing when you two go off on those long investigations?' 'I'll bet you come in your pants very time she shows off her legs,' mocked Holmes. 'Fucking bastard,' exclaimed David and lunged at Holmes, punching him so hard that he fell against the table. Ann heard the noise, switched off the tape and left the room to investigate. She could not believe her eyes when she saw the two men embroiled in battle like a pair of overgrown schoolboys. 'What the bloody hell is happening?' she screamed. An embarrassed David got up from the floor. 'Sorry guv, this bastard made a very personal remark and it got to me,' explained David. 'And what do you have to say for yourself, Holmes?' asked Ann. 'Not my fault guv, your boy can't cope with the truth,' explained Holmes. 'What do you mean by that?' Ann demanded to know.' Better ask pretty boy here, he will tell you why,' continued Holmes.

'Well whatever the reason, this is no way to behave. I suggest you settle your differences outside work,' scolded Ann. Both men apologised to her. Holmes left the room and David asked to be excused to tidy up in the men's room. Ann returned to the interview room. She turned the tape recorder back on and resumed questioning Jake. 'Mr Casey, forensics have revealed that the code book found at your brother's house has been written in the witch's code. Can you tell me what the code means?' Jake shifted uneasily in his chair. He replied hesitantly. 'I don't know anything about codes.' 'Oh come, don't play the innocent. You were as heavily involved in satanic worship as your brothers. You are facing a possible murder charge. If you cooperate, the judge might commute your sentence, 'she continued. 'Murder'? he stuttered. 'Yes, murder and for that, you are looking at a life sentence,' she replied. He remained silent for a few moments. 'I know some parts of the code, but if I reveal it to you, they will kill me,' he said. 'Who are they?' 'asked Ann. Jake ignored the question. 'We will offer you police protection if you help us,' she said. 'Bollocks, you know you cannot guarantee that for the rest of my life,' he shouted. 'So what alternative is there?' You will just have to trust me and start spilling the beans,' she urged. 'I tell you what we shall do. We have enough evidence to get a warrant to search your home. You will have to spend 24 hours in police custody while your house is being searched. You will have 24 hours to decide whether to assist us or not. The choice is yours,' she said. He was furious and demanded to see his lawyer. 'You have the wrong man detective. You had better be damned sure of your case because you remember how you cocked up the arrest of Sam Cain,' warned Jake. Ann said he would be allowed to contact his lawyer later that afternoon. Jake was taken to the holding cell. Ann turned to Tobin and informed him that David and Holmes had had a fight. She told him that she wanted them kept apart at work at all times. He agreed and assured her he would have a word with Holmes. She signalled for David to accompany her to her office. They walked in silence. When they were in her office she turned to David and said,

    'You will tell me in your own time what happened at the interview office today. But let me warn you, if it ever happens again, I will replace you-that is a promise,' she warned. David listened in silence. He promised to keep his temper under control and apologised for his lack of judgement. 'Now go and get us some doughnuts. I need plenty of sugar for my meeting with Edwards,' she urged. Ann prepared herself mentally for the encounter with Edwards, before she knocked on his office door. 'Yes, who is it?' boomed an agitated Edwards. Ann opened the door and peered inside. 'Stop skulking outside and get in here,' he shouted. 'I hear you have Jake Casey in custody,' he declared. 'We found a glove finger with his prints at the scene. He also does not have a watertight alibi for his whereabouts after 11. He was the last person to see his brother alive. A warrant would enable us to possibly find more evidence,' she explained. 'Does he have motive?' Edwards demanded to know. 'Well yes, he was also involved in the occult rituals and he resented George having exclusive rights to sexual encounters with their sister. This caused a great deal of resentment between the brothers,' she continued. 'But he has a partial alibi, his brother was with him on the night of the murder until 10pm,' said Edwards. 'The brother went to bed after 10pm, so if Jake sneaked out, he could have travelled to Surrey in 45 minutes,' continued Ann. 'I have the men checking the local cabs, just in case he went by taxi,' she explained. 'Okay, so we get the warrant and find nothing. You can't convict him on the evidence of a glove print if he admitted to leaving his gloves in the bin at the house. The boot print at the scene suggests another person was in the house and could have planted the glove finger at the scene,' he warned. 'Yes sir, that is why we need to search the house to find more evidence, 'said Ann. 'Get the bloody warrant and make sure you don't fuck this up Dixon. We already have negative press reports, no thanks to that Amy Baker,' he threatened. Ann always felt she had run a marathon after a meeting with Edwards. He drained her of all her energy and confidence. She added the last updates to her laptop and headed home.

  Josie was due to arrive late as she had deadlines to meet for a new line of fashion. She headed for the shower a soon as she got home. She poured herself a glass of wine and slumped into the armchair. Ann's phone rang, and she excused herself to answer it in the bedroom. It was Edwards who informed her that he had a warrant to enable the police to search Jake's house. He reminded her to be very thorough in their search as he did not want the police to bungle yet another investigation. She promised to do her best and contact him as soon as they had finished the search. She turned on her laptop to ensure that she had documented everything pertaining to the case. She knew that the police's reputation and hers was riding on the outcome of this case. Josie called out to her and threatened that if she did not join them for a drink, she would be carried back to the dining room by her and Adam.

Ann turned off her laptop and dutifully went down stairs. 'You are not allowed to work when your brother is visiting,' scolded Josie. 'Spoke to my boss. Could not get out of it,' explained Ann. 'Hey your case is really making headlines. Do you think it is the work of a serial killer?' enquired Adam. 'Not sure, we think it is a personal vendetta against the Casey brothers. A grudge perhaps or someone trying to stop the victims from revealing incriminating information,' continued Ann. 'Oh for goodness sake, don't encourage her, Adam. She spends too many hours at work anyway," complained Josie. 'It's a fascinating case you must admit, I would not mind tagging onto to some of it myself,' declared Adam. 'Hang on a minute, Sherlock Holmes, who appointed you to the Met?' enquired Ann jokingly. 'If you two don't stop talking shop, I won't get tickets for Tosca next Saturday,' warned Josie. This statement got their attention and they asked if she was serious about going to the opera. 'Would I joke about something so close to my darling's heart,' declared Josie. 'I take it you will both be able to attend?' she asked.

'Oh yes we would love to,' they chorused in unison. Adam stifled a yawn. 'You are sleeping here tonight, and I won't take no for an answer,' said Ann. Josie added her support. Adam was too tired to argue and settled for the sofa bed in the living room. Ann and Josie chatted into the early hours before falling asleep. Ann only regretted her large consumption of wine and getting to bed at 2.30am when her alarm sprung into life at 5.30am. 'Oh God my head is going to explode,' she complained as she made her way to the shower. She turned on the cold water to revive herself. The cold water made her shudder, but had the desired effect, and she appeared much more alert getting out of the shower. She scrambled her clothes together and dressed hastily. David was parked outside the door as she emerged at 5.50am. 'Good morning David. I hate these bloody early mornings,' she said. 'Morning guv, we are going to collect the warrant on the way to the Casey house, aren't we?' he asked.

'Yes, the forensic chaps will meet us there.' she said. Just then her mobile rang. The look on her face and the expletive she uttered told David something terrible had happened. 'We need to get over the station. Jake Casey was attacked in the showers and is in hospital,' she screamed in exasperation. David was stunned at the news but obeyed and turned the car around and headed for the police station. Ann jumped out of the car and hurried towards the holding cells where she had last seen Jake. The sergeant met her on route and followed her. She demanded to know what had happened. The constable who had been assigned to guarding Jake was called into an office to explain to Ann what had happened. He looked terrified because Ann was so angry that the officer thought he would be physically attacked. He stuttered as he spoke. 'Jake was fine until he went to have a shower. I left him to get on with it and when I came back half an hour later, he was lying unconscious, face down in the shower. He was taken to The Chelsea and Westminster Hospital. 'I want the names of everyone who was on duty last night and this morning,' shouted Ann. The constable and sergeant assured her that the list of names would be supplied to her later that morning. Ann asked to be shown where Jake's was found and immediately ordered the forensic officers to examine and take samples from the scene of the attack. D.I. Tobin joined her at the scene of the incident, and they discussed the details of the attack.

'Come on David, we need to find out how badly Jake has been injured,' she said. David did not attempt any conversation as they sped off to the hospital as Ann appeared most unpredictable in her moments of anger. They headed for the ward where Jake had been admitted when they arrived at the hospital. A policeman sat outside the intensive care unit as David and Ann entered. A nurse and doctor were with Jake taking a sample of blood. The doctor looked up at Ann as she approached the bed. She flashed her identity card and introduced herself. A Dr Evans told her he was in charge of Jake's care. Ann asked about the medical details. Dr Evans informed her that Jake had sustained a subdural haemorrhage due to a severe blow to the back of his head. There was substantial brain damage. He said that they had operated to remove most of the blood clot and had to wait for the swelling on the brain to subside before they could ascertain whether there was long term damage. The doctor said he was unable to say how long it would take. Ann gave a disconcerting grimace at the prospect of the unknown time factor. "I understand this man was arrested on suspicion of murder, Inspector," said Dr Evans. 'Yes, but it is more complicated and having an injured suspect makes my work very hard indeed,' complained Ann. She thanked the doctor for his help and took her leave.

She instructed the constable on guard outside the door that she wanted the number of officers doubled and the identity of all non- hospital staff vetted. A noisy group of reporters were waiting outside the hospital gates as Ann and David emerged. 'How badly is the suspect injured, Inspector?' asked one reporter. 'He is stable in intensive care. That is all I am going to tell you lot,' she said. They ignored her statement and persisted with their questions. 'The Met is very careless to allow a suspect to be attacked,' someone shouted. 'What do you have to say about that, Inspector?' said another reporter. 'The Met will call a press conference soon and then you can ask all the questions you want,' she said. They crowded around the car like a pack of wolves continuing to fire questions at Ann. 'Put your foot down so we can get away from this lot," said Ann. "bastards, they don't give up,' complained Ann. 'I will have to tell Edwards before he hears it from someone else. Let's stop at his office,' she said. 'The super wants to see you urgently,' said one of the sergeants as she got into the building. 'I am on my way to his office now," replied Ann. She told David to wait in her office while she braced herself for Edwards' wrath.

'What the hell is going?' You had better have a bloody good reply,' shouted Edwards. 'I can only tell you what I know," said Ann bravely. This is going to give the press a field day, and we are going to look like incompetent idiots,' he continued. 'I have ordered a full investigation and report. Got forensics working at the holding cells. I have spoken to Jake Casey's doctor who says he cannot predict the rate of recovery from the head injury. I have increased the security at the hospital," she said. 'Do we know why Jake was targeted,' he asked. 'This seems incredible, but I think he was attacked because there is an accomplice in the murders. "I want to know who was in or around the interview room yesterday. I want everyone questioned', he stated. Ann nodded in agreement and said she would have a report on his desk by the morning. Ann rewarded herself with a coffee when she got to her office. David was on his mobile and ended the call when Ann appeared. 'This is such a bloody fiasco. It has fucked up everything,' she complained. 'I will chase up list of names of the staff on duty at the holding cells yesterday,' promised David. 'Thanks, I will appreciate that,' said Ann. We will need to pick up the warrant and get to Jake's house this afternoon. Tell everyone the time has been rescheduled and ask Nathan to be at home so that we can gain access,' she added. 'Yes guv, I just spoke to Nathan who was very miffed at being kept waiting three hours before being told his brother had been attacked and we were not going to pitch,' said David. 'Just be nice to him and win him over. We can't afford to alienate him now,' said Ann. David immediately began phoning around to arrange everything. Ann got on with the report she was preparing for Edwards. The phone rang two hours later. It was D.I. Tobin informing that he and a team of forensic officers were at Jake's house. They hurried off to the car and headed for West London. Ann cursed at the heavy traffic which slowed them down. A dejected Nathan stood at the front door as David pulled up in the drive. 'I am so very sorry about what has happened to your brother and I want you to know everything is being done to find Jake's attacker,' she promised. 'That's exactly what you said when Tom died and since then another brother has died, a niece is missing and another brother badly injured. 'It doesn't inspire me with confidence, and it gives me very little trust in your ability to do your job Inspector,' said Nathan coldly. Ann was embarrassed at Nathan's criticism as his comments were overheard by Tobin and some of the forensic officers. 'Ann thought about a suitable retort for Nathan's condemnation of her, but desisted, took the front door key from Nathan and proceeded to instruct her officers to begin their work. The forensic officers began their work in the bedrooms upstairs, bagging and labelling Jake's clothes.

They focused their attention to his shoes as they were a size ten, same size found at the murder scene. Ann's attention was drawn to the photographs on wall of Jake's bedroom. They were of him while serving in the Territorial Army. They searched the cupboards thoroughly, looking for weapons and items related to the murders. They found a cloak, some candles in a box under the stairs. Ann examined the entry and points of the house and considered the possibility of someone leaving without disturbing the rest of the house. Exit was possible via the kitchen door and from the bedroom or living room windows as they opened easily without making a noise. Ann spotted the garden shed at the bottom of the garden and sent a forensic officer to inspect it. The shed door was unlocked. There were gardening implements in it and bags of fertilizer. Then in the semi darkness of a corner of the shed, the officer spotted a pair of boots. They were army boots caked in mud. The boots leaned against a large mallet. The mallet had mud and what appeared to be dried blood on it. He called out frantically to his colleagues. Ann heard the shout and rushed to the shed. I found these boots and this wooden mallet, guv,' said the officer. 'Bag them and get them to the lab,' said Ann. They continued the search, finding items relating to practises of the occult in the basement. A pentagram drawn on the floor of the basement suggested that rituals might have occurred there. The team spent many hours going over the house carefully. Satisfied that they had collected all they came for, Ann announced that they should wrap up the search and she would meet with them later. David drove her back to her office. 'The boots and the mallet are an important find and I hope will be match the boot print found at the scene,' Ann said hopefully. She slumped into her chair with exhaustion. It was 7pm. 'I think my stomach thinks my throat has been cut. I had no food today. I am absolutely famished,' she announced. 'Just give me half an hour to get this report done, then we can grab some dinner. She checked her phone for messages. There was a message from Josie reminding her to come home for dinner and forbidding her to eat out. She phoned Josie and asked if she could bring David along as they were both very hungry. David looked up from his paperwork and waved to Ann indicating a rejection to the dinner invite. Ann ignored his refusal and told Josie to prepare for an extra person for dinner. When she came off the phone, she informed him that she would not take no for an answer because Josie loved to cook and entertain.

'I will not have another word on the subject, get done so that we can get out of here,' she ordered. The whizzed out of the office by 8pm and sped off to Ann's home. 'They were greeted by Adam who had also been invited to dinner. Ann introduced David to Adam. Josie came out of the kitchen, kissed and hugged Ann. 'There will be no food for the guests who discuss work,' Josie announced. She ushered them to an immaculately laid dinner table. 'You have forgotten the place names,' quipped David. Josie responded by swotting him over the head with a dishcloth. 'I hope you don't have any food fads David. I have cooked a French dish that I hope you will enjoy,' she said. 'I am not fussy and as I am starving, any food will be just fine,' he replied. 'Whatever it is I am sure Josie never disappoints. She is an excellent chef. I keep urging her to open a restaurant,' said Adam. 'You are too kind, darling Adam. I doubt whether my culinary skills can compete with the great chefs out there,' replied Josie. They tucked into a starter of smoked salmon, figs and a garnish. This was followed by coq au vin served with petite pois, potatoes and vegetables. The dessert was crème brulee, which was followed by cheese, biscuits and coffee. There was a happy banter during the meal. David and Adam hit it off and discovered they had many shared interests. 'I suppose Ann doesn't give you much time off,' said Adam. 'Well that's just the nature of our work,' explained David. 'I pursue my hobbies and interests during my days off or while on leave,' said David. Ann was quite surprised that David played squash and did boxing. She was also surprised that he shared the love of photography and canoeing with Adam. The two men chatted away like old friends, while Josie flirted across the table with Ann. 'You should invite your sergeant more often, Ann. You will learn more about his pursuits of pleasure,' said Adam. 'Chance would be a fine thing. She works them into the ground. We are very lucky that her ladyship has deigned to join us tonight,' joked Josie.

Adam and David exchanged phone numbers. 'I don't think it's a good idea for you to socialise with my sergeant, Adam,' remarked Ann. "Why ever not, I don't have a pal I can drag along when I want to chill out. I don't complain when you go off playing squash with your MI6 heart throb, Owen Hammond,' teased Adam. 'Mind your own business and stop telling the world about my social pursuits,' retorted Ann. 'Just remember, work first. No gadding about with my brother and phoning in sick to get time off,' warned Ann. 'Told you she will put a damper on the fun. Time off does not feature in this lady's book,' joked Josie. The wine flowed freely and when Ann noticed David getting inebriated, she reminded him that he needed his full senses for work in the morning. David checked his watch and announced that he ought to be getting home. He thanked Josie for a superb dinner. Ann called a taxi and David left half an hour later. 'Nice bloke, your sergeant,' said Adam. 'I don't want your filling his head with promises of adventure. He has an important job to do,' said Ann. Adam moved close to Ann and whispered, "Your sergeant idolises you. Have you noticed how he watches you?' I would guess that he more than admires you,' remarked Adam. 'Don't be ridiculous. David and I are a great team and we have a good professional relationship. They stopped talking when Josie entered the room. 'Who is having a relationship?' enquired Josie.' I was just telling Adam what a good professional relationship David and I have. 'He is a great guy. I wish he could meet a nice girl,' said Josie. 'Chance would be a fine thing. He never gets out enough to meet a nice girl. His boss who will remain nameless work him too hard,' added Adam. 'Watch your mouth Adam Dixon or you will be banned from this house forever, 'said Ann hitting him over the head with a cushion.

    Adam thanked Josie for the meal and announced he was going to bed. Ann and Josie chatted while they finished washing the dishes. Josie embraced Ann and they kissed passionately. Ann broke away and said, 'No second dessert tonight, we have a guest remember.' 'Oh damn, I forgot,' exclaimed Josie. 'Never mind there is always the weekend' said Josie with a cheeky grin. Ann called at David's house to collect him for their visit to the hospital to check on Jake's progress. 'I hope he wakes up soon. It is damned inconvenient with him being unconscious. Everything is in limbo,' said Ann in frustration. 'Perhaps forensics will come up with someone to decode the book and that will give us a lead,' said David reassuringly. 'No chance of that happening. The forensic expert said that the coding was very personal and was probably written by two people who needed to decode the book together. We don't have a hope in hell of decoding it ourselves. Jake must know part of the code because he became very distressed when I questioned him about it. He was very afraid of the other party to the code. He said if he helped us to decode the book his life would be in danger,' she continued.

Chapter 4

The good news was that there had been no deterioration. Jake was stable but remained unconscious He promised to keep Ann informed of any significant improvement. She thanked him and left the unit. Just as she emerged from the Intensive care unit door, Eve and Harold Marshall arrived. 'Well isn't this nice, the Inspector visiting the hospital when she should be out there finding my daughter,' said Eve sarcastically. 'Mrs Marshall the police are doing everything in their power to find your daughter. We have her photo in all the newspapers. My officers have interviewed many people who are friends or associates of your daughter. Please just be patient and less critical of the police,' said Ann. 'The police have made no progress in their investigations of two murders How the hell can we trust them to find our daughter,' shouted Harold. Ann remained composed and politely promised them that she would do her very best to find Elaine. They snorted and walked off. 'Phew! he certainly woke up on the wrong side of the bed today,' remarked David. 'Never mind them for now,' said Ann.

'Let's get over to the holding cells. I want to interview those idiots who allowed Jake to be attacked,' said Ann. They were greeted by the constable who was minding the reception desk at the station. 'Inform all the staff here that I want to see them in the main office in five minutes,' ordered Ann. 'Yes guv," he assured her. 'Get hold of D.I. Tobin. I want him here too,' she said. The men went to the assigned designation promptly and Tobin appeared ten minutes later. 'Right I want to know how someone can walk into a police station and clobber a prisoner over the head without any of you lot noticing,' Ann demanded to know. 'D.I. Tobin, you were in charge of the holding cells on the night of the assault. Where were you, and more importantly, where was the constable guarding Jake Casey?' she continued. 'I had gone off to get something to eat, and I left constable Drake to stay with Jake,' he explained. 'What do you have to say for yourself constable Drake?' asked Ann. 'Jake Casey asked to have a shower. We were not busy, so I checked with sergeant Pollock here if it was okay to take Jake to the shower, explained the Constable. 'I left him in the shower for 30 minutes and went off to wait for him in the office down the corridor,' explained Constable Drake. 'You have omitted to tell us that the reason you went to wait down the corridor was because you and a female officer were having sex in that little office,' she shouted.

'You were so immersed in your sexual activity that you were unable to see when a stranger posing as a maintenance man and a fake identity slipped into the shower and floored Jake Casey. Is that not what happened?' asked Ann. Constable Drake was horrified that Ann knew the truth. He began to stutter as he replied. 'I am sorry Guv. It was a terrible lapse of judgement on my part, and I am truly sorry,' he said. 'You see I have good officers who are loyal to this force and who tell the truth. Your appalling behaviour has injured our prisoner and has given the press a field day questioning the creditability of the police,' she continued. 'Superintendant Edwards wants to see all of you. I can tell you my reprimand is the least of your concerns compared with how he will discipline you and possibly dismiss you from the force. I want a comprehensive report on the incident on my desk by the morning. Now get out of my sight,' she said. 'Fucking arrogant dyke. I hate her,' cursed Drake. 'I wish someone would put her in her place,' he said to Tobin. 'Watch your mouth, Drake. You were in the wrong, and she is only doing her job. Your negligence has dropped all of us in it, especially me as I was accountable for the security of the holding cells,' he said. 'What do you think will happen to me?' asked Drake. 'Well a reprimand if Edwards is in a good mood, but I suspect he will make an example of you as a warning to other potential misconduct. I would start to pack your bags. I think you will be shown the door,' he warned. Edwards wanted D.I. Tobin and Sergeant Drake in his office at 2pm that afternoon He was incandescent with rage did not mince his words telling them how outraged he was at Drake's behaviour and Tobin's negligence. 'You can clear out your locker. You are no longer part of this force. Now get out of my sight,' growled Edwards. The two men listened in silence, knowing any attempt to explain would incur Edward's wrath even more and left hurriedly. 'Bastard thinks he can treat me like dirt. I never wanted to be a policeman anyway. Did it to please my father,' complained Drake. "Oh well now you got your wish. You can contemplate your future while signing on the dole,' Tobin joked. 'I wouldn't advise contemplating any type of revenge, because life as locked up ex-policeman is a very grim one indeed,' was Tobin's parting words to Drake. Ann and David met with the C.I.D. Squad in the incident room where they discussed their latest findings on the two murders and the kidnapping. D.I. Ian Roberts lead the feedback. 'We had an eyewitness who was walking his dog on the morning of the murder of George Casey. He says around 4.15am, he saw someone in George Casey's drive, carrying something which looked like a large sack over their shoulder and putting it into the front seat of a Lamborghini which was parked in the drive.

The man said he hid behind a tree. He watched as the car drove off and saw a woman slumped in the front seat, as the street light shone on the car when it drove past him. She looked asleep of very drunk as her head rolled from side to side. He was unable to see the face of the driver as it was too dark. 'Why did he not come forward with the information sooner?' asked Ann. He said he had just moved into the neighbourhood a few weeks ago, and only came forward when he read about it in the papers. 'We must assume that Elaine Casey is still alive and being held captive somewhere,' said Ann. 'All the interviews with her friends and her associates yielded no clues. We discovered that she had a secret boyfriend who said they kept their relationship quiet until

Elaine had passed her exams at the bar. He said her parents did not want her studies interrupted. He had an alibi for the night of Elaine's disappearance, Ian Roberts informed the team. 'What have you dug up Tobin?' asked Ann. He recapped about the finding of a part of Jake's glove, which had his fingerprint, at the scene of the murder. His flimsy alibi, and the fact that he was the last person to see his brother alive. 'I have just picked up the report from Peter Drew at forensics. The boots belonging to Jake Casey which were found the garden shed at his house, contained mud from George Casey's garden, blood belonging to George. Carpet fibres were from the carpet in George's car and a hair belonging to a sibling of George Casey, presumably his missing daughter, Elaine,' continued Tobin. 'We interviewed Casey's hedge fund associates. He did not seem to have enemies, but the view was that they knew that George had powerful friends. They carefully mentioned that he had links to the underworld, so nobody would dream of trying to harm him,' said D.I. Tobin. 'Has anyone spoken to Sam Cain?' enquired Ann. 'I did. He was out chasing girls with his brother on the night of the murder and spent the night with a woman who has confirmed his story,' continued Tobin. 'I don't want you to rest on your laurels and assume that we have no more work to do, since Jake Casey is a suspect,' said Ann.

'Our suspect was attacked in the shower of the holding cells last night by someone posing as a maintenance man. He is unconscious and has been taken to intensive care. The idiots who were guarding him allowed this to happen and dropped us all in the shit. We have no idea when Jake Casey will recover but this will not halt the investigation,' said Ann. A buzz of disquiet filtered through the room. 'Okay there's no need to dwell on what is done. All I am asking you all to do your job with commitment and professionalism. The public and the press will be unforgiving and very critical, so I am asking for total discretion and dedication from all you,' said Ann. The team nodded in agreement. 'We have grounds to go over every bit of the property. You may have missed something,' said Ann. 'I don't want anyone speaking to the media. The superintendant will handle all press releases,' she warned. The team left the incident after the briefing and chatted amongst themselves as Ann gave orders to the senior officers. David told Ann that Peter Drew wanted to speak with her at her earliest convenience. 'Thanks David, tell him I will see him in the next thirty minutes," she said. Ann checked her watch and remembered that Josie had booked opera tickets for them at 7.30, but she wanted to know what Peter Drew had to say. She sauntered off to his office, hoping he had encouraging news about the case. 'Drag up a chair, Ann I need you to hear this,' he said with some hesitance. "I examined the shoes we think belongs to Jake Casey. I let his brother identify them. Nathan is not one hundred per cent sure if the boots belong to his brother, but he said Jake has a pair like the ones we have found in the shed. If you look carefully, you will see that the boots are caked in mud almost up to the laces. We have checked the boot prints left in the mud in the garden of George Casey's house. We are sure that the prints were made by these boots, as the mud on them has the same geological composition as the mud in George's garden. The blood belongs to George. The pattern of mud on the boots and the depth of the prints in the mud in the garden suggests that a man with a height of 6ft 3inches, weighing 12 stone and carrying a weight of around 8 stone.

    The killer must have carried Elaine Casey, as from the house to the car, across the muddy flower bed. This is consistent with the eye witness seeing a man carry what looked like a sack of potatoes over his shoulder and into the front seat of the car. The soil in the flower bed had been loosened by" the gardener and the water sprinklers came on at 3am. The soil had been loosened by the gardener and had two hours of soaking, which made whoever walked in it, leave deep prints. We need to establish Jake Casey's height and weight, and of course Elaine's weight when we find her,' he continued. 'I will get Jake's details from the hospital. I will get Sergeant Hughes to find out from the hospital and get the information to you as soon as possible,' she said. 'I must dash. Going to the opera tonight, must not be late, or I will be severely reprimanded,' she added. She charged through the front door of her house like a bat out of hell, as she had barely an hour to get ready. 'Hurry up slow coach,' scolded Josie as Ann raced to the bathroom. 'Get me a glass of wine. I need something to calm my nerves,' shouted Ann, as she disappeared into the shower. Josie was applying her makeup in front of the mirror in the bedroom, when Ann came out of the shower. Josie looked so tantalisingly provocative in her little black dress. The dress accentuated her beautiful curves. Ann lifted the hem of Josie's dress and slid her hand along the top of Josie's stockings, trailing her fingers past the suspenders to her crotch. Ann sighed as she anticipated the potential for an erotic evening. 'Oh, please stop. You are driving me mad with desire,' Josie pleaded. 'You smell divine, good enough to eat,' purred Ann. 'Oh don't start or we will never get to the opera,' Josie whispered as Ann's seductive words sent an erotic wave through her body. She pushed Ann away just as Adam popped his head around the door and enquired if they were ready to go. He smiled mischievously as he witnessed their embrace; apologizing for spoiling their fun. 'Weren't you taught to knock on bedroom doors before entering, cheeky sod?' scolded Ann. 'Just think of all the fun I would miss if I did that,' he said.

Ann drained the last drop of her glass of wine, put on the finishing touches of her makeup and raced downstairs after Josie and Adam. 'Do you have the tickets, Josie?' Adam asked. 'Yes, Mr Fusspot. Bloody hell, Adam! Do you trust anyone?' asked Josie. They stopped off at a restaurant after the performance. They were sated with soulful sustenance and liberal amounts of champagne. "Adam are you coming in to put us to bed?' asked a rather inebriated Josie. 'No, my darlings, I am going to leave you to continue the unfinished business you started earlier this evening,' replied Adam with a wink. 'Go home you wicked boy,' said Ann. They hugged and kissed him goodnight and went indoors. It was with feverish and joyous anticipation that Josie pulled off Anne's clothes. Both women were highly charged. When their bodies were exhausted from their orgasmic tsunami, they lay in each other's arms reminiscing about the love which bound them so securely. Their hopes of having Saturday morning lie in were dashed when a car hooted outside. Josie cursed at the noise, got up and looked outside the window. What does Hughes want at this time on a Saturday morning?' said Josie. Ann sat up in bed rubbing the sleep from her eyes. She slipped on a dressing gown and went to open the front door. 'Who chased you out of bed this morning, David?' asked Ann. 'Sorry to disturb you guv, we have had an anonymous tip off from a caller. Jake Casey has a lockup garage near Kings Cross. We were unable to reach you as your phones were switched off.' D.I. Tobin and the team are already at the scene,' continued David. They raced over to meet the rest of the team. The area was cordoned off with tape. Tim came out of the grubby garage, wearing his SOCO suit. '"Hi Ann, the body is that of a young woman aged early twenties was found in the boot of the car. It appears to have been stored in a freezer, then wrapped in heavy duty plastic and put in the boot of the car,' he said.

Tim led Ann to the boot of the car. He pulled away the plastic covering the body. It revealed a naked woman lying in a foetal position in the boot of the car. Ann gasped as she recognised the face of the deceased woman to be that of Elaine Casey. Her skin was marbled and extremely pale. Decomposition has been delayed due to the body being frozen. 'I think the body was kept in a freezer for some time, then dumped about two days ago. You can see the freezer burns where the skin was in contact with the cold surface of the freeze,' continued Tim. 'Do you know the cause of death?' asked Ann. A wound below the sternum, suggests a puncture of the aorta. Exsanguination, probable cause of death cause of death,' said Tim. The forensic team worked diligently, collecting and labelling samples and taking photographs and collecting evidence. D. I. Tobin joined Ann and began updating her on his findings. 'The car is registered to Dr James Muller. The lockup is in Jake Casey's name. We assume that both men shared the garage,', replied DI Tobin. 'Get the car and everything to the forensic garage,' said Ann. The teams spent many hours collecting evidence. Ann arranged for refreshments to be served to the teams to revive their flagging energies after hours of diligent work. When the forensic team had satisfactorily completed their work, they placed the body in the body bag and moved it to the police mortuary. Ann ordered urgent DNA tests as she wanted to establish the identity of the victim. The garage was sealed off and locked. Ann arranged for a 24hour police surveillance outside the garage. The media stood around at a discreet distance. They waited for Ann to walk to where her car was parked, where they raced towards her. 'Who have you got in that garage D.C.I Dixon?' asked Amy Baker. 'It is an unknown woman. We will need to wait for the pathologist and the forensic team to establish identity,' said Ann.

"Do you think the body is that of the missing woman, Elaine Casey?' asked another reporter.' "Read my lips. Haven't I just said, we need to establish identity, we do not know whose body it is?' shouted Ann. 'I am not answering any more questions. Steven Edwards will be doing an official press release later. You will need to be patient till then,' she continued. 'Do you think it is another serial killing?' asked Amy Baker, ignoring Ann's request for them to wait until the official release. 'I think you have been outsmarted, Inspector and I think you have lost your edge,' continued Amy in a spiteful manner. 'I don't care what the hell you think. The police are doing their utmost to solve this case,' replied Ann angrily. David opened the car door and coaxed Ann into the passenger seat, reminding her that there was no point in arguing the toss with the press. Ann kept silent despite a barrage of questions still being fired at her. They drove off swiftly, not uttering another word. 'Bastards, they never give up. Just like rats, gnawing at one's soul,' remarked Ann. 'Not worth getting into a spat with the press. They will only use it against you, and you will be viewed as the aggressor,' advised David. 'Let's speak to Peter to get us an urgent report on the forensics. Our next priority is to contact Eve Marshall and ask her if we can visit,' said Ann. They called at Peter's office. He smiled as Ann walked in. 'Coming to egg me on for your results, hey Ann,' said Peter. I will have them ready by this afternoon,' said Peter. David accompanied Ann to the incident room, where they began preparations for the briefing of the team on the body found in the garage. 'Schedule the briefing for 9.00 tomorrow, we should have all the information by then, Ann informed David. Peter rang her around 2.30pm. The dead girl is Elaine Casey. Her DNA matches, the hair and blood we found at the scene of her father's murder,' said Peter. 'Fuck," exclaimed Ann. 'Shit now I have the onerous task of telling her mother,' she complained. She thanked Peter for the prompt information.

She dialled Eve Marshall's number. 'D.C.I. Dixon here, Mrs Marshall. I wonder if it would be convenient to call at your house today. There have been new developments, but I need to discuss them with you in person,' said Ann. There was a brief pause. 'If you don't have news of my daughter, then you would be wasting my time coming to see me,' said Eve. 'Mrs Marshall, I would not be ringing you if I did not have important information to share with you. Please let me see you in person as the information I have is highly classified and cannot be said over the phone,' explained Ann. She could hear Eve asking her husband if it was okay for Ann to call at the house. 'I see no harm in the detective coming here,' she heard Harold say to Eve. 'Alright, you had better come before 4pm as we have an appointment,' said Eve. 'We will get there as soon as possible, traffic permitting of course," replied Ann. She ascended the steps to the Marshalls' front door with some trepidation. Harold Marshall opened the door. 'Hello! Inspector do come inside,' said Harold cheerfully. He enquired if they wanted tea. Ann sat opposite Eve and composed the statement she was about to make. 'Mrs Marshall, I am afraid I have bad news about your daughter. We were led to a garage where her body was found locked inside the boot of a car,' she said bracing herself for the reprisals that she expected would follow. Eve clung to Harold as the bad news was revealed. She let out an ear, piercing scream and leapt out at Ann, aiming to hit her in the face. David stepped forward and intercepted the blow, and got struck in the face instead of Ann. Eve became hysterical screaming and cursing as Harold and David tried to restrain her from attacking Ann. Ann looked on resignedly, understanding Eve's rage and not trying in any way to defend herself.

It took twenty minutes before Eve finally sank into a chair sobbing uncontrollably and saying Elaine's name repeatedly. When Harold satisfied that it was safe to leave Eve sitting by herself, he asked Ann if the police had any idea who the garage belonged to. Ann answered cautiously, replying that they would have let him know as soon as the police discovered the identity of the garage owner. She informed them that she would arrange when it was convenient for them to formerly identify their daughter. "Do you know how long Elaine has been dead?' he asked.

'I am afraid it is up to the coroner to determine the time of death, so we will need to wait for the post-mortem results,' replied Ann. Post-mortem! Nobody is going to cut up my daughter,' shouted Eve. 'I am afraid the law states that a post mortem has to be performed in cases of sudden or unexplained death or cases of suspicious death,' she continued. Are you saying our daughter was murdered Inspector?' asked Harold. 'The circumstances surrounding Elaine's death, suggests foul play,' she said. They sat in silence drinking their tea while the Marshalls tried to come to terms with their grief. Ann was the first to break the silence.

'Thank you for your time. I am sorry I could not bring you better news. My team and I at the station will be available at any time you have any queries,' said Ann. They were both relieved when they reached the safety of their car. 'What a wild cat, that Eve Marshall. She nearly had your eye out, Guv,' said David. 'Look at the situation from her point of view. Her only daughter visits her father and bang, she disappears and ends up dead in the boot of someone's car. All those agonising days of waiting and hoping, ends in a statement that makes her world come crashing down. You and I would react in a similar fashion, maybe not so vocal, but visibly outraged,' continued Ann. 'She would have killed us if she knew that the car and garage belonged to her in-laws,' replied Ann. 'Let's hurry back to the office. I need to fill Edwards in on the latest details,' said Ann. Her heart sank as she walked down the corridor to her office as Edwards waited for her leaning against her office door.

'In my office, now,' he demanded, ignoring her protests to see him in an hour. She followed him slavishly and sat down in his office. 'What the hell is going on, Ann?' I get a call from my chief telling me that he was informed about a dead woman found at a lock up garage belonging to Jake Casey and a James Muller. You can imagine the headlines tomorrow. It is going to make the police look like a bunch of amateurs,' said Edwards. 'We don't know all the details, but I assume that both men were involved in the murder. Tim says the state of the body suggests that Elaine was kept in a freezer after death, then wrapped in plastic and put in the boot of the car. So, supposing Jake killed her days before he was arrested, and James possibly could have transferred the body to the boot of the car in the garage. 'How did you arrive at this conclusion?' asked Edwards sarcastically. 'We have evidence to support the fact that Jake Casey was at the murder scene. He did not put Elaine in the car at George's house, because circumstantial evidence supports the fact that a heavier taller man carried Elaine to the car. Our eyewitness substantiates this fact. Tim Jones was not able to establish the post-mortem interval because the body had been frozen and left in the car for approximately two days. We need to wait for the post-mortem to find out more. If we have some way of knowing that James was in London at the time of the murders, we can categorically say that he was an accomplice to the murders,' she continued. Edwards listened without interrupting for a change. 'Have you briefed your team?' he enquired. 'I have a briefing scheduled for tomorrow afternoon. By then, Tim will have done the post-mortem,' she said. 'I am meeting with Jeremy Doyle, the guy from Interpol tomorrow evening. He might have some news about James Muller,' she said. 'Well I don't care what it takes to get a result, but you bloody get to it and wrap this fiasco up as soon as possible. I have the chief superintendant breathing down my neck,' he hissed glaring at Ann. This seemed to placate Edwards and he allowed her to go, warning her to keep him abreast of everything. David was waiting in her office when she finished her impromptu meeting with Steven. 'Rough going was it, guv?' asked David. 'Bloody man is so impatient and rude,' replied Ann. Her phone rang. It was Tim Jones. 'Hi Ann, I just ringing to say I will be performing the post-mortem on Elaine Casey tomorrow at 8.30. Do you think you can make?' he asked. 'I wouldn't miss it for it for the world. See you at 8.30 prompt,' she promised. 'Did you hear David?' PM being done tomorrow. Pick me up around 7.00 and I will treat you to breakfast,' she promised. 'Please ensure the team know about the briefing at 3.00 pm tomorrow. Yikes! It is going to be a hell of a day,' she complained. 'I am going to call it a day, David. My brain has gone to sleep, she announced at 9pm. 'Want me to drop you off, guv?' he asked. 'No thanks, I'll grab a cab as I am meeting Josie and some friends for a drink in Islington. He left promising to collect her at 7am the next morning.

The cab dropped her off at the Fox and Hound pub in Islington. She threaded her way through the crowd to the table where Josie sat with her friends from the fashion world. She beamed with delight as she spotted Ann heading in her direction. Ann kissed and hugged Josie gently as they met. "This is my partner, Ann Dixon, Josie announced proudly as introduced Ann to her colleagues. They smiled back and each shook her hand in turn. 'Josie says you are working on a serial murder case,' announced a girl named Tamara. 'Yes, you will probably read about it in the papers,' replied Ann. She gave Josie an admonishing look as she pinched her thigh under the table. "Let's give my partner a break from work, shall we?' ' I am sure she doesn't want to be reminded about work when she is here to enjoy herself,' announced Josie, knowing she was in for the high jump when they got home. The conversation switched to more conventional matters and the awkward moment passed.

The evening at the pub passed amicably. Ann saved her reprimand of Josie when they were in the cab going home. 'Are you telling the whole world that I am working on a serial killing?' asked Ann. 'No! my darling, Tamara Smith who asked you about your work was a former lover of the News of the World reporter, Amy Baker. Perhaps you would like to know that Amy Baker left Tamara for a constable on your team. So! Tamara's presence at the pub was no coincidence. I think she was a plant by Amy who knows you and I are together. I think Tamara hoped to catch you off guard, hoping you would reveal information she could pass on to Am,' Josie explained. 'I have turned you into quite a sleuth. Haven't I?' said Ann. 'Indeed, I am not just a pretty face. I do watch your back more than you realise,' replied Josie. 'Do you know the name of the constable she is dating?' asked Ann. 'I don't, but I could find out,' said Josie.

Ann lay awake for some time, mulling over what Josie had told her about Tamara Smith's link to one of her constables. She realised where Amy Baker might have got her classified information from, which she printed in the paper. 'Good Morning guv. Have you seen the papers today?' asked David as Ann got into the car. 'No what does it say?' asked Ann. David showed her the headlines. It read, 'Casey family virtually decimated by serial killer. Are the Metropolitan Police procrastinating while a family is being brutally murdered?' Ann skimmed over the article which implied that she was being outwitted by the killer and seemed to be out of her depth at solving the case. The article also contained forensic facts which had not been released to the press. 'Bastards! I will show them who is incompetent,' she vowed. 'I found out last night that Amy baker is dating one of the C.I.D. officers on my team. Find out who he is. I am going to skin him alive, and have him chucked off the force,' she said. He said he didn't know but would make a special effort to enquire who Amy was dating in the force. 'That explains why the newspaper published details not officially revealed to the press,' said David. 'Yes, that is precisely why Edwards had my guts for garters because he assumed that I had leaked information to Amy Baker, to cement my status with the media,' he called it,' she complained. 'I think we have a mole leaking sensitive and highly classified information, I want him found,' said Ann. 'Let's have breakfast at that workman's cafe in Eccleston Street,' she suggested. They drove in silence for the rest of the journey as Ann continued to read the inflammatory article. They ordered a substantial breakfast as Ann feared it would probably be her last meal for the day as her schedule was packed for the day. After breakfast they hurried to the mortuary. Tim looked up as they arrived.

He talked into the tape recorder as he began his examination of the remains of Elaine Casey. 'This is the body of a white female aged 23. Decomposition was delayed due to being deep frozen. Considerable body mass loss suggests this woman was starved or refused to eat over some length of time, prior to her death. There is no rigor mortis present. The length of time that the body was kept in the freezer is unknown. I cannot give you date or time of death. I would surmise three weeks plus or minus. There is evidence of bruising on face, wrists, ankles and thighs.

There is a deep cut below sternum, probably pierced the aorta. It appears that the wound was done with a dagger with a 6inch blade. The blade width is two inches. There is a 4cm cut over the jugular vein on the right side of her neck. Cause of death, exsanguination due to incisional cut of aorta,' he reported. 'Ann, the manner in which this poor girl was killed suggests it might have been ritualistic,' he said. 'Don't quote me on this, but you should go with your gut feeling and check out the Casey's satanic pursuits as you had originally intended to do,' he continued. The hair of the victim contained seeds, grass and insects. It suggests she was left in the woods before being put in the freezer. After taking photographs of the wounds, he began washing the body. There was a measure of sadness in his face as he performed this task. Ann always admired the professionalism and empathy with which Tim performed his post-mortems. He stopped washing the body as he stumbled onto what resembled a leaf in Elaine's hair. He collected the leaf debris cautiously and put it in the forensic bag. Then when he turned the dead woman's head to the left side to continue washing her body, he noticed something stuck in the left ear. He lifted it out gently with pair of forceps. 'Hmmm looks like a type of beetle. How odd, there was no evidence that any insects had visited the body. Perhaps this one crept in while the body lay on the ground to be moved. Let's see what forensics have to say about I,' he said.

His assistant helped him turn over the body as he continued washing. 'Livor Mortis on the back suggests she died face up," he added. He then began the process of opening the body and examining all the organs as he carefully removed them weighed them and continued a running commentary on their condition. 'The victim's organs appear in a good state of health,' he continued. When he got to inspect the pelvic organs and colon and rectum, he paused and expressed concern at what he found. Massive bruising of the vagina, and a tearing of both vagina and anus suggests either repeated, violent acts of rape and sodomy," he declared. The labia majora are missing. These have probably taken as trophies. 'The sick bastard who did this must be found,' said Tim as he gritted his teeth in anger. He examined the empty cavity of the thorax and abdomen after he had removed all the organs. 'Hmm I thought as much, the blade which pierced the aorta, was wielded with so much force that it cut into the vertebra. See here, the muscle and tissue are scraped off the bone,' he added. She nodded in silent acknowledgement. He took blood samples and scrapings from under Elaine's fingernails, bagged and labelled them and sent them to forensics. 'Please make her face as decent as possible because her mother is very fragile at the moment, so I don't want her freaking out by her daughter's battered face,' said Ann. 'Don't worry, my technician is good at his job. He will ensure that Elaine looks good for when her mother does the identification bi,' he reassured Ann. David had managed to pop in and out between spells of nausea during the post-mortem, much to Ann's amusement. Tim promised to send Ann a concise report on the post-mortem. She thanked him and promised to be in touch if there were any queries. It had been a long morning.

Ann looked at her watch with a gasp of consternation as she had barely thirty minutes to prepare for her briefing with the team. She checked her emails and was relieved to discover that both D.I Roberts and Tobin were unavoidably detained and would not be able to make it to the briefing. 'Thank God for that,' said Ann relived that she did not have to rush to do the briefing as she was not fully prepared. She was also pleased because she wanted to get the full forensic report on Elaine to present to her team. David breezed into her office bearing gifts of coffee and mouth-watering doughnuts. 'You truly are an angel of mercy,' she said gratefully a she munched away. She phoned Jeremy Doyle to reschedule her meeting with him for early afternoon. She was in luck because he had a slot in his diary for the time she requested. 'David, I want to ask Edwards he would fly you to Spain to interview Jack's son about the Russian girl, Saskia who hung out with the Casey's,' said Ann. I can't imagine him forking out money for an air ticket. He will give us chapter and verse on the constraints of his budget,' said David. 'Fuck his budget, if he wants us to solve this case, he will need to spend money,' replied Ann. 'All I can say guv is good luck with that one,' said David. 'I have got to follow every lead David. All our reputations are at stake here. We look like shit in the public eye,' said Ann fearfully. They worked out a rough plan for their team in preparation for the briefing which Ann postponed for two days later. 'Come on, let's hurry, we are meeting with Jeremy from MI6, at Novotel on the Euston Road. The traffic should not be too heavy,' Ann urged. Jeremy Doyle was a tall slender man. They met in the bar of the hotel which was unusually quiet. 'Nice to meet the woman I had heard so much about, face to face,' said Jeremy with abroad smile. 'Hopefully good things about me, I hope,' said Ann. '"Mostly good things, and the bad was only mildly bad,' replied Jeremy. 'Ah ha that's what I like to hear, only the truth,' said Ann beaming with delight. 'This is D.S. David Hughes," she said proudly as David stepped forward to shake Jeremy's hand. 'What would you like to drink?' Ann asked. 'It's okay, I'll get this round,' said David. He ordered while Ann and Jeremy set about the business at hand. 'You seem to have a hell of a difficult case,' Ann said Jeremy. 'It has been a bloody nightmare,' replied Ann. 'Thus far, we have two murdered brothers, an unconscious brother and a dead daughter of one of the murdered men.

Our efforts of finding the killer has been frustrated because the sly bastard has been planting evidence which sent us chasing the wrong people. There is a possibility that there may be two murderers working together. We think that the unconscious man might have had an accomplice, possibly James Muller, who unfortunately has not been found to date,' said Ann. She showed Jeremy some of the information on her laptop to get him up to date on what they had thus far. 'Did you get the photos I sent to you of James Muller,' she enquired. 'Yes thanks, we have begun processing the information,' he replied. 'Thus far, we can tell you that James Muller has been in London until a few days ago when he left for Brazil. We have no leads as to where he lives in London. He is not employed at any hospital or clinic as far as we are aware. He has not contacted his sister, Susan, since he left. We have circulated his photograph throughout the country and at all major ports and airports. We are also working closely with the FBI in Brazil as they have a greater network over there.

A few days ago, we received a report that James Muller left the Britain under the alias of Carlos Mendes. He travelled on a Portuguese passport. He seems to have something to hide. If he has been here three months ago, there is no doubt that he is involved in the killings,' continued Jeremy. I am going to head a team to Brazil and meet up with some guys from the FBI,' said Jeremy. 'Do you have any idea why Jake Casey was attacked?' asked Jeremy. 'We are absolutely sure, but I have a hunch that he knows something his accomplice does not want him to reveal. If they did the killings together, then his accomplice fears he will turn state witness. If it is about the contents of a coded diary written by his deceased brother, Tom, the diary must contain evidence implicating the accomplice,' said Ann. 'What chance does Jake have of waking up,' asked Jeremy. 'The doctor said a good chance when all the swelling on his brain subsides,' replied Ann. 'Have you checked James is not employed at any of the army bases," asked David. 'Hey that's somewhere we had not explored. I will get on to it tomorrow,' replied Jeremy. 'I don't care if you have to kidnap James Muller, to question him. Find him and get some answers,' urged Ann. 'I don't care what it takes, but I am accompanying your team to Brazil,' Ann urged with determination. 'We would love to have you come along, but your boss might not agree due to the cost of the trip,', replied Jeremy sympathetically. 'Sod the top brass, I will pay my way with my own funds,' Ann replied with annoyance. The beer had flowed freely during their long meeting. When Ann began to see double, she called time on their meeting and thanked Jeremy for his contribution to the investigation. When they were alone, she whispered to David to save her blushes by getting her home before she fell over and disgraced herself. He had to hold onto her to help her out of the car into the house. He enjoyed the brief moment he was able to hold Ann close to him. He savoured the heady fragrance of her perfume. He wished she was sober and was leaning against him in a loving embrace. They were met by a surprised Josie at the door, who helped David get her into the house. Ann mumbled a few incoherent words, before collapsing into a stupor on the couch in the living room. 'David, you won't pass a breathalyser test either. Sit down and have some coffee to sober up,' said Josie. She covered Ann with a blanket. Adam came downstairs when he heard the commotion. 'Hi, David, nice to see you again. Thanks for getting Ann home safely," said Adam. 'Oh, it's a pleasure. We had a heavy meeting with someone from Interpol. The meeting went on for five hours and I guess we did not realise how much we had drunk,' replied David.' 'I'll see you to the car"' said Adam.

Just as soon as they got outside, Adam tugged at David's sleeve and said, hold on, don't go just yet. 'I have some very important news I must tell you. It concerns the case, but I cannot tell you now. Let's arrange to meet in Scotland. Dream up a story for Ann. Tell her you are going fishing with a friend", said Adam. 'Ok, I'll ring you when I have secured the weekend,' promised David. David chose a suitable moment when Ann was momentarily distracted to ask for the weekend off. 'Oh, so you have met a nice girl, have you?' enquired Ann. 'No Guv, I am going fishing with my brother?' replied David. 'You have never mentioned him before,' said Ann, her piercing eyes boring into him. 'He has been away for a while so, we just made contact in the last few days,' said David. 'Okay, as long as it is only two days away. I need you here promptly on Monday morning,' she said. 'Now go and find me that forensic profiler's contact number, while I collar Edwards about sending you to Spain,' said Ann. 'If it is about the post mortem on Elaine Casey, I have already received the report, said Edwards as she entered his office. 'No actually, it is about another matter,' replied Ann. "If it is about supplying more officers, the answer is no,' said Edwards in anticipation of her request. 'During our interview with the Casey's old neighbour, Jack Slade, in Nottingham, we found out that the Casey brothers befriended foreign girls and lured them into their house and probably subjected them to all manner of perverse sexual practises. Jack's son, Andrew who now lives on the Costa Del Sol in Spain knew one of the Russian girls who visited the Casey's and she disappeared suddenly without a trace, while the Casey's were living at their old house. I would like you to fund DS Hughes flight to Spain to interview Andrew Slade. Edwards swung around with an indignant look on his face. 'How the hell do you think I am going to justify spending money to send your sergeant to Spain on a fact- finding mission, which won't bring us nearer to solving these murders,' he said angrily. 'That's where you are wrong, sir, the brothers' shared interest in the occult is the key to solving these murders. Someone attacked Jake in the hope of killing him to silence him. Andrew Slade grew up with the Casey brothers and he should be able to shed some light on the Casey's perverse practices. He had a Russian friend who might be a witness to the Casey's practises and Mr Slade's son is the only one who may have the answers. Please just give me a chance to explore what I consider a very important lead. Take the money out of my salary, if the Met are too mean to support my request,' continued Ann. Edwards sat down and said, 'Oh alright, I will speak to the commander and get back to you.' Ann smiled broadly and thanked him profusely. She rushed into her office and phoned David excitedly, telling him there was a chance that her request might be approved. There was a message on her mobile to contact Peter. She was so keen to know the outcome of the forensic results that she went to see Peter at his laboratory. He was typing a report when she arrived. 'You have got to sit down to hear what I am going to tell you. You are going to buy me dinner for all the hard work I have done," he said smiling mischievously. The sand found on the wheels of the car and from Elaine's body bag was found in the boot was traced to sand from Sherwood Forest. A knife with a 6inch blade was found hidden under the carpet of the boot. It contains old blood and DNA of two different females. We also found petrol in five litre cans in the boot. I am guessing that whoever killed Elaine intended to torch the car with the body inside. The entomologist had a look at the beetle found in Elaine's hair. It is a darkling beetle, native to Sherwood Forest. The species are found elsewhere in The United Kingdom, but, the fact that the beetle had microscopic traces of soil endemic to Sherwood Forest, narrows down the location of the beetle as having lived in Sherwood. The leaf found in Elaina's hair is from the sessile oak trees native to Sherwood Forest. The soil found in Elaine's hair is endemic to Sherwood Forest. The report from on her blood is even more astounding. Her blood and stomach contained a combination of Teonacatl and Ololuiqui. These substances are found in plants grown in Mexico and other parts of South America. The Aztecs are known to have given the ones chosen to be sacrificed, the mushrooms and seeds to ingest in order to make their victims hallucinate before they were killed. The victims knew their fate but were disabled by the effects of the plants they were forced to ingest. The effects of these hypnotic plants are like ecstasy. The victims suffer blurred vision, euphoria, increased sense of hearing, altered concentration, hallucinations and a sense of oneness with a divinity of their belief. A dose of 4 to 8mg is effective. Teonacatl or Peyote is an alkaloid mescaline. It grows in Huixol and Taraumara, Mexico. It has properties similar to LSD. Oliuqui or Turbina. Corymbosa is found in the seeds of bindweed, also grows in South America. The effect gives the victims a feeling of inebriation, being possessed of some entity, and hallucinations. The British pharmaceutical society lists these natural drugs under

Class A, dangerous drugs section. These plants are found in other parts of the world, but the species found in Elaine's stomach, contained soil endemic to Mexico. So, it is my calculation that these natural drugs were brought from Mexico, possibly by your Dr Muller," said Peter. I think Elaine was murdered in Sherwood Forest in some bizarre satanic ritual and kept in a freezer, before being brought to the garage. The killer planned for us to find the body. I think it was the killer who told Tobin about the garage,' he explained. 'Well I'll be damned,' she exclaimed when he had finished. 'It is abundantly clear that we are dealing with extremely dangerous and clever criminals who will stop at nothing to get what they want,' said Ann. 'We cannot possibly allow them to get away with murder. I will pursue them to the ends of the earth to bring them to just, I swear it,' said Ann. Tim put a consoling arm around her and reassured her that she would succeed, but also reminded her to proceed with caution.

She took the forensic report with her to her office to update her files and share the news with David. He could hardly believe his eyes as he read the report given to him by Ann. 'I want everyone at the briefing tomorrow, including the forensic team. I want a full report from all my officers, and nobody is to leave the room until I am absolutely finished,' she told David. He nodded in agreement and informed her that he had already made it very clear that it was an important meeting, and everyone needed to be there on time and ready to make a valuable contribution to the investigation. Edwards popped his head around the door of her office and informed her that he wanted to be present at the briefing. 'Ok Sir, I will send you the forensic report later today,' said Ann. 'I believe the findings are quite incredible. I look forward to reading it,' said Edwards as he turned on his heel and walked off. 'David do we know who owns the Casey's house in Nottingham,' enquired Ann. 'Jack Slade said that George Casey bought the house and paid the rest of his siblings for their share. I think I recall Jack saying that part of the animosity amongst the brothers was as a result of George buying the house,' said David. 'Let's find out from Eve Marshall if she has access to the house,' continued Ann. 'I will ring her now. Nothing like the present to get the ball rolling,' she added. She dialled Eve's number. Harold answered. "'Sorry to bother you, Mr Marshall, I wonder if it would be convenient to pay Mrs Marshall a visit as there is some very important information we need,' enquired Ann. She heard him relay the question to Eve and heard the sarcastic reply. My wife is still very angry with the police. She says she will think about your request and get back to you, Inspector,' said Harold. 'Thank you, I will be grateful if she could let us know at her earliest convenience,' continued Ann. "Damn difficult woman," said Ann as she came off the phone. 'I think I will send D.I. Roberts and yourself to question Eve. Perhaps not seeing me might elicit a more positive response,' said Ann with some irritation. 'Okay guv, I will contact D.I. Roberts as soon as Eve gives us the go ahead,' replied David. The time had flown.

They were both starving, so David did not hesitate when Ann persuaded him to join her for a meal at a pub near Sloane Square. He also anticipated that it was going to be a long night filled with discussions about the case. He didn't mind however, because it gave him a legitimate excuse to be with her; to admire her in secret. They sat at the tables outside the pub to avoid the deafening din inside which forced them to shout at each other to be heard. Just as fate would have it, David glanced over Ann's shoulder and spotted Josie's colleague, Tamara with D.C Terence Holmes. He moved closer to Ann and whispered to her to move away from the table, to avoid being seen by Holmes. They headed for David's car across the street from the pub. Ann asked, 'Is that D.C Holmes I just seen with Tamara Smith?' asked Ann. 'Yes guv, he must be the mole in our team. I can guess why he is dating Tamara. He has a gambling problem, and I am sure she is funding his habit. I am sure Tamara is using him to get information she is passing onto Amy Baker. That is why The

News of The World can print chapter and verse on our murder cases,' said David. "I want Terence Holmes tailed. I also want his house bugged. The bastard is not going to ruin my investigation because he needs to fund his gambling habit," said Ann with conviction. They sat in their car across the street from the pub and observed D.C. Holmes and Tamara in animated conversation at their table. They were so engrossed in their conversation, that they were oblivious to everything else. They seemed in earnest conversation. Tamara leaned in close to Holmes as if they did not want to be overheard. They were joined by another man who brought them a round of drinks.

Ann was seething with anger imagining how they were plotting to undermine her. 'I am going to speak to surveillance and nail the bastard who is passing information to Amy. I will not allow them to make fools of the force. We are already viewed in a bad light in the eyes of the public', she hissed. 'I will help you to nail the bastard, guv. You just tell me what I need to do, David reassured her. 'I will get the surveillance team to help me trap Holmes and somehow link him to the newspaper reporter who has targeted me. I will not leave a stone unturned to get this sorted,' Ann vowed.

Chapter 5

After watching them for twenty minutes, Ann announced that she wanted to be taken home. 'Remember the briefing is at 8.00, so please collect me at 7.00,' said Ann as she got out of the car at her the front door of her home. Josie was asleep. Ann tiptoed around the room while she prepared herself for bed. She got into bed and snuggled up behind Josie's back, kissing her in the neck as she moved closer. This manoeuvre never failed to ignite Josie's passion. The resulting exchange of sexual fury consumed them and continued until they were both spent. They hugged and kissed and continued to touch and stroke each other until they drifted off into a dream filled sleep. The hooting of David's car woke Ann and she fell out of bed, horrified that she had not heard the alarm. She ran to the door to let David in, apologising profusely for being late. She dashed into the shower, shouting for Josie to get up and help her find some clothes to wear. Josie came into the shower with a smile on her face. She handed Ann a towel and whispered, 'See what happens when you seduce a poor innocent girl.' teased Josie. 'Hmm I can still taste you, you wicked girl. Get out of here and help me to get dressed,' said Ann. Josie laid out a smart suit with matching accessories.

Ann got dressed hurriedly, bounded downstairs, grabbing phone and laptop. 'We can get coffee on the way,' she said to David. She kissed Josie and thanked her for getting her clothes. The radiance reflected in their faces, said it all. David guessed the reason for their elation and had to supress a wave of envy. They stopped at her office to collect the reports and relevant information for the briefing. Stephen Edwards was already seated in the briefing room when Ann arrived. The rest of the team filed in steadily until everyone was present. Ann had arranged all the photos and notes about the killings and kidnap on the incident board at the front of the room. She stood up and thanked them for attending. 'We have a very complex murder investigation. I am grateful for all your input and diligence and I don't want you to be influenced by the negative comments in the media. The latest murder of Elaine Casey brings us to the conclusion that there may be two killers. We have arrived at this conclusion because the eye witness described a larger, taller man putting Elaine Casey into the car on the night George Casey was murdered. The depth at which the boots worn by the man sank into the mud in the flower bed suggests that it was a taller heavy man and not Jake Casey who kidnapped Elaine. The fact that her body was found in the car belonging to James Muller, in Jake Casey's garage, we must assume that these men jointly responsible for the killing. The murder weapons used to kill George Casey were found in Jake's lock up. A gasp followed her last statement. Some of the men shook their heads in disbelief and muttered their disgust. 'I want D.I Roberts to contact the forestry commission of Sherwood Forest to grant us permission to do a search for the spot where Elaine was murdered. 'I can do better than that guv, I have found out that George Casey had a private ownership, public service with the forestry commission. George had his own woodland which he cared for but was supervised by the forestry commission. We should find out where it is in the forest and get a search, warrant based on the findings of the death of Elaine,' said D.I. Roberts. Everyone stopped talking. They were astounded that D.I. Roberts had produced such valuable information as the team had always looked down on him. 'Good work Roberts. I am sure Superintendant Edwards will get us the warrant to search the woods,' said Ann, smiling at Edwards as she spoke. He scowled and said he would need a few days to get the warrant. If you have any queries concerning the drugs used to sedate Elaine, speak to Tim, who will be able to answer any questions you have," she continued. 'Our task is very complex as we don't have either of the killers in custody. Jake is still unconscious, and James Muller is in Brazil,' she said. 'What has Interpol said?' guv, asked D.I. Tobin. 'I spoke to Jeremy Doyle, who is says that James Muller had been in London over the last three months but left on a Portuguese passport under the alias, Carlos Mendes, a few days ago. Jeremy is meeting with the FBI in Brazil to gather more information. "I have asked Superintendant Edwards to ask for funding to send D.S Hughes to interview the Casey's old neighbour, Andrew Slade about one of the girls who was possibly used in their rituals. I also want to get permission from George Casey's wife, Eve Marshall to search the Casey's old house which he now owns,' he continued. Edwards addressed the meeting endorsing what Ann had said and surprising her by announcing that he had managed to get approval for DS Hughes to travel to Spain for the interview. 'Okay, let me introduce our forensic profiler, Savannah Carey. Ms Carey has had a great deal of experience with the profiles of serial killers. Savannah stepped forward and acknowledged Ann's introduction. Her long blonde hair and curvaceous figure caught the eye of the officers and elicited a momentary whoop from them, which made her blush. 'Calm down boys, Ms Carey is here in an official capacity. Please give her the best of your professionalism,' said Ann with irritation. 'Hi team, I was called in to assess the profile of your perpetrator. It is my opinion after having studied the details of the murders that your killer is operating alone. He behaves normally but his psychotic behaviour manifests when he is challenged. He enjoys the buzz of being pursued by the law, hence the red herrings he has left, diverting the focus of the police. He is extremely clever and manipulative. He has a fully functioning frontal cerebral lobe which makes him very intelligent in his meticulous planning of these murders. He probably had a very controlling parent during his early life and has built up a sea of hate against anyone who prevents him from getting his way. He is a professional man who conducts himself respectably in his everyday life but is capable of extreme violence when the need warrants. He craves control in all situations and when his power is challenged, he will go to any length to maintain it. The degree of torture suggests that it is a revenge vendetta. It suggests that the murderer knew his victims. The attack on one of the brothers suggests that Jake Casey might have some information the murderer wants to suppress. If the murderer has an accomplice, it would be someone of lesser intelligence and subservient to the killer who makes all the decisions about the murders,' she continued. The officers questioned Savannah about various aspects of the perpetrators character. She answered their questions confidently and reassured the team that she would be available for discussions about the case whenever they needed her. The officers swapped various pieces of information they had gathered and shared it with one another. The whole room buzzed with conversation as the team chatted excitedly about details of the case thus far.

Ann and Edwards spoke to the other senior officers of the team, questioning them about their enquiries. The meeting dragged on for four hours. Ann, sensing that matters were drawing to a close, announced that it was evident that under no circumstances was anyone allowed to speak to the media. 'God help anyone who is found to leak information to the press or anyone outside this force,' warned Ann. There was a hushed silence as they digested her warning. 'I am proud of you lot, so don't let the team down. If there are no more questions, get out of my sight and come back with good results,' she said smiling as they walked past her, out of the room. Edwards came up to her and thanked her for a successful briefing. He asked about Savannah's professional background. Ann informed him that Savannah had a degree from Oxford and had helped to solve cases on several murders. She told him that Savannah was highly respected for her work. 'Well she had better know her stuff with our case,' he added. She reassured him he would not be disappointed. She thanked him for getting the funding for the trip to Spain. 'Just make sure it is not a wild goose chase or the chief will have my guts for garters and there will be not end to what you will suffer,' he said to Ann." It will be a valuable trip, I assure you, sir.' Ann replied. David joined her as they walked to her office. They helped themselves to a coffee in the corridor and went to drink it in Ann's office, while they mulled over the briefing. 'We can phone Andrew Slade today and ask him when it will be convenient for you to come,' said Ann. 'Okay, I am phoning Andrew Slade. Grab a pen so that you can jot down all the details for your trip to Spain. The phone rang for a while until a woman answered. Ann introduced herself and asked for Andrew. She was told that she was speaking to his wife, Rita, and that he would come to the phone shortly. Andrew took the phone from his wife and greeted Ann pleasantly. 'My father warned me that you would be ringing, Inspector,' he said. 'Yes, I wondered when it would be convenient for Sergeant David Hughes to come over to Spain to interview you about Sasha,' said Ann. 'Oh, next week would be fine. I will give you the details of how to get to our place,' he said. Ann repeated the address and all the details of the directions. She gave the phone to David to continue the conversation with Andrew.

Ann took the phone from David when he had finished the conversation and added, 'Please remind my sergeant that he is on duty, so no sangria, or any other form of alcohol. I don't want to have to read in the papers that a member of my team was carried off somewhere because he was inebriated, please Mr Slade,' continued Ann. A hearty laugh filtered through the phone and Ann chuckled mischievously. 'Please don't get back late from your weekend break. I need you here on Monday as we have to tie up many loose ends before you go,' Anne reminded him. '"Now I need to grasp the nettle and talk to Eve Marshall so that we can gain access to George's house in Nottingham. I will try phoning her in the morning,' she said. The briefing had inspired the team to continue their investigation with renewed vigour. D.I Tobin contacted Sam Cain for another interview with the hope that he would gain more information about how Jake and James managed the garage. D.C. Terence Holmes was the only one who came away from the briefing bearing a grudge. He was incensed, that Ann had made such an issue about the information leaked to the press. 'Arrogant bitch! Did you see her looking at me when she spoke?' 'It was though I had spoken to the press," he said angrily. 'And did you reveal classified information to the press, Holmes?' enquired Tobin. 'No, I bloody didn't,' he replied. 'You are banging Amy Baker's ex- girlfriend, aren't you?' asked Tobin. 'Yes, so what if I am. It doesn't mean I need to open my mouth to get laid,' he continued. 'If you have friends of the media, you will be considered a risk of confidentiality, even though, you say that you are not discussing details of the murders,' Tobin reminded him. 'So, I have to curtail my private life to please the Metropolitan police,' he complained. 'Yes, remember you are judged by the company you keep and your discretion concerning your acquaintances, are crucial to the stability of the force. If you are talking to the likes of Amy Baker, I will personally deal with you,' warned Tobin. Holmes uttered an expletive and walked out of the office. Tobin phoned Ann and told her that he had questioned Holmes about his association with Tamara and that Holmes denied leaking the information. Ann replied that Holmes was telling a lie and that she wanted Tobin to arrange to have Holmes tailed.

    Tobin promised to keep her informed. Steven Edwards arranged to meet with his chief, Michael Heath, to discuss the progress of the investigation and about the warrant for searching the woods. Michael liked Ann and admired her professionalism immensely. He listened intently while Stephen told him about the difficulties the officers had encountered during the investigation. Just as he was about to condemn certain aspects of Ann's method of investigation, Michael stopped him and reminded him about Ann's impeccable record over the years and about the time when her male colleagues confounded by the evidence in a previous murder, and Ann came up with a solution which solved the case. 'Steven, you cannot possibly allow your misogynistic prejudices to blind you to Ann's tremendous talent. She has survived tremendous odds, chauvinism, homophobia and has triumphed in bringing the criminals to justice, despite everything. There is no guarantee that the Metropolitan police would have made more progress, if a man headed the investigation,' Michael reminded him. 'Ann Dixon can hold her own against any male police officer. She worked for MI6 for a short while. She has trained as a special forces officer. Her track record in the force has been most commendable. She has the highest number of successful arrests which led to prosecutions in the UK. I will get you the search warrant, but you must promise me that you will give Ann your total support, no matter what your prejudices you harbour', continued Michael. Stephen listened to what Michael had said and nodded his head in agreement. 'I can't promise anything. I cannot change overnight, but I will try to be more civil to Ann. I will wait for the warrant and let you know how the lads got along,' said Stephen. Ann had managed to get Eve to meet with her at the Marshalls home.

Eve was still sulky when they first started talking, but Ann won her over by making the priority of the meeting about catching Elaine's murderer. Ann had to diplomatically and skilfully reveal to Eve that Elaine had been killed in Nottingham, and the police suspected that perhaps George's empty house might have been used to keep her body until she was moved to London. 'So, you see Mrs Marshall, you would be a great help to us if you gave us permission to search your husband's old house. Our officers will take the greatest care not to damage any valuables which may be in the house. You are at liberty to be nearby, so that you are able to check each day when the officers have finished,' Ann reassured her. The pain of losing her daughter was still very real, so Eve cried bitterly as Ann spoke. After an hour of contemplation and discussion with Harold, Eve agreed to let them search the house. Ann signed for the keys and thanked the Marshalls for their co-operation. She promised that she would keep them informed of any important findings at the house or overall. Eve hung onto her every word, hopeful that someone would pay for murdering her beloved Elaine. Ann bounded down the steps of the Marshalls' home in great spirits. Just as the car door slammed shut, she smiled at David and told him that she felt sure they would find something significant at the house. 'David, I want us to be at the house in Nottingham on Monday morning. I will give you the afternoon off today, so that you can have a longer break, but please don't let me down. I need you to be there with me, she said. 'Oh thanks, guv. I can leave earlier and get to my brother's by tonight,' he replied enthusiastically. 'Ok bugger off and have a good time before I change my mind,' she warned. David phoned Adam as soon as he left the station. 'Hey Adam, going off with you feels like cheating on the boss,' said David. 'We know why you feel that way, because you fancy my sister, like crazy and think nobody notices,' replied Adam chuckling away. 'I am not the only one who will be in trouble when Ann finds out. She is going to roast your arse too,' said David. 'Ok let's get serious. We are catching the 3.45 to Glasgow. I will hire a car to get to the fishing grounds outside of Glasgow. Don't be late,' he reminded David.

It was an anxious Adam who craned his neck looking out for David as the minutes ticked by at Euston station. There was only nine minutes left before the train departed. Then, just as Adam began to give up hope of David arriving in time, he heard his name being called. It was David running frantically towards him. They jumped on the train, just as the last call to board came over the speakers. 'Shit, you guys love to live life on the edge,' said Adam. 'Sorry, I had left my keys at work and had to get them and then of all the bad luck, ran into your sister who wanted to ask a hundred questions. I have never told her so many lies to get away,' continued David. Adam grinned at David's discomfort at lying to Ann. 'You have to remember the lies, because Ann has a memory like an elephant and she has a talent for tripping you up if you cannot repeat the lie chapter and verse,' warned Adam. The train pulled out of the platform slowly. David sighed with relief as the prospect of not having to think about work for two whole days was most satisfying. 'Do you get to see much of your brother?' asked Adam. 'No actually, we don't speak to each other. We had a terrible argument some time ago,' replied David. 'Must have been a big fight if you are not speaking,' said Adam. 'I'll tell you about it some time, but let's not talk about it now please,' said David. 'Okay, mate, don't stress, let's change the subject,' replied Adam. 'Actually, I have a confession to make. This is not a fishing trip. It was a ruse to get you to meet someone who has vital information about your case. I have a contact in MI6, a guy called, Nigel Phillips. He knows Rachel Levine, an agent with Mossad, whom I worked with a few years ago,' said Adam shuffling around somewhat embarrassed at his deception. 'Oh no, and here I was psyching myself up for a weekend of leisure,' said David, with a measure of regret. 'Sorry, about ruining your weekend, but you will realise how important the information Nigel has for your investigation,' replied Adam. 'Cheer up, it won't all be work. We will have a good piss up and go horse riding,' Adam reassured him. The journey sped by and soon they were pulling into Glasgow station.

They waited just outside the station entrance. A tall, muscular man walked up to them, smiled at Adam and stuck out his hand. 'Good heavens, Adam, you're looking good. Got a good woman keeping you in shape?' 'Hi, you don't look so bad yourself,' said Adam grinning. 'Meet DS David Hughes,' said Adam, pushing David forward. 'Hi nice to meet you,' replied Nigel, shaking David's hand vigorously. 'Come on you must be famished. I'll treat you to dinner,' said Nigel, leading them to his car. Fully sated with a hearty Glaswegian fare and numerous pints of lager, the three men retired to Nigel's home. 'Your room is just off the kitchen. I hope to don't mind sharing. The other spare room is stacked with all my diving gear,' said Nigel. 'We don't mind, just need a place to kip. It doesn't have to be the Ritz,' replied Adam. Nigel lit the gas fire to warm the chilly room and piled a few bottles of wine to keep them going while they talked. 'I was going to call Ann Dixon, but Adam did not want her to see the true picture until I had talked to you. 'Your murder suspect came on the radar of MI6 through our Mossad contact, Rachel Levine. They are very interested in James Muller aka Carlos Mendes because of his links to Hezbollah through the Mexican drug cartel, Los Zetas. There is a Brazilian drug link too, but James is directly involved with Los Zetas. There is no love lost with this strange alliance their only interest in one another is the money. Vast sums of money through the drug trade supports Hezbollah for the sale of arms, Los Zetas for drug money and Muller's neo Nazi troops for their fascist campaign. Muller is vital to Los Zetas because he ensures that their money is laundered. They protect him as if he was a bona fide gang member. Hezbollah don't care who shares their bed, as long as it supports their need for arms against the Jews. So even though members of this unholy alliance do not share one another's passion for their different causes, together they are a mighty force because their commitment to the common purpose of making lots for money. This is the true driving force which makes them formidable enemies. Rachel Levine and her colleagues are working on a very daring plot to kidnap Muller and fly him to Israel. It is a virtual impossible task, but it can be done if we all work together. You must realize that it is going to be a very dangerous mission, and I am afraid to say, lives will be lost during this mission. The most important reason to find Muller and bring him to justice is that our double agent in Brazil has told us that Muller knows Ann has put out an alert for his arrest. He is planning to take her out. We must act before he does. The team if everyone is agreed will consist of you, Jeremy and another MI6 colleague, Rachel and two DEA agent. Ann must not be allowed to accompany the team as it is too dangerous. Hopefully, Nigel can convince Jeremy to exclude her," continued Adam. "Forget it,

Ann has made it abundantly clear to Jeremy that she is going," David informed them. 'Oh shit, that means I definitely have to go too. I must protect my sister,' Adam added with impunity. The DEA agents and two local Brazilians who are working undercover in the Los Zetas camp. David, you need to tell Jeremy that Nigel called and you answered the phone. Contact Jeremy explaining that Nigel needed to speak to him urgently. Make some excuse that Nigel did not have Jeremy's direct line and as the matter was of the utmost secrecy, he needed to call Nigel. He has to tell Jeremy to work with Rachel and her Mossad operatives omitting the fact that I am involved,' Adam emphasized. There was a brief silence as David and Nigel assimilated what they had just been told 'Phew, pretty intense, makes one's hair stand on end, just envisaging the dangers,' said Adam. The obstacles are not insurmountable, but we need to plan the operation with military precision and work together as though our lives depended on it,' said Nigel. 'Ann must never know you are behind all the surreptitious planning, Adam. She will make our lives a living hell if she ever finds out,' said David. Nigel will introduce Rachel to Jeremy. Rachel will mention that they have an operative called Ben Hajjiof, who is me with an Israeli identity," explained Adam. Jeremy must not disclose Adams true identity as Ann will definitely not agree to Adams involvement", Nigel continued. "Jeremy is partial to sound suggestions. He is not as arrogant as his colleagues. He is our best bet to hopefully get all of us in the team to Brazil", Adam added enthusiastically. The three men talked well into the early hours of the morning. The next day they had a hearty brunch, then went horse riding. The rest of the day was spent consuming vast amounts of alcohol. The alarm echoed though the room a few times before rousing David from his deep sleep. He had a severe headache and cursed at having to go to work. Remembering he had promised to collect Ann early, he jumped out of bed and rushed around to avoid being late. He chewed gum to mask the strong smell of alcohol which still hung on his breath from the heavy drinking session he and Adam had on the Sunday before they returned to London. He stopped at Ann's home, hooted and waited. She greeted him cheerily as she got into the car. 'Bloody hell, I needn't ask if you had a good weekend, I can smell that it was a good one. The chewing gum hasn't worked'" she remarked. He shuffled uncomfortably and apologised for smelling of alcohol. 'I hope you are sober enough to do your job this morning,' she added. 'My brother and I had a late drinking session last night, but I feel fine this morning,' he lied. She suggested they go to the station and join the rest of the team who would be travelling to Nottingham. 'D.I. Tobin and his sidekick, Holmes will be going too, so I don't want a repeat of what happened at the station a month ago. Is that crystal clear, Sergeant Hughes,' said Ann sternly. 'Yes guv, I will stay out of his way,' David reassured her. The CID team were milling around at the station when they arrived. Ann checked whether they had all the equipment they needed for the search. The forensic team would also accompany them. Ann briefed them on the search and warned them to be careful not to damage any items inside the Casey home as she was accountable for loss and damage of items inside the house. It was considered that they would be flown to Nottingham by helicopter as time was of the essence. They were ferried to the helicopters and were flown to Nottingham. They were met by Nottingham CID who provided transport for the team to the Casey home in Edwinstowe. They disembarked from the cars and walked up the long garden path to the house. The house was in an immaculate condition, even though it was unoccupied for most of the time. Ann turned the key in the front door, opened it and led her men into the house. The furniture was covered with white sheets. The place looked as though nobody had lived in it for some time, but every piece of furniture was tidily arranged in the room. A thick coating of dust clung to the floor. Ann switched on the light at the entrance to the rather dark living room. A pair of shoeprints was visible leading from the front door towards the rear of the house. The thick layer of dust delineated the outline of the shoe very clearly. Ann ordered the forensic team to take an impression of the shoeprints. They moved forward and examined the prints before proceeding to take an impression. 'Looks like a man's size ten shoeprint," said an officer. Checking it was safe to proceed further into the room, Ann led the team to the next room. The forensic team went ahead and asked the CID to be careful where they walked in the house as they did not want any evidence destroyed as the house might have been a crime scene. They entered a large dining room, which lead off into another living room and a spacious kitchen. Stairs led to four large bedrooms, a study and two bathrooms. Everything was in pristine condition. It seemed as though a housekeeper had maintained the rest of the house, as it was in an immaculate condition. 'I want every corner of this house searched,' said Ann. David called out to the team as he found a door leading to what looked like a cellar. The door was heavily bolted. A small glass window in the top of the door had a metal grid over it. Ann and some members of the team rushed to see what David had found. 'We are going to have to cut the bolt to get into that cellar,' said Ann.

A constable who had bolt cutter cut the large lock off the door. David opened the door nervously, peering carefully around the door, not knowing what he would find. The rest of the team followed cautiously. The darkness hindered their search, so Ann called for a torch and told the men not to move. Ann shone the light into the cellar and was shocked at the sight that greeted her. There were chains, manacles, knives and a bed. 'Get the forensic team in here right away and the rest of you get out of here now," she shouted. The forensic team filed into the cellar. Ann shone the torch until they had found the light. They gasped as the light revealed a very macabre array of what appeared to be torture instruments. Dark patches on the floor appeared to be blood. The crude metal bed also contained stains. There was some dirty crockery and cutlery, and stale bread. A bag which contained soiled women's clothing, lay in heap at the end of the bed. Ann and David stood at the door while the forensic team photographed and collected items they thought were significant to the investigation. Ann shone her torch onto the ceiling of the cellar. A blood splatter pattern was visible on the ceiling. There was an assortment of daggers, candles, cloaks with satanic insignia and rope. One of the forensic officers found a large freezer hidden in an alcove of the cellar. It was covered with a cloth. When they opened the freezer, it had blood inside and a layer of thick ice as it was still switched on and in working order. They also found a chainsaw which was caked in dried blood and had fat and gristle on the blades. The forensic team set about photographing the cellar and collecting items of interest. The rest of the team searched the garage and gardens for anything remotely connected to the murders. Ann organized refreshments for the men as the search took a long time. The Nottingham CID officers mingled with Ann's team and discussed aspects of the case. Ann called a halt to the search at nightfall and told the men they could continue the following day. 'Come on you lot, all roads lead to the local watering hole. See you there in an hour,' announced D.I. Tobin. The team chorused their approval and departed noisily from the house. They all congregated at the Black Swan pub an hour later. They were joined by members of the local police, so it became very crowded inside the small pub.

  The deafening noise of enthusiastic police officers annoyed the locals who frequented the pub. There was a happy banter amongst the officers and for a few precious moments the men from the Met were able to unwind and forget about their onerous task of pursuing their investigation. 'Listen up. I don't want you lot pissed out of your skulls tonight. You need to be on your game tomorrow,' warned Ann. Her warning came too late for her sergeant who had consumed quite a large amount of alcohol. At one stage he called Ann by her name. She swung around and gave him an admonishing look. Despite his drunken state, he remembered Adam's warning about never dropping his guard around Ann. Terrified of giving anything away, made his excuses, and left for his hotel. The team was back at the house the next morning. They found a secret trapdoor which lead from the cellar to the rose garden. The door could only be opened from the inside of the cellar. The CID team searched the garden and a shed. They found some burnt out wooden torches in the shed which were strewn amongst the gardening tools. The forensic team took fingerprints off the torches. Ann surveyed the rose garden with a keen interest and was very tempted to have her team investigate the garden, but knew she had to adhere to only searching the house. The team was extremely pleased with their discoveries and were sure they were nearer to solving the case. Ann received a call from Edwards, informing her that he had managed to get a warrant from the wildlife trust of Sherwood Forest to search Treswell Wood which was managed by George Casey. The project was run by trustees who gave permission for the police to search the woods. "Listen up guys that was the boss. We have just got permission to search Treswell Woods,' she announced. A disgruntled jeer echoed around the group their faces filled with dismay at yet another day working in inclement weather. "Okay I will get you fed and watered first, then it's back to work,' she said.

They beamed with delight at the prospect of food. Their mood instantly transformed to one of enthusiasm. Ann used the lunch break to discuss the strategy of the search in the woods. The geologist had mapped out where the sessile oak trees grew in the woods. Ann instructed them to search for any clearing that would suggest a meeting place for the Satanists. She divided the officers into teams and instructed them how to proceed with the search. They were transported to the woods by the local police. They disembarked at the edge of the dark, dank forbidding verdant enclave. The teams separated and went their respective ways according to the plan set out by Ann. It took some time before the men were able to penetrate deep into the wood. Just as

Ann began to despair that their search would be fruitless, an officer shouted to signal that he had found something. His colleagues rushed to the over to where he stood. When they reached him, they saw a clearing hidden behind a clump of large oak trees. A wooden sawn of tree trunk stood in the centre of the clearing. There was pentagram drawn on the ground, near the trunk. There were many footprints on the periphery of the tree trunk. There were dark red stains on the ground around the trunk. The forensic team examined the curious red substance closely, hazarding a guess that it might be blood. They collected a sample, bagged and labelled it. The officers searched the undergrowth meticulously for the darkling beetle, which is indigenous to Sherwood Forest and which was found in Elaine's hair. The officers found the many samples of the beetle in the undergrowth. A few leaves of the sessile oak were also collected.

Many photographs were taken of the site and everything assumed relevant to the investigation. It was a totally exhausted team of officers who finally emerged from the woods as daylight faded. The samples and items collected at both sites, were carefully packaged and despatched by helicopter to the Metropolitan laboratories at Scotland Yard. Ann was pleased that they had found what they came for. There was a last count to ensure all the team were accounted for, prior to their departure to the hotels where they stayed. Evening entertainment was organized by the local police force at one of the hotels.

A meal was followed by a cabaret. There were no constraints on the officer's consumption of alcohol. David steered clear of Ann as he knew he had no control over his words when he was inebriated. The entertainment continued into the early hours of the morning. Ann had consumed a considerable amount of alcohol, but she managed to stay on her feet for most of the night. It was an early departure for the weary officers who were still wrestling with a hangover and sleep deprivation the next morning. They were transported back to London by helicopter. Ann's first meeting of the day was with Edwards and Michael Heath. 'Good to see you Ann. How did the search go in Nottingham?' he asked. Very well, sir. I do believe we have had significant finds linking Elaine's murder to Nottingham. Our forensic boys should come up with some interesting facts, based on the items we have found. I will let you know as soon as Tim sends his report," continued Ann. 'Do you think it will make it clearer as to who the killer is?' asked Michael. 'I cannot say for certain, as one suspect is out of the country and the other is unconscious. 'If their DNA or prints are on any items found in the cellar of the Casey's house, it will strengthen our case against our suspects,' explained Ann. 'Jolly good, well done Ann, I shall look forward to seeing the forensics report. Don't you agree, Stephen, Ann deserves credit for all her hard work thus far,' said Michael. Stephen forced a smile as he nodded in agreement. 'I will get the report to you as soon as forensics sends it to me,' promised Ann. 'Come on David we need to also prepare you for the trip to Spain. Let's grab a coffee on the way,' she added. She slumped into the chair at her desk and sighed with relief, believing that she was beginning to make some headway with the case at last. David entered the office with two cups of coffee and sat opposite her, fully focussed on the task ahead.

Ann opened a file on her desk which contained an air ticket and some documentation. She handed him the air ticket and began briefing him on details of his trip to Spain. 'You leave in five days. Please get to the airport in good time as you are notorious for being late at times,' she said. 'You fly to Marbella. Andrew will collect you at the airport. He will hold a card bearing your name at the arrivals lounge, so keep your eyes peeled,' she said. David perused the contents of the file and reassured her he would find out as much as he possibly could about the Russian girl whom Andrew had known. A knock on the door interrupted their conversation. David opened the door and was surprised to see Savannah. 'Hi, sorry for failing to warn you I was coming. I was in the building and thought I might catch you before you leave,' confessed an embarrassed Savannah. 'Oh, do come in, the guv has not left yet. 'Hi Savannah, how can we help?' Ann enquired. I was keen to know what you uncovered in Nottingham,' she added. 'We have a great deal of interesting forensic evidence. We are just waiting for SOCO to do the analysis and get back to us. The house and forest had evidence of satanic practices and torture. Come along to my meeting with the team when I reveal the SOCO results,' Ann stated. "I was about to leave. David can have a half day off. David, why don't you take Savannah to lunch?' I am afraid I cannot join you as my partner is anxiously awaiting my arrival at home. I have been away, so I will be in the dog house if I don't get home in time,' Ann explained. David nodded his head in agreement at Ann's suggestion but was most annoyed at her presumption that he wanted to have lunch with Savannah. The situation was made worse by the fact that he was spotted with Savannah by Holmes who quipped,' I see you have settled for second best. Better luck next time mate.' David gritted his teeth in anger but desisted from replying.

Savanah smiled as she noticed David's supressed anger. 'I gather that chap is not your favourite person,' she added.' No, he irritates the hell out of me. I would like to smash his face in if I can,' replied David with visible frustration and anger. 'Is it a professional rivalry?' she pressed. 'It is a personal thing and that bastard knows how to press my buttons to get me angry. He nearly got me chucked off the force when we came to blows,' David continued. 'Oh, my goodness it sounds serious. What does Ann think?' she asked. 'I prefer to leave Ann out of the equation', David replied. 'Let's have lunch and not talk about that bastard please,' David implored her. 'Sounds great, let's go, she replied.

Chapter 6

Ann swept through the front door and called out to Josie who shouted a reply from the bathroom. Ann raced up the stairs pulling off her clothes as headed for the bathroom. Josie was in the bath. She climbed in with her and smothered her with kisses. They migrated to the bedroom and spend the next hour making love with wild abandon. 'Well Inspector, it seems that your absence has given you a ravenous appetite. You should go away more often.' chirped Josie. 'Cheeky beggar, you won't get dessert," replied Ann slapping Josie's bottom. 'No time for dessert, your brother will be here soon, and you know he has not learned to knock before entering,' she added. 'True, let's get dressed and go down to the kitchen," Ann advised. Josie chatted about her forthcoming trip to New York. Ann listened with a disapproving scowl. 'Goodness what's with the face, I'll only be gone five days, darling,' Josie reassured her. Ann filled her in on the events in Nottingham. Josie listened intently, adding her comments as the story unfolded. She warned Ann to be careful as she thought the whole case sounded fraught with danger. Then Josie seized the opportunity to broach the subject of having her IVF treatment to have the baby they longed for. 'Ann don't forget you need to be flexible so that you can accompany me to the IVF clinic for the implantation. It will be in the next week', said Josie smiling with delight. Ann swung around in amazement at Josie's announcement. 'You are still interested in us having the baby, aren't you, Ann'? She thought for a while before replying. 'Yes, but you must realize I cannot guarantee to be free at a moment's notice,' she said apologetically. 'That is exactly why I want to discuss it now because you will never make the time because your work takes up all the time. Do you honestly still want this baby or not?' added Josie. 'Don't be ridiculous, I still want us to have the baby, but I also need enough warning to be able to be with you when it happens,' continued Ann. 'Real life is not so simple. I can't command my hormones to perform when Ann Dixon is available,' shouted Josie. 'I will just drag Adam along because I know you will not be around when you are needed,' said Josie tearfully. 'And while we are on sensitive subjects, when are we having our Civil Union?' Josie probed, annoyed at Ann's procrastination. 'Gosh, you got out on the wrong side of the bed today, haven't you?' 'All this talk about sensitive issues,' said Ann. 'Good gracious Ann, I love you so much and all I want is to cement out relationship with a special union and a baby we can love together,' replied Josie, with tears welling up in her eyes. She fled to the bedroom and shut the door. Ann regretted her insensitivity. She ran up to the room and went to sit on the bed beside Josie. She put her arms around her and began comforting her. 'Sorry my darling, I did not mean to be so cold. I suppose, I am afraid of the commitment in a way. I also care what my colleagues at the station would say when they found out,' explained Ann. She kissed Josie tenderly on her forehead and wiped away her tears.

'Okay, tell me when you need me to accompany you and I will be there, I promise,' said Ann. Josie looked up and smiled. 'Why are you so insistent on the Civil Union? asked Ann. 'You know that my entire family have ostracized me because of my lifestyle. Well I don't want them having any claim on our baby if anything should happen to me. The Civil Union will ensure that you are the legal guardian,' added Josie. The hurt in Josie's eyes spoke volumes. She never got over the fact that her family had excluded her from their lives when they discovered that she was gay. She vowed that Ann and Adam and Adam were her only true family. 'I have leave in two weeks from Monday. Let's tie the knot during those two weeks,' said Ann. 'Can we have Adam as a witness, please, please, please,' begged Josie. Ann shook her head and laughed. 'Oh! Yes, alright, because I will never hear the end if Adam is not included,' continued Ann. Josie hugged and kissed Ann and danced around the room with absolute joy and abandon. 'Anybody home?' Adam called up the stairs. 'We're in the bedroom,' replied Josie. 'Oh no you are not at it this time of the day, girls,' said Adam. 'Stop assuming things. Do you think our entire lives revolve around sex, you wicked man,' said Ann, flinging a pillow at him as he popped his head around the door. He grabbed another pillow and engaged the girls in a pillow fight which they invariably won and had him begging for mercy. 'What are you both doing at home so early?' enquired. I had work to do on my laptop, and Josie is just chilling out after her trip to Milan,' said Ann. 'Why do you look so happy?' enquired Adam. Josie smiled and looked to Ann for approval to share their good news. Ann sighed and nodded for her to tell Adam. 'Ann and I are going to get hitched this month,' said Josie with the broadest grin on her face.

'Oh, great news my favourite girls are tying the knot at last said Adam, as he lunged forward and scooped them in his arms. 'Have you named the day?' he enquired grinning in anticipation. 'No, we haven't, and I don't want you telling a soul, I really mean that Adam. You know how much flack I have had from my work colleagues. The last thing I need is to have gossip ringing through the police corridors about my civil partnership,' Ann warned. 'Oh, for goodness sake, Ann you are surely not going to be dictated to by an ignorant bunch of coppers who have nothing better to do than engage in idle talk. Your personal life is your own and you should not consider anyone's opinion,' he continued. Ann glared at him and said, 'You have no idea what I have endured, so for the moment, you will jolly well adhere to my request to shut up about my private life,' Ann replied sternly. An awkward moment followed, after which time Josie came to the rescue by hugging Ann and Adam and announcing that dinner was ready. She had such a knack for diffusing potentially volatile situations. A call from David asking Ann for a lift to the airport interrupted the conversation. Ann explained that she had an early meeting and told him to arrange with D.I. Tobin. Adam interjected and offered his help. Ann handed him the phone reluctantly. She listened to the conversation, and heard Adam arrange a pick up time for David. When he had finished the call, Ann asked, 'Since when have you joined the Met?' 'I don't mind giving David a lift. It is on my way to Reading anyway,' he explained. 'Yes Adam, I am not as daft as you think, I don't trust you and David Hughes as far as I can spit. My gut tells me you are up to something,' she said staring at him with her penetrating gaze. He was unable to look her in the eye as he replied, 'Problem with you sis, is that you are never off duty. You should believe in your flesh and blood more readily.' She dismissed his explanation with a smirk and walked away. Adam hooted impatiently outside David's flat the next morning. David came running out towards the car, clinging onto his cup of coffee. 'Come on, get in, your boss will never forgive me if you miss your plane,' Adam urged. 'Bloody hell, she must have given you some stick for volunteering to take me,' said David grinning as he slumped into the front seat of the car. "Stick is hardly the correct word. She bloody wiped the floor with me for offering to take you and accused us of scheming behind her back,' continued Adam. 'I swear she operates with radar,' David added.

'What are you going to do in Spain,' enquired Adam. 'I have to interview the Casey brother's neighbour's son. He was a friend of a Russian girl whom the brothers were friendly with, and who vanished without a trace. Ann thinks the girl might have been murdered by one of the brothers,' said David. 'Gosh, sounds like heavy stuff. Have you had any news from Interpol about tracing James Muller?' 'No, they have drawn a blank thus far,' said David. 'Damn, I know I can help them to find the guy. My South American contacts are very efficient,' replied Adam. I will wait for your return from Spain and then I will make some excuse to Ann that I need to go to Israel,' continued Adam. He pulled into the car park, got out of the car and accompanied David to the check in desk. They shook hands and promised to meet on

David's return. There were no delays and the flight left on time. David sipped his drink as he read through the instructions, Ann had given him for interviewing Andrew. He nodded off to sleep and was awoken by the stewardess announcing their arrival at Marbella airport. He removed his jacket, while standing in the queue at passport control, as the stifling heat clung to his body. He looked out for a man carrying aboard with his name on it as he emerged at the meeting place. A stocky man with a disarming smile held up a board with his name on it.

He walked towards the man, stuck out his hand and asked, Are you Andrew Slade?' 'Yes, I am he, you must be David Hughes,' replied the man. The two men shook hands and walked off in the direction of the car park. Andrew stopped as they got to a red Ferrari. 'Welcome to Marbella," he said as he invited David to get into the car. 'Thanks, I have never been in a Ferrari before," David confessed. 'It is my pride and joy. My wife says my car is the other woman in my life,' he continued. 'Yes, I am an avid racing fan too, but my work prevents me from racing my stock car. 'What a shame. You must come and stay with us when they stage the next big race,' said Andrew. "Thanks, I will keep that in mind," replied David. They sped along the Golden Mile, a glitzy, charismatic stretch of coastal paradise teeming with scantily clad, beautiful women who enticed the many millionaires who cruised around in their fancy Ferraris. 'David, we need to conduct out talks whenever we are away from my home. I beg you not to mention any of this business in front of my wife. She does not know about my life in Nottingham and I do not want her knowing anything about the Casey brothers. It is a part of my life I would rather forget. I will tell you what I know when we go out alone,' said Andrew. David nodded in agreement. They arrived at an exquisite villa after travelling for twenty minutes. A white Spanish styled house peeped out from the trees as they walked from the car. The pool shimmered in the morning sun, shaded in parts by some palm trees. Andrew led the way into the spacious living room. They were greeted by Andrew's wife, Rita. She shook David's hand and invited him to make himself at home. He sank into the plush leather settee which adorned the living room. He opted for a beer, after being offered an array of various cold refreshments. Andrew's two children appeared and cowered shyly behind their father when Andrew introduced them to David. Andrew offered to show David around the villa when he had finished his drink. He was taken to the guest room first.

He gasped silently as he was led to a vast, luxurious room with private balcony. He then followed Andrew around the villa, listening to the commentary about special features of the place and how it was built. He was informed about the time that lunch would be served but asked if he could skip lunch as he wanted to rest instead. He did not emerge from his room until 6pm that evening. Andrew was relaxing on the sun lounger at the pool and his wife and the children were in the pool. Andrew announced that they would all be going to have a meal at his favourite restaurant later in the evening. They sat and chatted around the till 8pm, after which time, Rita announced that the children were hungry. They set off for the restaurant around 9pm. Andrew parked outside a place called Pangea, one of the most luxurious restaurants in Puerto Banus. The place oozed wealth and status. Andrew was known to the waiters who ushered them to their table. Rita struck up a conversation with Andrew while they waited for their drinks. 'Andrew tells me you are here to quiz him about the shady dealings of his ex -business partner,' she enquired. David stammered a reply as he was totally unprepared for her question. 'Yes, we have quite a bit of dirt on this bloke and we thought Andrew might be able to help,' he lied. She wanted to press on with the matter, but Andrew intervened and asked her to allow David to enjoy the evening, and they would discuss the matter at a more appropriate time. Thankfully she switched to another topic. David made polite conversation as they enjoyed their meal. They left the restaurant around midnight and headed for home. It was an absolute pleasure to be woken by a brilliant sunshine which streamed through the partially opened curtains, the next morning. David lay in his bed and thought, 'I could get used to this lifestyle.' Andrew knocked on David's door and enquired if he wanted to go for a drive along the coast. David shouted back a reply that he would love to go along but needed a quick shower. 'Take as long as you need, I will wait for you on the terrace,' replied Andrew. They drove out past the ruins of the old Arab wall in the Orange Square which had been built in 1485. They passed ancient, stately buildings, tall trees, exotic plants, and as they approached the coastal road, manifestations of every water sport came into view. Andrew pulled off the main road, to a quaint little café which served a scrumptious breakfast. David looked up from his coffee at Andrew and said, 'You nearly dropped me in it last night. Why did you not warn me that you had given your wife a story about a business partner?' David exclaimed. Andrew laughed out loudly. 'Lucky 'you were quick on the draw and dug yourself out of the hole,' Andrew replied. 'Ok now we need to talk about serious business," said David. 'Come on, we will drive to a quiet spot and you can ask your questions,' continued Andrew. He drove to a secluded spot surrounded by trees and not another human in sight. David explained that he needed to record their interview. Andrew shuffled around in his seat, hesitant about divulging what he knew. 'Are you absolutely sure whatever I reveal to you will not be traced back to me?' asked Andrew nervously. 'I promise you that whatever you tell us will be kept in the strictest confidence,' David said reassuringly. When he was satisfied that Andrew was ready to be interviewed, he switched on the tape, establishing the date and time and saying Andrew's full name. 'How long have you known the Casey brothers, Mr Slade?' All my life as we lived next door to the family in Edwinstowe, Nottingham,' Andrew replied. Can you tell me about the Russian girl, named Saskia who was your friend, and also an acquaintance of the Casey brothers? David asked. "Saskia was an illegal immigrant whom I met in a pub in Nottingham. I was entranced by her beauty and her charm, but she also appeared very nervous and rather naive when we first met. She told me that she had recently arrived in England and lived with friends in Nottingham. Her English wasn't very good, but we were able to engage in conversation without much difficulty. I later discovered that her so called friends were none other than the Casey brothers. Saskia and I began meeting regularly and as time progressed and she began to trust me, she revealed that she was grateful to the Casey brothers for rescuing her from a gang of Albanian pimps who had her working in a brothel. She was terribly ashamed of her past and said she could never return to Russia, because she was unable to prove to her family that she had become a professional model. I suppose I became attracted to her beauty and her vulnerability.

We eventually fell in love, but I did not want to progress to a physical relationship as she was so damaged by her time at the brothel. I wanted her to be ready to take our relationship to the next level. We shared a great many interests. I discovered that she was very bright. She regretted not going to university, as her parents clearly wanted her to have a good education. She confessed to getting mixed up with a wayward boy at school who got her onto drugs and eventually resulting in her meeting a man who promised her a modelling career in England. She discovered to her horror that the man was an Albanian pimp who procured her for work at a brothel. She managed to get away and ended up meeting Tom Casey who allowed her to stay at his home. Saskia would disappear for days or weeks. I finally got used to her gypsy lifestyle. She phoned me after a short absence and told me that she was pregnant and needed to have an abortion as she was not able to support a child. I discovered that the father of the child was Tom Casey. I was angry but was unable to do anything about her situation as I knew taking on Tom or any of his brothers would be tantamount to suicide. I asked her how she could allow Tom to get her pregnant when we were in a relationship. She confessed that she needed money and asked Tom who suggested she agree to have sex with him and get pregnant. He told her that his cousin, a doctor needed babies for research, and that she would be paid two hundred pounds for having the baby aborted. I offered to take her to an abortion clinic, but she declined at first, saying that she was terrified of going through the abortion process. I did not see Saskia for weeks after our discussion. She did not return my calls or text messages. Then just as I had given up hope of ever seeing her again, she came into a café I frequented. She looked drawn and tired. She was embarrassed at not contacting me, and at first gave me a half-baked story about visiting a friend in London. I pushed until she finally confessed that she had the abortion, but not at the clinic. She said that Tom's cousin, James did the abortion and paid her two hundred pounds for the 24week old foetus. I protested that the abortion was not carried out properly as it would have been done at a designated clinic. Saskia hesitated for several minutes before telling me a very bizarre story.

She remembers going through the abortion process but was not shown the baby. She thinks she might have been drugged at the time that the baby was taken away. When she awoke, she asked to see the baby, but was told James needed to take the baby. Saskia said that Dr James told her he had to take the baby to the hospital without delay as he did not want to lose vital information for their research. Saskia was convinced that she had made a good contribution to medical research, so much so, that she introduced her cousin, Olga to the brothers. She said she thought she had found a good honest way of making money. I was horrified but was unable to intervene as it would have put Saskia at considerable risk. I tried to dissuade her from allowing the doctor to perform any more abortions, as I told her it should be done at a clinic or hospital. Dr James was her hero, and no matter what I said, fell on deaf ears. The two Russian girls wrongly believed the Casey's were good to them and agreed to the dangerous practise of getting pregnant and having frequent abortions. The girls did not care as they had somewhere to stay and were being paid for their contribution to medical research. I felt sorry for Saskia, but I was deeply hurt too, as I had fallen in love with her. The next time we met, Saskia was very distressed. She told me that Olga had disappeared, and she could not tell the police because they were illegal immigrants. She told me that Olga was pregnant and was due to have the abortion in two weeks. George Casey told Saskia that Olga had not come home, but Saskia knew Olga not to be irresponsible and would not have gone elsewhere. Saskia said there were other homeless girls who lived with the Casey's, who got pregnant and had abortions performed. I remember, an Irish girl named Mary O'Reilly, who was besotted with George Casey and took whatever he said as gospel. She spent a great deal of time at their home. She looked pregnant the last time I saw her and then like the other girls, disappeared without trace. I still remember where she stayed with her mother as her father had died in an accident. Mary was very wayward and gave her mother a hard time controlling her. I can give you her address if you would like. Mary had a cousin, Ellen O'Brien who also hung out with the Casey's. Saskia feared that we would lose touch, so she gave me her brother, Yuri's contact details in Moscow. I kept it safe in case I plucked up the courage to make contact one day. When she vanished fifteen years ago, I was too afraid to contact her brother, as I felt they would have held me accountable if anything had happened to her. I was also afraid that I knew about the abortions and might have been implicated in what the Casey's were doing. I was terrified of reprisals from the brothers because they were very violent. I thought it best to remain silent even though it came at a huge personal cost because I really and truly loved Saskia,' explained Andrew, supressing his emotions as he got up from his chair and walked a few paces from where David sat. He seemed very distressed at what her had recounted, avoiding eye contact; gazing into the distance instead. David listened in astonished silence. He gave Andrew time to recover. He then spoke into the tape signifying the end of the interview. They drove back to the house in silence, each immersed in their own thoughts, watching the sun sink over the horizon. Andrew's children ran up to greet them as he got out of the car. Rita jokingly said she had sent the police out to find them as they had been gone for so long. David explained that Andrew had a great deal of explaining to do as the case was complicated and Andrew had to give a concise account of what had happened. The explanation placated her, and she announced that she had prepared dinner. Andrew and David opted for double whiskeys and went to sit beside the pool. 'Oh, my goodness, it must have been a gruelling day if you need double whiskeys to calm your nerves,' remarked Rita. The men smiled at her comment and carried on with their conversation. A delicious dinner followed, which the men washed down with plenty of wine. Rita retired to bed with the children and *left* the men to continue their conversation. Andrew explained his rather chequered career in the construction business and his narrow escape from bankruptcy after his business partner defrauded millions of his company money. David arose at the crack of dawn to enjoy a swim before his departure to London. Andrew drove David to the airport. They discussed final details of the information on the Russian girls. David thanked Andrew for his cooperation and hospitality and boarded the plane for London. Adam met David in the arrivals lounge as he emerged through the arrivals exit. 'Come on, let's grab a coffee before we hit the road,' said Adam, as he carried David's carrier bag with alcohol. 'Oh, that's for you, by the way. I thought you might like some old famous grouse,' said David. 'Oh thanks, my supplies are running low, so this will come in real handy,' replied Adam. 'So how many Spanish belles have you conquered?' Adam purred suggestively. 'Chance would be a fine thing. Your sister gave me such a stern warning about partying that it put me off even contemplating having a wild time,' he replied. 'Anyway, it was a tight schedule as Andrew took off a few days for the interview with me, so we had to utilise every spare moment. The trip was worth it as it yielded information vital to our investigation. And before you interrogate me, I am not giving you a single detail. You already know too much,' continued David. By the by, her ladyship requests the pleasure of your company, so I was instructed to deliver you to her straight from the airport, and she specified, immediately you arrived.' said Adam. 'You promised to keep me posted about the happenings in Brazil. You will keep your word, won't you?' Adam pressured David for an answer. 'Yes, I will keep you posted, but if Ann finds out, you are going down with me and your name will be the last one on my lips when Ann thrusts in the dagger. Both men laughed at the visual image conjured up by David's statement. They left the airport and headed for Ann's house. She was working on her laptop when they walked into the living room. 'Hi David, how was Spain?' Ann enquired. 'Hello guv, it was a very useful trip. The information I gathered will advance our investigation to some degree,' David replied.

'We will go over the details later. Josie has prepared lunch, so let's eat before we get to work,' she said. Josie swept into the living room and welcomed David with a hug. He responded with, 'good to see you.' Adam fetched some wine and filled up each one's glass as Josie began to place the food onto the table. They tucked into the Sunday roast chatting away during the meal. David impressed everyone with his vivid details of the millionaire lifestyle of Andrew Slade. Adam was especially interested in Andrew's invitation to David to join him for the Monte Carlo Grand Prix. 'You are definitely in the wrong job, Hughes, always yearning for the greener grass in another man's garden,' Ann added. Josie momentarily forgot that she was not to speak about the wedding, when she blurted out to Ann that she had contacted a marriage officer who was willing to perform their wedding in the Lake District. She continued enthusiastically oblivious that everyone had stopped talking. Ann's angry expression spoke volumes. Only then did Josie realise her mistake at speaking out of turn. It was too late to do anything about it as David had heard the announcement and shifted uncomfortably in his chair. Adam sensing an imminent volcanic eruption came to the rescue. 'Ann and Josie are tying the knot, but don't want it to be public knowledge. But seeing as you found out inadvertently, perhaps the girls would need a second witness at the wedding. Adam looked across at Ann who was incandescent with rage.

'Nothing in this house is private anymore. It is like living at with the media,' said Ann as she banged her fist on the table. Josie and Adam ran to her and flung their arms around her apologising profusely. Determined not to appear unreasonable, Ann said, 'Well David since you inadvertently found out about my private life, I am sure you know that you will be expected to exercise the most stringent discretion,' she warned. 'I am very happy for you both, and I would be honoured to be a witness if needed,' said David. 'Please let him be a witness, Ann,' begged Josie. 'Alright if it will stop you two behaving like couple of spoiled kids,' said Ann suppressing a wry smile. Josie then launched into chapter and verse about details of the forthcoming marriage. The venue was to be at a country house at the Lake District in three weeks. David and Adam put the date in their diaries. Josie asked everyone to remind Ann to keep at least two days free before the wedding. 'Enough of this levity, David we have work to do,' said Ann leading the way to her study with David following behind. She enquired if Andrew was co-operative, and David told her Andrew was very helpful and answered all the questions without hesitation. 'Let's hear the tape shall we,' replied Ann. David played back the tape and they both listened to Andrew's testimony in silence. When the tape had finished, Ann commented that she needed to meet with the Michael Heath, to ask for permission to travel to Moscow, to find and interview Saskia. 'It is going to be a tall order, guv. I can't see them getting money for our trip,' added David. 'I am going to fight tooth and nail to get us there. If they want a result, I will leave no stone unturned to solve these murders,' replied Ann. 'I have arranged a briefing on the findings in Nottingham. I have asked Peter Drew to deliver his findings directly to my team at the briefing at 1pm tomorrow. 'You had better get home, so that you can be fresh and alert tomorrow. Thanks for going to Spain and getting the information,' said Ann as she ushered him to the front door. Josie and Adam chorused a goodbye and waved to him as he got into his car and drove off. Josie hugged Ann as she sat down beside her on the sofa. 'I have not forgiven you for the unforgiveable breach of trust today. Don't look at me with those doleful eyes, Adam, because you are also in the doghouse.

'No more cuddles and kisses for at least a month until you have repented,' Ann added sternly. David arrived promptly to collect Ann on the Monday morning. She ran through the schedule for the day to ensure they met with their deadlines. Her first appointment was with Peter Drew at 8.30am. 'Morning, Ann. Good weekend?' 'Not bad thanks. I worked for most of it, but had some rest,' replied Ann. 'We have some shocking evidence collected at the house in Nottingham,' Peter informed her. 'The cellar yielded most of the evidence and it seems it was used as a torture chamber by the Casey brothers. The most disturbing find was the presence of foetal blood, belonging to 15 babies, found in the cellar. They examined the forensic details and began preparing their presentation at the briefing later that day. Ann informed Peter that she would be presenting details of the taped interview with Andrew Slade at the briefing.

Ann repeated the time of the briefing and left with David. 'Next stop, meeting with the monster, but let's get some caffeine for courage,' said Ann as she grabbed a coffee and headed for her office. Stephen Edwards was surprisingly good tempered when Ann entered his office. 'Word has it that the investigation is going well,' said Edwards as he motioned Ann to sit down in his office. 'Yes indeed, sir we have made incredible progress. The trip to

Spain delivered invaluable information on the case and I have just spoken with Peter who has a wealth of forensic evidence which undoubtedly will advance our investigation. I will be most grateful if you and possibly the chief could join us for the briefing at 1pm today. 'I will try to get the chief to be at the briefing. Look forward to hearing what Peter has for us,' he replied. Ann was bowled over by Stephen's good temperament and pinched herself to ensure she was not dreaming. David jokingly reminded her Edward's good mood was short lived. The briefing room buzzed with excited conversation as the officers shared information and discussed it among themselves. Ann called everyone to attention when she was sure that everyone was present. She thanked her team and the forensic unit for their diligent work and welcomed Peter and Steven to the meeting.

She was pleasantly surprised that the chief had made a special effort to be at the briefing. Ann addressed the team by saying that she would leave Peter to tell them about his forensic evidence found at the house in Nottingham and Sherwood Forest. Peter had photographs taken at these sites. He pointed to the relevant photographic evidence, with a running commentary of what they had found. He pointed to the bed, and a set of chains found in the cellar. He said that the items contained human hair, tissue and blood belonging to the murdered Elaine Casey. He explained that her skin was also found in the freezer kept in the cellar. So! they now knew that Elaine was held hostage in the cellar before her death. He added that she was murdered in a clearing known as Treswell Wood because the improvised alter had large amounts of Elaine's blood on it. He said that the same species of indigenous oak leaf and beetle found in Elaine's hair were found at the wood. Peter paused to allow his audience to assimilate the information before continuing. He expressed his concern that hair and samples of blood found in the cellar belonged to as many as 5 different women and fifteen different foetuses. Foetal blood had also been found near the tree stump in the woods. The forensic team were able to collect fingerprints off the wooden torches found in the cellar and shed of the property. Some of the fingerprints were a match to Tom, George, and Jake Casey. The shoeprint in the hall of the house was a size ten man's shoe. It matched the shoeprint found at both crime scenes. They also found traces of semen from some unknown males. One was a match to Jake Casey. Peter's report was followed by a stunned silence. Only Ann's query, regarding questions, mobilised the men into motion. 'What do you think happened at that house, guv?' asked D.I. Tobin. I would like D.S Hughes to tell you about his interview in Spain before I answer your question,' Ann replied. David played the taped interview with Andrew Slade. When the tape had finished, Ann asked if it had made it clearer about the forensic evidence. Some of the team members nodded, indicating that they had a better understanding, and some pressed for more answers. She urged that it was imperative that some of the girls were traced to verify what was done with the bodies of the babies. She emphasized the importance of finding James Muller. She instructed D.I. Roberts to return to James' sister to extract more information. She asked David Hughes to accompany him to the interview. Ann realised that as the importance of tracing witnesses who would contribute to the gathering of evidence, she seized the opportune moment to request funding for a trip to Moscow. Ann expressed the need to explore every lead in order to solve the case. Peter Drew, realising, Ann's brilliant move, supported her on the idea of going to Moscow. Stephen Edwards shifted uncomfortably in his seat as he realized he was put on the spot by Ann's suggestion and would have been deemed mean and uncooperative if he refused outright. He looked to the chief for support as he promised half-heartedly to assess the available funds. The chief rubbed salt into wounds by saying he was sure they could squeeze some money from the Met somewhere. Ann gave the address of Mary O'Reilly to D.I. Tobin, instructing him to trace her or her cousin. She gave D.I. Roberts details for Saskia Stravinsky who lived at a shelter in Nottingham before she met the Casey's. Ann enquired if anyone had checked on Jake Casey. She was told that he remained in a coma, but his condition was stable. A member of the team asked Ann if Interpol had tracked down James Muller. Ann replied that she had a meeting with Interpol later that week and would ask them to step up their enquiries as James Muller needed to be found. She added that there was no doubt that James had a hand in the murders and was accountable for illegally aborting the foetuses and possibly killing them too. The team began dispersing after they had taken their instructions. Michael Heath walked over to Ann, patted her on the shoulder and said, 'Splendid work, Ann. I am proud of you,' he continued. Ann blushed at the compliment and hastily added, 'It's thanks to my team who have worked very hard to get us this far,' she replied.

'Give me a call in a couple of days. I will try to get you funding for your trip to Moscow,' he said reassuringly. 'Sir, will it be possible for D.S Hughes to accompany me?' Ann enquired nervously. 'Yes of course, Ann, you will need you right hand man to accompany you,' he continued, patted her on the shoulder and left the room. Steven Edwards had overheard the conversation and made it clear that he was not in favour of the Moscow trip. 'What the hell do you think you will achieve by going to Moscow?' he asked. 'We have a contact number and address. I believe we will succeed in finding the Russian girl. She may be our only witness to the murders in the woods,' Ann replied. 'Come on David, we have a trip to prepare for,' said Ann.' 'Let's grab some lunch, I am famished,' she announced as she grabbed her coat and coaxed David to join her. They sauntered off to a pub in Victoria who was still serving lunch at 3pm in the afternoon. 'Michael is going to get enough money for both our tickets,' announced Ann triumphantly. 'That must have put Edward's nose out of joint,' quipped David. 'He damn nearly had a heart attack when Michael said he would get the money,' said Ann giggling mischievously. They waded through lunch voraciously, pausing briefly to comment on the briefing. 'David, I want a thorough interview with James' sister. I suspect she knows more that she is willing to say. I don't know whether it is because she is afraid of him or is protecting him. Perhaps I should go with you to assess her,' said Ann. 'Ring her today, if you have her number. I would quite like to see her as soon as possible,' continued Ann. David had the number and promptly dialled Susan Muller's number. A crisp sounding voice replied. David identified himself and asked when it was possible to meet with Susan. She was most reluctant to meet with any of the police. Ann took the phone and explained that she wanted to accompany her sergeant as they had some new information. Susan finally agreed after some persuasion.

She scheduled the meeting for the following morning. David and Ann went their separate ways after lunch and agreed to meet at the station the next morning. It was an irate Susan Muller who answered the door the next morning. 'I suppose you had better come inside,' she said to Ann and David who stood outside her front door. She motioned them to sit down as they entered the living room. 'I don't know what you think I can possibly tell you after the exhaustive questioning I endured the last time with your officers,' said Susan crossly. Ann knew she had to reclaim Susan's loss of confidence in the police, so she invented a ploy that she hoped would change Susan's mind. 'Miss Muller, I am very concerned that as you have not heard from your brother, any number of things might have happened to him. I don't know whether you realise that South America is a dangerous continent. The law as we know it is not practised democratically. Killing of innocent people happen every day and the police over there are bribed to look the other way in most cases. You know that the drug cartels of Mexico also have jurisdiction in Brazil and there is no policeman brave enough to challenge these thugs who rule many of the South American countries. There has been kidnapping of the local people and foreigners, and some of them have been killed. We are concerned for your brother's safety. We know that your brother had foreign friends, and we need to trace these friends in order to find him. Did your brother ever mention the names of people he knew?' Susan looked bewildered and frightened. Her eyes darted from Ann to David, but she was unable to reply. "We have reason to believe that James is in Brazil, but we are not sure of his exact location. Does he have a relative in Brazil?' asked Ann. Tears began to well up in Susan's eyes. 'Do you think he has been harmed?' she stammered. 'Well we don't know, but it would help us if you tell us where he might be in Brazil. We could help him if he is in trouble,' explained Ann. 'We have an Uncle in Curitiba. His name is Jurgen Muller. James may be with him. I do not have a contact number,' replied Susan hesitantly. 'You must promise not to tell my brother that I told you about my uncle, please,' she begged. 'Susan, has James hurt you in any way?' 'No, no, he would never do that,' she said repeatedly, almost trying to convince the police and herself that her brother was incapable of violence. But Susan's vulnerability had not escaped Ann's radar, and she pressed on with the questions, probing stealthily in her professional manner.

David sat in silent admiration of Ann's unique interview technique- making the person being interviewed, feel that they were the most important person in the room, and that their role was vital in securing the safety of their loved ones. Ann's approach secured her the answers that had eluded the officers at the previous interview. Ann had a special talent for getting the job done and anyone who realised her brilliance would give her full marks for being an exceptionally bright member of the force. Her performance had only solidified the professional bond between her and her sergeant. Ann asked to use the toilet. Susan told her where it was situated. When she got to the top of the landing, she slipped into Susan's bedroom and removed some hairs from Susan's hair brush and put it safely in a plastic bag. She returned to the toilet, flushed it and joined Susan and David in the living room. Ann thanked Susan for her time she gave Susan her card and urged her to phone if she needed to talk or had any important information. Susan smiled as she nodded in agreement, taking the card from Ann and bidding the detectives a warm farewell. 'Well done, guv,' said David as he eased into the driving seat of the car. Ann bristled with satisfaction as she replied. 'Yes, I thought that went rather well. I stole some of Susan's hairs to give to forensics and we also have a name and place to start with', she declared triumphantly. 'David, I want you to arrange another interview with Sam Cain. We may be able to squeeze something more from him. Please drop me off at home. I have just remembered Josie has invited me to some party to lure new clients to her fashion house.

Ann's phone sprang into life. It was Josie, in a panic about them being late for the party. She urged Ann to hurry as David stopped at their front door. 'Hi David, are you coming too?' asked Josie. 'No thanks, I'll pass this time. I need to do some essential domestic chores at home. Next time, maybe, thanks,' replied David as he drove off. Josie hugged and kissed Ann as she welcomed her home, then gently urged her to hurry as they barely had 45 minutes to get to the party. She rattled off some names of important guests who were going to be present and who were going to make a significant impact on her business. Josie looked ravishing in her black dress; a sight which never failed to tantalise   She dashed out of the shower and swept Josie onto the bed. 'Forget the party, we can have one of our own right here,' suggested Ann provocatively. 'You bad girl, behave yourself and get dressed," said Josie as she jumped off the bed and continued to apply her make up. Ann reluctantly complied with Josie's commands. They arrived at the party with minutes to spare. The VIPs from Milan and New York arrived an hour late. Josie was furious but could not complain because she needed their support for sales of her new line of fashion. When all the formalities had been settled, liberal amounts of food and wine was served by a team of efficient waiters. Josie proudly showed Ann off to her new clients. An Italian VIP named Matteo took a shine to Ann and stayed with her for most of the evening. He seemed quite dazzled by Ann, much to Josie's annoyance. Tamara Smith seized the opportunity to inflame Josie's temper by commenting that she observed the inspector seemed entranced by Matteo's attentions. Ann was oblivious to the debate that raged about her conversation with Matteo. She discovered that he was an archaeologist, who accompanied his brother, Marco, the fashion designer to the party. Ann had a huge interest in archaeology both on a personal level, and in regard to her work. They soon became completely engrossed in the machinations of excavation. Tamara navigated her way around the room to where Ann stood and said, 'Hello Inspector, have you caught any bad guys yet?' Ann smiled and replied, 'Hi Tamara, just as well I can tell the good guys from the bad ones. You might want to tell the bad guys I always get my man,' said Ann. The remark wiped the smile off Tamara's face, and she turned on her heel and made a hasty retreat. Josie could no longer tolerate having Ann stuck in one place for what seemed and eternity. She walked towards Ann and took her arm, apologising to Matteo for having to steal Ann from his company. She explained that some guests were just dying to meet Ann. When Matteo protested that it was a pity she had to go, as they were enjoying their talk on archaeology, Josie replied, 'Well that is even more reason that I need to rescue Ann as she knows subjects about work are banned at my parties.' Matteo held onto Ann's hand and made her promise that she would keep in touch. When they were out of earshot, Ann said, 'I hope your behaviour is not as a result of your conversation with that poison dwarf, Tamara. I saw you speaking to her earlier. She passed a comment to me to get me riled, but I did not rise to the bait.' "No, I was just annoyed at your prolonged chat to Matteo who, in case you failed to notice, was not only interested in archaeology, he was practically undressing you with his eyes,' said Josie with some irritation. 'Oh, I think the lady is very jealous,' Ann remarked with a smile. 'I have a host of people who want to meet you, so come along,' said Josie grabbing Ann's hand and rushing towards a group of people in the centre of the room. The guests turned around as Josie called out, 'Hi everyone, meet my partner, Ann. The party continued into the early hours of the morning. Josie drove them home. Adam was still awake when they got home. 'Dirty stop outs, what time do you call this?' he enquired cheekily. He noticed that Josie had her dress on inside out. "Wow it must have been some party. Did the party rules require dresses being worn inside out?' he quipped. 'Don't be so nosey,' Josie scolded him, beating him about the head with her scarf. 'What are you doing here?' Don't you have a home of your own?' asked Ann. 'Don't you love your brother anymore?' 'Yes, I do, but when he visits too often, it dilutes the love to some degree. 'Ouch! That was painful. I thought you loved your brother totally,' added Adam. 'Oh, stop trying to put me on the spot, and get us some coffee,' Ann scolded.

'I can do better than that. I can add toasted croissants,' declared Adam. 'Oh! that sounds wonderful,' said Josie coming out of the shower with a towel around her hair and sat down at the table. 'Thank God it is the weekend. Will you be free next weekend, Ann?' asked Josie. 'Hmmm I need to talk to you about the next couple of weeks,' replied Ann. Lord, this sounds ominous,' exclaimed Josie. 'David and I have to go to Moscow on an important assignment in the next three weeks.

I will know more nearer the time, but if money for our travel is made available, it may be as soon as the end of next week. 'Why do you need to know if I am free?' asked Ann. 'I thought it would be nice to go to the Lake District and check out the venue for the wedding. Adam had stopped what he was doing and focussed all his attention the conversation. 'Dare I ask why you and not Interpol need to go to Moscow?' he asked. 'No, you may not. I need to go to Moscow because I am heading up the investigation,' replied Ann curtly. 'Don't tell me we may need to postpone the wedding date,' exclaimed Josie disconcertedly.

'Yes, there seems to be a possibility that I may not make it on the day,' said Ann apologetically. Josie groaned with disappointment. 'Never mind, Josie, you and I can amuse ourselves while the big chief is away,' said Adam in support. 'Don't push your luck, I might ban you from this house indefinitely,' warned Ann. 'You would send a search party to find me the moment I disappear because you really love having me around,' replied Adam. Ann smiled because she knew he was right. 'Let's make the most of this weekend, shall we?' said Josie. "Yes, let's get out of London and do some exploring in the countryside," suggested Adam. They were just about to leave when a text message arrived on Ann's phone. It was from D.I. Roberts. It read, 'Guv, can we meet urgently. Have important surveillance information. The look of resignation on Ann's face spoke volumes. 'Don't even attempt to justify what you are about to say,' said Josie angrily. Ann knew it nothing would placate Josie, so she just kissed her on the forehead, apologised and walked to her car. She phoned David to join her at the agreed meeting place with Roberts. D.I Roberts and his constable were there to meet her. They sat down at a quiet spot in the pub. David took everyone's order and went to get the drinks. 'Guv, we have bugged D.C. Holmes' house, and recorded this information.

He played back the recording. It was a conversation between Holmes and Tamara. Tamara was heard to say, 'That bitch is going to have a heart attack when she reads the Monday papers. Why, has Amy found out that Josie is cheating on her partner?' asked Holmes. 'No, it is nearer to the bone than that,' replied Tamara. 'What could possibly be worse than a scandal linked to Ann's partner?' enquired Holmes. 'Classified information which is going to freak her out,' replied Tamara. 'How the hell did you access the information?' asked Holmes. 'A very obliging little bird tweeted the information to Amy,' said Tamara. 'Shit that is bad news for me as the Met already suspect me of giving you information,' said Holmes. 'Aha, but they can't prove anything. Great for Amy if she can dazzle her boss with exclusive information and sell papers,' she said. 'Fuck, I don't care about Amy. I could lose my job, and never be able to work in the force again,' shouted Holmes. 'Come on baby, you need me to pay your gambling debts, and Amy helps sometimes. You keep your side of the bargain by keeping quiet, and Amy bathes in the glory of an exclusive,' continued Tamara. Holmes was outraged and the conversation descended into a shouting match. A door was banged loudly and then silence prevailed. Roberts looked up at Ann whose knuckles turned white as she gripped the edge of the table. 'I don't care if you have to bug the whole CID unit. I want the bastard found, who is leaking information to the media,' hissed Ann. "What are you going to tell Edwards?' asked David. 'I don't know, but I want you all to keep this recording quiet. I want to catch whoever it is red handed. Edwards will tell everyone. I need you to set up an undercover surveillance so that everyone's movements are reported to me.

I want to know everything about everyone, even when they shit,' she said caustically. Roberts reassured her he could devise a system which would encompass keeping tabs on the movements and associations of her team. David pledged his support to the best of his ability. They discussed their plans and strategy at great length and came up with a workable plan. Ann went home, but sleep eluded her as she contemplated a bruising encounter with Edwards if the papers contained the damaging article by Amy Baker the next morning. She sent David a reminder to get the newspaper on his way to collect her. It was a miserable night as Josie sulked because Ann worked all weekend. Ann was dressed and ready when David arrived at her house. Ann grabbed the newspaper which was on the front seat as she got into the car. Blazoned across the front page were the headlines: 'Police find evidence of human sacrifice and satanic ritual at the Casey house in the forest.' The article contained information which Ann feared would undoubtedly stifle the progress of her investigation. She bit her lip as she read; the veins visible on her forehead as she supressed her rising anger. David carried on driving and remained silent as he knew only too well not to speak to her when she was angry. She got out of the car when they arrived at the station, failing to return the greeting of the constable at the entrance when they walked past. Edwards stood waiting at her office door as she walked down the corridor. 'Get into my office,' he growled as she got to the door. 'Yes, in a minute, Sir when my sergeant has fetched me a coffee. Something tells me I am going to need a considerable amount of caffeine for what you have in store for me,' she replied sarcastically. Edwards was taken aback somewhat as she had never dared to backchat ever. David ran to get the coffee, smiling silently, that she no longer allowed herself to be bullied. 'I am not far away if you need anything, Guv, just shout,' said David in support. Ann thanked him and went into Edward's office. "Explain this,' he ordered showing her the newspaper article. 'I can't explain it because neither members of my team, or I, would jeopardise the investigation by leaking information to the press. You will agree with me that my officers strive for excellence, so I do not see the logic in them cancelling their chances of promotion by currying favour with a nobody like Amy Baker,' said Ann.

Have you considered the mole may not be amongst the CID, but in the allied units connected to the Met?' It seems to be someone who works very closely with our team. Edwards shuffled uncomfortably in his seat as he realised Ann's deduction made sense. 'What happened to that Holmes fellow who you suspected earlier,' he asked. "He no longer goes out with Tamara Smith. She is back sleeping with Amy again,' replied Ann. Edwards raised his eyebrows in astonishment that Ann had chapter and verse on Holmes. 'How do you propose to find the culprit?' he enquired. 'I have spoken to Roberts at our last briefing, and he has come up with a plan to find the mole. Edwards was amazed that Ann was one step ahead. 'How did you know that the media would print this article?' he probed. 'I didn't, I just followed my famous instincts that as Amy had tried to undermine our investigation in the past, she would not stop at a warning, but press on for the duration of the investigation. Ann had managed to turn around a potentially fiery meeting to an amicable understanding. Edwards even offered her a drop of brandy in her coffee. 'What do you suggest we do for damage control?' he asked. 'I think you should call a press conference and redress the balance,' suggested Ann. 'Okay I will get that arranged for later this week. Will you be around this week?' he asked. 'Yes, I should be. David and I are planning to have another talk to Sam Cain this week. I think he knows a lot more about the Casey's than he is prepared to reveal,' she added. 'Have you heard any more about the funding for Moscow?' enquired Edwards. 'No, Michael said he would let either of us know when it comes through,' she said. 'That reminds me, I have a meeting with our auditor. Better dash. Call me as soon as you hear from Michael,' Steven reminded her. She left Edwards with a triumphant smile. Gone were the days when she trembled at the mention of his name. He had become astonishingly approachable, and Ann suspected that Michael Heath had had played a part in Steven's change in attitude.

David was busy working on his laptop when Ann walked in, smiling contentedly. "Wow that smile says the boss has told you we have funds to go to Moscow,' said David in amazement at her good mood considering she had been with Edwards for 2 hours. 'Oh no, my elation is because, I have managed to transform the ogre to a gentle giant. He wanted to sweep the floor with me initially, but I had him eating out of my hand in minutes,' said Ann triumphantly. 'Good for you, Guv. It is by time that you are shown some respect from the top brass,' added David. Have you managed to contact Sam Cain for a briefing yet?' enquired Ann. 'No, I waited for you in case you were not available when he could make it,' said David. 'I'll ring, give me the number,' said Ann savouring her coffee as she reached for her phone. Ann got through to Sam on the first attempt. 'Who is it?' was Sam's angry reply. 'Oh my, Mr Cain, why are we in a bad mood today?' enquired Ann jokingly. "I have had a bloody rotten day, and I don't need you, Inspector to add to my stress,' he replied with some irritation. 'I am sorry to bother you, but I wondered if you could spare the time to have a chat,' she asked. 'I know about your chats Inspector, they end up getting one arrested,' he added. 'I will see you without your lapdog, Sergeant Hughes. I still have the bruises from the hand cuffs he so readily shoved on me when I was arrested,' said Sam. 'Shall we say tomorrow morning, around 11am?' asked Ann. 'Alright then, but I only have an hour. The police have wasted too much of my precious time,' he added impatiently. 'Sounds like you are not in Sam's good books because of the brutal arrest,' said Ann with a bemused smile. 'I don't mind, guv. I have plenty to do tomorrow. Just mind yourself around that lot. Sam Cain is not as innocent as he professes to be,' warned David. 'By the way, guv, Peter Drew said we could pop in to see him before lunch,' said David. 'Let's go now before I get bogged down with work,' replied Ann. Peter Drew was studying some files when they walked into his office.

'Hi, Ann, David, I gather we have been keeping you busy with all the forensic information at Nottingham,' said Peter. 'Yes, thanks we are grateful to you for all your hard work. I am here on another matter,' said Ann. 'It sounds very serious. I'll get you some coffee and then we can talk,' added Peter. They sat around his desk, sipping their coffee while Ann explained that someone was leaking classified information about the case to the media. Peter listened intently, nodding in agreement at Ann's concern that the leak could jeopardise progress. 'How loyal are the guys in your team, Peter?' asked Ann. 'Ten members of my team have been with me for fifteen years. The newer members are very dedicated too. I believe they are team players and would not jeopardise the integrity of the team for personal gain,' he said. 'Do you know if anyone in your squad has a grudge against the Met?' she enquired. 'Not to my knowledge, but if there is, I will do a secret surveillance to find the bastard,' he vowed. 'We will be eternally grateful, because the leaks are a blight on all our reputations,' she continued. 'I don't want you to make the team aware that they are being watched. I don't care whose human rights might be compromised. I just want the culprit caught and prosecuted. I will get the surveillance boys to come and see you about putting taps on your land lines,' she continued.

'I will need a list of the mobile phone numbers of all your staff please," she added. Peter frowned at the prospect of being complicit in spying on his colleagues and employees. He looked dejected as he agreed to Ann's plan. She thanked him and promised to keep him posted of any new developments. 'I don't blame him for being reluctant to help. Spying on his team is very near to the bone when one works closely with people over the years. I do understand how he feels,' said Ann. 'Yes, guv, especially with all the hype about phone hacking,' replied David. Ann's phone rang persistently while she talked to David. She was obliged to answer it. 'Ann Dixon, who is it," she asked irritated. 'It's Eve Marshall. Have you seen the papers this morning, Inspector?' 'Yes, I have. What about it?' 'There are facts in the article you have withheld from me, and I want to know the reason,' enquired Eve.

Ann turned over her eyes in exasperation as Eve spoke and David realised it was going to be a long telephone call. Eve rambled on almost incoherently about being deceived and misled. Ann tried in vain to explain to her that the reason for not revealing certain facts about her daughter's death, was to avoid informing her killer of the police strategy in finding him or her. Ann gritted her as teeth when she finally ended the call. 'This is exactly what I feared about the impact of the leaks on our investigation.' She said with marked vexation. 'Sod it, let's get lunch. I have had it up to here with work just now,' said Ann as she walked to her car. David suggested they head for Pizza Express. Ann agreed and swung the car in the direction of Covent Garden where they could reserve out a quiet spot at the restaurant. Ann remembered that Josie had the day off. She called her as they sat at the restaurant asking if she wanted to join them. She explained that her and Adam were decorating the spare room and were covered in paint and no fit state to go out. Ann was disappointed but accepted that Josie could not join them. 'Who was that on the phone,' shouted Adam from the ladder where he was painting the ceiling. 'Your beloved sister. She wanted us to join her and David for lunch. I told her we were unable to as we are painting,' replied Josie. 'Did she have any cheeky comments?' asked Adam. 'No, she just sounded disappointed and said she would see us tonight,' explained Josie. 'I hope she is going to like this aquamarine colour. It will be suitable for either a boy's room or a girl's room,' replied Josie. Yes indeed, the decorating in is being done in good time. It will give it enough time for the paint smell to fade by the time the baby arrives,' added Adam.

'I never dreamed I would actually get pregnant after all Ann's procrastination, and then you were there when I needed you. said Josie, grinning at her recollection of Ann's reluctance. Ann and David had a busy afternoon setting up meetings with various teams, to implement their plan to find the mole within the force. 'What time are we meeting with Jeremy Doyle?' Ann asked. 'We are meeting at the Fox and Hound pub, in Chelsea at 6.30pm. It is already 5.45. We have 45 minutes, depending on the traffic,' replied David as he checked his watch. 'Oh God, I'll never get done in time. Edwards wants this report for the briefing with the press at 2pm tomorrow. Damn, this means l will need to work at home after the meeting. Come on we had better not keep Jeremy waiting," said Ann. David sped through the busy roads to make it in time for their meeting. They arrived ten minutes late with Ann apologising profusely. Jeremy smiled as he shook her hand and said, 'I would begin to wonder if there was a problem when you guys arrive on time at all.' he said with a smile. 'Oh, we are not all that bad at time keeping. Don't you agree, David?' He laughed at her attempt to persuade him to agree to lie. Jeremy ordered the drinks and brought them to the table. 'You're drinking gin tonight, Ann?' 'No! I have a mountain of paperwork I need to do tonight, so I had better keep my head clear,' replied Ann. 'Do you have encouraging news for us, Jeremy,' enquired Ann. 'Well our boys in Brazil have established that James has in fact arrived there. We were however unable to locate him in Brazil. The Immigration boys out there appear to have lost him after his arrival there. They suggested that he might have travelled by road to Colombo or Mexico. They were oddly tight lipped and very unhelpful. They were not even tempted by a modest bribe. My boys think they are withholding information and are probably being paid a lot more than we can afford. We were able to establish that James is a VIP and may be protected by someone in a high position," he added. "David and I revisited Susan, James' sister and she told us that they have an uncle in Curitiba, one of the German settlements in the south of Brazil.

She said that they have been out of contact with him for a while, but James may have gone to live with him. There's no address or contact number. 'We have an MI6 operative, Nigel Miller who works with DEA agents in Brazil. He contacted me and warned me that Muller has ordered a hit on you, Ann,' he announced gravely. 'I am meeting with Nigel to check his credentials. He also has a contact who works with Mossad. The Israelis are interested in Muller because of his links to Hezbollah,' Jeremy continued. 'You know that this is a very high profile and sensitive murder investigation, and we cannot allow some unknown Indiana Jones to push his way in without the proper checks,' said Ann gesticulating frantically. 'Ok, we will need help. If this chap is as good as you think he is, we can use him,'he assured them. Ann excused herself from the company and headed for the cloakroom. Look I need to meet alone with you. There is information I cannot reveal to Ann. You must trust me on this,' urged David. They stopped talking as Ann approached the table. 'I just need to inform both of you that I will insist on being kept informed of every part of the plan. Withhold information at your peril,' she warned. 'If there is no more to discuss I would like to go home, because I have plenty to do. David led the way out of the pub, with Ann and Jeremy following close behind.

They parted outside the door and went their respective ways. Ann was somewhat prickly when she arrived at home. It was a clear indication that she be left to her own company. Adam received a text message from David, requesting an urgent meeting. He replied that he would see David the following evening. Ann worked into the early hours of the morning and fell asleep on the sofa. Josie came looking for her and snuggled beside her for the remainder of the short night. David had to hoot continuously when he arrived at Ann's home the next morning, as she had not heard the alarm. He always marvelled at Ann's ability to get showered and dressed in fifteen minutes. She breezed into the car in a jovial mood, and thankfully did not harp on the debate of the previous evening. "Check the briefing room is set for the press meeting this afternoon, while I am away seeing Sam Cain please,' she reminded David.

He was glad of being alone for the morning, because he could plan his strategy for Jeremy, and ensure there were no loopholes. Ann scurried about between her office and Steven's until 10.00, and then announced she was off to see Sam. Sam Cain greeted her cheerily when she arrived at his home. 'Good morning, Inspector Dixon, I see nothing has changed much. You are reliably late as usual,' said Sam. 'Yes, I do apologise. There was an accident on the motorway which I did not anticipate,' she explained. 'Do come inside, please,' he coaxed. 'So, three murders and nobody arrested as yet,' he commented. 'I am afraid it is a very complex case. We seldom have an instant result in these circumstances,' she added. 'I see even the great Inspector is stumped,' he mocked. 'Cut the crap, Mr Cain. I want to know what you are not telling us. You were close enough to the Casey's and their sister to have gained inside knowledge that would not have been privy to anyone else. 'I am particularly interested in the satanic rituals performed by the brothers, and don't pretend you don't know about this. Jake told me that you know because you spent a great deal of time with the brothers and their sister, Yvonne confided in you,' continued Ann. 'You must choose your words carefully Inspector when you make such statements. I know that satanic rituals were performed, but I was not present at any of them.

My information is second hand. Don't think for one moment that you are going to coerce me to stand up in court and give evidence about rituals in never witnessed. Whatever I say to you today is off the record and I trust you that you have no hidden recording equipment to entrap me,' he said. "I give you my word, I will not deceive you, but by the same token, I appeal to you to help us catch the Casey's killer. We have some leads which indicate that it may be two killers working together. We know that the satanic rituals are an important part of the killing,' she continued. 'Do you know any of the people who participated in the rituals? Did Yvonne ever mention names?' she asked.' 'Yvonne said there was a doctor who delivered foetuses, but she did not know what happened to them. She did not know the doctor's identity as she said he wore a mask. She was told a doctor would do the abortion to reassure the girls they would be cared for by someone who was medically competent. Tom and George repeatedly raped Yvonne during these rituals.

She said she was drugged for most of the time, so it was pretty much blur of what really happened. They aborted the pregnancies as a result of the rape," he continued. 'Why did Yvonne allow her brothers to rape her, and not tell anyone who could have stopped it,' asked Ann. Her father sexually abused her. Her brothers witnessed the father doing this and blackmailed her into allowing them to do the same to her or they would tell her mother. Yvonne blamed herself for allowing the abuse and was unable to get them to stop until Luke Cowan came into her life. Mr Cowan knows much more than he is willing to tell you. He showed a great interest in the rituals, and that is how he met the Casey's. He was only ostracized when he married Yvonne and took her away. They wanted Luke and Yvonne to remain in the family home, but Luke moved to another side of the county. He did not know what the brothers were doing to her. Yvonne was terrified that if he found out, he would leave her. She confessed that Luke had a violent temper. She also said that he indulged in sadomasochism. He tried to interest Yvonne in the depraved practise, but she declined. This did not discourage him from forcing her to participate in his sick indulgences. She often had to hide the bruises caused by his sick fantasies,' he revealed. 'If you are desperate to learn more about the rituals, Mr Cowan is your man. The question remains, Inspector, what are you prepared to forfeit to get your answers? If you are prepared to indulge in sadomasochistic sex games, Mr Cowan will without a shadow of doubt accede to any request you have. He is addicted to depravity. "I am not suggesting you would do such thing, but consider it might be an option,' he added cheekily.

Ann did not indicate whether she though it was a good suggestion. She became deeply immersed in thought as she contemplated the possibilities. Sam had to call out to her to bring her back from her transient daydream. 'Sorry, I just had so much information to process, that I just got lost in thought,' she confessed. 'If that is all you need to know, Inspector, I must go now as I have an important meeting at 1.30,' said Sam apologetically. 'Oh Yes, thank you for your time and the information. I am sorry I took up so much of your time. I assure you, all you have said will be kept in the strictest confidence. Ann knew what she had to do but had to satisfy herself that the sacrifice was worth the reward. She that knew that she had to dig deep in the recesses of her conscience to justify what she was about to do. There were moral and obligatory responsibilities to address and only she could decide if her actions compromised her loyalty to the woman she loved. The deafening buzz from the briefing room confirmed that the media were already assembled there ready to fling their vitriol at the Met. Ann ensured she was not seen before the meeting so as not to upstage the chief. Steven met with her briefly and went over the facts to ensure he would not be tripped up. He entered the room and called loudly to get everyone's attention. The noise stopped immediately as they waited for him to begin his statement.

He began by saying that he was very disappointed about the sensitive details contained in the News of the World article. He stated that the media were supposed to work with the police not against them. He pointed out the potential damage which was done by the publication of the article. He said that the public would lose their trust in the police and the media if certain people in the media worked in secret with rogue members of the force who leaked classified information. 'The information you so proudly shared with the public about Elaine Marshall was withheld from Elaine's mother to save her the devastation of learning a member of her ex- husband's family might have murdered her daughter. We consequently would never have uncovered the evidence we did. Please note our investigation points to possibly two killers. They are extremely clever and have managed to send us on a wild goose chase by planting evidence at the crime scenes. We still have a long way to go but had an important breakthrough over the past month. No matter what your prejudices are against the police, I urge you to work with us, to solve this case. The Met has to withhold some information to ensure we do not give the killers the advantage of eluding capture,' Steven appealed to them passionately. His words seemed to sink in as a moment of total silence followed before the mob of reporters began their onslaught of questions. 'Chief Inspector, will Jake Casey ever regain consciousness, and is he one of your two suspects?' asked Amy. 'The doctors cannot predict if Jake when Jake will wake up, if ever. Items implicating him in the murder have been found, but there are extenuating circumstances, which his defence team will put forward. 'If you know about a second killer, why has he not been caught?' she continued. 'Yes, Ms Baker, it would be possible to arrest him when we find him. Perhaps your informant who so readily provides you with information, would be so kind as to tip you off as to the killer's whereabouts,' said Steven with some satisfaction. Amy blushed with embarrassment at the put down. She could not resist having a dig at Ann. 'Well DCI Dixon, you seemed to have lost the knack of catching the bad guys. Doesn't seem that there'll be any chance of promotion in the New Year,' she said cattishly. 'Oh, I don't need the promise of promotion to do my job. It is just a matter of time before my team and I solve this case. If you check my track record, you will see I always get my man. Our bonus will be catching the bastard who is betraying this unit,' replied Ann triumphantly.

Angry that she had been rumbled, Amy sat down and kept quiet. The other reporters asked relevant questions and were circumspect in their approach. The reporters were encouraged to speak directly to Ann for all their queries, and she gave them her word that she would answer all their queries as promptly as she could. When everyone had simmered down and the questions fizzled out, Steven drew the briefing to a close. He handled the briefing admirably and there was a measure of co-operation instead of the usual striving to score points. The media left the meeting feeling that they had come away with some tangible facts they got from the horse's mouth. Edwards thanked Ann for her support. She was amazed at his invitation to join him for lunch. She declined, promising to be available later in the week. He replied that he would hold her to her promise. 'It went very well, guv. Wouldn't you say Edwards has undergone a total transformation? remarked David. 'Yes, I was most impressed, but listen to the best part. He invited me to lunch. 'Good God he must be unwell,' replied David with an enormous grin on his face. 'Did you accept?' 'No, I postponed it till later. Can't let him think I am easy,' joked Ann. 'Come on, that coffee is long overdue. Grab some of those yummy doughnuts I saw in the incident room, on your way back. Her phone rang as David left the office. 'Hi, am I speaking to the grumpy, sexy Inspector?' said Josie on the other end of the line. 'Listen, cheeky, you're not allowed to speak to an officer of the Metropolitan police like this. Don't you have work to do?' replied Ann trying not to laugh at Josie's cheeky enquiry. 'And let me guess the laziest man in England is spending the day with you, painting. I must be in the wrong job, because my boss expects me at work every day,' replied Ann cheerily. 'Oh, what a fuss pot! You should be grateful that this famous fashion designer and a handsome, brilliant journalist are decorating your house, without demanding any money,' said Josie. Ann could hear Adam laughing in the background. 'Have you two been drinking?' "Good gracious, no we are hard at work. We just took some time off to invite you to dinner because we haven't been able to talk to you recently. You can bring that lovely sergeant with you, if he is free,' continued Josie. 'Wait till I get home,' said Ann just as David returned with the coffee. 'It's Josie. She has invited us to join her and Adam for dinner tonight. Are you free?' 'Yes, thank you, I would love to come,' replied David grateful for the opportunity to meet with Adam without having to concoct a lie to get away from Ann for the evening. They tucked into the doughnuts while Ann poured over her laptop checking that she had dealt with the urgent matters for the morning. 'Finish your coffee and close that door,' she instructed David. 'Right we have work to do concerning the rat in the force. We need to set a honey trap for Amy. This is what I have in mind,' she said to David, keeping her voice in a very low tone. We have an undercover cop called Julie Cunningham. She has done some splendid work for us in the past. Amy will find her irresistible. She would give her eye teeth to have Julie. I am going to get Josie to organise a party and invite all partners of her employees. To ensue Amy goes to the party, Josie must ensure that she invites the disgraced Italian designer, Franco who got caught in bed with his male lover by his wife. His acrimonious divorce made headlines around the world. Amy would give her eye teeth to get close to Franco. When Julie gets lucky with Amy, she will be in the house to plant the surveillance devices. The surveillance will at some stage uncover who is giving Amy her information. We just need to wait patiently," said Ann with a satisfied smile. 'It sounds very workable, but what happens if Amy doesn't like Julie, and can't get into the house,' replied David sceptically. 'It will work. You need to think like a gay woman,' continued Ann. David smiled at her impatience at his retarded understanding of love amongst women. Julie will give a star- studded performance. I know she will make the plan work,' said Ann. 'Where do we find this wonder woman?' said David mockingly. I will contact her through Michael Heath," she replied. 'Will Michael support your plan?' enquired David. 'Michael never says no to me. I know I can rely on his full support,' replied Ann with conviction. 'In fact, let me phone him right now. There's no better time than the present. Just as luck would have it, Michael answered immediately.

Ann apologised for the impromptu call. He reassured her he was available anytime. She asked if she could pop over and tell him about her plan to catch the mole in the force. He invited her over to his office straight away. She was delighted at his prompt response. 'Come on David you are driving, let's go," she urged. They sped over to Michael's office, hopeful and happy. Ann knocked at the door of Michael's office and waited for a response. He opened the door and invited them inside. He offered them a whiskey and poured himself one too. "Okay, let's hear what you have in mind,' he said. Ann told him her plan. He listened until she had finished. He said that it sounded feasible, but he had concerns about the surveillance and if the devices were found, Amy may find out that Julie had planted them in her house. 'Amy is no fool and did not get this far in her career by being unobservant. She has a nose like a bloodhound. Ann, I know how much we need to nail the bastard who is leaking information, but we need to be cautious that the means do not defeat the end.

I am going to discuss your plan with Alec Sawyer who heads the undercover unit and get back to you. We need to proceed with a great deal of care as it is too delicate to mess up now that we have made such progress,' said Michael. Ann was a little deflated, as she thought her plan was workable and that valuable time was lost by more procrastination. They had talked into the early evening. Ann glanced at her watch and made her excuses to leave. 'Don't worry, I won't keep you waiting. I will get back to you later this week,' he said reassuringly. She smiled, shook hands and left with David. 'Damn, I hope this Sawyer guy is not one of those steeped in the bureaucratic soup of delays, and realms of paperwork,' said Ann disconcertedly. 'Cheer up guv, he didn't say no, it was a conditional yes,' replied David enthusiastically. 'Let's get home, before the chef bans us from her dinner table for being late,' she replied. They were met at the door by a smiling Adam. He hugged and kissed Ann and patted David on the back. 'The chef was just wondering if you would be disgracefully late,' he said with a broad grin. 'Yes, I would like to have a few words with your chef who makes nuisance calls to an officer of the law,' replied Ann. 'I heard that Inspector.

Be careful not to upset the cook as you may not be given dinner,' said Josie flinging her arms around Ann and kissing her lovingly. 'I'll get the wine. What is everyone drinking?' asked Adam. He memorized their requests and went into the living room. Adam poured the wine while Ann helped Josie bring the food to the table. Everyone indulged in the repast with enthusiasm and expressed glowing compliments for Josie's efforts at creating a new dish. The evening passed amicably. Adam left with David, the excuse being that he wanted to spend the night at his own flat. Ann cheered his decision saying she was glad of her and Josie being afforded some privacy. Adam and David continued their discussion on their proposed trip to Brazil into the early hours of the morning. Ann and Josie finished washing up the dishes and headed for bed. Ann seized the opportunity to inform Josie about her plan to put Amy under surveillance. "Josie, do you remember reading that article about our murder investigation last week,' enquired Ann. 'Yes, I did, and I remember how stressed you were when your chief tried to pin the blame for the leak on you,' said Josie. 'Well, I need you to be an honorary sleuth, to help me,' said Ann. 'Wow do you mean that?' asked Josie beaming with joy. 'Don't get carried away. I need you to organize a fashion event with an after party. I want you to invite Franco. I also want you to invite Amy. I would be even happier if you could send Tamara away. So that she is not present at the party. I also want you to send an invite to a girl called Julie Cunningham,' said Ann. 'Can I ask why,' enquired Josie. "Absolutely not! This is on a need to know basis and you only follow instructions. No questions please,' said Ann emphatically. 'Okay, when do you want this party organized?' asked Josie. 'I want it done thoroughly, so don't rush. It is important that it all goes smoothly. We only have one shot at this. There is a great dealing riding on this opportunity, so no mistakes. 'Oh, I think I could grant that, depending on the price of the reward,' replied Ann. 'A wedding date in the near future perhaps?' asked Josie, half expecting a look of disapproval from Ann. To her astonishment, Ann replied, we can arrange it for when I get back from Moscow. I did not forget about it. Yes, I do still want to tie the knot with you.

Stop being so afraid and insecure. I don't want anyone else. Does that put your mind at rest?' asked Ann, playfully pulling Josie's ear. They hugged and snuggled in next to each other. Sleep did not come easily to Ann as she toyed with the myriad of thoughts and plans that bombarded her brain. David phoned Jeremy early the next morning to arrange a meeting. He asked Jeremy not to say anything to Ann just yet, as he had some explaining to do. Jeremy arranged to meet later that morning, as he was keen to hear what David had to say. Ann had some meetings which did not include David for the morning, so he was grateful that he could get away without telling lies. Jeremy and David met at a coffee shop in Chelsea. 'Drag up a chair and tell me all,' said Jeremy enthusiastically. 'Nigel will meet with you, but you will only meet with this guy, Ben Hajjioff in Brazil. He will talk to you but his associate, Rachel Levy will give you security clearance for him. She has worked with Hajjioff and can vouch for him. You will need Ben as he is fluent in Portuguese and knows our double agent with the drug cartels. He also knows the equatorial forest, and some of the forest inhabitants. He lived with them when he did the documentary on native American tribes. He trained as a commando before becoming a journalist. He is a valuable ally. I spoke to our Mossad contact, Rachel Levy. Her MI6 contact has informed Rachel that James Muller is protected by the drug cartel in Brazil and that he would move heaven and earth to stay alive. I other words, whoever pursues him is in grave danger of being killed.

You must convince Ann to stick to the request of these agents and not insist on a face to face meeting. You must dig your heels in on this. I know this is her investigation, but she must follow their protocol as we need their help,' urged David. 'Hmm you seem to have it all worked out. The difficulty will be convincing Ann of your importance in the Interpol team. I can emphasize that you are needed because you are closely involved with the investigation and have close ties to our contact. I will need to speak to this Ben and check him out, before I sanction his participation in this investigation. Give me a couple of weeks. I will then return with concrete information to give to Ann. 'Send me the contact details for Ben, and I will get on with it,' promised

Jeremy. The two men parted company, with the understanding that they would stay in contact by phone only as they feared emails would be read or traced. David phoned Adam to tell him he had met with Jeremy and had sewn the seed about going to Brazil. Adam said that Rachel would get his new identity as Ben Hajjioff set up. He told David he needed two weeks to get everything arranged.

'How much is Jeremy going to tell Ann of all of this?' Adam asked nervously. "I have asked him to inform Ann on a need to know basis. We are in luck that it is Interpol jurisdiction, so Ann won't be able to demand to know every detail. Jeremy agreed, so we are safe for now,' added David. 'Meet me at the Dog and Duck in Islington after work on Friday,' said Adam. 'Okay, see you there, must rush before Ann gets back from her meeting,' replied David. Ann got back at lunchtime. She went looking for David and found him in the incident room going over some of the forensic reports. 'Hi David, can you come to my office, I have some feedback from Michael. 'On second thoughts, let's grab some lunch,' she said. They headed for a Pizza Express in Covent Garden. 'I don't care what you order, I am famished,' she said. 'Had a busy morning guv?' he enquired. 'Yes, quite busy. I met with Michael, and Stephen about our funding for the Russian trip,' she added. David leaned forward expectantly. 'Did we get it, guv,' he asked. 'Yes, we got it. I told you Michael never says no to me,' she purred confidently. 'That is fantastic news. When do we go?' asked David. 'Hold your horses, cowboy, we have to contact the Russian equivalent of the CID and get a liaison officer to take care of us when we are there. It might take a few weeks. Time to celebrate. Let's have a glass of wine.

They finished their drinks and Ann asked to be dropped off at Peter Drew's lab. He explained that he was meeting with DI Roberts. David went straight to the Incident room where Roberts was working on his laptop. 'Hi, did you get our report on the interview with Susan Muller?' 'Yes, indeed, I did,' he announced proudly. 'I say, even though Ann muscled in on what should have been my interview,' said Roberts sarcastically. 'I know, I was not able to prevent her doing it. You know when the gu'vnor wants to do something herself, she just goes ahead and does it,' added David sympathetically. 'I went to Nottingham to find Mary O Reilly. The family moved years ago. They were a disjointed family, according to some of the neighbours who knew them. Mr O'Reilly was a drunk and left Mary's mother when she was very young. Her mother had no control over her. She grew up running wild. They remember her being involved with the Casey boys. She had a younger sister, Ellen who does not live in Nottingham any more. Mary also had an uncle who might know what became of Mary. I left my contact details with the neighbour who said she would contact me if she is able to find an address for the uncle,' explained Roberts. 'Well you didn't do so bad yourself. Ann will be pleased with the information,' he added. 'No, she will pick holes in my work as she always does. She's never satisfied with anything. I don't know how you can put up with her probing and questioning,' he said. David patted him on the back sympathetically and whispered, you just need to practise some patience. Anyway, let's go over the Nottingham information again to ensure we haven't missed anything,' said David.

Terence Holmes entered the room singing, 'From Russia with love.' He smiled at David and said, "Rumour has it that someone is going on a Russian honeymoon', he teased. 'Cut the crap, Holmes, I am warning you,' said David angrily. 'You will have plenty of opportunity of banging her; a dream come true,' he said with a smirk. David had reached boiling point. He lunged forward, punching Terence on the nose. The two men wrestled with each other on the floor. Papers and chairs went flying as the fight escalated. Their fellow officers watched and cheered as the two men threw punches and kicked each other. David was the better and stronger fighter, but Holmes was a dirty fighter when he was felt he was losing. He bit David's ear until he drew blood. David retaliated by bashing Holmes' head on the floor. He managed to beat Holmes into submission. The commotion was heard down the corridor. Order was only restored when Edward's voiced boomed over the sound of the cheering bystanders. 'What the hell is going on here?' he demanded to know. He turned the air blue with a barrage of expletives, to express his anger at their behaviour. The bloodied fighters stared at the floor while they were reprimanded. Holmes had a broken nose, and David's torn ear was hanging by a piece of skin. The room looked like a bomb site. Blood was spattered on the floor, broken chairs and the on the files. 'Get out of my sight. Just remember, the damages will be deducted from your salaries,' he warned as he turned on his heel and walked off. Both men were taken to the nearest casualty for medical treatment. Edwards phoned Ann to inform her about the fight. She swallowed hard as Edwards criticised her lack of control of her sergeant and suggested she put him on a lead or have him replaced. Much as she was tempted to defend him, she was forced to eat humble pie as she knew nothing excused David for fighting on duty. She was shocked but kept her cool and calmly asked which hospital David had been taken to. She apologised profusely for her sergeant's behaviour and thanked him for informing her.

She sped to The Chelsea and Westminster Hospital, preparing the lecture she was going to give David. She made her way to Casualty where she showed her badge and explained she was looking for Sergeant Hughes. The staff informed her that he was undergoing repair to his ear in the minor surgery suite. Ann managed to track down Holmes who had just had his broken nose reset. He could not look at Ann. 'I demand to know what led to this despicable behaviour?' she said angrily. 'It was just a disagreement, guv. David is very sensitive and does not like being teased. He hit me so I retaliated, and it got out of hand,' explained Holmes, sheepishly. 'I don't care who was to blame. You are a disgrace to the force if you cannot control your emotions and your temper. Edwards wants you both or sacked. There will be an internal enquiry and you both will be severely reprimanded and disciplined. I get hauled into the shit with you because I am accused of not being able to control you,' she continued. Holmes apologised profusely and promised it would not happen again. 'There won't be a next time because you won't be working for the force much longer,' she warned. 'Go home and stay there until you hear from the chief,' she said. She fetched a coffee from the machine on the ward and went to wait for David to return from surgery. She worked on her laptop while the time ticked away. Roberts joined her while she waited. 'What the hell happened today. I believe you witnessed the whole incident,' hissed Ann. 'Yes, indeed, I had the unfortunate pleasure of seeing two grown men knocking the shit out of each other. I didn't see the start of the fight as I popped out to get a coffee. Next best thing, when I got into the room, blood and chairs were flying everywhere,' he explained. 'So why the hell didn't anyone try to stop them. I hear the men were applauding the fight as though it was an official boxing match?' she enquired. 'What? Only a madman would have intervened. It was obvious they were intent on killing each other. I have no idea why. The men present said that Holmes entered the room singing, 'From Russia with love' and began taunting Hughes who struck the first blow,' said Roberts. "They were caught brawling a few months ago, and I warned both of them,' she added. 'I believe you and Hughes are due to go to Moscow in pursuit of a witness testimony. Will the chief allow Hughes to go along, considering his aggression record?' asked Roberts.

'I will do my level best to convince the chief he has to go, because he is a good copper, but I have a horrible feeling he will be disciplined, which will inevitably delay our trip. I am going to see Edwards after speaking to David when he wakes up. 'Okay, I will catch up with you tomorrow. Got to dash as I have a meeting in an hour,' he replied as he put on his coat and prepared to leave.

Ann drummed her fingers on the table as she waited impatiently to speak with David. The nurse came to tell her that David had woken up and would see her. A very groggy David tried to sit up in bed as Ann approached. She glared at him; her anger omnipresent. 'What have I told you about having disputes at work and behaving in such a despicable manner?' she asked. David held his heavily bandaged ear and grimaced with pain.' 'Oh God, my ear, my head, it feels like I have been hit by a bus,' he complained, as he held onto his head. 'If it was up to me, I would ensure you were hit by a bus. You deserve to be punished. I don't know what Edwards is going to say. He may even stop you going to Moscow. You will be disciplined, and it will impact on our investigation time. We have already procrastinated too much. Why were you fighting? I do not want a stupid excuse. Were you and Holmes fighting over a woman?' she demanded to know. 'It was about a woman but not in the way you think. It was what he implied in a very lewd way that sparked the fight,' replied David. 'I want to know exactly what he said. If you don't want to tell me, Edwards will demand that you mention all the details in you statement. So, the choice is yours,' she added. There were a few moments of silence before David replied. Holmes insinuated that you and I guv were going to Moscow to have an affair. I punched him because I found his remarks unsavoury and disrespectful to you.' David looked down towards the floor, not daring to meet Ann's gaze. 'Why could you not walk away, and leave me to deal with him,' she asked. 'Well because we guys settle our arguments differently to women.

I could not stand by and allow a rogue like Holmes to get away with spreading malicious gossip which is untrue. Sometimes when dirt is thrown around often enough, it begins to stick and that is unfair to the person who is talked about,' he said with conviction. The effects of the analgesia took effect and David began drifting off to sleep. Ann realised that it would be pointless pursuing the questions. Just as she was preparing to take her leave of David, Steven popped his head around the door. 'I thought you might be here. What the hell happened?' he asked pulling up a chair. 'I believe it was as a result of Holmes' insinuation that David and I were off to Moscow to conduct a clandestine love affair,' she explained. 'What preposterous poppycock,' replied Edwards. 'Yes, my sentiments entirely,' said Ann. 'Why the hell can't you control your boys?' added Edwards. 'With respect sir, I signed up to solve cases for the Met not teach grown men how to behave,' replied Ann crossly. 'Why did Hughes take offence?' Good God, he is not secretly in love with you, is he?' stifling a laugh. Ann smiled, sensing he was making fun of her. 'Well perhaps if I can persuade him to change his sex, he might be in with a chance,' she replied. 'His behaviour was disgraceful, and I believe it is the second fight these two men have had. I will not tolerate such lack of control amongst members of my force. They will be disciplined, and I think it may be good to move him to another unit for a while. I will let you know,' said Edwards. 'What does the doctor say?' Will his ear recover fully?' he asked. 'The doctor has said he will make a complete recovery. He will be discharged tomorrow and be back to work next week,' she explained. 'I'll be off. See you at my office tomorrow,' he said as he headed for the corridor. Ann was very thoughtful as she drove home. She was fearful that David would not be allowed to accompany her to Moscow. She had not realised how she had enjoyed working with him, until Steven mentioned separating them. They were a great team, and she wanted them to complete the investigation together.

She knew that she had to manipulate the situation to her advantage, to keep David as her assistant. She had to play her trump card to make that happen. She phoned Michael and told him what had happened. He sympathised and agreed to meet with her the following day. The expression on Ann's face spoke volumes when she walked through the door. 'Goodness who has died?' asked Josie as Ann sat down. 'Oh, don't you add to my problems. I have had a rotten day,' replied a dejected Ann. Adam stopped what he was doing and went to sit next to Ann on the sofa. 'What's the matter sis. Has misery guts Edwards been on your case again?' he asked sympathetically. 'No, it's David. He is in hospital. He had a fight with another officer. David's ear had been bitten off and the other guy also sustained injuries,' she continued. 'Bloody hell, I thought coppers were supposed to fight the criminals not one another.

Is David going to be ok?' he asked. Yes, he will be discharged soon,' Ann replied with some irritation. 'May I ask what the fight was about?' asked Adam. 'No! it is none of your business. If David wishes to tell you it is entirely up to him. Besides you are too nosey when it comes to business about the Met,' replied Ann. 'Oh, that's put you in your place,' replied Adam. You know Ann gets techy when it involves her David,' added Josie with a grin. 'And you can take the smug look off your face and keep your opinion to yourself, and by the way he is not my David,' added bluntly. 'Ok, I'll just slink into the kitchen to avoid the slings and arrows that are flying around here,' said Josie. 'Oh; you are like a couple of kids, you two. Come on, I am going to take you to dinner,' said Ann. 'I have a bone to pick with you Adam Dixon. You had the nerve to take Josie to the fertility clinic without consulting with me,' snapped Ann. 'Yes, it was under exceptional circumstances, you must agree, and the result was pretty amazing, wasn't it sis?' continued Adam.

'I feel like doing something bloody amazing to your head. You have the audacity to presume you can waltz into people's lives and make decisions without their knowledge and pat yourself on the back for the consequence of your actions,' said Ann. 'A thousand apologies for acting without your permission, but I did it to help both of you,' he protested. 'And I suppose you know that Josie is pregnant,' said Ann. 'Yes, she told me last night and I am delighted for you both. Congratulations,' he purred. 'Come on you wicked man, drive us to dinner,' said Ann. Josie announced during dinner that she was going to spend ten days in New York. Adam said he had a meeting in Paris and would be away for two weeks. They were surprised that Ann did not complain about being on her own. Her thoughts were on a mission to discover the truth. The very next day she made an appointment to meet with Luke Cowan. She ignored his sarcasm and pressed him for a meeting. He reluctantly agreed to meet her at his home the next evening. 'I appreciate you making time to meet with me Doctor Cowan," said Ann as he showed her into his living room. 'The pleasure is absolutely mine,' replied Luke as he invited her to make herself at home. He offered her a drink which she gratefully accepted. 'I will come straight to the point, Doctor Cowan, said Ann. "We have reason to believe that you had been involved in the satanic rituals with the Casey brothers,' continued Ann.

Well, well, you certainly have been very busy inspector. I hope you can back up your suppositions with concrete evidence. Do you really believe I could be bothered to go chanting mambo jumbo with a group of mindless individuals?' I think not,' he added. 'I assure you we have reliable witness who saw you with the Casey's during their mambo jumbo practices,' said Ann. He suddenly became serious and got up from his seat. 'You can't prove anything, my lawyer will overturn whatever accusations this witness levels at me,' he said confidently. 'Don't be so sure, I always get my man,' replied Ann. 'I need your help, doctor Cowan. I am not here to accuse you or to fight you. You are not a suspect. Whatever you reveal to me would be confidential,' said Ann. 'I want you to take me to the place where they meet for satanic rituals. Don't pretend ignorance because I have it from a reliable source that you have witnessed these rituals,' Ann informed Luke. 'My word, you are very assured about your information Inspector,' Luke added mockingly. 'My information comes at a price. I hope you are willing to pay,' he continued. Luke walked over to her and ran his fingers along her cheek.

She did not resist or reproach him but watched to see what he would do next. 'So, the great inspector wants my help. I am afraid you must agree to a forfeit of my choosing. My help comes with certain conditions. Let me show you my little secret parlour. It will pique your curiosity," he continued. She followed him to a cellar which was only lit by candle light. It was decorated in dark red and black. There were a collection of whips and handcuffs on a table. A bed covered in red satin sheets stood in the centre of the room. He turned towards Ann, saying, 'see inspector, this is my private domain. Not a shred of satanic worship in sight, but I indulge in something much more exhilarating.' He reached over and held her face in his hands. He kissed her passionately. She responded at first, then bit his lip and drew blood. This inflamed his passion and he began to rip off her clothes. She embraced him and raked her nails down his back, drawing blood. He arched his back with the pain, but her actions only served to arouse him. He was distracted for s few moments. Ann grabbed the opportunity to handcuff him. She pushed him onto the bed and tore off his shirt. She reached for a large candle which contained a significant amount of melted, hot wax. She proceeded to pour the wax over his chest. The hot wax ran to his groin. His erect member stood proud and pulsated, seemingly electrified by his suffering. He screamed with pain and ecstasy. She pulled him off the bed and chained him to a chair. She grabbed one of the whips and began beating him. The bloody welts on his skin sent him into a sexual frenzy. This aroused him even more and he begged her to continue to hurt him. She then untied him, and he put a chain around her neck. He beat her with a whip until she bled. He bit her on her buttock till he drew blood. He savoured the blood that oozed from her wounds. He pushed her onto the bed with her back towards him. He forced her into a kneeling position. He gazed at her exposed buttocks, and, glistening vagina which inflamed his ardour. He kept a hold on the chain to control her movement, just as one would control a dog. He thrust his engorged manhood into her, violently as she screamed in ecstasy.

They continued their violent engagement with abject, bestial carnality, for what seemed hours, until they were spent and collapsed on the bed, totally exhausted. They slept until the next morning. Luke brought her a cup of coffee. He had a smirk on his face. 'So, the great inspector has an Achilles heel. 'Fuck off Cowan, don't get above yourself, we had an arrangement. It is business, that is all,' said Ann. 'I'll tell you something inspector, you are a fucking good lay. I had to have a wank after I met you. You have a divine body. It is wasted in your job. I wonder what your lady love would say if she knew you were screwed by me,' he said mockingly. 'You leave Josie out of this. You agreed to take me to the forest and witness the ritual, so you had better keep your word,' she continued. 'So desperate to get the answers you require, that you would risk everything,' he continued mockingly. 'You bastard, if you double cross me, I will not stop at anything to teach you a lesson,' Ann replied menacingly. 'If you didn't make me so fucking randy, I would tell you to piss off,' he said. 'Okay I will help you. I will let you know when they have their next ritual,' he said. Ann put her coat over her torn clothes and sped out of the house to her car.

There numerous of messages on her phone when she switched it on. One was from an irate Edwards who demanded she come to his office. She raced home to shower and change. She was shocked and disgusted at the bruises on her back, neck and thighs. "God, I hope these are faded by the time Josie gets back," she thought. She wore a scarf to her meeting with Michael the next morning. 'Good to see you Ann. Grab a chair. 'I'll get my secretary to bring in some coffee, or would you prefer something a little stronger?' asked Michael. 'No thanks too early for me, I'll settle for the coffee,' replied Ann. 'What's with the scarf?' asked Michael. 'Oh, some rash that looks unsightly, so I decided to cover it up,' replied Ann 'So your boys have been engaged in a bit of fisticuffs,' he said. 'Yes, and now Edwards wants to move David to another unit, and he did not start the fight. I want him to accompany me to Moscow because he knows the logistics of this case. I want you to block Edwards and stop David being moved, please sir", pleaded Ann. 'Ok, I will do my best, but how do I convince Edwards this will not happen again as it is not the first encounter these boys have had,' he said. 'DS Holmes needs to be moved. He will continue to agitate Sergeant Hughes. But you must convince Edwards that Holmes is the aggressor,' said Ann. 'Ok, if I can convince Edwards, you must be ready to travel to Moscow in ten days. I have spoken to the Russian CID leader. Seemingly nice fellow called, Sergei Kiminsky. I am going to give you his number, so that you can update him on the case. I just prepared the way in a diplomatic sense for you. He gave me his assurance that you would be supported every step of the way,' added Michael. 'Thank you, sir, I am most grateful. I will phone Sergei sometime today. 'By the way, how is Jake Casey getting along?' 'Has he shown any signs of recovery yet?' asked Michael. 'I'm afraid, not. The doctor says he is stable but still unconscious,' replied Ann. 'Do you still believe that Jake was an accomplice rather than the prime murderer?' asked Michael. 'Yes because of the many variables in the case. Nothing is clear cut. Either we have a very clever murderer who is not Jake Casey, or Jake's cousin, James committed the murderers with his help. We will have to see if we can track down this Saskia in Moscow,' replied Ann. 'Good luck, I will certainly support you in all of this,' said Michael.

'Thanks, sir, I am truly grateful,' said Ann, shaking his hand. She was able to speak to Sergei later that day as she had sent him a comprehensive email of both cases and explained the reason for their visit to Moscow. She was able to have a visual teleconference with Sergei and his sergeant, called Dimitri. The two men were very excited about Ann's visit. They said the case was fascinating and challenging. Sergei reassured Ann that he would arrange their accommodation in Moscow and would have them collected at the airport. She thanked him and promised to phone him nearer the time of their visit. Her next call was to check on David. 'How are you?' she enquired when a groggy sounding David replied. 'Not too bad, guv. The ear still feels very painful,' he added. 'Serves you bloody right for fighting,' said Ann. 'Oh no not now, guv. You can fight with me when I am totally better. Right now, I just want a bit of peace and quiet,' he pleaded. 'Alright you have a week's sick leave. Come into the office at the end of the week. I want to prepare for Moscow. We travel in ten days. Please try not to have any more accidents in the meantime,' she said. David sighed with irritation, 'Ok I will remember that,' David replied. Josie informed Ann that she was regrettably delayed for another week. Ann was grateful of the extra time for her bruising to fade. She was racked with guilt, so she phoned Owen to arrange a meeting. 'What's up?' You sounded deathly depressed on the phone,' enquired Owen. 'Oh God I have acted foolishly and recklessly. Please help me,' pleaded Ann. 'I had sex with a person of interest in our murder case in exchange for vital information,' Ann confessed. Owen listened intently as she blurted out her reckless encounter. He raised his eyebrows as she told him she was going to the forest to meet with her informer to take her to the Satanist place of ritual. 'I don't condemn you. I understand your motivation for doing what you did but I am concerned that you are at some risk accompanying this guy into the forest. If he is the loose cannon you say he is, what stops him from attacking you and bumping you off?' asked Owen. 'That's why I have you on my side. We are going to Treswell woods, Nottingham. I will tell you when and you are going to follow us and be my bodyguard,' added Ann. 'Phew, same old Ann. Still sailing close to the wind. OK, I will be there for you,' Owen assured her.

Luke contacted her three days after their meeting informing her that the meeting of the Satanists, was scheduled for the time of the full moon in two days. Ann insisted on travelling in her own car, with Luke leading the way. The clement weather ensured they had a smooth journey to Sherwood Forest. Luke stopped a few hundred metres from the edge of the forest and got out of his car. Ann alighted from her car and walked to meet with Luke. 'Ok Ann, this is no time for heroics as the people who indulge in these practices are deadly serious and very dangerous. The perimeter of the forest where they do the rituals are booby trapped. They also have lookouts who are armed and dangerous. It is vital for both our safety to stay close to me and be very quiet. I will make a sound by which the lookouts will know I am not the enemy, but they must not see you,' he urged. She nodded in agreement and followed him as he walked ahead. The full moon broke through the stark darkness that engulfed the forest. They stuck to the thick undergrowth, moving slowly until they got to a large tree. Luke whispered to Ann that he would help her to ascend the tree, reminding her to be very quiet. Luke crouched so that Ann could put her feet on his shoulders to ascend the tree. She managed to reach the first sturdy branch and heaved herself up onto the arm of the nearest branch. Luke stuck a knife into the main trunk of the tree to get a foothold before heaving himself up with Ann helping him to ascend. They snuggled in the small space on the horizontal branch. Their position gave them an excellent view of the forest clearing. The eerie silence was only punctuated by the hooting from nesting owls. It seemed like an eternity before a grating noise revealed the opening of a hatch which had been concealed by the undergrowth. Hooded figures emerged from the hatch which seemed to lead to an underground tunnel.

  The figures dressed in black formed a circle around a central alter. A figure dressed in white emerged from the tunnel and the rest of the group bowed to him calling him master. The group began to chant. Moments later, a woman dressed in white was carried out of the tunnel and placed on the alter. She seemed asleep or drugged as she did not protest or cry out. A live goat was also brought into the centre of proceedings and tied to the side of the alter. The chanting continued for what must have seemed like an hour. The figure in white then walked over to the goat and cut its throat. Blood gushed out. A black cloaked figure collected the blood in a large chalice. The figure in the white cloak drank from the chalice. It was passed around to each person in the black cloak. The remainder of blood in the chalice was poured over the girl lying in the alter. The figure in white then ripped off the girl's clothes and took off his clothes. He mounted the alter and began to have sex with the girl. The girl woke up from her drugged state and began to scream. Her attacker became more violent in his rape of her and proceeded to sodomise her. The other figures cheered as the attack continued. When the white cloaked figure had satisfied himself, he cut the woman's wrist and proceeded to drink her blood. The girl passed out during her ordeal. The figure in white thrust his hands into the air glorifying Satan. His followers did the same. They carried the girl back into the tunnel and disappeared into the darkness. Just as the last figure descended the steps into the tunnel, the moonlight revealed his face. Ann gasped silently as she recognized the face as that of the DS of the Nottingham division. The man who had led the search in the forest with her team some months ago. They waited until the last of the lookouts had gone before descending the tree. Luke lead her safely out of the forest. Cramped, and shocked at what she witnessed, Ann whispered, 'Do you think they killed the girl?' 'Well that is for you to determine, Inspector.

I did my job to take you to the venue. Whatever happens next is nothing to do with me. We still have the little interlude we had which may be considered as payment. You can't deny have been to my place as your dabs are all over my handcuffs and my candles. Your visit is on my CCTV. Good luck and goodbye,' he said sarcastically as he drove away in his car. Ann sat quietly contemplating her dilemma. She could confide in nobody about the events of the past week. She knew nobody would understand her actions, least of all Josie. She knew that her trip to the rituals was not a wasted one as it confirmed her suspicions about it being linked to the murders. She just needed time to link these events. She got home in the early hours of the morning and was glad that she was alone and did not need to give an account of herself to anyone. Her bruises had still not faded. She prolonged her shower. No amount of scrubbing could erase her sordid encounter with Luke.

Hey how did you manage to get away without being asked one hundred questions,' asked David when Adam appeared at his front door. 'Oh, I just told them a white lie about meeting someone at the pub,' he replied. 'How are you doing, my friend?' asked Adam. 'Painfully well,' replied David. He then explained to Adam what had happened. "Still defending my sister's honour. I see" added Adam. "Yes, that bastard was totally out of line. I had to teach him some manners. Your sister didn't see it that way. She just thinks I am a thug with no discipline", added David." Rubbish! don't let her hard front fool you she admires your chivalry. 'Anyway, I managed to meet with Jeremy. I filled him in on Rachel and the MI6 operative. I gave your name as Ben Hajjioff. I also gave him contact numbers for them and told him that you would only be contactable in Brazil. I warned him not to tell Ann the information came via me,' said David. 'Sounds good. When do you think you and Ann will return from Moscow?' asked Adam. 'To tell the truth, I may not be allowed to go to Moscow as the chief wants to transfer me to another unit because of the fight,' said David. 'Don't worry, that will never happen. My sister will fight tooth and nail to ensure you go, Mark my words,' said Adam with conviction. 'The plan for Brazil is that you and Ann will be met by Rachel and Nigel.

I will request that you join me when we go into the forest to meet my DEA connection. We will finalise everything nearer the time. But you must convince Jeremy to only deal with my DEA guys because there are a few crooked ones amongst those in the mainstream,' said Adam. 'I'd better be getting home now,' said Adam. David arrived late for work the next morning, much to Ann's chagrin. 'You are appearing before the chief constable for review of your position as a result of your fight with Holmes. I hope you will not be moved to another unit, or worse, demoted' said Ann regretfully. 'I hope so too, guv. I want to see this investigation to the end with you,' said David. 'Well you should have thought of that before you behaved like an idiot and put your career at risk,' said Ann. 'Now get out of my office, your appointment is in 15 minutes,' said Ann with some irritation. David obeyed and took his leave of her. The disciplinary hearing was brutal and intense. Worse still, David was none the wiser at the end of the hearing as to what had been decided. The chief constable informed him he would be notified about his fate when a decision had been reached. He expected the worse as the enquiry was gruelling and damning. He headed for Ann's office as he knew she would be more supportive. 'Well are you in or out?' she asked as he stuck his head around the door of her office. He slumped in the chair looking as dejected as someone who had been given a prison sentence. 'I have no idea what they have decided. They said they would inform me when they have made a decision,' he replied. 'Oh, for goodness sake, cheer up. You have a good record and I am assuming that will tip the balance in your favour,' said Ann slapping him on the back. 'You have done me a favour by delaying the Moscow trip, because Josie and I want to tie the knot. If you have no plans on the 12, that's a week away. I want you to be one of our witnesses,' she added. 'I would love to be, guv, just text me the time and venue and I'll be there,' he replied. 'And remember, not a word to anyone,' added Ann. David smiled and nodded in agreement.

Ann had been so busy arranging their Moscow trip that the days sped away and before she knew it, the eve of her wedding had arrived. Adam and Josie ran around frantically making the arrangements for the wedding as Ann had so little free time. The modest gathering at the venue in the Cotswolds celebrated the marriage of Ann and Josie. David and Adam were the witnesses. Ann hoped that the registrar at the wedding would not remember her name as she appeared on TV in connection with the murders. The short ceremony was followed by a lavish champagne lunch. Josie looked stylish in a cream silk dress. Ann wore a silver- grey silk suit. They had to put the honeymoon on hold as Ann anticipated her trip to Moscow would follow soon after the wedding. She booked them into another hotel as she had every intention of thwarting Adam's plans to booby trap their bedroom. She enjoyed the look of surprise and disappointment on his face when she ordered a cab to whisk her and Josie to a secret location. He could not resist telling them not to go wild on the wedding night as Josie should remember she was carrying his nephew. He and David sauntered off the nearest pub with the intention of getting disgracefully drunk.

The three days passed quickly. David was summoned to the chief superintendant's office at 8am on the Monday morning. 'I don't know why they are so lenient with you, if I had the chance, I would have had you removed or sacked,' said Edwards glaring at David. "You can remain here and continue the murder investigation with DCI Dixon. DS Holmes has been transferred to Bexley Heath Division,' said Edwards. David nearly collapsed with relief. 'Thank you, sir, I am very grateful. I will endeavour to keep on the straight and narrow,' replied David humbly. 'One more step out of line and you are gone, now get out of my office,' he added. Suffused with elation and relief, David sped to Ann's office to share his good news with her. 'Guv, I'm off the hook, they are letting me stay,' beamed David. 'Oh, that's great news, David. Grab a chair. I am just about to do a video conference with the Russian detectives. Edwards and Heath will be here I want you in on this, so don't wander off,' said Ann. 'Ok do you think we have time for a quick coffee before we start?' asked David. 'Hurry up because Edwards will blow a fuse if we are delayed, and you know how much he loathes you at this moment in time,' she added. David dashed off to get the coffee while Ann made last minute preparations for the meeting.

There was aloud knock on the door. The door opened, and Edwards walked in followed by Michael Heath. David appeared soon after. 'Don't even think of bringing that coffee to this office. What the hell do you think the Russians will say if they spotted you sipping your coffee during the video conference. We British are already labelled as lazy and seeing you enjoying a coffee might give them the wrong impression of us, so you can chuck that away for a start,' said Edwards. David scowled as he ditched the precious coffee down the sink. She wasted no time in getting the conference underway. They got a good satellite link. The Russians appeared on the screen and their CID chief Sergei greeted them in his broken English. He introduced them to his colleague. Dimitri. Ann returned the greeting and thanked Sergei for agreeing to help the British with their enquiries. Sergei had been sent all the information on the details of Saskia. Sergei reassured Ann that they had located the whereabouts of Saskia's parents. The two teams made final arrangements for Ann and David stay in Moscow. Sergei reassured Ann that he would meet them at the airport. Dimitri came to the rescue whenever Sergei struggled to explain.

The video conference lasted two hours. Edwards shuffled in his seat impatiently which was cue for Ann to end the conference. 'Well they seemed pretty efficient,' said Michael. 'I want to know what happens when we have spent all this money time and effort, and it comes to nothing,' said Edwards. 'It won't be a fruitless search. Saskia's brother was close to her and he will lead us to her when we tell him how important it is,' replied Ann. 'What if this whole bloody expensive trip is a total waste of time?' asked a pessimistic Edwards. 'It won't be a waste. We have done our homework. Give us some credit, Sir,' replied Ann indignantly. 'Anyway, The Russian guys sound very committed to helping us, guv,' said David. 'Yes, they are very enthusiastic, which is very much in our favour. We leave tomorrow. If there are no further questions, I would like to get on and prepare the paperwork for my trip please,' replied Ann.

'David, grab us some coffee. My withdrawal symptoms are bad. How the hell can Edwards deny us our sustenance?' exclaimed Ann. David rushed to the machine and came into Ann's office bearing the black gold she had become addicted to. They sat down at her desk while Ann began planning her strategy for their investigation in Moscow. It is going to be bloody cold when we get there. I hope you have warm clothes,' Ann warned. 'Yes guv, I will use my mountaineering underwear and a warm jacket,' he assured her. 'I don't know how organized their police force is but judging by the efficient way they traced Saskia's parents, I think we will work together very well,' she added. 'Dimitri seems to be on the ball and very keen. We need such enthusiasm,' said David. 'He reminds me of you; mouthy. Forward and a taste for the good life. I am not so sure you should meet him. You will come away being even worse than you are now,' said Ann, suppressing a smile. 'I must leave for home now as I have a couple of million things to do, David,' said Ann grabbing her coat and heading for the door. 'Come on David, join us for a brief dinner and then you can have an early night,' Ann said.

Chapter 7

Ann and David settled comfortably in their seats, as they prepared for their flight to Sheremetyevo airport. Just as the emerged into the arrivals lounge, Ann spotted two men holding up a board with her name on it. 'Look! David, there's Sergei and Dimitri, Let's wave in case they have not spotted us. The airport thronged with noisy travellers. Ann and David threaded their way to their hosts who smiled broadly as they approached. 'Ah, at last we meet in person,' said Dimitri as shook Ann's hand and drew her towards him, kissing her on both cheeks. Ann blushed at the gesture but composed herself and shook hands with Sergei who followed Dimitri's example. making her blush even more. David was amused at Ann's discomfort and couldn't resist saying, 'When in Rome, guv.' Dimitri's English was much better than Sergei's, who spoke with a heavy accent. Dimitri offered them coffee, but Ann declined, requesting to be taken to their hotel to freshen up before joining them at the police head office. The extreme cold of the Russian winter took their breath away as they emerged from the warmth of the airport building. 'Whatever you do, never take your gloves off outside. Wear your gloves when you hold or touch any object outside, even your phones, if you don't want to be permanently attached to them,' warned Dimitri. They diced with maniacal yellow taxi cab drivers who tore through the traffic, cursing and swearing and making obscene gestures at other drivers who dared to challenge them. They arranged with their hosts to collect them in an hour. The hotel rooms were clean, but rather basic, probably in the 3star rating. They got ready promptly and were back in the car heading for the police station. Dimitri ushered them to a large dimly lit room. They were introduced to the rest of the Russian criminal investigation team by Sergei who added that he had the best team in Russia. Dimitri smiled, and added that Sergei always thought he had the best of everything. Coffee was brought into the room and the team members took their seats. Sergei was the equivalent of a DCI and Dimitri of a

DS. David helped Ann to display pictures of the murder and a photo of Saskia. The team listened intently. Sergei paused, for a few minutes. A few of his officers asked questions which he interpreted for Ann, who answered. Ann emphasised that she thought the killings were linked to rituals of the occult which was the key to the murders and that Saskia probably held the clue to who may have been behind these murders. Sergei informed Ann that they had tracked Saskia's parents to a house near the forest. The meeting carried on for some time as the police got to grip with the essentials of the investigation. They poured over the gruesome photographs of the victims, making notes of the details of the investigation. Ann was in mid conversation with David when she overheard an officer making lewd remarks about her. She walked over to the officer and in fluent Russian rebuked him for his disrespectful comments. A deafening silence prevailed, and all eyes were fixed on her. Dimitri stepped forward and asked what had happened. Ann whispered in his ear. He stiffened with rage and lunged forward at the offending officer. An angry exchange of words followed, and the officer was forced to apologise to Ann. Dimitri apologised profusely for his colleague unforgiveable remarks and promised it would not happen again. Dimitri suggested they join him and Sergei for dinner.

Ann accepted, but requested they take her to the hotel first. 'Let's grab a drink before dinner,' Ann suggested to David as they walked into the hotel reception. 'You're a dark horse, guv, fancy being fluent in Russian,' said David. 'Oh. it isn't as fluent as I would like. I learned it when a Russian student boarded with us and then learned it properly when I was training for MI6. I haven't spoken it for years,' replied Ann. 'Was that idiot's comments very near the bone?' asked David. 'Let's say if you had heard what he said, you would have bitten off his ear,' replied Ann. 'Never mind, pass me my drink, I am parched,' she added. 'Do you think Saskia's parents will help us to find her, guv?' 'Don't know, they might refuse to cooperate if they think her life is in danger,' replied Ann. Dimitri and Sergei walked in through the swing doors of the hotel. Dimitri looked rather dashing in his dark blue suit. His tall, large frame filling every fold of his shirt as it defined his muscular torso. Sergei was less well dressed, having only changed his jacket. They were ushered into the car and were driven off. Dimitri continued to apologise for his colleague's inappropriate remarks. Ann reassured him she was made of sterner stuff and would not allow it to get her down. They drove along the Bulvar, the road around the Kremlin that had stretches of park between the lanes, benches and statues of famous writers and revolutionaries. The roads were grid locked with traffic. It required the skill of a racing driver to negotiate a path out of the choked roads. Sergei pointed out the places of interest and gave a brief history as we continued our stop start journey. Dimitri spotted a parking slot at the embankment along the river and raced towards it with the tenacity of a racing driver. The crooked outline of the rollercoasters of Gorky Park loomed across the dark water of the river as we emerged from the car. He suggested we walk the rest of the way to the restaurant.

The Bulvar was populated with loud teenagers, boozers and prostitutes. A noisy din emanated from the restaurant as we approached the floating restaurant. A band played Latin American music rather badly. They were intercepted by a waitress who motioned them to a table. Ann and David peered over the menus carefully as they did not want to choose an unpalatable item on the menu. Ann and David chose lamb. Dimitri and Sergei chose the sturgeon shaslik. The side orders were Azeri pancakes stuffed with cheese aubergine rolls filed with walnut stuffing served with pomegranate sauce. All of this was washed down with copious amounts of vodka. Their table was situated at a window, which afforded Ann the opportunity to see the imposing statue of Peter the Great beyond the bridge. Dimitri proposed a toast to the teams of the two countries, clinking their stumpy vodka glasses against David and Ann's. 'Nasdrovia,' said Sergei and was followed by a chorus from the other three. They discussed the highs and lows of their careers and poked fun at the bullying of their superiors. The evening passed pleasantly, and it afforded them all the opportunity to get to know one another a bit better. Ann announced that she was exhausted and in need of a goodnight's sleep. She woke up with a pounding headache as her body tried to flush out the excess of vodka. 'Never again!' she moaned to David as they met in the hotel lounge. He was also worse for wear and so were their hosts when they drove up to collect them. They were taken to Sergei's incident room where Ann and David met the rest of the CID team. They were briefed on the details of the case and were informed that they were in Moscow to locate and interview Saskia who had vital information linked to the murders. Ann suggested to Sergei to divide his team into units which worked more effectively to getting results. The meeting continued into the late afternoon. When they had finished, Sergei suggested they go to a different restaurant. Ann declines as she said she was still tired from the previous night and wanted to go to bed at a reasonable time. David agreed and they opted to eat at their hotel and meet with Dimitri and Sergei in the morning.

Sergei arrived in a heated car the next morning to collect them. It was a long drive to Saskia's parent's home. Happy banter accompanied them on the journey. Dimitri familiarised them with the odd customs of the Russian people. Sergei teased Dimitri for thinking he was more English than Russian. 'My English is perfect compared with Sergei,' Joked Dimitri. They arrived at midday. Sergei knocked on the door and was greeted by a grey, haired man who called himself Boris. He invited them in and introduced them to his wife, Tatiana. She appeared frightened and nervous at the sight of so many police officers. It helped to allay her fears when Ann also spoke to her in Russian. They were invited to sit down, and tea and coffee served. Sergei explained that the two police from the UK were in Moscow to speak to Saskia as she knew the people who were being investigated. Tatiana became very distressed at the mention of Saskia's name. Boris explained that Saskia had disobeyed her parents and instead of going to university, she went to London and has not been heard of since she left their home. Boris explained that he was working for the Russian space programme and was paid very well, so he could afford to educate his children and provide for them. He said they had a son, Yuri who is a scientist. He said Yuri still had contact with his sister. They gave Sergei Yuri's phone number. The meeting had continued into the early afternoon. Tatiana served a lunch of herring, gherkins, homemade bread, washed down with copious amounts of beer.

    Sated and happy that they had gained a contact number, they thanked Boris and Tatiana and left. They discussed how they would approach Yuri to gain his trust and his fullest co-operation on the journey. Ann declined dinner with Sergei, opting instead for her and David to eat alone in order to allow them time to review the details. Ann also wanted to update Edwards and Michael Heath on their progress. Dimitri managed to contact Yuri who reluctantly agreed to meet with the police. The meeting was arranged for that evening when Yuri had finished work. He lived in a salubrious part of Moscow. The interior of his apartment was very tastefully decorated. He lived alone. He was fluent in English and very pedantic in his approach. He asked many questions before answering any of theirs. He paused for a while before informing them that he had not spoken to Saskia for 5 years. He informed them that she was working at a brothel for a man named Oleg Berezofsky. He explained that Oleg was also a trafficker of young girls to wealthy business men. He had a respectable club in Moscow where he lured the girls to dance, then they disappeared. The police were on his payroll, so he never gets caught. Sergei shuffled uncomfortably when he heard that the police were involved in such nefarious practices. Yuri said that he knew Saskia had two good people who she could trust at the club. A girl called Masha and a man called Vladimir. He said he did not have their contact numbers, but if the police went to the club as clients, they may find these people there. Sergei explained that Yuri would need to accompany them there as he could identify them. He reluctantly agreed after some persuasion from Ann. They thanked Yuri and agreed to meet with him at the club at the weekend. It was decided that David would go with Dimitri and Yuri. They arrived at the club at around 9pm. It was crowded with some very sleazy characters, who were drinking lavish amounts of vodka and champagne. The girls working at the club were scantily dressed tantalising the men with their curvaceous bodies and enticing them to spend lavishly.

They were herded into a dimly lit corner and two women began flirting with them. A large bottle of champagne was placed in an ice bucket on their table. One of the girls sat on David's lap and began kissing him. He played along, much to Dimitri's amusement at his discomfort at the unwanted attention. Yuri asked the girl if she knew Saskia. She replied that Saskia had left and no longer worked there. He then asked if Vladimir still worked for the club. The girl became very nervous and told him she was not allowed to give information about the staff. Yuri lied to her telling her that Vladimir owed him a favour and handed her a wad of notes to induce her to tell them what they needed to know. She hesitated and looked around nervously, telling them that they could wait at the backdoor when Vladimir went off duty at midnight. She then got up quickly and went to another table. They stayed until just before 12, then left and headed for the back door. They waited patiently, then just as they wanted to give up, a tall, thin man emerged from the building. He got into his car and drove off. The men followed at a discreet distance and followed him to his home. David advised them not to speak to Vladimir immediately, but to meet with Ann the next morning and discuss the strategy they needed to employ. Ann waited for David to get home as she was eager to hear how they had got along. She was pleased that David had exercised caution about approaching Vladimir. The team met the next morning at the incident room. It was decided that as Yuri was known to Vladimir, he should approach him about Saskia's whereabouts. They asked Yuri who was most reluctant as he said it would place him in danger. Ann's persistence was rewarded, and he finally agreed. The team parked their car some discreet distance from Vladimir's home. When he emerged to get into his car, Yuri stopped him and asked if he could spare 5 minutes to talk. Vladimir was furious. 'Do you think I am Saskia's keeper?' He retorted angrily. Saskia has gone away. She no longer works for Oleg", he continued. Yuri knew he was lying, because he had never reacted so defensively. He pushed past Yuri, got into his car and sped off. The team met with Ann at lunchtime. Dimitri suggested that they deal with Vladimir Russian style. He suggested that they kidnap Vladimir's wife and children and force him to tell them where Saskia is being held. Ann opposed the idea saying she would not be part of thuggery. 'Ann with respect, sometimes it calls for drastic measures if you want a result", replied Dimitri. 'We will ensure the wife and children do not get hurt,' he assured her. She looked at David for support and asked what he thought. 'It is your call, guv. Sounds plausible to me if we need the information and they guarantee the family's safety,' he continued. 'Yes, and when it goes wrong and the shit hits the fan, it is my neck on the line,' said Ann. 'It is how you say, killing two birds with many stones", replied Sergei. 'Kill two birds with one stone, you idiot. I told you he can't speak English,' said Dimitri. Ann finally agreed reluctantly. They agreed not to share the kidnapping with the rest of the CID team in case there was a mole in the police.

Dimitri and Sergei chose a disused building normally kept as a safe house. The kidnapping was scheduled for the next evening. They had already removed Vladimir's wife and three children from the home when he got home that evening. The police took him at gunpoint. He swore and cursed all the way to the safe house. They took him into a separate room, next to the one where his wife was held. They had a recording of his family's distress. He did not know they were the police, which intensified his fear. They told him that Oleg had taken Saskia from her family who had hired them to find her even if it meant killing him and his whole family. They began beating him to prove that they meant business. He denied all knowledge of

Saskia, but when the screams of his children became intolerable, he agreed to give them information. He told them that Saskia was Oleg's mistress and lived with him. He said that Oleg operated his human trafficking from a disused factory which he had renovated to suit his needs. He also said that Oleg had a helicopter which was kept on the roof of his building. He showed them on map where the factory was located. He also knew how many armed guards were in the building and the drew a map of the layout of the building. He said that the only way into the building would be if they posed as clients interested in buying the girls who were on offer. He said that the girls were sold for up to a million pounds.

The interrogation went on for hours. Dimitri looked triumphant as they emerged from the building. 'Sadistic bastard. I hope you are not proud of your despicable behaviour,' said David. 'You English are too soft. You should have been in the Russian army. It would toughen you up", replied Dimitri. 'Who cares, we got our information,' said Sergei. David returned to the hotel where an anxious Ann waited. 'Got our information, guv, but it was pretty tough for Vladimir,' he added. 'Oh God did they harm the children,' she asked anxiously. 'No, they just frightened the children and their screams got him talking,' he replied. 'I wish this was over, can't stand the tension,' she said.' Come on let's get some coffee sent to the room. I want to phone Josie and Adam. 'Someone must be missing me. What's with the early call?' said the voice on the other end of the line. 'I do miss you so much, and I wish I was home already,' said Ann. 'We miss you too, even the baby. He just kicked when I mentioned your name,' said Josie. Adam interrupted. 'Hi Sis, are they treating you well over there. When are you going to be back?' We miss you,' he added enthusiastically. 'We are going to be awhile yet. You just take good care of my family,' she added. 'How is David?' asked Adam. 'He is working really hard,' she replied. 'Tell him to take care of you,' said Adam. 'Will do. Speak soon. Love you, lots,' said Ann. They met with the CID team the next morning. They did not reveal how they got their information but told the team that they knew where Saskia was being held. Ann spoke first. She told them that David would pose as a client to buy the girls. Dimitri would act as his bodyguard. The team agreed. Sergei proposed that they would access the building via an access hatch which was outside of the protective fencing of the building. The access hatch was in a disused area frequented by tramps. The hatch had a lock and chain on it and was left unguarded as Oleg probably thought it posed no risk as only tramps frequented the area. David has ten seconds to get from the outer door to the inner door before it shuts. We have no code to open the inner door,' said Ann. 'Who supplies funds for the girls?' asked Ann. 'No problem,' interrupted Dimitri. 'We have a Krishka. In Russia everyone needs a Krishka to take care of them. It is like a fixer who protects and provides when necessary. Our Krishka is an oligarch who will give us the money. He has an old score to settle with Oleg. Money no problem,' said Dimitri. 'Thank God for that. Can you imagine what Edwards would have said if we asked for that kind of money?' said Ann. 'I can imagine his words would have been choice to say the least,' replied David. 'I will get David fitted with a designer suit,' said Dimitri. "By the way, has anyone got a message to Oleg informing him Vladimir he will be away for a few days?' asked Ann. 'Yes, we got him to phone Oleg and tell him he was away as his mother is ill. Oleg accepted without question,' replied Dimitri. 'Ok, we will schedule the assault for when the next sale of the girls take place. Our computer geek has hacked into his secure site and has secured David a bidding slot as Alfred Gray,' said Dimitri. They poured over the arrangements for hours trying to anticipate and deal with potential problems. 'This is the final blue print for our plan.' David and Dimitri will enter the building with all the legal papers as potential clients. According to Vladimir, David will be shown to the viewing room where he will remain for an hour, choosing a girl. When he has made his choice, he will be shown to another part of the building where he will be given his phone and access to his laptop to transfer the payment for the girl into an off shore account. When he has done this, he will send a text message to Ann and Sergei giving them their cue to attack. I will have joined David by this time, so he needs to send a coded message on his radio in case the phones are not working. David then announces that he needs to use the toilet which is the corridor opposite to the security access for the door to Oleg's apartment. Vladimir has given us the access code for the first door. The inner door will open but closes in ten seconds when you have passed through the outer door. David will have to run like hell to get inside the apartment, as we don't have the code for the inner door. David will need to wait until the guard at the door does his half hourly checks of the lower end of the corridor to get through the outer door. Sergei, you and your men will enter the tunnel via the disused car park.

It is a 10foot drop so you will need ropes and fluorescent sticks to light up the tunnel. Prepare yourselves for fierce resistance.' warned Dimitri. Everyone nodded their approval of the plan. 'Please do say if there is anything you are not happy about or concerned about,' said Ann. Sergei then addressed his officers. 'All your phones will be confiscated for the next 3 days, except Ann's, David's, Dimitri and mine. Our officers will stay at a safe house and won't be allowed out in case we have a traitor amongst them,' continued Sergei. 'On the day at 7pm, Ann will travel with her team, posing as the food delivery guys. She will hijack the real delivery men and tie them up in the back of the van. She will wait for David's signal, and alert Sergei that she has started the assault on the entrance to the building. This should coincide with the time that David reaches Oleg's private suite,' explained Dimitri. 'I will have to go in disguise as some of the guards are ex-soldiers and may recognise me,' said Dimitri. 'Sergei has arranged for a makeup artist to disguise my face,' said Dimitri. 'Ok lads that about sums up everything. We had better get home as there is a great deal to do,' said Ann heading for the exit. David followed her and hailed a taxi as they got to the street.

'Rather exciting, wouldn't you say, guv?' said David. 'Yes, and bloody dangerous too. Some of us might be killed,' replied Ann. David was taken to the tailor for his suit and Dimitri went off with the makeup artist. The rest of the team checked their guns to ensure it was in good working order. Ann rechecked the schedule and ensured that everyone was familiar with the plan and timing.

The completed suit was delivered on the morning of their departure. It was decided that Ann would go with the team in the food van and Sergei would accompany the team to the access hatch at the tunnel. David sauntered up to Ann wearing his chic grey designer suit with a royal blue shirt and gold tie. He looked very dapper. Ann gazed at him for a while surprised that she never noticed how handsome he looked as his muscular torso accentuated the lines of his immaculate suit and his groomed dark hair added the finishing touches. She sauntered up to him and adjusted his tie. 'Hmm looking very handsome Sergeant Hughes. You had better not get used to this life. Remember it is only pretend,' said Ann smiling at his discomfort. Dimitri joined them, looking mean and rugged. The makeup artist had done a great job with his disguise. 'It's so bloody good, I am sure your mother would not recognise you,' said David. 'You look damned good too,' replied Dimitri. 'Ok, we need to get going as we need to be there at six. Ann waved them off as they drove off in the smart black Bentley.

    She phoned Josie and Adam to reassure them she was okay, before starting her preparations for the assault. She phoned Sergei to check that his men were ready. Satisfied that the plan was ready to be mobilised, she took a taxi to her rendezvous with her unit. Checking the map with the driver, they set off on their journey. They waited in a siding for the food van, which was scheduled for around 6.30. It would take them thirty minutes to get to the factory. Their assault would be synchronised so that they got to the gate of the compound as simultaneously as Sergei's task force entered the tunnel via the disused car park. Ann organised the road block minutes before they spotted the vehicle entering the road they patrolled. The van stopped at the road block. Ann, dressed in army uniform instructed the driver to get out of the van, explaining in fluent Russian that they were authorised to check all vans for a fugitive on the run. The driver and his companion got out of the van. They were despatched swiftly by one of the police officers. The police officers got into the van and crouched out of sight on the seats. Ann and the Russian sergeant sat in the front seat. The sergeant took the steering wheel. They synchronised their watches, sent a message to Sergei informing them they were on their way to the compound. He acknowledged their message. Meanwhile David had already arrived at the compound, alighting from the Bentley. Dimitri followed him into the building. He was apprehended at the entrance and asked for his papers.

    A man dressed in a smart silk suit read through the papers and waved David into a hallway. A guard blocked Dimitri's entry and asked why he was with David. Dimitri explained he was David's bodyguard. The man in the suit motioned for Dimitri to follow David after checking Dimitri's credentials. They took David's laptop for safekeeping and told him he was only allowed the use of his laptop to transfer the money if he chose to purchase a girl. David nodded and followed the man who led him to a kiosk. Dimitri was told to stay outside the kiosk. There cubicle has a window which looked out onto a centre stage. David sat silently going over the strategy of his role in his head. A bell sounded and 10 beautiful young women stepped onto a carousal in the centre of the stage. The carousal had vertical poles along the whole of its circumference. The girls wore no clothing except diaphanous gowns. Another bell rang and the girls grabbed a hold of the poles on the carousal and began a ritual of dancing. Their acrobatic dancing was designed to show off the most intimate details of their bodies to titivate their potential buyers. Vladimir told them if chosen, the women would be considered for role in films in Hollywood and for modelling. David watched for an hour, then pressed his buzzer indicating that he had made his choice. A man appeared at the door of his cubicle and escorted him to another room, where he was met by a smiling official, who assured him that he had made a good choice. He was handed his laptop and began the process of transferring the £300000 into the Oleg's account. When he had finished, he asked to be shown the way to the toilet. He was pointed in the right direction and walked slowly observing the guard who sat guarding the entrance to Oleg's private quarters. David went into the toilet and held the door ajar to watch the guard when he went to do his routine checks along the corridor. David rushed to the door, punched in the code and observed the inner door opening. He raced to get through it in the ten second time span.

    The suite seemed empty but as he approached the living room, a young woman was sitting in a chair. She gasped at seeing David and was about to scream when he lunged forward and covered her mouth with his hand. She tried to struggle free. He spoke to her in a low voice telling her he was sent by Yuri. The mention of his name seemed to calm her, and she went silent. David had his back to the door. He did not see the massive figure that crashed into him. He only felt himself being catapulted across the room with incredible force. He picked himself off the floor and came face to face with a monster of a man. The bodyguard had found him. The giant figure lumbered towards him and lifted him into the air like a rag doll. He was thrown across the room and smashed into a large mirror which shattered on impact. He picked himself up quickly and using his body like a missile lunged at the man, but instead of pushing his attacker off his feet, he bounced off like a rubber ball. David grabbed any heavy missile he could find and threw it at the guard. His kicks and punches made no impact, and this invincible creature continued his relentless assault. David jumped on his assailants back sank his teeth into the big man's ear. His attacker groaned in pain but kept punching David. The guard held David in a headlock and began tightening his chokehold. David knew he had very little time before he would pass out. In one last desperate effort, he grabbed hold of a shard of the broken mirror on the floor and plunged it into his attacker's neck. A fountain of blood spurted out from the hole the glass had made and after a few seconds, the guard slumped to the floor, dead. The girl had been cowering in a corner during the fight.

A man rushed into the room and called the girl Saskia. He spotted David still lying on the floor. He shot at David, grabbed the girl by the hand and rushed out towards the escape tunnel. David was bleeding profusely from a wound in his chest. Just as he despaired that there was no backup Dimitri entered the room.

Where the hell have you been?' David demanded to know. Dimitri walked over to the dead guard and let out a whistle. 'Bloody hell you did not need my help, you killed the giant on your own,' he exclaimed with some amusement. I will get you for that, you bastard. I am dying here, and you have time to joke,' croaked David coughing up blood. 'No time to waste, I think Oleg has taken Saskia and are headed for the helicopter. We must stop them,' David urged. Dimitri helped David to his feet, and they hobbled along the corridor towards the helipad. They heard gunfire behind them as they headed for the helipad. The wind generated by the helicopter engines nearly knocked them off their feet, Dimitri and David ran towards the helicopter which was trying to take off and grabbed hold of the feet- clinging on desperately as the machine hovered over the helipad.

The occupants in the helicopter began shooting at the men clinging to the feet of the helicopter. Dimitri returned fire and began firing at the blades of the helicopter. Just when it seemed they were losing the battle, Sergei, Ann and the other officers appeared. They managed to abort the take off. The pilot and Oleg were handcuffed and led away. 'Why the hell did you take so long?' David demanded to know. 'We had heavy opposition in the tunnel,' explained Sergei. 'We also had one hell of a fight with the guards at the front of the building. Not exactly a walk in the park. If you were not wounded, I have a good mind to give you a clip around the ear,' Ann scolded. 'Come on, we had better get David to the hospital. How many dead amongst out chaps,' asked Ann. Five, I think,' replied Sergei. 'Pity, there should have been none,' added Ann. 'Too bad, that is how it is,' Dimitri explained. 'Our timing was perfect. We ambushed the van, got through the gate and surprised them. We must have killed 20 of the guards. The other captured guards were placed in handcuffs and put in police vans. Ann accompanied Saskia to a safe house. David was sent to hospital. He had been shot in the right lung Ann's fluent Russian helped to gain Saskia's confidence. A police woman was left to stay with Saskia. Ann wanted to ensure that she had got over the shock of the events of the day before questioning her. Ann declined Sergei's offer of copious amounts of vodka, in favour of a shower and a comfortable bed. Ann phoned Michael Heath to inform him that she had managed to find Saskia. 'Bloody good job. I hope Hughes did his bit,' Said Michael. 'He was a hero, sir. He got pretty badly injured and is in hospital. We lost five officers,' said Ann. 'Rotten luck, poor sods,' replied Michael. 'When will you be back?' asked Michael. 'Another couple of days. Probably just as soon as David is well enough to travel,' said Ann. 'I need you to furnish us with papers to enter the UK, Sir,' Ann urged. 'Ok, that will not be a problem. I will get it couriered to our embassy in Moscow and you can collect it there,' replied Michael. 'Ok will do. I will keep you posted if there are any changes,' said Ann. 'You have a good night. You deserve it,' said Michael. Ann and Dimitri went to check on David the next morning. He complained of a great deal of pain. 'Feels like I have been in a cement mixer. A few broken ribs and lots of tissue damage. 'Don't worry you won't die, you killed Goliath, just like in the good book,' said Dimitri grinning at David. 'You bastard, you were supposed to be my bodyguard, but arrived after the fight,' replied David. 'When will you be out?' asked Ann. 'They said I would be in here for a week,' replied David. 'I will use the time to interview Saskia and visit you each day to keep you posted. I have reported to Michael who sends his best wishes,' said Ann. 'We can start the interview with Saskia this afternoon,' said Dimitri. 'Does Sergei want to be present?' asked Ann. 'No, he is recovering from a hangover, and won't be at work till tomorrow,' replied Dimitri. 'Come on Ann let me take you to lunch. We can then meet with Saskia,' he added.

They mulled over the details of the interview during lunch. They informed Yuri that they had found and rescued his sister. He was elated and wanted to see her urgently. Ann informed him that they might ask for him to be present as Saskia might be more willing to talk if her brother was in the room. Saskia looked frail and anxious when they entered the room. Ann reassured her in Russian and said she would only proceed with the interview if she felt well enough to do so. She objected to Dimitri being present. Ann explained that it was imperative that Dimitri remained in the room. She reluctantly agreed. Ann informed Saskia that the information they needed was nothing to do with her time spent with Oleg. They needed to know about her time in England.

She became very distressed and refused to answer Ann's questions. Saskia told Ann that she would only talk if her brother was present. Ann motioned Dimitri to follow her as she exited the room. 'We will have to get Yuri to be present when we talk to her. Can you phone him and ask if he is free to join us tomorrow,' said Ann. Dimitri nodded in agreement and left. Sergei contacted Ann, asked her to join him for a working dinner. She reluctantly agreed not wishing to be part of his lengthy drinking episodes. He chose a relatively quiet place. She was glad that Dimitri had been invited too. She informed Sergei that they would interview Saskia when her brother could be present. He appeared irritated at the delay and asked when her brother would be available. Dimitri interrupted, informing them that Yuri had agreed to be present the following afternoon. Ann asked if they had released Vladimir and reunited him with his family. Sergei told her that it had been done and they had moved the family to a safe house outside of Moscow. They would give Vladimir a new identity and move him to a place in Switzerland. He has agreed to testify against Oleg who would be charged with human trafficking, drug dealing and murder. Ann said that if Saskia agreed to testify against the Casey brothers, she would be flown to England and resettled somewhere of her choosing in Europe. Ann curtailed her stay soon after dinner explaining that she needed to see David. Dimitri accompanied her to the hospital. They found him sitting out of bed. 'Hmmm you seem to be recovering in leaps and bounds Sergeant Hughes,' said Ann. 'Yes, if only I felt as good as I appear to look. Everything hurts like bloody hell,' he replied. 'How did you get on with the interview?' asked David. 'She is too traumatized to talk. She wants her brother to be present. He has agreed to be there tomorrow,' said Ann. 'Should be interesting to hear her side of the story,' said David. 'Yes, I am sure her version will be quite a story. You must be very bored in here,' she added. 'No, actually Josie and Adam call regularly. Josie is very excited about the baby, and Adam is also over the moon,' said David. 'Yes, they carry on like a couple of teenagers. Sometimes I wonder if they should spend so much time together,' added Ann. 'Well we had better let you get some sleep. See you tomorrow to brief you on the interview,' said Ann.

Ann updated Edwards on their progress. He told her that preparations had been made for Saskia to be brought to London and that Ann could collect the papers from the Embassy in Moscow. She phoned Josie. 'A little bird told me you have been phoning Moscow everyday but strangely I didn't get a single call",' said Ann. 'Oh methinks the lady is a trifle jealous,' replied Josie. 'You should let David recover, not bombard him with millions of calls, and that goes for your side kick too,' replied Ann. 'Oops who rattled your cage?' You should not be causing anxiety to a woman in the late stages of her pregnancy, Inspector,' said Josie. 'Just you wait until I get home, I will deal with you, regardless of your condition,' said Ann. 'Promises, promises,' replied Josie, chuckling at Ann's frustration. 'Joking aside, when are you coming home?' asked Josie. 'I think by the middle of next week, if David is fit to travel,' replied Ann. 'Goodnight, dream of me, love you,' said Josie. 'Love you too, kiss the baby for me,' replied Ann. She lay awake for a long time after the call, thinking of her new role as a parent with some trepidation. She was in the middle of brunch the next morning when Dimitri came to collect her. 'Sorry I am so late. I fell asleep in the early hours of the morning, so woke up very late,' said Ann. 'Don't worry, I will have some coffee while you finish your meal,' said Dimitri. 'Yuri will be with us at 2pm,' said Dimitri. 'We set up the tape in Saskia's room. It will be better if I go in with Yuri. You will be able to listen to our interview in the next room,' said Ann. 'Yes, that will be a better option for Saskia. She will be more at ease,' replied Dimitri. They finished their leisurely brunch and made their way to meet with Yuri. They took Yuri to Saskia and left them alone for some time. When he indicated it alright for Ann to join them, she did so. Saskia had been crying and Yuri was also tearful. Ann chose her moment to begin her questioning. She began by telling Saskia that George and Tom Casey were murdered. She explained that she needed to know if there were other men who joined their parties at the house and whether Saskia knew any of them. She hesitated for a long time before answering. She told Ann that she met George Casey at a local pub. He invited her to his home where she was introduced to his brothers Tom, Jake and Nathan.

    During her association with the brothers, she was thrown out of her accommodation as she was not able to pay. George offered her a room at his family home. She offered to clean the house and do the shopping to earn her keep. This worked okay for a short while, then one night, Tom seduced her. The brothers had parties at their home to which they invited many foreign girls. The parties would go on till the early hours of the morning where they had sexual orgies with the girls, including her. She became pregnant and was very worried as she had no job to support a baby. She was approached by their cousin, James Muller who said if she was prepared to abort her baby to help medical science. She would be paid for her help. She readily agreed as she thought it would help her out of her dilemma and she was doing something good for medicine. The baby was aborted at 24 weeks and taken away. They continued to have sex with her, and she fell pregnant again six months later. The same offer was made to her and the baby taken away. Her cousin, Olga who had come to England found herself in financial difficulties. She sought help from Saskia, who asked the brothers if Olga could stay at their home. They agreed, but soon they were having sex with Olga and got her pregnant. They aborted her baby and took it away. This happened four more times. One day, Saskia heard Olga having a heated argument with James about the abortions. Olga told him she was not going to have another abortion and threatened to tell the police. James grabbed Olga by her hair and warned her that if she went near the police, he would kill her. The same night, Saskia found a tunnel leading from the house to the forest. She followed the brothers who were wearing black hooded cloaks. They gathered around a tree trunk in the forest and placed Olga's body on the tree trunk. Olga seemed drugged as she lay very still. Another hooded figure in red appeared and all the others called him Master and chanted as he approached. The master got on top of Olga and began having sex with her. When he had finished, he plunged a dagger into her chest and cut her throat. He collected her blood in a cup, drank it and passed the cup around to the other figures. They cheered and gave thanks to Satan. Saskia began to cry as she recalled this event. She was shaking and asked to be allowed to stop. They gave her a break for an hour before asking to resume the interview. 'Did you see what he did with Olga's body?' Ann asked. 'No! I had to hide before they spotted me,' said Saskia. 'I waited until they had all gone out the next day, then I took some money belonging to George Casey and bought a ticket back to Moscow. She told Ann that there were some Irish girls who were made pregnant and their babies taken away. Ann asked if all the brothers were present at this meeting in the forest. She said that Nathan never got involved in any of the sexual acts or the meeting that night. She said that she saw Tom, George,

Jake and James dress in the black cloaks. She did not know the identity of the master. Ann enquired if there were any other names, she could recall. She replied that the brothers did not allow any other men to join their circle of debauchery. Yuri asked for the questioning to stop as he said his sister was very distraught. Ann agreed and apologised for putting Saskia through such a rigorous interview. She assured him that she would ensure Saskia's safety. He thanked her for all she had done to rescue his sister and left. Dimitri just shook his head at what he had heard when Ann joined him in the next room. 'Shit I thought the Russians were sadistic bastards, but the English are not far behind,' he said. 'If she agrees to testify, I am going to nail that bastard, James Muller's arse,' said Ann. 'Problem is we have to find him first,' she added. 'Come on let's go tell David,' she said. "Well, guv, did she spill the beans?' asked David. 'Yes, every detail,' replied Ann. "James Muller, top of the hit parade,' she added.

'Have you told Edwards yet,' asked David. 'No, I am going to phone him when I get back to the hotel", she replied. 'You hurry up and get better, we have a great deal of work to do,' she said. She phoned Edwards as soon as she got back to the hotel. He sounded relived that her witness gave her the information she needed but did not compliment her on her achievement. Michael Heath was chuffed about Ann's success and showered her with compliments. Dimitri stayed with David after Ann had left.

'Your boss is quite some woman. She is as tough as the best of my Russian guys. She is good looking and has a great body. How do you keep your mind on your work?' said Dimitri. 'She is great to work with and I suppose her conduct demands respect and co-operation of her team. A guy doesn't dare think of anything else,' replied David. 'Oh, come on, you are a man first. You can't say you have not noticed her great legs and her lovely arse,' said Dimitri. 'Hey stop right there. Ann is married to a lovely lady and they are expecting a baby. If you let her know I told you about this, I will kill you with my bare hands,' David warned him. 'Wow, really, what a shame. Doesn't she like guys at all?' asked Dimitri. "No and don't go stirring up trouble by assuming anything,' said David. 'Enough about Ann, let's talk about something that will be of greater interest to you,' said David. 'Ann wants you to travel with us because I am not fully recovered, and Saskia will need protection. I want you to meet Ann's brother, Adam. He is a journalist with a great deal of experience in capturing fugitives. He has international links with important people. When Ann and I go in search of James Muller in Brazil, Adam will be joining us, but Ann does not know about this. I will ask Adam if you can be included in our team as we will need your army skills. You must remember not to speak about any of this in Ann's presence. I will find time when you are in London to get Adam to speak to you in private,' said David. Speak to Sergei and warn him that Ann wants you to accompany us to London,' continued David. 'Sergei won't mind if I go. I have some leave owed to me, so he won't need to find the money for my ticket. I was saving to go to Italy for my leave, but I will go to London instead,' said Dimitri. 'Ok, not a word to Ann, until I have spoken to her,' said David. Ann made the final arrangements for their return to London. She spoke at great length with the doctor who had been caring for David and was assured that he would be fit to travel. David persuaded Ann to have Dimitri accompany them to London.

She reluctantly agreed, telling David she was sure that he had conspired with Dimitri to accompany them. Ann arranged with Michael to organise a safe house for Saskia and accommodation for Dimitri. She thanked Sergei for all his help and support and took her leave. They arrived at a rain swept London. Michael and Edwards met them at the airport. They took Saskia to the safe house. The female Russian policewoman who spent time with her, was allowed to stay with her. Ann, David and Dimitri were driven to her home. Josie beamed at the door when she saw Ann. She hugged and kissed Ann, while David and Dimitri looked on. Adam appeared a few minutes later. Ann made the introductions and invited Dimitri to make himself at home. 'Wow sis, it is so good to have you home. 'You have managed to steal the best officer in the Russian police, I see,' he added. 'You must forgive my sister, Dimitri, she often takes things that doesn't belong to her. She can't help it really,' said Adam grinning mischievously. 'You are going to get a thick ear in a minute,' said Ann, smacking him on the head. Dimitri and David laughed. 'You must be starved. Come along, sit down, I have cooked dinner,' said Josie, ushering them to the table. She grabbed Ann by the hand and led her to the kitchen. 'Oh, my darling, I missed you so much,' she said as she embraced Ann. Ann surprised her by not pulling away as she usually did but held her too and told her how much she was missed. She guided Ann's hand to her stomach, and said, 'feel baby's kicking. Ann felt the baby move and smiled. There is only a month to go,' said Josie. Ann kissed her again. 'Does anyone out there, care about the starving dregs out here,' shouted Adam. Ann gritted her teeth. 'I am going to crown that brother of mine before the end of the night,' said Ann. 'Perhaps if the fellow with the big mouth volunteered to help serve the dinner, he might not starve,' Ann shouted back. Adam rushed to the kitchen to help them carry the food to the table. David served the wine.

  The evening passed pleasantly. Dimitri was taken to a bed and breakfast near Ann's home. Adam offered to take David home. During the journey, David updated Adam on his conversation with Dimitri. They agreed to set up a meeting with Dimitri. David informed him that he was still recovering, so was not expected to be at work for another week. Josie noticed the bruises on Ann's body as she came out of the shower. 'Oh God look what they have done to your body, exclaimed a horrified Josie. Ann grabbed a towel to hide the bruises. 'It's nothing, just a few bruises,' exclaimed Ann. She was riddled with guilt but grateful that the trip to Moscow had given her an alibi. They talked about the imminent birth until the early hours of the morning. Ann drove to work. She missed David's promptness in the morning. Her office seemed cold and empty. Her in tray was stacked high with mail. She leaned back in her chair and savoured the cup of coffee brought to her by one of her junior staff. She was jolted out of her daydream by the ringing of her phone. 'Hi Ann, have you landed at your office yet?' said Michael. 'Yes, I am at my office, but haven't found my bearings yet,' she replied. 'Ok, can we meet with Stephen this afternoon. He is rather keen to hear the tape,' said Michael. 'Where are we meeting?' she asked. 'My office is more private. Say around 2.30?' he added. 'See you then, sir,' she replied. Michael arranged for lunch to be brought to his office for their meeting. Ann played the recording with Saskia. The two men listened in amazement at the revelations on the tape. Michael praised Ann for her diligent work and success at rescuing Saskia. She paid tribute to the Russian police and expressed regret at the loss of life. Edwards was quick to condemn her for the loss of life. She replied by explaining that the rescue occurred in exceptional circumstances. 'What happens next?' asked Edwards. 'Well, we need to have another search of the Casey property in Nottingham. We need to find the link to the forest and get SOCO to examine the garden and the basement again. If they were killing babies, there must be human remains on the property,' said Ann. 'I will get my team to hear the tape and we will plan our next move from there. 'Can you both be available at the incident room tomorrow morning, at 8.00 please,' she said. They agreed and she left Meanwhile, Adam, David and Dimitri met at David's flat. David supplied the beers while they chatted. Adam filled Dimitri in on their plan and asked him to add his thoughts to the plan. 'How much does Ann know about your involvement, Adam?' asked Dimitri. 'Oh shit, nothing, she will do her nut if she finds out I am involved. She will demand that I am pulled out,' he added. 'I will arrange a meeting with our MI6 man and work out a plan including you, Dimitri. Your military background will be a bonus to our mission. 'Would Sergei agree to your involvement in this, and who would pay for your airfare etc?' asked Adam. 'You forget I have a Krishka who will fund me, and I will use my leave to stop questions being asked by powers above Sergei,' replied Dimitri. 'We need to have your total commitment because it is going to be a massive project especially as Mossad is involved. They will insist on the greatest commitment and attention to detail because they want their man, so no mistakes. I want to organize a meeting with us, MI6 and Rachel, our Mossad link while you are here,' said Adam. Dimitri nodded in agreement. 'David, you will need to dream up a plausible excuse to get away from Ann for a few days. Be bloody convincing so that Ann does not rumble you,' added Adam. Dimitri smiled.

'Your sister is an incredible woman. I wish she did not have someone in her life. Perhaps I could have changed her mind", said Dimitri. 'Yeah, dream on, I think chances of that happening is pretty impossible. My sister knows exactly what she wants, and she is stone in love with Josie. Wild horses would not be able to drive her away from her commitment to the relationship, especially with a baby on the way,' added Adam. 'Well we had better leave now to get home well before her ladyship gets home, to avoid a thousand questions. Josie is preparing dinner,' said Adam. 'Give me some time to shower and change, then I will join you,' said David. 'Okay, we will wait in the car, hurry,' replied Adam. 'What have you boys been up to all day?' asked Josie. 'Just driving around. We showed Dimitri some of the sights and then stopped off for a pub lunch,' replied Adam. 'Come on make yourselves useful, set the table please. Ann will be here in half an hour,' said Josie. 'David, you can serve the drinks while we are waiting,' said Josie. Ann arrived carrying a stack of files. Adam took them from her then kissed her on the cheek. 'Good day at the office, sis?' he asked. 'Frantically busy. I missed David. I want you to come to the meeting of the team tomorrow, David,' she added. 'There will be no talk about work until after dinner, madam Ann,' said Josie embracing her. 'Okay, I surrender, take me to the dinner table, I am starving", said Ann.
'So how did you spend today?' Ann asked Dimitri. 'I had a very interesting day. The boys showed me around,' he replied. 'Good,

you are welcome to join us at the CID meeting tomorrow. We will discuss our time in Moscow and reveal the contents on the tapes,' said Ann. 'I will look forward to meeting your team,' replied Dimitri. 'No dessert for those who discuss work at my dinner table. Is that clear children,' scolded Josie. 'Sorry, darling, I just wanted to catch Dimitri before he was whisked off by Adam,' replied Ann.

'Good morning team. I would like to introduce you to Detective sergeant Dimitri Zhukov. He played a significant role in the rescue of our witness Saskia in Moscow,' said Ann. Dimitri stood up in acknowledgement of Ann's introduction. 'I am going to play the relevant parts of the recording of my interview with Saskia. This young woman is very nervous and afraid. She will remain at the safe house with a Russian female member of their CID team. The man who was her lover and kept her a virtual prisoner was arrested. Sadly 5 of their squad members died in the rescue of Saskia. I have passed our condolences and gratitude to their families. The whole recording is too long, but you will gather enough information from the parts I am playing,' said Ann. 'The team listened in silence and only voiced their opinions when the parts about sacrificing the foetuses were revealed. Ann called them to order, appealing for patience. When the tape had finished, some members of the team flung a barrage of questions at Ann. 'What's the next step, guv?' asked DI Tobin. 'Well we need to visit the Casey's family home. I am sure there are remains of the babies under the floor boards or in the grounds. They must have buried them somewhere. I will speak to the CID squad at Sherwood Forest. I will also meet with the forensic archaeologist. The murderer of the babies is James Muller, according to Saskia. He may also have murdered her cousin, Olga. Whatever the search uncovers in Nottingham will point us in the next direction. A trip to Brazil is on the cards, as we have no guarantee that Muller will return to the UK,' said Ann. 'By the way, has Jake Casey woken up yet?' Asked Ann. 'No guv, he is stable, but still unconscious,' replied Tobin. Ann walked back to her office with

Dimitri and David. Ann collected coffee from the machine for all of them and invited Dimitri to join them in the office. 'Your team are very enthusiastic,' said Dimitri. 'I am glad about that they are eager to solve the case. We have been criticised severely by the press on our delay in solving the case. I am glad we found Saskia. I am sure we will find many clues in Nottingham. I am sorry you will not be here when the search takes place,' said Ann. 'Oh, but I will be here for two weeks. Perhaps I go with you,' he replied. 'What about you, David, will you be well enough to go to Nottingham?' asked Ann. 'I have another week of sick leave, guv,' he replied. 'Damn, what a bind, I could have done with you", she replied. 'Actually guv, Dimitri would be a good replacement,' said David. 'Don't shirk your responsibilities Hughes. I said all that play acting in an Amani suit would go to your head,' said Ann smiling at his discomfort. 'Let's do some work. Get me the forensic archaeologist on the phone. Let's arrange a meeting. Also need to speak to the Nottingham squad,' she added. She managed to arrange a meeting with the forensic archaeologist in two days. The Nottingham Forest DCI said he would organise a SOCO team to meet with Ann at the house in three days.

'Pain or no pain, I want you at my meeting with the archaeologist,' said Ann to David. 'Don't look so miserable. I will bribe you with dinner tonight,' said Ann. David left with Dimitri while Ann had a lastminute chat with Edwards. The archaeologist stretched back in his chair after listening to the tape. 'You've got a bloody complicated case. How sure are you that we will finds human remains on the property?' 'What if they dumped it in the forest,' asked Phillip Chambers. 'I am damned sure we will find remains around the property because the arrogant murderers thought they were unstoppable and that nobody would dare to descend on their property while they were living there,' Ann stressed. 'Sounds feasible.' he added. 'When do we start?' he enquired. 'Tomorrow. I am meeting with the Nottingham CID who did the first search. We will need to check out the forest where they had their satanic meetings too,' said Ann. 'I will call you when we arrive. You will of course give us the address and inform Nottingham of our involvement,' said Phillip. 'We will keep in touch and make the final plans when we meet in Nottingham,' replied Ann. 'She's like a child going to the fun fare when she goes on these missions,' said Josie as she noted Ann's hyperactive frame of mind.

'She never takes her beloved brother anywhere on her adventure,', lamented Adam. 'Yes, beloved brother, has anyone reminded you that you are not a member of the Met. Have they also reminded you that as the imminent uncle, you have maternal responsibilities?' she added. 'Quite right too, start putting the dinner on the table,' said Josie. Adam suggested the men accompany him to the pub as Josie and Ann declined. Ann helped Josie with the washing up and retired to bed. They snuggled close together. Ann rubbed Josie's large abdomen lovingly. 'Not long to go now. Are you going to be with me at the birth?' asked Josie. 'I will do my utmost to be there, my darling,' replied Ann. 'Hey, we talked about you setting up Amy to find the rat who is their informant. Do you think you will be up to arranging that soon, because we don't want classified information getting out especially with our new quest in the investigation,' said Ann. 'I am so sorry I was not able to arrange it sooner. So many things happened which prevented me from setting up the perfect scenario. I will get onto it soon as you leave for Nottingham. You can pay me in kind in advance,' suggested Josie with a cheeky grin. 'Devious little madam, you always know which buttons to press,' said Ann ravishing Josie with an avalanche of kisses. Ann and Dimitri set out early the next morning. Ann outlined the plan to search the Casey property. She updated Dimitri about what the police had discovered with the last search. He added his views and made a few suggestions about finding the tunnel based on his experience when he served during the Serbian conflict. 'When do you think you will travel to Brazil?' asked Dimitri. 'A great deal will depend on our findings at the Casey home, finance and the assembly of our task force,' replied Ann. 'Anyway, you need not concern yourself with our mission in Brazil. Your team have helped enormously by assisting us to find Saskia,' said Ann. 'I disagree. This case is as much as ours because if Muller has murdered Olga who is Russian, you cannot exclude us from further involvement in this case,' said Dimitri. 'Hmmm, forgive me for thinking that David Hughes has opened his big mouth to persuade you to speak to me about Brazil,' replied Ann with some irritation. 'Yes, David and I talked, but I decided that we should be part of the Brazil trip as a Russian national has been murdered and we have as much right to have a say in the matter. Let's face it, Muller's capture will not be a walk in the park. You will need personnel skilled in armed combat. I have a military background and have seen active service for a number of years,' Ann explained.

If you are taking on the drug cartel, you will need the expertise of guys who can do the job and survive. Your two DEA guys and the Mossad team will need some extra help. I have some leave and my Krishka will finance my trip,' said Dimitri. 'Bloody hell, you have been well informed. I am not refusing help, but it is not up to me. My superintendant and the MI6 and Interpol chaps will need to consider your involvement,' she added. 'Anyway, your wife will be most appalled that we drag you into this dangerous mission. What will we tell her if you are killed?' continued Ann. 'I am divorced. I have two teenage children who live with their mother. I have a very good relationship with my ex-wife. She knows my work has many dangers,' he replied. 'I am not promising anything. You will need to wait until I have spoken to my superiors,' said Ann. 'We are approaching Nottingham. We will rendezvous at the Casey home, so watch out for the turnoff towards the forest,' Ann instructed Dimitri who was driving. When they got to the Casey property, they were met by the Nottingham DCI, SOCO and the forensic archaeologist. She introduced Dimitri to the assembled group and gave a brief account of his involvement in the case. The group was split up into teams, with Ann suggesting that they should start their search in the cellar where she believed they might locate the entry to the secret tunnel. The archaeologist began their search using ground penetrating radar in the rose garden and the grounds of the house. Ann surveyed the walls of the cellar, looking for a possible concealed entry to the tunnel. She leaned against the side of the bookshelf and accidentally pushed a lever which resulted in a grinding noise as the bookshelf moved aside and gave way to the mouth of a gaping dark tunnel. There were excited shouts as the officers rushed towards the sound. There were calls for lights as the officers gingerly proceeded into the tunnel. They walked into thick spider webs, dust and dirt as they made their way cautiously down the tunnel. The roof and sides of the tunnel was securely supported by solid steel frames. The tunnel continued for half a mile before they reached the end. 'Look for a lever. This must be the exit hatch just above your heads,' said Ann looking up towards the roof of the tunnel. They shone their torches searching anxiously for a lever. 'Here, this must be it said one officer pulling on a long steel handle. A grating sound and a moving shaft revealed the exit to the tunnel. They clambered out into the forest and found themselves at the cut off tree trunk used by the Satanists in their rituals. 'Right, get SOCO to take samples of everything on the alter. Get us some better lighting. We need to examine the inside of the tunnel properly,' she continued. The SOCO teams were split themselves into groups so that there were officers collecting and photographing samples in the cellar, in the tunnel and in the forest. Ann returned to the archaeologist, anxious to know if they had located any human remains. 'The tunnel leads to the forest. Any luck on your find, Phillip?' Ann enquired. 'I am afraid not Ann. We have checked the ground in at the front and side of the house,' replied Phillip. 'You know I just had a thought. These Casey brothers did not respect life, but according to their neighbour, they were very meticulous about their rose garden. Why would a bunch of murders care about gardening so much?' said Ann. 'You have a point there. I will start with the rose garden in the morning. I will have to wrap up now as the light is fading. Care to join me for dinner? said Phillip. 'No thanks, I promised to have a drink with the Nottingham squad,' replied Ann. She collected Dimitri and went off to the pub. She left for her hotel as soon as she knew Dimitri was comfortable amongst the other officers. Ann was up at the first light of day. She collected a rather hungover Dimitri and drove to the Casey's home. Phillip had the equipment lined up to search the rose garden. Ann's hunch was rewarded as the radar revealed a vast collection of human bones beneath the soil. The large area was divided into rectangular grids. The forensic archaeology team set about excavating the ground. They worked with trowels and brushes, carefully sweeping away the sand around the bones and using sieves to sift the soil. Ann greeted the find with a mixture of triumph and sadness as there were so many skeletons of babies. Three hours later, they uncovered the skeleton of an adult. 'How long do you think they have been buried?' asked Ann. 'I would hazard a guess at ten year,', replied Phillip. He examined the pelvis of the skeleton and declared it was that of a female. 'Do you know who the skeleton might be?' asked Phillip. 'I don't know but it might be Olga, the Russian girl or an Irish girl who went missing after she met the Casey brothers. 'God knows who they ensnared in their den of iniquity,' said Ann. 'How long do you think you will take to unearth all of it?" Ann urged "Probably two to three weeks,' replied Phillip. 'I will hang on for a few days until SOCO has completed their work then return to London. We will await your findings with great anticipation,' said Ann. The team gathered at the pub at the end of the fifth day of their search. They were in buoyant mood and toasted their success with copious amounts of alcohol. Ann was shocked at Dimitri's consumption of alcohol. She intervened when she thought he had drunk too much, and frog marched him to the car to the cheers of the other officers. Dimitri was barely able to stand when they got to their hotel. He put his arm around Ann's shoulders to steady himself. When they got to his room, Ann opened the door, but

Dimitri paused and leaned with all his weight against her. He embraced and kissed her muttering endearments in Russian. His powerful arms held Ann for a few moments before she was able to break free and push him away. She led him to the bed and left the room hastily. She stood outside his room momentarily catching her breath and chiding herself for allowing him to kiss her. When she got to her room, she phoned Josie. 'How are you my darling?' I miss you and the baby,' said Ann. 'Uncle Adam and I are just sitting here talking about you. When will you be home? 'she enquired. 'I will be home on Sunday,' replied Ann. 'Was your trip successful?' Adam shouted down the phone. 'Mind your own business Adam Dixon,' said Ann with some irritation. 'Goodnight. See you soon,' said Ann. It was a very subdued, embarrassed Dimitri who joined Ann for breakfast the next morning. 'I am so sorry about my behaviour last night. Please forgive me Ann,' said Dimitri. 'Oh, so the alcohol did not affect your memory.

'All I have to say to that is never ever cross the line again. I thought you were different. All the men I have met disapprove of my relationship and are under this misguided belief that if I slept with them, I would change my preference in an instant. I want you to remember that our relationship will have only a professional relationship. You are not my friend. Just remember your place,' continued Ann. They finished the breakfast in silence and journeyed to the excavation site. Phillip had found a third adult female skeleton. The neat back garden looked like a bomb site with heaps of soil, sieves bags, and men milling about with equipment and cameras Ann collected copies of the photographs taken at the house and set off with Dimitri back to London. Ann's first stop was at Edward's office. He was very pleased with their progress and even managed to compliment Ann on her find. He arranged a meeting with Michael Heath later that day. She asked David to be present at their meeting. Michael invited them to join him for lunch at his private members club. Michael gushed with pride as Ann revealed their findings. 'We will have a meeting with the team as soon as we have all the Information from SOCO. The forensic team will take at least three weeks to process their findings. We will release the information as it unfolds,' continued Ann. 'What is your next move?' asked Michael. 'Well based on the information we have, Saskia's testimony and what we find at Nottingham, we have a strong case to go after James Muller,' said Ann. 'I don't know where the hell you think the funds are coming from,' protested Edwards. 'Oh God, Be reasonable Stephen. We are on the brink of achieving the most amazing result and all you can worry about is the cost,' said Michael. 'There is another issue I wish to discuss with you,' said Ann. 'Going after Muller will not be easy. We have assembled a good team, but I had a request from Dimitri who wants to join us because he says if Saskia's cousin, Olga has been murdered, then the Russians have a legitimate role in joining us,' said Ann. Edwards exploded with rage.

'Why the hell does he want to tag along and who is going to pay for him?' Said Edwards. 'He has leave and will be funded by some benefactor,' replied Ann. 'Hold on, before we all get hot under the collar. Let's check with MI6 and Interpol, if they will allow Dimitri to join us. Ann you brief Tobin and the rest of the team some time tomorrow. Take the rest of the day off. You have earned it,' said Michael. 'Thanks Sir, I will keep you posted,' replied Ann. She left with David and headed home. 'This is all your fault, David. You could not keep your trap shut. You had to share classified information with Dimitri who did not hesitate in telling me about the great Brazilian trip,' said Ann. "He was very persistent in his questioning,' stuttered David. 'Yes, and while he tightened the thumb screws, you simply could not stop yourself spilling the beans,' said Ann angrily. 'Sorry, guv, I just thought he might be useful owing to his experience,' replied David. 'You could have had the courtesy to ask me before speaking to him,' replied Ann. "I am so very sorry, guv it won't happen again. I have good news for you. Josie had the part and got Julie to hook up with Amy. She swallowed the bait line and sinker and Julie was able to plant the bugs in Amy's home. We have gathered interesting information, but not been able to nail the informer", said David. 'Great, I sure we will find the mole,' replied Ann. 'You had better collect Dimitri on the way home,' said Ann. Josie was delighted to have Ann home so early. 'Where is Adam?' asked Ann. 'He will be home at six. He went to meet a friend,' replied Josie. 'You and David keep Dimitri company. I have some paperwork to do,' said Ann. The volume of noise rose as Adam entered the house. 'Hey this is nice. Did you enjoy the hospitality of the Northerners, Dimitri?' asked Adam. 'I did. They are very much friendlier than the people in London,' replied Dimitri. Ann joined them, hugging Adam as she entered the living room. 'Hmm dinner smells great,' said Adam. 'Yes, you can do the salad and get someone to help you serve the dinner,' said Josie as she sank into the armchair.

"We might have to carve out room for your tummy at the table,' said Adam patting Josie's growing abdomen. 'Come on stop messing about, I will help you with serving the dinner,' said Ann. Adam took Dimitri and David home while Ann cleared up after dinner. They snuggled up together catching up on their news. The boys stopped off at the pub on the way home. 'Wow, your sister is frightening when she is angry,' said Dimitri. 'Oh yeah, what caused her anger?' asked Adam. 'I was drunk, and I kissed her,' confessed Dimitri. 'What?' Are you insane?' 'You are lucky you escaped with your balls intact,' said Adam. 'She waited until I was sober to inflict her venom. She was so angry,' said Dimitri. 'Look here my friend, don't you ever do that again. Ann does not deserve such disrespect. I told you she is committed to her relationship. Forcing yourself on her will alienate you. You don't want Ann to be your enemy, I promise you,' said David angrily. 'Sorry guys, it won't happen again", continued Dimitri. "I talked to Ann about the Brazil trip", said Dimitri. 'Yes, you bloody idiot, she wiped the floor with me about it,' said Adam. 'I don't believe in beating about the bush, as you English say. I approached her head on as I want to be included in your team for Brazil. She said she would check with her superiors and get back to me,' replied Dimitri. 'We can expect a meeting with all involved soon", said Adam. 'Yes, I think she will meet while I am here,' replied Dimitri. 'I had better warn Rachel at Mossad. She will want to be present at the meeting,' said Adam. The men chatted late into the night, making tentative plans for their part in the Brazil trip. The shrill ringing of the phone jolted Ann out of her deep sleep. 'Hello, who's speaking,' said a groggy Ann. 'It's me, guv. Have you seen the papers?' asked David. 'No, I haven't. Do you know what bloody time it is?' It is my day off as well. Why the hell would I be reading the papers at this time?' asked Ann.

'Get a copy of the News of the World, and you will see what I mean. Sorry to disturb you guv. See you later,' said David. He had piqued her curiosity to such a degree that she was unable to get back to sleep. She dressed hurriedly and dashed to her local newsagents to buy a newspaper. Emblazoned on the front page was the heading: 'Russian woman provides police with vital information regarding family serial killing.' Ann let out a flurry of expletives as she raced home. 'Fucking Amy. I could kill her,' shouted Ann when she got home. 'What on earth is going on,' said a sleepy Josie as she walked down the stairs. 'Read this,' said Ann slamming the newspaper on the table. 'Oh, I see. I guess Edwards will have your head for this,' said Josie. 'You can bet on it, and it's the rat who is to blame. When we catch him or her, I will personally deal with them,' vowed Ann.

The doorbell rang. Ann answered the door. 'Come in David. The shit has hit the fan. I don't care what methods you employ. I want the bastard caught who is leaking this information. This places Saskia in grave danger,' said Ann. 'Julie has put the bugs in place, guv and it will just be a matter of time before we catch the mole,' said David. Her phone rang. It was Edwards blaming her for the newspaper headlines. She explained that her team was in the throes of catching the informer. He ignored Ann's explanation, berating her for her incompetence. She slammed down the phone vowing to punish Edwards for all the abuse she has endured. Josie and David calmed her down and pledged their support. Ann received the results from SOCO following the search at Nottingham. She called a meeting of the team requesting that Edwards and Michael also be present. 'Good afternoon everyone. We have the results from Nottingham. Numerous samples of human and animal blood, hair and skin was found in the cellar, tunnel and the alter. There was writing in Russian on the wall inside the tunnel read 'They have killed my babies and I am afraid they are going to kill me. 'Someone, please help me,' sighed Olga. Olga is Saskia's cousin and someone Saskia believes had been murdered by James Muller. The forensic team are still busy finding out the identities of the three adult female skeletons found in the rose garden. There were 35 foetal skeletons found with items of clothing, knives and pairs of gloves. The foetal skeletons had knife marks on the frontal surfaces of the cervical vertebra, suggesting their throats were cut possibly during the rituals.

Two of the female victims had knife marks on the ribs and sternums, suggesting the knives were plunged into their chests. They will have died instantly as a result of puncture of their aorta. The third woman was strangled, and a ligature was found around her neck,' continued Ann. Silence was followed by an indignation and disbelief that such barbarism still existed. 'Please keep your opinions to yourself. You are here to solve the crime and not engage your personal feelings,' shouted Edwards. The team asked numerous questions and Ann tried to answer them as best she could. 'Have you been able to track down Mary O'Reilly?' asked Ann. 'No guv, we have spoken to neighbours who knew her cousin and they have said both girls were not seen for the past ten years. Family have said that the girls were very wayward and left Ireland to live in London. They stayed with an aunt in Nottingham for a while but when they got involved with the Casey brothers, they had an argument with the aunt who threw them out. We have put numerous appeals in the papers with their photographs, but nobody has come forward yet,' said Tobin. 'Have you checked the death register?' asked Ann. 'Yes, no luck. Not even in Ireland, Guv,' replied Tobin. 'We will let you know what happens next,' he added.' We have a mole in our midst. Further information will not be released. You will all be informed on a need to know basis,' continued Ann. The team dispersed and Ann, David, Edwards and Michael proceeded to her office. 'Well that went well. When do you think you will hear from the archaeologist?' asked Michael. 'Phillip said that the strontium tests on the bones of the women would ascertain where they were lived. The reconstruction of their faces will take another two weeks. I will call you as soon as I hear from him, said Ann. 'When are you going to find the mole in your team,' Edwards demanded to know. 'Just as soon as the little bug we placed in Amy's house delivers the golden goose, Sir,' replied Ann disdainfully. 'I will arrange a meeting with MI6 and Interpol and Mossad. I believe your Russian chap wants to join you,' he continued.

'Do you think he is up to the job?' asked Michael. 'Absolutely. He is very skilled. I have no doubt he will be an asset to our team. He also believes he has a right to be with us because two Russians are involved in the case,' continued Ann. 'Okay I will be guided by you, Ann. Let's arrange a meeting for early next week,' replied Michael. 'Alright. Will keep in touch, sir,' replied Ann. 'That bastard, Edwards is like a dog with a bone. He always finds a whip to beat me with,' complained Ann. 'You should not let him get to you, Guv. He is jealous of your success. His record as DCI was unimpressive. He wished you would fail, but all your hunches paid off. He is especially miffed because you are a woman. Don't allow him to get to you. You are so close to getting a result,' said David. 'Yes, I suppose you are right. What the hell. Come and join us for dinner,' she said. 'Thank goodness you are more cheerful,', said Josie as Ann walked through the door. 'Yes, we had a good team meeting. I have invited David to dinner. Do you mind?' asked Ann. 'Of course not, silly. David is part of the family. He is always welcome here. I wanted to ask if he could be Godfather,' continued Josie. 'It is amazing how decisions are made over my head and I am always the last to kno,', said Ann shaking her head. 'Adam wondered if it would be nice to ask David as he was a witness at our wedding,' replied Josie. 'Well why am I not surprised that my brother has put his penny in the plate once again. Do you see how I am passed over, David,' protested Ann. Just then Adam walked in with Dimitri. 'Did I hear my name being mentioned?' enquired Adam. 'Yes, and I feel like crowning you for making suggestions without consulting me,' replied Ann. 'I would never assume anything without consulting you, Sis,' said Adam. 'Don't play the innocent. Josie says you suggested we make David the baby's godfather,' continued Ann. 'Oh, that, I would have asked you first. It was just me thinking aloud,' replied Adam. 'Well this is our baby, so keep your thoughts to yourself. Josie and I will make our own choice,' said Ann. 'Come on stop bickering. Dinner is ready,' said Josie. Michael convened the meeting with all parties concerned for the Brazilian mission.

Two members of Interpol and Mossad also attended. Rachel was not at all like Ann imagined her. She was a rather short, woman. It was only when plans for the trip unfolded that Rachel's talents emerged. She was very well informed about James Muller's history and his criminal background. She stressed that it was a dangerous mission and everyone on the trip would be expendable. She expressed her concern that Ann had very little army experience. Ann informed her that she had trained with the special forces when she was opted for the army before joining the Met. Dimitri hastily added Ann's impressive role in rescuing Saskia. They spent many hours working out a strategy for kidnapping Muller. 'We must take him alive at all costs,' said Rachel. 'There will be nine members in the group. The ninth man, Ben Hajjioff will only join us in Brazil. He has local knowledge and speaks the language. He is also ex- army", continued Rachel. They prepared for very emergency and agreed to leave in a week. Rachel informed them that her spy confirmed Muller was still hiding in the jungle near the Colombian border. 'We need to get him before he decides to move elsewhere,' said Michael. When the meeting ended, Michael invited them to dinner. The group were more relaxed and became better acquainted. The wine flowed freely, and they all went home quite inebriated. Ann hid her fear that she might be killed on the Brazilian mission by drinking more than usual. Rachel met with Adam and updated him on the mission. David called at Ann's house three days after the meeting to give her the good news. He rushed in through the door, chattering excitedly. 'Calm down Hughes. I can't understand a word you are saying,' said Ann. 'We got him, guv. We have nailed the mole,' said David, beaming all over. 'Bloody hell! David, are you sure?' said Ann. 'Yes, guv, you will never believe who the culprit is,' continued David. 'Come on then, don't keep me in suspense. Spit it out,' urged Ann. 'It is Sergeant Neil Havers. He is the detective constable working with DI Mason. 'We've have got him, guv. The evidence is irrefutable. I have sent a report to Edwards and Heath,' said David.' I would love to see Edward's face when he finds out,' said Ann. 'Hmm it will take the heat off you, guv,' replied David. 'Come on, join us for dinner,' she said.

'Josie has cooked a great meal,' said Ann beaming with delight. 'Hey, could not help overhearing what sounds like terrific news,' said Adam rushing down the stairs. 'Listen inquisitive, you should keep your nose out of police business,' replied Ann hitting Adam playfully on the head. 'Well could not help overhearing since you both talked at the top of your voices,' said Adam. 'Hurry up and sit down or the dinner will be stone cold when you get to eat it,' urged Josie. The meeting of members of Ann's task force took place at a private room at Michael Heath's gentleman's club. Michael, Stephen, Ann, David and Dimitri met with Clive and Roger from MI6 and Joe and Reece from Interpol. 'Welcome everyone. Glad you could make the meeting. You have been briefed by Ann and about this very complex case. I am going to set out our preliminary plan for when we get to Brazil. We all travel to Sao Paulo. We will be met by the Mossad operatives,

Rachel and Abie. We meet up with the DEA chaps, Eric and Douglas in Manaus. Our internal flight will leave for Manaus on the evening of our arrival in Brazil. We have told the Brazilian government very little because their will offer no help, and we cannot risk a leak if there are any drug cartel contacts in their government. We know that our suspect lives in a compound near the Brazil, Venezuelan border. He is protected by the drug cartels living in the compound. We also know that Muller travels to rendezvous with a terrorist cell, 10 kilometres from the compound. Every 3 days. He travels with an armed escort. We cannot attempt to take him on his route out of the compound because beside his armed escort, there are armed men all along the route. We will be outnumbered. We have to draw up a plan to take him inside the compound. We are sure that we can pull this off because our team is skilled in SAS combat. You will all endeavour to protect Ann if needs be. She is competent but perhaps not at SAS level. All things considered it will be a highly dangerous mission. There is the possibility some of you may not return. Now I would welcome any thoughts and suggestions you have,' continued Michael. 'How are we going to get out once we have captured Muller?' asked David. 'The DEA guys will arrange a land rover to get you to an airstrip where a plan will pick you up. Mossad are responsible for supplying the plane that will ferry to your destinations and to safety,' replied Michael. 'What arrangements have you put in place if we have hostile fire from the cartels and the plane is unable to land?' asked Ann. 'The backup plan is to escape by river. The DEA have local connections in Icana where a boat will be kept in reserve. will organize the boat. Please remember, the cartels will not spare your life when they find you. You must kill them on contact. One of our Mossad agents, Ben has a comprehensive knowledge of the forest. He will be your guide. He speaks the local tribe dialect and will have one tribal member with him. You leave in a week. It will give you enough time to coordinate everything and iron out any potential problems", continued Michael. Ann staggered into the house inebriated by consuming alcohol over 6 hours at the meeting, to extinguish thoughts of dying on the mission. 'Good gracious, I have never seen you so pissed,' said Josie helping her onto the settee. Ann mumbled a few incoherent words and passed out. David apologised for Ann's condition explaining that the meeting went on for many hours and drink flowed freely. 'But I have never seen her so drunk for age,' protested Josie. 'I think she freaked out at the prospect of our trip to Brazil,' said David. 'Ann never panics about anything. Why is Brazil so different?' asked Josie. 'My lips are sealed. Please don't say I said anything. She probably hates leaving you in your condition,' said David. Ann's reckless inebriation troubled Josie. She waited for Adam to get home. He arrived in the early hours. 'Hi Josie, has ghosts chased you out of bed?' 'No, I waited for you. We need to talk. 'Oh, that sounds serious. A woman in your condition should not be engaged in serious talk,' joked Adam. 'I am concerned about Ann. She arrived very pissed tonight. Why would she do that?' The Brazilian meeting must have worried her, and drinking was her only solution to cope with the stress,' said Josie. 'Now you are being ridiculous. When has Ann ever allowed the responsibilities of work force her to resort to alcohol. I admit it must have been a very important meeting. She simply joined the lads at the end of the meeting to relax,' said Adam reassuringly. 'My gut feeling tells me a different story. I think she is really worried about something,' replied Josie. 'I tell you what, I will find out discreetly how the meeting went,' said Adam. It was a rather dishevelled, grumpy Ann who sauntered into the kitchen. 'Hi sis, I have made you a delicious breakfast. Are you going to join me?' said Adam. "Good meeting last night? he enquired. 'Mind your own business. I am not in the mood for conversation,', said Ann curtly. 'Well your inebriated state worried Josie very much last night. She thinks you drank excessively because of your Brazilian meeting. 'Yes, and I can imagine how you fuelled her insecurities by agreeing with her need to feel stressed,' said Ann. 'On the contrary sis, I reassured her and defended your corner,' continued

Adam. 'Well that was good of you but let me sort out matters with Josie in person,' replied Ann. David hooted outside. 'Thank goodness, rescued from the chamber of interrogation. Excuse me, I need to go. See you tonight,' said Ann grabbing her coat and slamming the door behind her. 'Hi David, thanks for being prompt. We need to get the team to the incident room for 2pm. The forensic report is ready. I want everyone including Heath and Edwards at the meeting. The incident room was crowded. Everyone was keen to know the archaeologist's findings. Stephen Edwards addressed the meeting. 'Thanks for coming. Allow me to introduce Phillip Chambers, the archaeologist who has done sterling work on the remains found in the garden of the house belonging to the Casey brothers", said Edwards.

The board was had a vast array of photographs taken at the excavation site. There were photograph of numerous skeletons of infants and partly intact skeletons of three adult skeletons. Absolute silence prevailed as the sight unfolded to the people present in the room. Chambers began revealing his findings. 'I must hand it to the brothers. Their gruesome secret of their garden would never have been discovered, because only the outer rim of the garden had real roses. The centre of the garden, where their continued to bury the remains of their victims consisted of a removable plate with artificial flowers. The garden always looked immaculate because only the centre was disturbed, but the replacement of the artificial flowers ensured their secret was not uncovered. The head of the forensic team revealed that DNA isolated from items in the tunnel, the cellar and the car which contained the body of George Casey's daughter belonged to the same person. Ann had managed to secretly obtain hair samples from the brush and toothbrush in Susan Muller's bathroom. The DNA at the time indicated that the DNA in the car belonged to Susan's sibling. Since it was known that the James Muller used Jake's car, it was concluded that findings at the burial site was linked to James Muller. Phillip also informed the team that he used strontium to trace the birthplace of the women. One woman was traced to Minsk, Russia and the other two to Donegal in Ireland. Two reconstructed faces starred out from the plinth they were placed on. 'This is the reconstructed faces of the dead women. Dimitri will arrange for Saskia's aunt and uncle to identify the face and we will check their DNA to establish if it is that of their daughter, Olga", said Phillip. 'How much information does your team have on tracing the O'Reilly family?' asked Phillip. 'We will need to obtain the DNA of Mary's cousins and get them to identify the face to confirm identity. Hopefully they will help us to confirm whether Ellen O'Brien, Mary's cousin is the other victim,' replied Tobin. 'We have sufficient evidence to justify our need to pursue James Muller. We have a task force that will be headed by DCI Dixon. If you are wondering why Ann is needed to accompany the task force, we want to bring Muller to the UK to be charged and stand trial. The Israelis want him too, but we have priority. The Israelis will argue that they need to question and prosecute him, for his terrorist ties are greater. We will leave that to MI6 to settle", continued Michael. "We have assembled a very capable task force.

    The men and women have served in the special forces in their respective countries and undoubtedly will execute their task to the best of their ability. The mission is fraught with danger as they will need to capture their quarry in drug cartel territory. You will appreciate that in the interest of the safety of the task force, we cannot reveal more information. I also want to inform you that we have found the mole amongst us who have been leaking classified information to the tabloids. He has been dealt with accordingly,' said Michael. 'Thank you for your patience gentlemen. If there are no questions, you are free to go,' said Edwards. The team dispersed, leaving the senior members to continue their discussions. Michael informed Ann that he would her know when the rest of the task force had decided on a date of departure. She returned to her office with avid and Dimitri. She informed Dimitri that he could contact Sergei from her office and sent David in search of much needed coffee. Sergei popped up on the Skype screen. 'You have stolen my sergeant, Ann. When are you sending him back?' said Sergei. 'You had better ask him yourself. I think he has got used to the lazy British life of lying about all day,', said Ann. Dimitri cut in on the conversation. 'These English women tell so many lies. You should not believe them,' replied Dimitri. He then continued the conversation in Russian updating Sergei on all the latest findings of the investigation. Sergei expressed his opinion at hearing of Dimitri's trip to Brazil with expletives. Ann reminded him that he ought to mind his language. He apologised and continued the conversation. Dimitri informed him that he would be returning to Moscow in a few days and would return to London to join Ann for the Brazilian trip. David entered bearing coffee and doughnuts just as Dimitri completed his call. 'David, you and Dimitri can take a photo of the bust of Olga and get Saskia to formerly identify it. Also get Sergei to take samples from Olga's parents, if she is the girl in the photo and get him to send it to forensics. I have a few things to tie up. I will see you tonight,' said Ann tucking into her doughnut hungrily. Her mobile rang. 'How is the hangover?' enquired the voice at the other end of the phone. 'Hi. There was no time to have a hangover.

We had a very important forensic meeting. Just finished and in the middle of having my first meal since last night", said Ann. 'Have no fear of starving. Adam has invited David and Dimitri to join us tonight. He is treating us to a meal. He said something about making amends for your encounter this morning", said Josie. 'Oh God, I wish Adam would just back off and leave us in peace for a while. I wanted to have some quiet time with you tonight. Do we have to go with them?' asked Ann. 'Come on cheer up. He means well. Do it for me, pleas,', continued Josie. 'Alright, I can't imagine why I let you and Adam bully me into doing things I don't want to do. See you later. Love you,' replied Ann. She completed her report on the findings at the meeting and sauntered off to Michael's office. She knocked loudly on his door. 'Come in", said the voice inside. 'Hello, sir, hope I am not disturbing,' replied Ann. 'Good heavens, no you are a lovely distraction,' replied Michael shaking her hand. 'Sterling work on your case. Edwards is most impressed, but he refuses to tell you to your face,' continued Michael. 'I am not bothered. All that matters, is that we achieve a good result,', replied Ann. 'Are you ready for Brazil?' enquired Michael. 'Ready as I will ever be. I am also bloody fearful.

My partner is expecting our baby and the prospect of my possible demise leaves me with sleepless nights?' replied Ann. 'Yes, it is very worrying indeed, but you have a bloody good team. The boys will protect you with their lives", Michael reassured her. "Can I tempt you to dinner?' he asked. 'That would be nice, but my brother is taking my partner, Dimitri and David to dinner. I will reserve an evening for us next week,' replied Ann. Adam chose an expensive restaurant in Mayfair for their dinner. 'This is so lovely, thanks Adam,' said Josie after the dinner. 'You do realize, Adam will be penniless after this meal. It must have cost a pretty packet,' said Ann. 'On the contrary, I had a win on the horses, so I shall not be skint. Would you ladies like to join us for after dinner drinks?' said Adam. 'No thanks, Josie and I want to spend some quality together, so we shall love and leave you", said Ann heading for the car.

'Can you imagine how Adam will fuss over the baby when it is here,' said Josie. 'I dread to think what he will be like. I doubt whether you will be allowed to hire a baby sitter. He will want to spend every minute with the baby,' replied Ann. 'Such a shame he has not met anyone. He would make a lovely dad,' added Josie. 'He never really got over Rachel. I think he is in denial about his feelings for her, so he hangs around us to escape the truth. Anyway, I thought we wanted to get away from the men tonight to spend quality time together, so no more about Adam's love life', said Ann snuggling up next to Josie. They talked about the future of their unborn son until sleep overcame them.

Chapter 8

Dimitri left for Moscow the next morning, looking rather worst for wear after a heavy drinking session. Ann and David were summoned to Edwards office where Michael was also present. 'You leave for Brazil in 3 days. Your code name for the mission is Jaguar. You will identify your assault team by that code. You will fly to Rio de Janeiro where you will rendezvous with Dimitri and MI6. Mossad and the DEA chaps will be at Manaus to meet you. The MI6 fellows will be solely in charge of intelligence and surveillance. Mossad has 3 agents to ensure the assault crew is full quota. Prepare yourselves to travel by boat to the forest. You will be taken by helicopter with your captive to San Carlos in Venezuela. The rest of the journey will unfold when you get to San Carlos. You both can take leave from today as I am sure you have a great deal to prepare.

Good luck. I have no doubt that you will succeed. You have proved yourselves in the past and I am confidant you will get your man and bring him to justice,' said Michael. 'We will do our very best, sir,' replied Ann. 'Have you been sent home for good behaviour?' asked Josie when Ann and David walked in through the door. 'You will be happy to know, we are on leave as of now,' said Ann. 'Oh does this mean you will be leaving soon?' asked Josie. 'Yes, I am afraid. Three days to be correct,' replied Ann. 'Come on, get some lunch down you. Adam will be home soon,' replied Josie. The fateful day of departure had arrived. Josie did not hide her anxiety. She was tearful as she kissed Ann goodbye. Ann promised she would be home soon and reassured her that she had left Adam to take care of her. Even though she appeared in control Ann suppressed her fears and doubts about the trip. She slept for most part of the long flight. David read for some time then fell asleep the rest of the way. The plane touched down at Rio de Janeiro in the early hours of the morning. They cleared passport control and walked to the agreed meeting point. Two men approached Ann and David and called out the code word,

Jaguar. 'Hello, you must be Ann. We are Clive and Roger,' said one of the men. 'This is my DS, David,' said Ann shaking their hands. Dimitri approached them wearing a broad smile. 'Hi, did you have a good flight?' asked Dimitri. 'Yes, I slept most of the way,' replied Ann. 'We only have an hour to our connecting flight. Let's head for the domestic departure lounge,' said Clive. The flight to Manaus was rather pleasant. The group became better acquainted during the flight. They landed at Eduardo Gomez airport, Manaus in the late afternoon. The group made their way to the designated meeting place. They were met by a motley group of people who identified themselves by revealing the operation code. They introduced themselves as members of the Interpol team and two members of Mossad. The team was missing Ben from the Mossad team. They were told he would be joining them the next day. Ann was grateful that Rachel's presence upped the numbers for women in the group. 'Let's head for the hotel,' said Ann anxious that their presence did not arouse suspicion. They stepped out of the airport building and were enveloped in the suffocating, cloying tropical heat. Manaus was a pocket of urbanity nestling in the middle of a large jungle. The perfusion of exotic sights and sounds as they drove along the busy streets was seductive. Two taxis ferried them to 10 De Julio. Their hotel was a rambling building with large sterile rooms and communal basic shower units. Their hotel was situated near the Teatro Amazones, built during the rubber trade and was now an opera house. Everyone headed for the showers. A long session of consuming cocktails and beer preceded a large dinner. The team discussed the preliminary assault plan, adding backup plans for every eventuality. They were in contact with the Eric and Douglas, the DEA team. They were informed that Ben would join them in the forest as he had to two members of the Yanomami tribe to be their guides in the forest. Ann learned that Ben had made a documentary on the tribe a few years ago and knew the men who were to be their guides. He also spoke a few words in their dialect. Eric and Douglas had stashed the weapons for assault at a place near the forest where they were to rendezvous. The next day, they were flown by helicopter to Boa Vista along the Rio Branco river. They were taken to a disused warehouse where they met with Eric and Douglas. They were supplied with their weapons. Sniper rifles, Mac10 submachine guns, army revolvers, grenades, a rocket launcher and a collection of knives. The team checked the weapons and ensured they were in working order by testing them. It was decided as it took 12 hours to get to the part of the forest where James Muller was in hiding, they would leave at midday. 'Night falls quickly and decisively in the tropics,' Eric told them. A meal of beans and bread was served for dinner and beers supplied while the team made final arrangements for the assault.

A boat was moored on the river equipped with food and supplies for their journey. An ex drug cartel member, Luis who was trusted by Eric and Douglas was assigned to take them to their destination. The boat was rather dilapidated and appeared as though it might sink at any moment. The upper deck had a table and basic cooking facilities. The middle deck had an array of hammocks. The lower deck had a primitive toilet. Luis advised them to stay in the middle deck as too many people on the upper deck might alert some drug cartel members who may be patrolling the forest. They began their journey in the heart of darkness of the Amazon. Some of the team members spoke quietly to one another to calm their nerves. Other members of the team snatched a few valuable hours of sleep. Two stayed awake to keep watch. Ann was unable to sleep. She kept thinking about Josie and hoped she would be back alive and in time for the birth of the baby. Rachel sensed her anxiety and reassured her that they would succeed. They reached their destination at around 8pm that night. The team communicated with Ben and his natives by mimicking animal sounds known to Eric and Douglas. The team alighted from the boat. There were three men waiting on the bank. There were two Yanomami Indians and a man wearing a black ski mask. The code was exchanged. Rachel walked a little distance away from the group and talked awhile. She returned to the group and informed them that they should spend the night on the boat and would be collected at 4am the next morning.

They had a brief meeting before retiring to bed. Eric told them that they were given inside information by an ex- drug cartel member who had been a guard in the compound where Muller lived. He told them there were 50 guards, on each shift. The compound was surrounded by barbed wire. The building had a flat roof where 10 of the guards kept watch day and night. The back of the building had a 2metre wall. The inside of the wall housed live alligators which led all the way to the back of the house. The ventilation shaft access was on the roof. It was decided that the guards would be engaged with knives and darts to disable them. Firing would alert the whole compound and give the guards time to call for help where more guards were at a recess a mile away. The cacophony of animal sounds deprived them of sleep and the heat added to their discomfort. They were grateful of the dawn. Breakfast consisted of cold beans, bread and hot coffee. The Yanomami Indians appeared at the meeting point. They told the group in their broken Portuguese that Ben had gone on a reconnaissance of the forest and would join them later. They were warned about the dangers of the forest and instructed to watch out for snakes and other dangerous wild life. The heat had begun to rise as they walked through the damp undergrowth. Dappled sunlight stole through the verdant canopy. They only stopped for toilet breaks and brief periods of rest. Ann went off a little distance from the group to relieve herself. Just as she went down to squat, she noticed a snake sliding towards her. She froze on the spot, terrified but remained calm. She and the snake stared at each other momentarily. The snake lunged towards her. A strong pair of arms grabbed her. The figure thrust her to safety and spun around with a machete, cutting off the snake's head in one swoop. Ann could hardly believe her eyes. The Ben Hajjioff she had met in the dark was none other than Adam. 'What the hell are you doing here, Adam Dixon?' asked Ann in bewilderment. A blackened face starred back at her, grinning from ear to ear. 'Shouldn't, thanks for saving my life be your first words, sis,' asked Adam. She did not reply but hugged him with relief. 'Who is with Josie?' asked Ann anxiously. 'Josie is in the safe hands of a private midwife who is living in the house. She urged me to come here,' he replied. 'Wait until I get home. I am going to sweep the floor with her,' said Ann as they walked back to join the group. Everyone cheered as they appeared. 'You bastards, you knew all along. Now I know why there was all this secrecy surrounding this mysterious Ben who never took of his ski mask and never spoke. I suppose you David Hughes knew all about Adam's involvement from the start. You know, I had this gut feeling that all your meetings in London was a subterfuge for scheming. I am going to recommend that you return to the beat,' said Ann pointing her finger at David. 'I am sorry to disappoint you, guv, but the big chief gave me his blessing,' replied David. 'He is right sis. We planned this to ensure your protection. I have been on dangerous missions in the past. I did a great deal of work with Mossad agents, especially Rachel. I am an honorary Mossad agent. Capturing Muller is no walk in the park. He will not stop at anything to avoid being kidnapped. Besides, who would have rescued you from the big bad snake?' said Adam hugging her. 'Meet my Indian guides, Gongalo and Gustado,' said Adam proudly. 'Okay, now we need to assign tasks to all of you. I suggest that David, Dimitri, Eric, and Ann and Gongalo take the rear of the building. Dimitri is an accomplished knife thrower and Gustado is handy with the darts. I want Alex, Rachel, Joe, and Reece to man the rifles and the ammunition. You can prepare your camouflage suits and get into position on my signal. Not a single shot is to be fired. We need to take out the guards with sniper fire. The big guns must only be used if they manage to summon reinforcements. We cannot let that happen as it will jeopardise our kidnap plan. Clive, Abie and Roger have organised our escape from the building by helicopter. Does anyone have any questions?' asked Douglas. Everyone nodded as they agreed to their role in the mission. The sniper squad asked about their rescue. Adam reassured them that he and Gustado would monitor and help them to the second helicopter. It took 10 hours of walking to reach the edge of the forest near the compound. The compound was visible from their vantage point. Their binoculars allowed them a good view of the building and the guards. A truck arrived at the gates of the compound. It stopped in the grounds of the compound. Two men with their hands tied behind their backs were roughly pulled out and pushed onto the ground. They were pushed to the ground and kicked violently. Another truck was parked in the grounds. The men were tied to the back of each of the vehicles with a rope. The drivers climbed in the vehicles and drove off with the men still attached to the vehicles.

Within minutes the stones in the ground had torn and battered the bodies of the two men. The vehicles continued driving, even though it appeared that their victims had died in the merciless torture. Their bloodied battered bodies were finally cut loose and picked up by a farming tractor and dumped on what looked like a cultivated patch of land in the compound. Two men chopped up the bodies of the deceased with an axe. The got into a tractor and ploughed the two bodies into the ground as though they were compost. 'I am glad you witnessed that. You see there is no room for error. These guys cannot even spell the word, mercy. The buzz word is to kill on sight. Do your job to the very best of your ability,' said Douglas. The team waited until around midnight when the lights in the building were extinguished. It is thought that he guards became more complacent once the lights were out. Dimitri aimed his knife at the guard smoking a cigarette behind the back wall. The knife struck its target and the guard fell like a stone. The second guard at the side of the wire was brought down by a dart fired by Gongalo. The remaining eight guards fell like flies as the darts and knives hit their targets. Ann ran towards the compound and clambered up the wall. She signalled using her torch to the sniper team. A few seconds later guards on the roof fell over as the bullets hit home. Rachel followed next and helped

Ann secure the cable. The rest of the team at the rear followed Ann onto the wall. David fired the grapple iron into the wall of the building. The iron had wires leading from it. Wheels were threaded onto the wire and one by one the team slid across towards the building. Dimitri reminded them to draw up their legs as they slid across to avoid being brought down by the alligators that were languishing in the yard. Ann located the access point of the ventilation hatch. She opened the lid and cautiously crept inside. She shuffled along on her belly and the rest of the team followed. They followed the sound of a television coming from one of the rooms. They had been told that Muller's room was the one at the rear. They moved more cautiously as they realized they were in the ceiling of his room. They were able to discern him sitting in an armchair watching television through the grate of the ventilation exit hatch. The access point was behind the chair. Ann opened the hatch carefully and slid out onto the floor. Muller swung around as he heard the thud. Ann used the taser and he fell after a few seconds. The rest of the team piled into the room. They checked the rest of the room for the presence of guards. They peered out into the corridor. Two guards were playing cards and had their backs toward Muller's bedroom door. Eric killed them with his pistol which had a silencer. The men slumped forward. The team penetrated the rest of the building shooting the guards they encountered. Douglas and his team had killed the guards at the front and at the gate of the compound. And finished off all the resistance they encountered on their way into the grounds of the building. Confidant that they had secured the building, they went into the building in search of their team mates. Dimitri and David had succeeded in getting Muller onto the rooftop. Ann stayed in the building to meet with Douglas and the team. The helicopter hovered over the roof while they strapped Muller in the harness. David hung onto the harness and was winched up with Muller. A second helicopter arrived to pick up the rest of the team. During their exit an enemy helicopter arrived and started shooting at them. Douglas and Alex positioned their air to surface missile and blasted the helicopter out of the skies. The commotion had alerted the reserve guards further down the forest. They raced to the compound in their jeeps. They began firing at the team on the roof. The airlift seemed to take ages, especially with the guards at their heels. The engine of the helicopter spluttered as if it was about to fail but sprang into life at the last minute. Adam and Douglas were still on the roof when the last man was winched up into the helicopter. They stood their ground firing at the guards who clambered up onto the roof. The helicopter swooped down to pick up the two men, but their attempts were thwarted by the gunfire from the guards on the ground. Just then Adam flung a grenade at the group of guards who had been firing at the helicopter. It felled them instantly and the helicopter was able to collect Adam and Douglas safely.

Nobody uttered a word until they had crossed the Venezuela border. There were whoops and cheers at the relief of a successful mission. Muller had begun to regain consciousness. They landed at San Carlos and were taken to a safe house. Muller was put in a locked room in handcuffs. He demanded to know why he was being taken into custody. Ann informed him that he was wanted for questioning regarding a number of murders. He smirked and replied that he had good lawyers who would get the charges squashed. 'Good luck with that Mr Muller. We have a very strong case against you. Let's see what the jury says,' replied Ann. 'Come on team, you have two hours to eat and freshen up, then we fly to Asuncion. While the team relaxed, Ann asked Reece to get her a connection to Michael Heath. 'Hello, sir, we are in San Carlos with our quarry,' said Ann. 'Well done, Dixon, I am proud of you. Any idea when you will be back?' he enquired. 'I think in a few days, sir. I will give you plenty of notice to organize the reception committee,' replied Ann. The next call was to Josie. 'Oh, my darling, it is so good to hear your voice. I have been out of my mind worrying about you,' said a tearful Josie. 'Remind me to strangle you for scheming with Adam,' said Ann. 'Oh that. We were only thinking of your welfare,' replied Josie.

'How are you and the baby?' asked Ann. 'We are doing well, but I am finding it more difficult to move around. My feet are swollen. I can't wait for the bump to be born. Get here quickly,' said Josie. 'See you in a few days. Love you, lot,', replied Ann. The Mossad team organized a plane to get them to Asuncion. They spent a night on Asuncion before continuing their journey to Barbados. Ann had to fight very hard to convince Mossad to allow her to take Muller to London. Rachel cast her vote in Ann's favour. Adam thanked his Indian guides and parted company from them.

    The Mossad team left for Israel. Ann, Adam, David and Dimitri and Muller took off for London the next morning. They each took turns to watch Muller in between short periods of sleep. Michael, Edwards and some of the CID team met Ann at the airport. They bundled Muller into a police car and sped off to the holding cells. Michael patted Ann on the back and congratulated her and her team on their outstanding performance. They went to Michael's office where they had the debriefing of the whole assault mission. Three hours later a relieved Ann headed for home. Josie flung her arms around her as she entered the house. Adam joined in the hug. David and Dimitri seated themselves on the sofa while Ann and Josie had a catch up. Adam served the drinks. They recapped on their Brazilian adventures during dinner. Adam filled Josie in on his miraculous rescue of Ann. 'Yes, don't think your heroism lets you off the hook,' said Ann. 'Come on, guv, if he didn't rescue you, you would not be here with us no,', added David. 'You keep out of this. You are in enough trouble as it is, David Hughes,' said Ann giving him an admonishing look. Ann scheduled the interview of James Muller for 8am the next morning. David watched from the next room. Ann switched on the recording tape. 'It is 8.33 am October 1993. People present in the room is the accused, James Muller, DI Tobin. 'James Muller, I must warn you and caution you that am charging you with the murders of Olga Mirinov, Mary O'Reilly and Ellen O'Brien. I am also adding the charges of suspected murder of Tom and George Casey on the 14 July and 2 August 1993. Your car, found in the lock up garage of Jake Casey, contained the body of Elaine Casey who had been murdered at the Casey home in Nottingham. We have found your DNA in the car. I also have two witnesses who will testify that you murdered some of the foetuses aborted by the women you and your cousins held captive at their home. 'Excuse me for being a touch obstructive, but I have been living in Brazil for the past few months,' replied James. 'On the contrary, Mr Muller, your sister told us that you only left the UK in June of this year. We also have checked and found that you travelled out in June on a Brazilian passport using the name Carlos Mendez,' said Ann. Muller shifted in his seat uncomfortably. 'I demand to have my lawyer present,' he shouted. 'Yes, so you shall, after this interview,' replied Ann. 'We have a witness to the satanic rituals you and your cousins performed in Nottingham forest. We also have the remains of three women used in the rituals and murdered by one or two perpetrators during the rituals,' said Ann. 'Don't look at me. I had nothing to do with any murders. My cousins are to blame for all that happened. By the way, how the hell do you know it was me?' I did not give you my DNA. 'We visited your sister, Susan and obtained her DNA. The DNA in your car revealed that you were siblings. We will be taking DNA samples from you in due course. You were living with your sister and she was unable to provide an alibi for your movements around the time of the Casey family murders,' said Ann. Muller began to panic and demanded to have his lawyer present. After 6 hours of questioning, Ann terminated the interview and instructed the officers to take Muller back to the holding cells. She met with Edwards and Heath and discussed the details of the interview. She called a meeting of her team in the incident room later that afternoon. The team applauded as Ann and David entered the room. It was such a different atmosphere than Ann had been used to in the past. 'Great job guv,' shouted the team. 'You bastards, I nearly lost my life having to prove I had balls,' replied Ann. 'The drinks are on you at the pub tonight,' said Tobin. 'Okay, it's a date,' said Ann. She did a brief talk on the mission and capture of

James Muller. She informed them that after they have confirmed his DNA, Muller would be implicated in the murders of the three women murdered at the Casey's family home. 'Saskia will testify to Olga's murder,' she added. 'Oh guv, Jake Casey has regained consciousness. He is in rehabilitation under guard,' said Tobin. 'Gosh that is extremely good news. I will see him later. How is his memory?' asked Ann. 'Not great, but he remembers being in custody. His is unable to walk unaided,' said Mason. 'We have received the DNA samples from Olga's parents. It is a match. She is their daughter. We also got the samples from Ireland. The other female body is Ellen O'Brien, Mary's cousin. The meeting ended on a high note. 'Come on David, my stomach thinks my throat has been cut. Let's get some food and then go to see Jake,' said Ann. Jake Casey sat in a wheelchair beside his bed. 'Hi Jake, how are you?' enquired Ann. 'Oh I have seen better days, but I am bearing up,' replied Jake.

'Do you remember much of what happened before your accident?' asked Ann. "I don't remember a great deal, except that I was in a holding cell", replied Jake. 'Do you remember me asking you if you could decode a book we found at your brother, Tom's house?' asked Ann. 'Vaguely, yes,' replied Jake. 'Can you help to decode the book?' asked Ann. 'My memory is not fully functioning yet. I will need time to recover but I can help with the decoding,' replied Jake. 'You do know that the evidence against you still stands. We have arrested your cousin, James and are hoping he can cast some light on the murders,' said Ann. 'You should be so lucky. James would sell his own mother to protect himself,' replied Jake. "Okay, we will leave you to rest, but I will be back to question you again later,' said Ann. 'Do you think he is pretending not to remember?' guv, asked David. 'I think in view of his accident we need to give him the benefit the doubt. If he knows his sentence will be reduced, he may co- operate more willingly,' replied Ann. 'Bloody hell, I am knackered. Drop me off at home pleas,', said Ann. Josie was home alone. She said that Adam had taken Dimitri for a drink. 'Great, we need to be alone.

Let's snuggle up and eat ice cream in bed,' said Ann. 'It sounds decadent, but lovely. I don't think I will grow any bigger,' said Josie. 'You are getting rather large. Don't worry only one week to go. I will be away for a few days this week. I am needed in Nottingham. I will be meeting with their CID about the skeletal remains. Josie scowled with disapproval. 'It's so unfair, Adam is also going away to Scotland. I will be all alone,' complained Josie. 'It's alright darling I will not be far away. The Met will fly me home if there is any urgency,' Ann reassured her. I have asked David to stick around if you need him. Ask him to sleep here if you are worried. I will not miss the birth, I promise you,' said Ann. 'I sent the midwife away she is too bossy. I don't want David here, only you,' said Josie. They snuggled next to each other, falling asleep in each other's arms. Ann started out on her journey early the next morning. She reminded David to check on Josie from time to time.

Josie got a call from Jake in the late afternoon. Josie told him that she could not meet with him anymore. He sounded desperate and anxious. He asked her to collect him from the rehabilitation unit. He persuaded her that he needed her to take him to collect a code book to help him decode a book for Ann. Josie felt sorry for him, so she agreed to his request.

She drove out to the rehabilitation centre and found Jake in his wheelchair in the car park. 'Hurry, we need to get away quickly,' he said. "Why all this urgency and secrecy?" asked Josie. 'Just trust me and get me to a safe locker. I need to collect a book to decode another book for Ann,' he replied. Josie got him to the locker and helped him collect the book. 'Drive me to your home, I want to talk to you,' he said. Josie obeyed, because Jake was so insistent. She wheeled him into the living room and went to the kitchen to make coffee. She heard voices coming from the living room. She went to investigate. There was a man dressed in black and wearing a ski mask. He had a gun and was threatening to shoot Jake. "Where is the code book?' shouted the man. Jake denied having the book. The man shot him in the knee. He screamed in agony, still denying having the book. The man shot him in the other knee. Josie was terrified but grabbed a kitchen knife and lunged at the man in the ski mask. He grabbed her by the hair and tied her hands behind her back. 'You just be patient, my love, I will deal with you later,' said the man. 'Kill me, but don't harm her,' pleaded Jake. 'You can watch while I enjoy her,' said his assailant. The man then pulled off Josie's clothes and raped and sodomised her. She screamed, 'you are harming my baby, you, cruel bastard. Josie managed to free her hands during the assault and grabbed her assailant's hands. She lunged forward to strike her assailant but missed. He knocked her on her head with the butt of the gun and she passed out. 'You bastard, I will never give you the book,' said Jake. His assailant shot him in the head and fled. David stopped at Ann's house on the way home. He rang the bell but there was no answer. He went around the side of the house and peered through the window. He saw Josie lying on the floor. He kicked down the door and rushed inside. She was still breathing but unconscious. Jake was dead in the wheelchair. David rang for the emergency services.

    He rang Ann and informed her that Josie was hurt and had been taken to hospital and to get back to London immediately. He informed Heath and Edwards. The house resembled a bomb site as the police and emergency services arrived almost simultaneously. David accompanied Josie to hospital. He informed Adam who was stunned at the news. Ann arrived at the hospital by helicopter. Josie was already in the operating theatre having a caesarean section and surgery to her brain. She had suffered a serious head injury. They allowed Ann into theatre during the operation. The baby boy was placed in her arms as soon as the surgeon extracted him from Josie's womb. She was ushered out of the theatre to the nursery. The little boy looked so helpless in her arms. She kissed him on the forehead and whispered, 'My darling boy, your mum can't enjoy the moment she lived for,' David watched her through the nursery window. She beckoned him to join her. 'Hello guv, I guess congratulations are in order. He is a handsome lad. The circumstances are exceptional. I am so very sorry that I got to Josie so late. I had lots to do at work,' he continued. 'It's not your fault David. I don't know all the details. Please stay with the baby. I am going to see if Josie is out of theatre,' she added. Josie had been taken to intensive care. The surgeon called Ann aside and told her that Josie's chances of recovery were very slim. He said the brain damage was extensive. Ann's mind was in turmoil. She blamed herself for not doing enough to protect Josie. She sat at Josie's bedside and talked to her hoping she could hear. She apologised for not spending enough time with her and going away too often. She told her that they had a beautiful boy and that he was waiting to meet his mum. Ann walked to the waiting room while the staff did some procedures on Josie. Michael Heath joined her in the waiting room. 'Ann I am so very sorry. We think Jake phoned Josie to fetch him. He did a runner when the officer guarding him went off duty and there was a delay in arrival of the relief officer. The perpetrator must have followed them from the rehabilitation centre,' explained Michael. Jake has been shot dead. 'How the hell does Josie know Jake?' She never ever mentioned meeting him and why did they end up at my house?' asked Ann. Their conversation was interrupted when they saw the crash medical team running to the ICU unit. Ann followed but was told to wait outside the unit. Michael led her back to the waiting room. A nurse brought them some tea. The doctor emerged 10 minutes later and called Ann aside. 'I am so sorry Inspector Dixon, we were unable to save your partner, she is gone,' said the doctor, putting his arm around Ann's shoulder. The look on her face when the doctor walked away spoke volumes. Michael comforted her, but Ann was inconsolable. She returned to the unit to spend some time with Josie's body. Adam arrived much later that evening. He wept uncontrollably. Ann kept asking why Josie had been with Jake. Adam then explained to her about Josie's accident with Jake and how they met. 'It was her guilt about the accident and her fear about keeping it a secret, so she agreed to have dinner with Jake to buy his silence. Nothing happened between them. She would never cheat on you,' said Adam. 'Why the hell did you not tell me,' asked Ann, 'I kept my mouth shut because I did not want to betray Josie's trust,' he replied. 'Your silence has cost Josie her life,' replied Ann. 'Oh come on sis you don't mean that. You are distressed and very angry right now,' pleaded Adam. David joined them and was told the sad news. He put his hand on Ann's shoulder reassuring her that no stone would be left unturned to find the perpetrator. David led Adam to the nursery to see the baby. Edwards entered the waiting room and expressed his condolences to Ann. It was so unusual to witness the once aggressive superintendant display such remarkable empathy. 'We have arranged for you to stay at a hotel until SOCO has finished their work. We will leave a police officer on a 24hour guard at your house. David can accompany you to collect whatever you need once SOCO gives us the nod,' said Edwards. Ann joined Adam at the nursery. 'Oh, he is so beautiful. Have you thought of a name?' asked Adam. 'Josie wanted him to be called Adam.

I want to change that to Joseph Adam,' said Ann. 'It sounds great. Josie would have loved that,' replied Adam. 'She is not here to call him by that name,' said Ann. 'I promise I will never leave you sis. I will help you raise him. I give you my word,' said Adam. Adam accompanied Ann to her hotel. He offered to stay the night. She accepted his offer as she suddenly felt terribly lonely. When she had composed herself, she concentrated her thoughts on finding Josie's attacker. Ann was given compassionate leave and another DCI brought in to manage the case. Ann was reluctant to take time off work, but she had no choice considering the circumstances. David and Adam spent a great deal of time with her. She toyed with the idea of returning to the house. She needed to see the crime scene for herself.

One evening she drove to the house. The officer guarding the house was nowhere to be seen. She let herself into the house and made for the living room. The house was in total darkness. She heard a door close and she dived behind the sofa. She fell next to an object. She began to explore the object with her hands in the pitch darkness. As her hands travelled over the object, she was able to make out that it was a body. She ran her hands over the body, running over the chest. She encountered metal bars on the shoulders which made her realize that the body was probably that of the police constable who was left to guard the house. Her hand moved over the victim's chest where she found a sticky wet spot. Her fingers followed the wet spot up to the victim's throat where the sticky trail led to a gaping wound in his neck. A noise in the darkness, made Ann hold her breath and crouch down low. A deathly silence followed. Ann was able to see the beam of torchlight flitting across the room.

It was impossible to see in the darkness, but as the beam of torchlight flashed around the room. The silence was broken by a message bleep on her phone. She fumbled frantically in the dark to switch off her phone but realized that the figure in the room had heard the noise. A dark figure lunged towards her. She rolled out of the way just in time and somersaulted back on her feet. By now her eyes has adjusted to the darkness and slivers of moonlight helped to outline the shape of her attacker.

Ann kicked her assailant off-balance, followed by flinging a chair at her assailant. The two of them exchanged vicious blows. Her assailant was very strong, but Ann stood her ground and retaliated viciously. She rained a series of attacks which found their mark and denied her attacker the advantage. Then, in an unguarded moment, Ann was kicked forwards and landed on her stomach, hitting her head. She was momentarily dazed which gave her assailant the advantage. The man held her neck in the crook of his arm. 'If you don't keep still, I will break your neck. Ann desisted and had her hands tied behind her back. 'Do as I say, and you won't get hurt,' said the man dragging her backwards across the floor. He was wearing a ski mask, but she recognised the voice. She erred on the side of caution and did not let on that she knew the identity of her attacker. 'What the hell are you doing in my house?' Ann demanded to know. 'I came back to collect an item belonging to me. I wouldn't want your lads at SOCO tying me to the crimes,' said the man. 'You killed my partner. I will not let you get away with her murder,' said Ann. 'Now temper, temper. It wasn't personal. Your partner just got in the way. Must say she is a fantastic screw. Let's face it, two women fumbling about, can hardly be called fucking. Pity you don't have a cock to know what I mean. I am going to screw you to the point of torture. Only difference is there will be no rules when I torture you. You will be my ultimate fantasy,' boasted her assailant. I bugged the Casey brother's phones and their houses, so I knew exactly where they were and what they were doing,' he continued. By now Ann had been hog tied and suspended by her arms. 'You just hang there and let me find what I came for and then we will have some fun. 'Why did you do kill Jake?' Ann demanded to know. 'Jake had the ability to decode the book which would have implicated me for the murders linked to the rituals and he refused to give it to me,' said the man. 'You must speak to James Muller. He should shoulder the blame for killing the girls,' he replied. 'Did you murder the Casey's?' Ann demanded to know. 'Got it in one. I did and if I had a chance, I would do it all over again. They deserved all they got.

They abused my wife when she was pregnant with my baby. They aborted the baby and sacrificed it in their satanic rituals. She died as a result of septicaemia after that abortion. I was away at the time, but I got back in time to hear it from her before she died. I decided then that no sentence would do justice to the punishment I had planned for them. I delighted in every aspect of the torture that I meted out to them,' said the man. 'Did you kidnap and kill Elaine Casey?' asked Ann. 'Yes, that was my piece de resistance. I got her father to screw his own daughter. You should have seen his face. He was terrified I would kill her right there at his house, so he did not have a choice but to fuck his own daughter. Before he died, I whispered to him that I was going to rape and kill his little girl and boy did I enjoy her. I tortured her for hours and then screwed her in every way I could. Such sweet revenge,' he continued, glorifying his evil deeds.

'You! contemptible rat, but you will not get away with it,' said Ann. 'Oh yes, I will get away with it because you won't live to tell them what I have told you. Can't pass up a chance to screw you, but first I must find the clasp of my watch. When I wrestled with your partner, she tore my watch off and the clasp was lost somewhere in this room. I am sure the clasp has some of my DNA,' he continued. He began searching earnestly for the missing item. His was so focussed on his search that he did not notice the two men enter the room and launched themselves on him, until the last moment. He was incredibly strong, but their combined strength pinned him down and knocked him out. David and Adam had come to Ann's rescue. She was bruised and battered and covered in blood. They untied her. She was seething with anger. 'You deserve to die, you piece of shit,' said Ann menacingly. They pulled off the man's ski mask. 'I don't believe it, it is Luke Cowan,' gasped David. 'How did you know where to find me?' asked Ann. 'We put a bug in your car and were able to trace you. I suspected you would return to the house to look at the crime scene,' replied David. 'How much did you hear of his confession?' asked Ann. Adam arrived before I did. He waited for me before we jointly attacked him. We heard most of what he said. Adam suggested we wait to see his next move before we stepped in to help,' continued David. You both did not hear us as your battle was so intense,' replied Adam. David offered Ann his handkerchief to wipe the blood that ran down her forehead. 'I recognised his voice but did not let him know as I was not sure what he would do. We must find that watch clasp,' said Ann. They shone extra lighting on the floor and table surfaces to find the item. During their search, Ann accidentally knocked over a flower pot on one of the little tables. She bent to retrieve the pot and while she was replacing the soil in the pot, she found the metal clasp. It appeared to have dried blood and skin on it. She carefully placed it in a clean freezer bag and labelled it. 'This must be what he returned for. It looks like the clasp of a watch,', said Ann. They had called for backup, so once again the house was buzzing with police and paramedics. Edwards and Heath arrived too. 'Your life is never without drama. Good God, you might have been killed,' said Michael. 'Yes sir, I am sorry, but I just had this gut feeling that the murderer would return to the crime scene,' replied Ann. Luke had woken up by then and had his rights read and taken away by the police. 'Pity about the officer on guard. Hughes, you will need to inform his family,' said Edwards. 'Yes sir, I will go as soon as we have finished here. Who will take care of Ann?' asked Heath.

'I will take my sister to the hotel,' said Adam. They stopped at the hospital and went to spend time with the baby. Adam held the baby and spoke to him, telling him, he would take care of him as if he were his own. Ann asked Adam again why Josie had kept her meeting with Jake from her. 'Look sis, Josie loved you with all her heart. Her meeting with Jake was to buy his silence. She felt guilty as hell meeting with him, but she also felt guilty about the accident and was manipulated to communicate with him. She never slept with him or encouraged anything beyond dinner and a drink. I think she collected Jake from the hospital at his request. I think it had something to do with the code book. Remember he promised you that he would decode the book. perhaps he felt vulnerable in hospital and needed to be at a safe location to do what he needed to do. I believe he was watched and followed. If the murderer got to Jake in jail, what stops him from watching Jake at the hospital. Think about it, Josie was the only neutral person he could trust. There was no way you would allow him out of hospital unguarded,' he said. 'I should have been at home and not gone to Nottingham when I did. She asked me to stay and I did not listen,' said Ann tearfully. 'Oh God, Adam, I am to blame for causing her death,' she hissed. Adam put his arms around her and hugged her and the baby reassuringly 'Adam there is something I must tell you,' said Ann. 'I overstepped the bounds of my authority by entering into an illicit deal with Luke Cowan. I had sex with him, sadomasochistic sex,' said Ann bowing her head ashamedly. 'I know sis. I overhead your conversation with him before David joined me. Thank God he did not hear it. Why in God's name did you do such a thing?' Adam demanded to know. A tearful Ann replied, 'It was the only way I could find out more about the satanic rituals. I knew there must been a tunnel to get from to house to the spot where they performed the rituals He knew where they gathered for the rituals in the woods and agreed to take me there if I had sex with him. I learned from Sam Cain that he would do anything for sadomasochistic sex. The only problem is if he reveals this to Edwards, they will find my DNA at his home and my visit to his home on his CCTV,' continued Ann. 'No bloody way, not if I have anything to do with it,' replied Adam. 'You are not going to be implicated in any of this. That bastard deserves what he gets, but he is not going to drag you down with him,' said Adam angrily. 'No Adam, I can't waive my responsibility. I am guilty and must own up to what happened,' insisted Ann.

'This is the one time I am not going to listen to you, sis. If it becomes public knowledge, your career is over. That piece of shit is not worth sacrificing your career for,' replied Adam. 'I am so ashamed. I feel I have betrayed and cheated on Josie and perhaps my punishment was her death,' continued a distraught Ann. "I won't allow you to think that. You did what your instincts dictated. Nobody knew that he would murder Josie in the process. Life happens. Shit happens and sometimes we have no control,' he urged.

Michael Heath asked Ann to call at his office the next day. She was terrified of what he was going to reveal. She knocked on his door and was invited in. 'Sit down Ann, I think you know why you have been called to see me,' he said. 'Yes sir, I would like to explain what happened,' she said. 'No need, your brother called to see me last night,' he continued. Ann bit her lip angrily. 'With respect Sir, I don't need my brother to fight my battles. I am quite capable of shouldering the responsibility of what happened,' she said. 'Ann I fully understand why you did what you did. It was done in extraordinary circumstances and your actions achieved a phenomenal result. Edwards and the chief constable will never see it like that. They will condemn you and demote you. Your brother had my permission to remove all evidence of your presence at Cowan's house including the CCTV evidence. He did so last night. If Cowan makes an allegation, no evidence linking you to having been at his home, will be found. You must give me your word that you will accept my ruling and that you will let it go. You must not blame your brother for intervening. He would give his life to protect you and I agree with him, you are worth all the sacrifice,' said Heath putting a reassuring hand on her shoulder. 'You have been put forward for promotion to superintendant.' Michael proudly announced. 'I will decline the promotion in view of the circumstances, sir and I don't want you pressurizing me to accept it,' she continued. Adam was waiting for her outside Heath's office.

She hugged him, not uttering a word. They clung to each other in silence. David spotted them as they got into the car. 'Fancy some lunch,' he said. 'Oh, that would be nice," replied Adam. David chose a quiet little bistro near Kensington. 'I believe congratulations are in order Detective Inspector Hughes,' Ann announced proudly kissing David on the cheek. 'That calls for champagne. Allow me to treat you,' declared Adam, shaking David's hand vigorously. 'Surely, they are going to give you the supers post, guv?' said David. 'They did and I turned it down because I wanted to keep my hand in the active side of the investigations. I am not cut up to be an office potato just giving orders,' added Ann. 'Shame not to have you as our boss but it is also great to be working with you in the field,' said David. 'You will be replacing D.I. Tobin,' said Ann. During the meal they discussed Cowan and Muller's impending trial. David informed them that both men would get three life sentences with no chance of parole. Besides the overwhelming DNA evidence, Saskia's evidence will seal their fate. The bite marks on Josie's buttocks was a match to Cowan and his DNA was found on the clasp of his watch. David enquired when Josie's funeral would be, and Ann said it was scheduled for the following Friday. The chapel at the little crematorium was packed with police officers. Every member of her team had made the effort to attend. Josie's sister, June and brother, Martin was present but kept their distance. Ann held the baby, but a nanny took the baby from time to time. The solemnity of the funeral and the support of her colleagues touched Ann deeply. She did not hold back her feelings but allowed herself to express the grief she felt so very deeply. Holding onto the baby was her only tangible reminder of the woman she loved so dearly. Her team shared that grief and lent their support throughout the ceremony. Edwards delivered a heartrending speech which moved Ann to tears. She could hardly believe that the man who hated her initially had such an incredible understanding of her loss. When everyone had left, Ann, Adam and David stood at the door of the crematorium sharing a group hug. Adam whispered softly. 'Sis, we will always be there for you and Joseph,' Adam reassured her. Ann cradled the baby in her arms and the three of them walked away together in silence-each preoccupied with the memories of the Josie they adored.

The End

Dedicated with love to the memory of Roy Du Toit

Printed in Great Britain
by Amazon